A MORGAN'S GROVE NOVEL

TRACI BORUM

Love Starts Here

Red Adept Publishing, LLC

104 Bugenfield Court

Garner, NC 27529

http://RedAdeptPublishing.com/

Cover Art by Streetlight Graphics

For my sister, Karen, whose enthusiastic support has meant the world.

Chapter One

Jill McCallister always knew when she entered "the zone," that moment when her fingers skated across the keyboard and nothing else in the world mattered. Not the snowfall outside her window, not the whining of her roommate's cat from the apartment corner, not the looming stack of mail waiting to be sorted. Jill could easily tune out those distractions and step straight into the story she was tapping out, where the characters, the setting, and the scenes all became her vivid reality. When people asked what it felt like, to write a novel and disappear into the story, "euphoric" was the most accurate word Jill could find.

If only she could find that euphoria again.

Fingers hovering above the keyboard, Jill stared at the cursor and blinked back with a generous sigh.

"Not today, apparently." She balled her fingers into fists then shut the laptop with a frustrated click.

It had been four months since she'd felt the spark of any significant creative idea, eight months since her literary agent had begun harassing her ("Where's the new book?"), and twelve months since she'd published her last novel, killing off her main character and officially closing out her popular series. Jill had grown tired of writing murder mysteries and wanted to pivot to a fresh project. But months of brainstorming had produced... nothing.

Has the well finally run dry?

Jill pushed down the familiar panic and eased backward into the sofa's cushion as she stared blankly toward her living room walls, which were decorated with serene nature photos and motivational posters. Her eyes drifted down to the bookshelf, which held, among other books, all four of the novels in her published series. There they sat, perched together in order, seeming to mock her and to ask whether future books would ever join them on the shelf.

Jill stood up and circled the couch, threading her fingers through her chestnut hair and massaging her scalp, attempting to ward off a headache. She needed a distraction, something *else* to work on. As she came around to her spot on the couch again, an idea hit. It wouldn't be the grand solution for a new novel, but at least it would keep her writing muscles flexed and intact.

Jill grabbed up her phone and tapped the screen for Miranda's New York number.

"Jill! I hadn't expected to hear from you so soon," Miranda told her.

"Not a bad thing, I hope?"

"Of course not."

"Listen, I was wondering if you could give me another piece to write. Human interest or maybe travel?"

"An excuse to get you out of a writing rut?" Miranda asked.

Jill shifted her weight. "Sort of. I need to restart my brain, shift gears."

"I totally get it. Let me see if I have anything for you..." Her voice trailed off, and Jill imagined her clicking through her ongoing, endless list of article topics.

Miranda Jenkins was Jill's college roommate from twelve years before. After graduation, she'd created an online magazine that had quickly blossomed into a savvy place for readers to find book reviews, fashion tips, human-interest stories, and travel pieces. Jill had been one of Miranda's first freelance writers and had continued to write occasional articles for the magazine throughout the years. When Jill's first novel was published and she'd found some actual success—and started receiving enough royalties to live on—Miranda had begged her to keep writing occasional pieces for the magazine. "You're the only writer I have who can find the 'heart' of a piece," she'd said.

Jill's most recent article, a piece about a wounded veteran named James, whose therapy dog was hit by a car, had been published last month. The community had reached out and ended up paying for two surgeries, and the dog had survived. The focus of Jill's story, though, had evolved into the special bond between dog and human. The moment James told her, "This dog saved me, so I had to save him," Jill knew she'd found the article's heartbeat.

"Okay," Miranda said into the phone. "I think I've got one for you. How does genealogy strike you?"

Honestly, it didn't strike Jill at all. She was glad they weren't on FaceTime together, so Miranda couldn't see the lines of her frown. "You mean, family trees, heritage, that sort of thing?"

"I know you're not big on fads and trends, but genealogy is hot right now," Miranda explained. "People are searching for their roots, their history. You could do something really new and fresh with this. Find an interesting angle or make it personal. But I'd need this piece by Christmas day, no later. Or I'd have to give it to another writer..."

Less than five weeks away. That translated into a few precious weeks of valid excuses to push her novel-writing aside, and to become rejuvenated in the process, or so she hoped. Plus, Jill was scheduled to speak at a huge writer's conference immediately after the holidays and had been struggling to come up with a strong topic for her session. If nothing else, she could use this article as a current piece of writing to discuss with the participants.

"I'll take it," she said.

"Perfect. I'm glad you called today. Listen, gotta run," Miranda told her. "Have a great Thanksgiving. We'll stay in touch."

After they rang off, Jill sat on the couch again and propped her socked feet onto the table then reached for her pen and legal pad. Handed a new purpose, she stared hard at the mustard-colored page and scribbled "genealogy" in its center. *Have I even spelled it correctly?* She squinted at the word, tapping the pen against her thigh, realizing she knew next to nothing about this topic. It would require some in-depth research.

A scuffling noise and raised voices at the front door told Jill that someone was about to knock. She recognized her roommate's voice. Lindsey was probably struggling to find her key again. Jill abandoned her notepad and headed swiftly for the door, watching Lindsey's skittish cat, Hercules, scamper off to the bedroom.

Opening the door, Jill braced herself for the inevitable burst of brittle-cold Colorado air then watched a tiny cyclone of snowflakes swirl at her feet.

"Hey!" Lindsey said, facing backward, crooking her neck. She struggled to hold the tip of a tree, while her boyfriend, Charlie, carried the base from a few feet away.

"A Christmas tree? Already?" Jill opened the door wider, watching Lindsey take awkward steps backward into the apartment.

"I know, I know. Gripe at me later. This thing is heavy."

"How can I help?" Jill offered.

"Guide me," Lindsey said, still stumbling into the living room, her petite stature dwarfed by the tree. "I'm headed toward that corner by the window."

"Keep walking straight back." Jill leaned over to shove aside the coffee table seconds before Lindsey could bash her knee into it.

Charlie shut the door with his foot and paused. "I've got it now."

He grunted then moved his tall frame to grab the center of the tree and ease it away from Lindsey, who stepped aside to stand with Jill. In one graceful movement, Charlie lifted the tree, brushing the ceiling with the tip of it, and carried it to the designated corner. The fresh smell of pine instantly permeated the room.

Lindsey removed her scarf and pushed out a long breath. "I'm exhausted," she told Jill. "Up two flights of stairs. My legs feel like jelly." She placed a hand on the crook of Jill's arm. "I know we didn't talk about it yet, getting a tree. But Charlie had first pick—his uncle runs that tree lot, remember?—and so we took the nicest one. Pretty, don't you think?"

Lindsey beamed toward the tree, which was tucked cozily into the corner of the room, as though it had been specifically designed to stand in that space.

A perfect fit. "It's beautiful," Jill admitted.

"We can decorate it tonight!" Lindsey insisted. "It'll be even more beautiful then!"

Charlie had joined them, brushing the pine needles off his gloved hands. He and Lindsey had been dating for over a year, and Lindsey was hoping for an engagement ring as a Christmas present. Although Jill would be ecstatic for her—they were one of those couples she could picture together decades in the future—she was also selfishly saddened by the prospect. It would mean finding a new roommate.

Jill had met Lindsey two years before at a local Denver writers' group. Lindsey was struggling with her children's book idea, and Jill had been asked to visit the group as a guest speaker. The two went for coffee after the session, where Lindsey peppered her with curious questions about the writing and publishing processes. The conversation had glided easily onto other topics, and as their personalities clicked and they realized they had similar tastes in music and books, they knew the seeds of a genuine friendship had sprouted that night. Weeks later, when Lindsey told her she was looking for a new apartment, Jill offered up her guest room, and they had been roommates ever since.

"Hey, I'm starved. Wanna get some food before the decorating starts?" Charlie suggested.

Jill's evening had changed with her call to Miranda—she was hoping to get started on the new article. But she knew she couldn't do it properly on an empty stomach.

"I can get us some Italian," Charlie suggested, making his pitch even more irresistible. Jill wouldn't even have to leave the apartment and brace the cold. Charlie knew their orders by heart—the Italian restaurant down the street was a place they either visited or ordered from once a week. When everyone agreed, Charlie gave Lindsey a quick peck on the cheek then headed out the door.

"You guys are cute," Jill told Lindsey.

"But not obnoxiously cute, right? Not the sit-on-the-same-side-of-the-booth type." She rolled her eyes at the image.

Jill chuckled. "Nope, you're adorable-cute. Very tolerable."

As Lindsey moved toward the tree, beaming up at it and probably mentally decorating it, Jill noticed Hercules peeking his furry head around the corner of the hallway then disappearing again when he saw the tree.

"I can't believe Thanksgiving is tomorrow," Lindsey said, slipping off her coat, the collar brushing against her short dark hair. "I think you'll like my family. They're loud, but they're welcoming."

The week before, knowing that Jill had no plans for the holiday, Lindsey had invited her to the big family celebration. At first, Jill had politely protested, saying she wouldn't be alone—like the year before, she'd planned to volunteer at a soup kitchen, surrounded by *lots* of people. But Lindsey was insistent and finally wore Jill down.

Jill joined Lindsey at the tree and touched one of the needled branches with her fingertips. "Can't wait."

DROPPING SOFT PILLOWS of marshmallows onto the sweet potato casserole, Jill doubted whether anything could be more

Thanksgivingy. The kitchen bustled with activity around her: three women overlapping in boisterous conversation, two eager dogs waiting for crumbs to fall, and one middle-aged man retrieving a soda from the fridge. Across the room, a toddler cried out for "More! More!" as he tugged on his mother's pants leg. Muffled cheers drifted in from the living room as the men watched a ball game on TV. An oven timer beeped its final announcement that the chestnut stuffing was ready.

Anyone peeking in on this domestic holiday scene might assume it was a Norman Rockwall painting come to life, an average American Thanksgiving. And that might have been true for most all the participants. But even as welcoming as Lindsey's family had been, with wide smiles and friendly greetings from the moment the door had opened, Jill still struggled to find her place in the gathering, to locate her comfort zone.

"That looks lovely!" proclaimed Lindsey's mother, peering toward Jill's sweet potato masterpiece.

"Thanks. I was trying to be creative," she admitted, tilting her head with a shrug. Jill had dotted the casserole with a slanted diamond pattern of marshmallows.

Jill wadded up the empty bag. "What else can I do?"

"I can't think of anything. We've got it mostly under control. Take a break and rest your feet. You've been hard at work." Lindsey's mother turned to the crowd. "Dinner's almost ready! Ten minutes!"

This news didn't seem to have the desired effect. No conversations paused, and no TVs clicked off.

"Oh! I meant to tell you. Lindsey gave me your book for my birthday... the first one, I think. *In Harm's Way?*"

"That's the one," Jill confirmed.

"Well, I haven't had a chance to read it yet. But I *will*," she assured Jill. "I don't seem to have time to read anymore. And now, with another grandbaby on the way..."

"I totally understand."

With a sparkle in her eye, Lindsey's mother added, "It must be *exciting* to be a famous author." Although phrased as a statement, it was clearly a question Jill was meant to answer.

Exciting wasn't the word Jill would use, not anymore. Fame was a funny thing, like a puff of smoke, tangible for a fleeting moment, but then disappearing as though it had never happened. Years before, two of Jill's books had hit the *New York Times* best-seller list for a few glorious weeks, and there had been considerable buzz surrounding her third and fourth releases. Jill McCallister was being hailed as "the next Sue Grafton" by certain smitten critics. But those next releases were met with lukewarm reception, and she knew she'd been dialing in the plots, which had led to her ultimate decision to end the series. Her heart wasn't in that character or that genre anymore. The books actually continued to sell at a steady rate, though, and Jill still considered herself a fairly successful midlist author.

Since it was too challenging to explain all of that in one polite sentence, Jill responded, "Well, thanks. I don't think of myself as 'famous,' but I'm happy with how things are going." In an effort to change the subject, she cleared her throat and asked, "Where's the powder room?"

"Around that corner." She pointed. "You can use the bathroom in the master."

On her way out of the kitchen, Jill passed behind one of Lindsey's aunts, who was discussing the "unacceptable behavior" of Hayden's preschool teacher, then rounded the corner and caught Lindsey's eye from the living room as she snuggled on the deep sofa next to Charlie. Jill gave her friend a reassuring wave. *I'm having a great time*, the wave said. *Glad you invited me.*

As Jill moved down the tiled hallway, she heard clicking and clacking behind her. She pivoted and saw that one of the dogs, a shaggy sheepdog, had followed her. She leaned down to scratch his head as he grinned up at her, wagging his tail and blinking behind all that fur.

"Happy Thanksgiving, boy," she told him. "I didn't bring any food with me. Go on back to the kitchen. I'm sure they'll sneak some for you..."

He gave a whine as she patted him one last time then straightened up to enter the master bedroom at the end of the hall. She closed the door, still aware of the activities going on in the house. A collective shout from the men erupted, no doubt praising an incredible play made by their favorite team.

Jill stepped farther inside the room and noticed the pristinely made bed, the cozy chair near the window, and the shelves lined with important-looking medical books owned by Lindsey's father, an anesthesiologist. As she walked deeper into the space, she noticed something else, a dresser topped with at least a couple dozen family photos in various frames. Hoping no one would walk in and catch her snooping, Jill moved toward the photos for a closer look. Some were older, black and white with stern faces peering out, while others were more modern and colorful with people wearing smiles and wild seventies fashion. Front and center was a recent photo of Lindsey with her arms lovingly wrapped around Charlie.

Jill wondered if she would have walked right past the photos had it not been for her new genealogy assignment. That always happened—whenever she had a new article or novel to research, the topic captivated her, seeping into almost everything else she did. She often became quietly obsessed with an idea, and this one was no different. She'd barely had time for a Google search the night before, but as she stared at the photos, she realized her research had officially begun.

Genealogy. Right here, on top of a dresser tucked inside someone's bedroom.

The photos symbolized more than cardstock inside pretty frames. They declared a rich history, a deep heritage, each photo telling the same story of nurtured relationships and lifetime bonds connected by one obvious element: family.

Jill couldn't help but personalize it, feeling a small ache inside as she remembered the sincerity in her mother's voice from their phone call last week: "Next year, honey. We'll spend the holidays together. I promise." But Jill knew it wouldn't happen next year, either. Her mother was a wanderer, a drifter, and had been ever since Jill's father passed away many years ago. They hadn't spent a single holiday together since Jill had graduated from college.

A particular photo caught Jill's eye, a recent family portrait with all twenty-something of the Lombardi clan smiling brightly for the camera. There were grandparents, parents, siblings, cousins, young children, and even a couple of dogs. Jill wondered if they knew how fortunate they were to have each other on a day like Thanksgiving—and every other day too.

Hearing another cheer raised from the living room, Jill resumed her mission and found the bathroom. She rinsed her fingertips of the sticky marshmallow film, dried her hands, then peered into the mirror and wiped away a smudge of mascara at the corner of her eye. Her hair, straightened in a hurry this morning, delicately grazed her shoulders. Staring at her reflection, she widened her brown eyes, puffed out a deep sigh, and willed herself to make it through the rest of the afternoon.

Passing by the photos again without a second glance, Jill opened the bedroom door to find the shaggy dog lying in the hall, waiting for her.

"Hey, boy." She squatted then scratched the fur under his chin. "That's a noisy kitchen. Are you taking a break from things too?"

He blinked his response.

Rocking on her heels, she clasped her hands together at her knees and looked him deep in the eyes. "Well, it's time to get back out there and join the party. This is Thanksgiving, and we have a lot to be grateful for, don't we?"

The dog gave her hand a hesitant lick then followed her back to the warm kitchen.

JILL ENTERED HER APARTMENT to the spicy scent of cinnamon and the soft tones of Bing Crosby crooning about Christmas. In fact, as she scanned the room and nudged the door closed with her elbow, she noticed that Christmas was *every*where, with miniature Santas and elves on tables, mistletoe overhead, a nativity scene on the coffee table, thick garland along the mantel, and a string of fairy lights framing the kitchen island. Lindsey had apparently awakened that morning with a singular mission: decorate everything in sight.

"Still snowing?" Lindsey asked from her favorite spot—on the floor, cross-legged, with her elbows propped on the coffee table while she graded math questions or cut shapes out of colored cardboard. As a second-grade teacher, Lindsey's workday usually extended well into after-work hours at home or even into the holidays.

Jill plopped her shopping bags onto the sofa then unraveled her scarf. "I think it's worse than this morning," she confirmed. "Traffic was a nightmare. I thought you were going to a late lunch with Charlie."

"He had to cancel. A work thing." Lindsey made a pouty face. "Wanna order Chinese later?" Consumed with her latest project, she barely glanced up as she spoke.

"Sure." Jill wriggled out of her coat and slung it across the back of the chair then headed toward the table to join Lindsey. Hercules was stretched out on the carpet nearby, intently focused on the flashing Christmas tree lights and likely plotting out which ornament to attack first.

"What are we working on?" Jill tried to make sense of the multitude of supplies spread out on the table: multicolored construction paper, glue bottles, glitter packages, cotton balls, markers, and popsicle sticks.

"Here. Grab a marker. It's a project for Monday. The theme is the Star of Bethlehem. I'm creating examples for the students. They can choose between drawing the shepherds, wise men, or angels. We can add cotton balls and glitter on the angel wings for some sparkle."

"Sounds exciting."

Lindsey grinned. "Well, at least this will keep them occupied for an hour or so. Those first days back from Thanksgiving promise to be *crazy*. I'm bracing myself. It will take the kids all next week to come down from the high of the holiday."

"Eighteen kids, at that age. I seriously don't know how you do it." Jill uncapped a marker and reached for a purple piece of construction paper.

Lindsey snickered. "Neither do I, most days. But I can't imagine doing anything else." She paused her coloring and looked across at Jill. "Teaching is the hardest job on Earth. But at the end of the most exhausting day, where everything has gone wrong—Matthew has put glue in Tabitha's hair, or Andrew has been in time-out because he won't stop using a curse word—I can still get into my car and know that I've accomplished something. That maybe, someday, these children will benefit from what I've modeled, whether it's how to handle a conflict or how to be loving to an unlovable classmate. Or maybe I've sparked an interest about science or reading that will affect their career choice down the road. It sounds dumb, saying it out loud—a total cliché. But teaching sort of... fills me up."

Jill understood completely. Teaching was Lindsey's zone, the thing that made her happiest.

"What is it?" Lindsey had paused her project. "You look... contemplative."

"I like hearing you talk about teaching. You really are making a difference."

"And what about you? That article last month, on the veteran and his dog. I was in tears by the end of it."

"Thanks. Yeah, that one was amazing to write. I wish all my writing could be that easy, though. I'm struggling with this new article, trying to find my focus."

"The genealogy topic?" Lindsey resumed her pasting of shredded cotton balls to an angel's wings. "I peeked at your notes..."

Jill threw a backward glance toward the cluttered mess of papers and spiral-bound notebooks she'd left on the sofa in frustration the night before. After coming home from Lindsey's parents' house, Jill had stayed up late, brainstorming, scribbling notes, researching online, and emailing a couple of professors at local universities, even though she knew they were on holiday break. On a piece of paper, she'd written *why?* then branched out possible reasons people would conduct genealogy searches in the first place: *medical history information, bragging rights (searches for famous people), strong interest in history, seeking a connection to the past, school projects, sheer curiosity.* But even after all that thought and effort, Jill didn't have a true starting point to work with.

"I thought I'd had a breakthrough," Jill admitted, "but it didn't work out. So I took today off. Ran errands, paid bills, the boring stuff."

"You piddled."

Jill lifted her marker into the air then paused and smirked. "Piddling is a vital part of the writing process. And I actually prefer the word 'lollygagging.'"

"Great word! I need to teach my students that one. Lollygag."

Jill resumed her coloring. "I was hoping to come back to the article fresh tonight, maybe be handed some inspiration on a silver platter."

"Oh, *that's* how it works."

"Sometimes, it actually does," Jill mused, capping her marker and reaching for another. "I only wish the gaps between inspiration weren't so long and frustrating."

Lindsey had pressed down on her angel's wings to secure the cotton. She kept her fingertips there but looked up at Jill suddenly with raised eyebrows. "Hey, I have an idea about the article. Why don't you experiment with it yourself?"

"What do you mean?" Jill hovered the marker in place, more interested in Lindsey's idea than the construction-paper project.

"With your own genealogy. Didn't your mom send you a subscription a while back to one of those ancestry websites?"

Jill's mother was notorious for buying quirky gifts, usually ones Jill couldn't hold or unwrap, such as subscriptions to online sites, stocks and bonds, or a notification that she'd had a star named after her. Jill could see where Lindsey was going and felt a rush of recognition.

"Yes. She did! It was months ago." Jill abandoned her marker then pushed aside the mess of papers and sat on the sofa, brought her laptop to her knees, and cracked it open. "In fact, I'm pretty sure I even created an account and put in some information. But then I never bothered to go back and check it."

She did a quick search of her inbox and skimmed the results. And there it was, the original gifted subscription from MyGenealogy.com.

"You already know most of *my* heritage," her mother had told Jill, trying to explain her gift over the phone. "French-Italian—but we don't know much about your father's family history. So I bought you a year's subscription. Let me know what you find out!"

Jill had forgotten the password ages ago, so she clicked the link to reset it then paused. "I'm not sure about this, though," she told Lindsey. "I don't write articles about myself. That's the fun of writing for the magazine. The same is true for my novels. I get to explore other people."

"You mean hide behind them." Lindsey grinned.

"True. I guess it's easier that way. Safer."

Lindsey clicked off Bing's song and joined Jill on the couch, peering curiously at the screen with her.

As Jill typed in the updated password, she considered the new possible angle. *Why* can't *I write about my personal experience? Or at least explore my own genealogy to get an idea of what the search actually feels like for someone else?* Jill had been doing her research all wrong. She had been tackling the project from the outside in, as someone who didn't particularly care about the topic of genealogy. Until now, the word had meant very little in her own life—it always evoked shady images of strangers buried deep in the past, of ghostly figures she had never met and never could meet. She couldn't fathom what good it would do to dredge up the past or what relevance it would have to her daily life. But as she recalled that dresser full of photos at Lindsey's family home, Jill realized Lindsey was right. In order to find the heart of it, the article *had* to be personal. There was no other way.

"You're in!" Lindsey proclaimed as the site accepted the new password.

Excitement grew as Jill clicked on her account information. She vaguely recalled, months before, having entered only her father's name and his parents' names, which was as far back as she could remember. As she watched the site generate its report, Jill tempered her expectations. *What information could the site possibly glean from on-*

ly three names and some basic information about them? But when the report appeared on her screen, she saw a significant family tree that traced her father's lineage backward for four generations.

"Look at *that*," Lindsey whispered.

Jill wanted to slow down and take everything in. The moment felt suddenly weighty, and she needed to absorb it. She saw her own name perched at the top of the family tree: *Jill McCallister*. She followed the line downward and recognized the first two names: Nicholas, her father, then her grandmother, Amelia Sandifer McCallister, where the family tree continued to branch off. Past that, Jill had been totally clueless about her history. But not anymore.

The next branch led to her great-grandfather, Cody Sandifer, born in 1920. Jill had hoped for a coordinating photo or link, but none was available. A couple of "cousin" branches splintered off, but Jill was most interested in the direct lineage, so she followed the main branch further down toward Cody's parents—Richard Sandifer and Morgan (Stout) Sandifer. No photos or links, unfortunately.

The tree branch halted noticeably at Morgan's father.

"Alfred J. Stout," Jill said aloud.

"Your great-great-grandfather."

"Add one more 'great,'" Jill said.

"Oh. Right."

Curious, Jill clicked on the black-and-white photo of Mr. Stout, born 1858, which expanded to a grainy family portrait of an unsmiling man with a bushy beard and piercing eyes, a willowy-looking wife, also unsmiling, and a little girl with ringlets, who wore a drop-waisted dress with lace-up boots. She was grinning ear-to-ear, which made Jill return the grin, there on her apartment sofa, over a century after the photo had been taken.

"My great-great-grandmother," she whispered to the photo.

"She looks like you," Lindsey confirmed softly, as though the discovery deserved some quiet reverence. "It's the eyes."

Jill saw it, too, that familiarity, that connection. Pulse racing, she clicked back to her family tree, finally understanding what all the fuss was about. Jill realized she *was* interested in knowing where she got her wide brown eyes, and especially, her unruly, naturally curly hair. But the biggest thrill of the search was the invisible unlocking of doors, of mysteries being solved before her very eyes, of history taking shape and filling in the gaps of her past. Jill had just opened a portal in time and was reaching inside, shaking the hand of someone she shared DNA with, someone she'd never met before.

"Is that a link? On Alfred's name?" Lindsey pointed at the screen.

"Looks like it..." Jill clicked it and was immediately taken to a website: *Morgan's Grove, Texas: The Most Beautiful Town You've Never Heard Of!*

"That doesn't seem right," Jill murmured with a frown. She scanned the main page and its photo of a charming town square filled with shops and a center courthouse decorated in festive lights. People walked, children played, shoppers shopped. It was small-town America in all its glory.

"What does a town in Texas have to do with Alfred J.?" she wondered aloud. Perhaps it was an incorrect link—one wrong letter in a URL address could make all the difference.

"Wait," Lindsey said. "Morgan. That was the name of Alfred's daughter..." She pointed at the town's *About* link. "Try that page."

Jill clicked, and there it was—that stern, now-familiar face of Alfred J. Stout. And beneath the name was a caption: *Founder of Morgan's Grove.*

"You've struck gold," Lindsey said, gently grabbing Jill's sleeve. Her excitement was contagious. "Keep reading..."

Jill read the blurb aloud. "Alfred J. Stout was a billionaire from New York, NY who gained his wealth from his business ingenuity, building several textile mills after the Industrial Revolution. He married a small-town Indiana girl then moved her to Central Texas in 1908, where he built a luxurious mansion for her. Shortly after, Stout purchased the derelict town nearby then rebuilt it with loving care. He named the town after his young daughter, Morgan."

When she finished the paragraph, Jill realized the screen had turned blurry because of unexpected tears. She had no idea that clicking on a family tree would draw out so many emotions in only a few minutes. She was gazing at her heritage, pieces of history from her father's background. The reminder of him could still prick a place inside Jill's heart, even years later. She wished her father could have been there, sitting beside her, discovering the new revelations right along with her.

Realizing Lindsey was still quietly clinging to her sleeve, Jill wiped a falling tear and smiled toward her friend, glad she had someone to share the moment with.

Lindsey whispered, "I think you found your story," then leaned in to rest her head against Jill's. After a beat, Lindsey pushed away with a small gasp and stared at Jill. "You should go."

"Go?"

"There!" She pointed at the screen. "To Morgan's Grove. Find out more, do some on-site research, stay awhile. A new place to write, a fresh environment. It would be good for you."

Jill tilted her head, allowing the idea to take shape. "I've never been to Texas," she mused.

"I'm shocked! I assumed you'd lived in all fifty states by now," Lindsey teased.

She knew all about Jill's childhood—how, after her father passed away, her mother had moved them nearly every single year afterward. New apartments, new schools, new jobs. This habit had followed Jill into adulthood, and since college, she'd lived in a few different places herself. In fact, for a thirty-year-old, Jill had accumulated remarkably few possessions. Much of the apartment's furniture, including the couch they were sitting on, was Lindsey's. Jill always tried to keep her life simple and clutter-free. *"Transportable," some might say...*

"Seriously," Lindsey continued. "Visiting Morgan's Grove might be inspiring. You could even end up writing a whole book about this journey—a search for your heritage, and how you basically own a whole town."

"I do *not* own a whole town." Jill snickered, glad for a lighter moment. She slid the open laptop toward the table. "Besides, you're talking about nonfiction. I write fiction. I get to pretend, to create storylines and whole worlds from thin air. I don't have to be chained to facts."

"Well, okay. Then forget your book for now and focus on the article. How can a town square like that not be inspiring? Especially at Christmastime, all decorated. It's charming and cozy, like a painting."

"It's probably Photoshopped." Jill smirked. "Too good to be true."

"You won't know until you get there!" She leaned forward to click another page on the website. "Let's see... there's a visitors' page. Horseback riding, shopping, nature hikes, hay rides, and 'other seasonal activities.' And look." She clicked a new link. "Here's Alfred J. Stout's mansion, the one he built for his wife. I'd go there first, if I were you. Hey, you might not own the town, but you could claim ownership of the mansion!"

Jill shook her head. "You've been watching too many Hallmark movies. Things don't work that way in real life." Still, she stared deeper into the photo and saw the pointed gables, the grand front porch, and the manicured lawn, and she imagined herself there...

"And look"—Lindsey pointed to the caption beneath the town's name—"this is located 'on the outskirts of Austin.' A teacher-friend of mine went there last year—Austin has this big social scene, clubs and restaurants, live music, and a huge university. Very metropolitan. You could take a couple of side trips to the city if you got bored."

"That's true..." Jill entered Morgan's Grove in her mind, walking deep inside a mansion that her great-great-great-grandfather had built. She pictured browsing the quaint shops, staying at some cute B&B, riding horses, and driving to Austin on a side trip or two. Plus, the weather in Texas would surely be warmer and milder than Denver, which in itself was incredibly appealing.

And even more, she wondered whether a research trip could be a hiatus *from* her writer's block, as Lindsey had suggested, a retreat away from the pressure and madness of forcing herself to invent new characters, creative settings, and fresh storylines. The more Jill seemed to focus on grasping desperately for ideas, the more they flitted further away from her as if they were teasing, playing a game. So maybe she should gain the upper hand again, turn her back deliberately on the Muse for a while, and let her trip to Texas be a much-needed escape.

Suddenly, the seed of an idea had blossomed into a tangible plan. Jill knew she couldn't resist. "Okay. I'll do it."

"I'll help you pack!" Lindsey pushed off the sofa and clapped her hands.

"Now? But I thought I'd wait a couple of days, keep researching online, book a flight and a hotel, check weather reports—"

"I can do all that for you." Lindsey waved away her friend's concerns. "No time like the present, right?"

Jill stood to join her roommate and puffed out a nervous sigh. "Looks like I'm going to Texas!"

Chapter Two

Jill clicked off the audiobook's narrator in mid-sentence, not caring that the name of Agatha Christie's murderer was about to be revealed. She had more important things on her mind. Gripping the steering wheel, she moved all her attention to the highway once again. After sixteen hours of driving split between two days, she didn't want to miss the Morgan's Grove exit.

It had been Miranda's idea for Jill to drive to Texas rather than fly. When Jill had told her about the new angle for her article, including her personal connection to an obscure little town in Texas, Miranda had thrown out the notion of a road trip so that Jill could experience for herself the changing landscape and shifting temperatures all the way from Colorado to central Texas. It could become part of her research, part of the journey. The road-trip idea was particularly attractive to Jill, since it meant avoiding altogether the nightmare of crowded holiday air travel.

So after spending the next day packing for a possible two-week stay, making B&B arrangements, and carefully studying the route, Jill had waved goodbye to Lindsey, climbed into her car, and headed southward. She'd spent that night in an Amarillo hotel, compiling her notes and observations, brainstorming more of the article, then getting some much-needed sleep.

On the second leg of the journey, Jill had watched the landscape change right before her eyes. As she entered Texas more deeply, she marked the vast differences in terrain from Colorado—there were fewer trees, heavier winds, and flatter lands. She had half-expected all the snow and cold temperatures to halt promptly at the Texas border, but Amarillo was snow-covered, and the white patches only disappeared as she reached Dallas to get gas.

As she approached the outskirts of Austin, Jill eagerly searched for the exit ramp she needed. Finally, two miles later, the Morgan's Grove sign came into view.

She took the exit then followed the street signs, craning her neck and slowing her pace. As she edged closer to the town, she wanted to absorb everything: the streets branching off with lovely neighborhoods, the old-fashioned houses—some already dotted with Christmas lights—the enormous and impeccable front yards, and the official sign that welcomed her to the town. *Population: 1,377.*

Soon, the Morgan's Grove town square, the crown jewel she'd been so anxious to see, appeared. Jill rolled to a stoplight and idled her Toyota to view the town's dusky skyline. She peered through the windshield and first saw the courthouse. It mirrored exactly the photo she'd seen on her laptop of a historic two-story building decorated with tiny white lights.

Smiling, Jill scanned the rest of the town square, including the grand library beside the courthouse then a string of shops wrapping all around the lengthy block. There was an old movie theater, an antique store, a barbecue restaurant, a candle shop, a bookstore, a music store, and others, all pristinely trimmed in white lights. A beautiful, stately maple tree stood in front of the library, its leaves colored a deep crimson. Dozens of people browsed the square. Some crossed the street with shopping bags, some walked dogs along brick sidewalks, and others perched on benches, sipping drinks.

Before the stoplight turned green, Jill snapped a quick photo of the square with her phone. She could text it to Lindsey later to prove that the photo of Morgan's Grove hadn't been Photoshopped.

At the other end of Main Street, she found the quaint bed-and-breakfast, painted a pale yellow with a wraparound porch. Jill located a parking space at the curb and snatched up her purse. She could bring in her luggage after checking in.

Inside the B&B, Jill heard Nat King Cole's voice floating through the air as she crossed the room toward the garland-decorated front desk. A four-inch Santa stood beside the guest book, welcoming visitors.

"Hello there," said a woman on the other side. She set down her paperback romance and laced her fingers together on top of its well-worn spine. Her plump cheeks widened into a bright smile. "I'm Paula Haversham. Welcome to Morgan's Grove."

Her accent was as twangy as Jill had expected, and every bit as charming.

The woman squinted and cocked her head. "You look familiar, hon. Have you been here before? To our town?"

"No, it's actually my first time in Texas."

"Well, I could just *swear* I've seen you somewhere…"

Internally, Jill made the possible connection as she spied the bookshelf against the back wall, stuffed full of paperbacks. Mrs. Haversham was obviously an avid reader, so perhaps one of Jill's novels had made its way onto one of the shelves once upon a time.

"I guess I have one of those faces."

"Guess so. Whereabouts are you from?"

"Denver."

"Oh, then you're used to these freezing temperatures. It only reached fifty-six today!"

Jill wanted to snicker at the notion of fifty-six being considered freezing, but out of politeness, she kept it to herself. Mrs. Haversham would never have survived the fifteen below that Denver experienced the winter before. "What's the weather usually like?"

"Sixties and seventies, even in December. But we've had historically low temperatures this season, and this body of mine can't get used to it." She shivered and rubbed her sweater-covered arms then retrieved the guest book. "So how can I help you, sweetie?"

"I have a reservation. Under Jill McCallister."

"Well, that name sounds familiar, too! I guess I'm having a real déjà-vu moment, here." Mrs. Haversham perused her guest book then paused. "Would you spell that for me, hon? Is it M-a-c or just M-c?"

"M-c," Jill verified.

Mrs. Haversham used her index finger to scan the list. "Mc-Callister! There you are." But then she shook her head. "That's not right..." She swiveled to check an old-fashioned key box on the wall behind her. With a tsk, she told Jill, "I can't believe I'm saying this, but... it seems we're overbooked." Her expression was fretful. "Let me check one other document."

She stooped to retrieve another book and flipped through its pages. She scowled again, worry lines showing in her forehead. "Oh, dear. I'm afraid your reservation starts tomorrow. Says here you're staying for two days?"

"I was hoping to stay longer, but I was told it's all you had, so I took it."

"Well, there's no room at the inn tonight. I couldn't be more sorry about this. There's no tellin' what happened. Maybe Becky—that's my niece—wrote down the wrong date. In any case, it seems we're full up."

Jill tried not to let the disappointment show as she wondered whether an updated computer system rather than an antiquated guest book would have prevented an overbooking in the first place. She wasn't upset with Mrs. Haversham—mistakes happened, human error and so forth—but Jill had driven such a long distance to get there. She had originally hoped there was enough daylight left for her to browse a few shops, but suddenly, her priorities had shifted. She would be spending the rest of the evening finding a place to lay her weary head.

"This is our busiest season," Mrs. Haversham explained with a wince. "In fact, I'm surprised we had a spot open, even for a couple of days. Tourists from all over come to see the festivities—there's a parade, a festival, a concert. And we have all sorts of quaint shops where people can buy Christmas gifts for loved ones—" She interrupted her own thought. "Sorry. I'm getting off track. Not trying to make excuses for our mistake. Only wanted to explain."

"I understand. Do you have any suggestions for another place nearby? Maybe Austin?" Jill wondered.

Mrs. Haversham tapped her index finger on the counter, her lips pursed in deep thought. Then, she snapped her fingers. "I have a solution. Lucille, a lady in town, has a room—in fact, she's trying to rent it out, but no luck yet. I'll give her a call."

After a moment on the phone, she nodded and set down the landline's receiver with a definitive click.

"It's all settled, honey." Mrs. Haversham found a thin newspaper, flipped to the back page, then handed it over and tapped the photo. "Lucille Wright, that's her name, is more than happy to put you up tonight. It's on us—you won't pay a penny."

"Oh, that's not necessary—"

"You'll learn fast that we don't take 'no' for an answer 'round here. It's that stubborn Texas pride of ours," Mrs. Haversham insisted with a grin. "Generous to a fault. You might as well get used to it."

"Well, okay. Thank you. It's very kind."

Jill skimmed the ad: *212 Tulip Lane. Tidy room for rent above garage. No pets, please. Daily breakfast included, chats optional.*

How quirky, Jill thought. The accompanying black-and-white photo showed a two-story house with a neatly clipped lawn.

"Lucille's a wonderful lady," Mrs. Haversham assured her. "You'll get along like two peas in a pod. And her house is a stone's throw from here. Just drive back through the square and find Tulip Lane. It's the first house on your right, corner lot."

Jill folded the paper. "Thanks."

"You're entirely welcome. I hope you enjoy your stay in our fair city."

"I'm sure I will."

COASTING BACK THROUGH the town square in her Toyota, Jill realized most of the shop owners were closing up, the street lamps were flicking on, and the tourists were thinning out as the sky continued to darken. She would have to wait until tomorrow to see the town in all its glory.

Jill suppressed a yawn as she scanned the street names for Tulip Lane, then slowed the car and made a right turn. She parked at the curb, removed her suitcase from the trunk, then turned to stare at the house. It was a life-sized doll house with crème-colored exterior, lacy trim, sharp-pointed gables, and a generous wraparound porch. The photo hadn't done it justice.

Jill snapped a quick photo of her own for Lindsey then rolled her luggage toward the porch, which held a swing at one end and a full-sized Christmas tree at the other. The branches shivered, but there was no wind to account for it. Curious, Jill approached the staircase and discovered the source of the shivering. A silver-haired woman knelt at the tree's base, struggling to string lights across the thick layer of bottom branches. She paused to rub her lower back then wheeled around when she saw Jill's shadow.

"Oh! There you are!" The woman abandoned the Christmas lights, hoisted her body up with a grunt, and walked forward with a slight limp. She was a thin, petite woman, no more than five feet tall. "I've been expecting you. Jill?"

The woman dusted off her palms then extended a hand as Jill climbed the final step to meet her.

"Yes. Jill McCallister." She set down her luggage then shook the woman's hand.

"How lovely. Sounds like a song." Her Southern accent was light around the edges. She had crystal-blue eyes and wore peach lipstick that matched her creamy skin tone. Jill guessed she was close to seventy years old. She wondered what Lucille had looked like when she was younger.

"Wait. McCallister? You look familiar..."

"I have that sort of face, I guess."

"You're a writer. Aren't you? That mystery series!"

"Guilty," Jill said, then realized her unintended pun.

"We read your first book a couple of years ago in our book club! I was in the middle of the second one but wasn't able to finish it. Oh, not because I didn't enjoy it, mind you. It's just that... it was a particularly hectic time for me, and—"

"I understand. No need to explain." Jill shuffled her feet, never knowing how to respond to those "I've always meant to read your work but never got around to it" or "I haven't been able to finish the whole series yet because..." type of statements.

"Are you working on something new?" Lucille wondered.

It was a harmless question, but in the mind of a writer struggling desperately for new ideas, it was a loaded one. "I'm in between books at the moment." Then, hoping to change the subject entirely, she added, "And you're Mrs. Wright?"

"Oh. Yes. Sorry! I got a bit starstruck. Call me Lucille."

"Your house is beautiful."

"Why, thank you. It's almost a hundred years old. A nightmare for upkeep, but it's home to me. Worth every bit of trouble." She studied Jill's face. "Whereabouts are you from? I don't hear an accent.

I was about to assume New York or California, but not all writers come from there, I suppose."

"I live in Denver."

"Beautiful place. I used to camp in Colorado with my husband, Frank, during summers a long, long time ago..." Her eyes held a wistful shadow, but then she blinked and cleared her throat. "What brings you here to our town? If you don't mind my asking."

Jill remembered the *chats optional* line in the ad and grinned at the battery of personal questions right up front.

She hadn't considered whether or not she would tell any townspeople about her article, about her suspected ties to Morgan's Grove. To keep things simple, she replied half-truthfully: "Well, I needed a break from things and heard about this town's holiday spirit. I thought I'd come and see for myself."

"Christmas is the perfect time to experience Morgan's Grove at its best."

Jill could hear Lucille's affection for the town in her voice and could see it on her face. It was the same expression Mrs. Haversham had worn for her initial greeting—they took genuine pride in their city.

"Well. Let's get you inside, shall we? It's too cold out here!" Lucille insisted. "And you're probably exhausted from your journey."

"I am," Jill admitted, following Lucille to the screen door.

"Are you hungry?" Lucille paused with her fingertips on the door handle. "I can heat up some leftover pork chops for you."

"Oh, thanks. But I had a late lunch. Still full."

"Maybe you've saved room for dessert. I was about to bake off some fresh gingerbread when Paula called about your room situation. How about joining me in the kitchen for some cookies and milk before I show you the room?"

Leery of saying "no" twice in a row to the kind stranger who was taking in a stranger of her own, Jill agreed, even though she secretly hated gingerbread. "Sure. That sounds nice."

Jill followed Lucille through the screen door, carefully bumping her luggage through the doorway, and heard a clacking sound she couldn't identify. But then, she saw two spunky, squatty dogs race to the front door. They came to a simultaneous halt at their owner's feet, panting wildly, tongues lolling.

"Hello, my little ones," said Lucille, stretching down to pet them both.

Jill couldn't identify the breed. They had splotchy blond-and-white coloring, long bodies like dachshunds, triangle ears like Chihuahuas, button noses like foxes, and soulful eyes like Labradors, but no tails. When the dogs finally focused on the stranger standing in their house, she could swear they actually smiled at her.

"They're adorable. A mixed breed?" Jill watched them sniff eagerly at her pants legs and then her suitcase.

"They're corgis," Lucille said.

"Oh, I've heard of those. Didn't the Queen of England raise several of them?"

"That's right. They're small dogs with big hearts. My husband gave me these two as a gift three years ago. George and Gracie," she said, pointing to one then the other. "They're brother and sister."

"Named after Burns and Allen?" Jill stooped to let them sniff at her fingers. One of them tentatively licked the back of her hand.

"Exactly. I'm surprised you know them."

"Oh, I love that era. My grandfather and I spent a whole summer together, watching *Burns and Allen* reruns on TV when I was a little girl."

"Impressive!" Lucille stepped through the corgis to make her way deeper into the house. "Please forgive the mess." She shoved an empty box aside with her foot as Jill noticed a few more boxes scattered around. "I'm finally pulling out all the decorations," Lucille explained, moving forward. "I say 'finally.' People around here start decorating for Christmas before Thanksgiving even arrives!" She snickered. "Guess I'm late to the party this year."

Jill followed Lucille past a staircase and down a long hall, the corgis tap-dancing behind them, toward the kitchen at the back—a sunny-looking space with warm, buttery colors. Jill set down her purse and luggage near a breakfast table then noticed an unusual area near the back door. A three-foot-wide wall stood completely covered in photographs, nearly floor-to-ceiling. She stepped forward for a closer look.

"This is amazing." Jill crossed her arms and browsed the photos from several different decades.

Much like Lindsey's family dresser filled with frames, Lucille's wall collage contained no particular rhyme or reason to the order of things—black-and-white photos intermingled easily with more recent pictures containing bright color and activity. *Someone's whole life, there on a kitchen wall.*

"Thank you," Lucille said, removing her cardigan. "That's my memory wall. It makes me happy, seeing photos displayed rather than stuck in some photo album to dust off every five years. I prefer seeing their faces every day. My loved ones. And friends. Some still around, some long gone..."

The picture in the center caught Jill's attention. She recognized Lucille standing between two men—one, possibly in his sixties, wearing a suit and tie, and the other, likely in his early twenties, donning a graduation robe.

"That's my husband, Frank." Lucille stepped closer, pointing at the photo. "And Rick, my grandson."

The tall young man with dark eyes tipped his graduation cap down toward his grandmother. His demeanor seemed gawky and unsure, but his grin for the camera was warm and proud.

"My, time flies." Lucille sighed. "That was almost ten years ago. University of Texas graduation, master's program."

"What field?"

"Computer science. I'm proud of what Rick has become. And so was Frank." Jill heard a tremble in her voice. "Rick is very successful in his business out in California. He calls me every other day, religiously. He's a good grandson. Usually joins me for Thanksgiving, but he wasn't able to make it this year. Couldn't get out of an important meeting. He said he'll come for Christmas, though."

The corgis had found a cozy spot near the patio door. One of them rolled all the way over onto its back, and its stumpy legs dangled in the air.

"Well." Lucille clapped her hands together. "I guess I'd better get going on these cookies I promised you."

"May I help?"

"No, no. You're my guest. Have a seat." Lucille gestured toward a barstool at the tall center island.

As Jill obeyed, Lucille pulled out a wax-paper-covered disc from the refrigerator and set it on the island. "Time to roll the dough and cut the shapes. This is my favorite part."

The moment Lucille peeled back the paper from the dough, the mixture of spices, presumably cinnamon, nutmeg, and ginger, hit Jill's senses. She'd always thought of gingerbread the way her mother thought of coffee—she loved the rich scent of it but not the taste.

"Smells amazing," Jill said, taking a deep whiff.

"It's my great-grandmother's recipe." Lucille sprinkled a healthy amount of flour onto the island then spread the dough out, first using the heels of her hands. She rotated the dough a quarter turn then pushed on it again. "I'm gonna be honest. I would love to barrage you right now with a bunch of questions about your profession—writers absolutely fascinate me—but I won't be that sort of hostess, trapping a guest here in my kitchen and digging for personal information. So, instead, what if I tell you more about our fair city?"

"I'd love that!" Jill hadn't expected to hear about the town from a local so early. She knew *that* was where the most interesting stories would come from, rather than some short, sanitized blurb on a website. Jill was tempted to whip out her laptop and take notes, but that would put Lucille on the spot, and it would expose Jill's primary purpose for being in Morgan's Grove. Instead, she would take detailed mental notes and jot them down later.

"Where to begin..." Lucille reached for the rolling pin and dusted it with flour. "The founder was a billionaire from New York City, Alfred J. Stout. What a name, eh? He made his fortune with some big industrial company... I always forget what type. Anyway, in the early 1900s, he decided to build himself an enormous mansion about a mile from this very spot. An abandoned, run-down town stood nearby, so he bought the whole thing, fancied it up, and named it after his daughter, Morgan. Then he let his wife name all the streets. She was a gardener, so she chose all flower names."

Jill recalled some of the street signs as she'd passed through town: Petunia, Gardenia, Rose Petal, Tulip...

"There's a plaque dedicated to the family, right in front of the courthouse. And the founder's mansion is on the outskirts of town. It gets a lot of traffic this time of year."

"I'll bet." Jill would visit the next day, first thing.

As Lucille rolled the dough into a wider, thinner disc, she barely needed to watch her own hands. She'd probably done it hundreds of times in her life. When she grabbed a nearby cookie cutter, her elbow nudged the half-full bag of flour, knocking it off the island and onto the floor. She muttered, "Oh, gracious."

George and Gracie's heads snapped to attention, ears perked, to see what the fuss was about.

"Here, let me help." Jill spied a broom and dustpan in the corner and rushed toward it. She knew from earlier observation on the porch that Lucille couldn't bend very easily.

"Thank you, dear." Lucille stood still as Jill swept away the white powder around her ankles.

"No trouble at all." Jill finished the job, tipped the dustpan into the trash can, then replaced the broom back in the corner. "Listen, I'd love to cut out some shapes with you. It looks fun."

"It is!" Lucille spread out the cutters on the counter. "You get first dibs."

Jill gave her hands a quick wash then rejoined Lucille at the island to sift through Christmas trees and gingerbread men. She found a snowman-shaped cutter and drew it out.

"Excellent choice. That was Rick's favorite too," Lucille noted. "He used to help me make these when he was a little boy. He refused to call them gingerbread, though. He had a special name for his cookies... I haven't thought of this in ages. What did he call them? Molasses... something. Molasses crinkles! That was it. Can you imagine? A boy of, oh, seven or eight, blurting out 'molasses crinkles'? I have no idea where he thought of it."

Soon, the empty tray was filled with cookie shapes ready to be baked. Lucille lifted the tray into a hot oven, set the timer for nine minutes, then returned to the island and kneaded together the remnants of dough, massaging them into a new disc for the next rolling out.

"This is quite a process," Jill said. "Making the dough, refrigerating it, then rolling it off and baking it. Must take hours."

"And don't forget the icing at the end! Yes, it's a long process. I always make a double batch and end up freezing half the cookies. But the effort is worth it for that very first bite. It's the flavor of Christmas." She floured the dough and pin, focusing on her task.

When the timer beeped, Lucille pulled on a thick oven mitt. "This was Frank's favorite part. He would always insist on removing that very first pan. As though *he* had helped in any way. Ridiculous man."

The mist in her eyes confirmed to Jill that Frank was likely deceased. She wondered how long he'd been gone.

The moment Lucille opened the oven door, the comforting scent of gingerbread infused the entire kitchen. It only took a few short moments for Lucille and Jill to make the icing—powdered sugar and water stirred briskly together—as the cookies cooled.

Lucille finished icing her first cookie then said, "I can't wait. I'm having one now."

Jill followed her lead. She swirled a dab of icing onto the snowman's head, dreading the next moment. Her one and only experience with gingerbread had been as a little girl, when her mother handed her a stale cookie one Christmas and told her to try it. The burnt, overly spiced flavors had made little Jill's nose crinkle in disgust. She'd spit the half-chewed piece into her hand when her mother's back was turned.

But now, for sheer politeness' sake, Jill was forced to have a significant bite. And to pretend to enjoy it.

You can do this. She lifted the snowman to her lips and tasted the sweet frosting with the tip of her tongue. Hopefully, it would be enough to mask the rest of the cookie's strong, spicy flavors.

Instead of being sheepish about it, Jill chose to dive in and be bold, to wrap her mouth around a significant bite. *All in. No turning back.* Lucille at least deserved a full tasting from her, after the time and trouble she'd spent on the cookies.

Jill clamped down on the bite and started to chew. Immediately, surprisingly, her taste buds welcomed the cookie. The delicate mixture of spices wasn't overwhelming at all. They were subtle, perfectly balanced, light and flavorful. And the texture wasn't crispy and burned, as she'd expected. Instead, the cookie was soft and chewy and decadent, practically dissolving in her mouth. She wanted more.

Jill stared widely at Lucille and held the rest of the cookie in midair. "Lucille. These are... fantastic. Seriously. Fan-*tas*-tic."

"Well, thank you!"

"No, I have a real confession to make. I sort of... lied to you earlier. I don't actually like gingerbread. But I was embarrassed to tell you. In fact, I haven't had gingerbread in twenty-something years. So I was worried about tasting these. But..." She took another bite, savoring it, then swallowed. "These are seriously incredible. You've converted me. I'm a gingerbread believer."

Lucille chuckled. "I know that not everyone loves gingerbread. It can be positively awful if the spices aren't blended well. But this is a special recipe. It's won several awards at our local county fair over the years."

"I can see why. You could even sell these!" Jill finished off her cookie and accepted the cold glass of milk that Lucille had poured for her.

"It's funny you should say that. Once upon a time, I considered opening my own bakery."

"Why didn't you?"

"Let's just say life got in the way..."

One of the corgis yawned in the corner with a loud, garbled groan while the other one stretched its stumpy legs.

Lucille finished her final bite then dusted her fingertips. "Now, about that room. Let me show it to you and make sure it will meet your needs."

"Thanks again for putting me up on short notice."

Lucille waved a hand. "No trouble at all. I like having the company. How long were you planning to stay in town?"

"Possibly two weeks. I'll search for a new place tomorrow, maybe in Austin..."

"Nonsense. Stay the duration here, at the upstairs apartment, if you like. You'll have more privacy than a B&B, and you can come and go as you please. The apartment can be your home base while you're here."

"That's very kind, but what about a potential boarder showing up? I know you're trying to rent the space."

Lucille retrieved her sweater from the nearby chair. "I don't think anyone will be interested over the holidays. Most people don't move until after the new year. So this could work out for both of us."

Jill recalled what Mrs. Haversham had said about trying to take "no" for an answer in this town. "Thank you. I'll definitely consider it."

She followed Lucille out the side kitchen door and toward the detached garage, which was lit by strong floodlights. To get to the room above, they climbed a narrow-but-sturdy staircase that ended with a square wooden platform and a green door. Jill bumped her luggage up the steps behind her.

"It's not much," Lucille warned as she unlocked the green door then opened it wide, flicking on the main light. "But it's cozy. New paint, new flooring, even a pretty bedspread. And I bought one of those—what do you call them?—a mini-fridge. It's there in the corner."

Jill stepped inside. The first thing she noticed was the strong scent emitted from a glass bowl of potpourri nearby. Then she saw the whitewashed walls, bright and cheerful, similar to a summer beach house she and her mother lived in for a few months, once upon a time. The only window in the room, which faced the street, was open slightly, letting in the chilly breeze and the faraway sounds of dogs barking and children laughing.

"It's charming," Jill admitted. She could instantly see herself happy in the space.

"It has both heating and cooling—you never know which one you'll need this time of the year. Weather can change in a heartbeat. One possible drawback, though..." Lucille winced. "You'll be able to hear the gears grinding underneath the floor whenever I have to take the car out of the garage. But I'm not out that often—mostly for church and errands and such. And never late at night. So hopefully, it's not a problem."

"That won't bother me. I can always hear my roommate, Lindsey, snoring down the hallway, even with both our doors closed. I've learned how to tune it out."

"Oh, and there's a small bathroom behind this door," Lucille pointed out. "The water pressure in the shower is strong. I had the man check it yesterday."

"This is perfect, all of it." Jill bounced her purse onto the mattress.

"Now, I promise that I won't be a bother and expect you for meals," Lucille told her. "I'll give you space and privacy. But you're welcome to join me, especially for breakfast. Once in a while, wouldn't it be nice to have a companion, someone to eat with?"

It would, Jill thought, nodding.

"Oh, and I always leave the kitchen door unlocked in the daytime. So, if you ever need anything—batteries, bottled water, a lightbulb, whatever—come on in and find them if I'm not here. Come and go as you please." Lucille wriggled the apartment's key free from her chain then handed it to Jill. "I'll let you get settled in."

Lucille clicked the door shut, and Jill sat on the edge of the bed, watching the hypnotic billowing curtains float in the Texas breeze against the dark sky. Somewhere during the few seconds when Lucille had removed the key from its chain and placed it into Jill's cupped hand, she had made her decision to stay for the duration. It already felt like home.

Chapter Three

The gray morning light sifted through the curtains in Jill's room as she stretched and yawned awake. It took a moment to remember where she was, and when she did, the original excitement returned. As tempting as it was to visit all of Morgan's Grove in one big rush, Jill knew she needed to slow down, savor her experiences, and ease her way into things. She couldn't lose sight of her ultimate purpose. Although she had a general focus in mind for her article—to explore her own family history as it related to the town—the concept was still much too broad. She needed a central hook, a strong through-line. And finding it would take time. It couldn't be forced.

Jill's cell phone jingled on the nightstand, and she rolled over to view a text from Lindsey: *That town is adorable! Glad you're settled in. Keep me posted on everything.*

The night before, Jill had texted her roommate a brief update about Lucille, the corgis, and the cookies, accompanied by photos of the town square and the apartment's interior. Jill responded to Lindsey's text with a smiley face then noticed the time on her phone: *10:30!* She'd wasted half the morning sleeping. She tossed her phone onto the comforter then pushed herself out of bed and headed for the shower.

Almost an hour later, thanks to her lengthy hair-straightening ritual, Jill walked down the outside steps attached to the garage. She wore a light jacket, grateful to have abandoned her usual thick sweater, double socks, down coat, long scarf, and heavy gloves that Denver required.

As she made her way down the lengthy driveway, Jill heard a rustling noise and turned to view the source—once again, the front porch's Christmas tree branches were shivering.

Jill quickened her pace and drew closer, calling out, "Lucille. Need some help?" She remembered the six-foot ladder perched against the edge of the house yesterday and knew Lucille had intended to finish the tree all by herself.

As Jill climbed the porch steps to the top, the shivering subsided. A man emerged from behind the tree, dusted off his hands, and stared down at her. His face was rugged and handsome, with at least a three-day beard, and when he locked eyes with Jill, she could sense the hint of a smile underneath.

"I'm not Lucille." His voice was husky and resonant, with only the slightest trace of a Southern accent.

"Clearly." She chewed her bottom lip, suppressing a grin.

The man, who stood as tall as the tree itself, wore faded jeans and a flannel shirt. She assumed he was either a helpful neighbor or a hired handyman, paid to finish the tree. But something about the intensity of his dark eyes looked slightly familiar.

He took a couple of steps closer, his boots scudding along the porch's planks, then pushed his hands into his pockets. "You're looking for my grandmother."

Grandmother. The familiarity made sense. "You're Rick," she said then noticed his confusion. "I saw you yesterday on Lucille's wall," she explained with her hands, realizing she wasn't making much sense. "The photos in her kitchen, I mean. She pointed out your graduation picture when she was making cookies."

"Mm," he said with a nod.

"Anyway, I'm Jill." She pointed at herself, pushing down a light, unexpected nervousness, then stuffed her hands inside her jacket pockets.

She'd had time by then to study the details of him more close-ly—the deep-set brown eyes that matched his thick brown hair, the way his broad shoulders filled out the flannel shirt. He was no longer the gawky twentysomething in the graduation photo.

"She mentioned you last night," Rick said. "The B&B mix-up..."

"Your grandmother was a lifesaver. I would've been driving blind around Austin, otherwise, trying to find a place to stay. Are you here for the holidays? Lucille said you'd be coming, but closer to Christmas."

"What *else* did she say about me?" His smirk was jovial. He was surely used to a proud grandmother talking about him to perfect strangers. "She wasn't expecting me. I had some time off and wanted to surprise her. I came in late last night."

That explained the slam of a car door, which had briefly woken her the night before.

"I'm making up for lost time. I usually do this over Thanksgiv-ing." He pointed toward the half-trimmed tree.

"I caught her trying to decorate it herself, yesterday. In fact, that's how we met." Jill noticed the boxes of ornaments sitting to the side. "Can I help? It would make the job go faster."

Rick shrugged. "Why not?" He moved toward the tree while Jill unlooped her purse from her shoulder and set it down on the porch ledge.

"I'll hand you the lights," Rick offered, returning to his original position behind the tree. He extended a hand toward Jill, and she took the string of lights from him, brushing his fingers in the process. She draped the bulbs along her side of the tree then passed the rest toward Rick, whose hand awaited on the other side. They worked silently and steadily for a few minutes. Then Rick swirled the lights up to the top, where Jill couldn't reach. He clearly didn't need a lad-der.

Tucking a strand of hair behind her ear, Jill leaned down toward the box and chose an ornament to hang. As she approached the tree again, the multicolored lights suddenly flashed on, and she let out a small gasp.

"Do they all work?" Rick asked from behind the tree.

"Yes. Beautiful," she said, anxious to see the lights in their full glory at night.

Rick met her on the other side and found an ornament of his own to hang. "I told Gran she didn't need an outside tree *every* year, but she's stubborn. Told me she has to 'contribute to the neighborhood.'"

"I can see that about her," Jill agreed. She barely knew Lucille but was still able to imagine her saying something exactly like that.

"Well, look at the two of you!" a voice said nearby.

Somewhere during the decorating process, Lucille had managed to step through the screen door without either of them noticing. Hands still wrapped around the ornament she was placing, Jill craned her neck to see Lucille closing the door with her foot. The corgis were nowhere in sight, so they must've been sectioned off in the kitchen.

Lucille paused, holding a plateful of gingerbread cookies. "I see you two have already met." She beamed up toward her grandson then turned to Jill. "When Rick tapped on the door late last night, I almost didn't answer it, thinking some teenager was playing a dirty trick on me. But there he was, suitcase in hand, ready for a long stay. Such a surprise!" Her gaze drifted past Rick and toward the tree. "What's all this? You didn't need to finish it for me."

"We wanted to," Jill insisted. "And you've been so good to me, it's the least I could do."

"No trouble at all," she clucked. "I simply offered you what I already had... a spare room."

"And cookies," Jill said, eyeing the plate.

"It was Rick's idea, when he was a little boy, to have cookies for *breakfast*," Lucille said. "Well, brunch, by now."

"Gran..." Rick quietly protested, shaking his head and showing his embarrassment.

"What? It's true! 'They're not any worse than sugared cereal or syrupy pancakes,' he would tell me."

"Convincing argument," Jill agreed. "May I?"

"Of course." Lucille extended the plate to Jill then to Rick, and they each selected a cookie and began to munch. Lucille set the plate on the porch ledge and moved closer to her grandson. Her leaning against him accentuated his tall stature even more.

Rick placed a gentle arm around his grandmother as he took a bite of the cookie. "Better than I remembered," he told her.

"Delicious," Jill agreed, feeling pride that she'd helped make them. The cookie, still fresh, was soft and flavorful, and the icing was luscious and sweet.

"Did Jill tell you what brings her here to Morgan's Grove?" Lucille asked Rick. "She's a writer."

"Really?" Rick raised his eyebrows.

Lucille looked sheepish. "Sorry. That probably wasn't my information to tell."

"It's fine. I'm not hiding it." Jill glanced at Rick. "I write mysteries."

From Rick's unchanging expression, it was clear he had never heard of her, which was weirdly refreshing. He nodded politely as he chewed his cookie.

"Our book club actually read one of her books a while back," Lucille explained.

"So you're here in Morgan's Grove to write?" Rick asked Jill.

"I'm actually here *not* to write," she murmured. "I'm between books at the moment. My brain needs a break."

Jill wondered if it was time to start mentioning her article to people who continued to ask why she was there. But she didn't yet want the well-meaning townspeople to look over her shoulder and ask about her progress. She needed to keep her main mission private, at least for the time being, and let the article take shape without any outside influences.

"Have you always wanted to be a writer?" Lucille asked, pulling away from Rick to reach for a second cookie.

That was a question Jill never minded. It took her back to her early experiences with writing and all the reasons she first fell in love with it. "Yes, ever since I can remember. I dabbled as a kid, wrote stories and poems. I thought writing was like magic—words appearing on a page. Later, I found out that it's a mixture of inspiration and incredibly hard work. I wrote my first novel at eighteen, but writing was only a hobby then," Jill confessed. "I knew I couldn't pay the bills with it, so I went to college and majored in marketing and small business."

"But you kept writing?" Lucille prompted, evidently eager to hear the rest.

"I did. *And* getting rejected. I took odd jobs for a while—transcription work for a doctor's office, statistical analysis for a toy company, some minor accounting for a dentist's office. I even got a teaching certificate and taught ESL night classes at a junior college for two semesters. I get restless pretty quickly. Finally, an agent said yes and got me a book deal."

"Persistence paid off!" Lucille smiled. "Well, you'll have plenty of privacy in that garage apartment, if inspiration hits while you're here. Did you decide to take me up on my offer to stay?"

Without Rick standing there, Jill's response would've been a fast and hearty "Yes!" But with his presence, things had shifted a bit. "I don't want to be in the way," she assured Lucille. "And since your grandson is here, he probably needs his room back..."

Lucille moved closer to Jill. "You're already settled in. Besides, that was never Rick's room. He's always stayed inside the house, upstairs. He won't mind your being here."

Jill peered toward Rick to see a polite expression appear. She couldn't tell if it was genuine or mostly there for the sake of his grandmother.

"Sure. Stay." He popped the final bite of cookie into his mouth.

"Well, okay," Jill conceded. "I'd really like to."

"Good. It's settled," Lucille said with a firm nod. "Oh, and you can park your car near the garage. There's an open spot for it near the outside staircase."

"I'll move it this afternoon." Remembering her full day ahead, Jill reached for her purse. "I'd better get going. I wanted to take a look at the town today, do some browsing."

"Sounds like a plan. And I'll help Rick with the last of these ornaments," Lucille replied.

Jill watched as Rick's lips parted in possible protest, but he closed them again, likely knowing it was futile to tell his grandmother "no."

"Have a good day," Jill offered as she made her way down the steps.

As she rounded the corner of Lucille's curb, Jill tried to shake off the lingering image of Rick's gaze in those first few seconds when they'd met. Something *behind* the gaze intrigued her, an element she couldn't name or identify, which made her think he was holding back, keeping it tucked away from people. She hadn't felt such a visceral first reaction to a man in a long time. Her senses had dulled since her last relationship ended over a year before, when her boyfriend took a job in Canada. After the breakup, Jill had immediately buried herself in content edits for her last novel, swearing off men for the foreseeable future. But that tiny jolt she'd felt while talking to Rick, hanging onto his every word and movement, told her that her senses might not be so dulled after all.

Unsettled by those unexpected thoughts, Jill moved closer to the main square and firmly reminded herself: *I am not here for a man. I'm here for Morgan's Grove and for this article.*

Her focus purposefully shifted, intent on her mission at hand, Jill mentally ordered her day. She would visit the mansion first, then maybe a couple of shops. If there was time, a local restaurant for a late lunch, then back to the apartment for some work on the article.

Jill's phone buzzed, and she paused on the sidewalk to withdraw it from her purse. A text from her mother appeared: *Disembarking. Will call later.* It was the first text since the brief "Happy Thanksgiving" message she'd sent several days before.

Jill knew that "later" could mean days, weeks, or even months. Her mother was currently on a lengthy holiday cruise in the Bahamas, alone. Since Jill had graduated high school, her mother had taken off to travel alone but would often make new friends during each journey. She prided herself on her independence and loved her freedom to come and go, no strings attached. A wealthy aunt had left her a hefty inheritance years before, enabling such a comfortable traveling lifestyle, which satisfied her constant craving to be on-the-go.

Jill pictured her mother wearing a broad-brimmed hat, expensive sunglasses, and a flowy skirt as she walked along the giant ship with flair. Jill wondered what color her mother's hair was at the moment—it was always changing.

She tucked her phone back inside her purse, planning to tell her mother about the genealogy "find" during their next phone chat—she couldn't possibly explain it all by text—then continued toward the square.

On her way, she watched the domestic activities around her: children played on lawns while mothers watched, an elderly man collected his trash can from the curb, and squirrels chased each other up and down winter-bare trees.

A bicycle's bell startled Jill, and her first instinct was to step aside and let the cyclist pass. Instead, the bike came to a full stop beside her, and she paused out of politeness. A man in his mid-fifties wore a blue ball cap that showed he was faithful to the Texas Rangers. A sprig of holly dangled from his handlebars.

"Good morning!" He smiled to reveal coffee-stained teeth.

"Hi."

"Beautiful day, isn't it?" He stretched his arm up toward the sky, as though Jill hadn't already noticed the enormous, puffy clouds making a pilgrimage overhead.

"Yes. It really is."

"First time in Morgan's Grove?" he prodded. His accent was strong with the twang Jill had fully expected from practically every resident of this Texas town. He was probably a native.

She chose a vague answer. "Yes. I'm here for the festivities."

"You're in the right place. Perfect town to spend the holidays. I'm Bob." He extended a hand, and Jill grasped it.

"Jill."

"Welcome to the friendliest city in Texas. Of course, there are a few folks who keep to themselves. The Griffiths on Petunia Street. Or the Milgrams on Azalea Road. They have a newborn, though, so that probably keeps them occupied. Hard to get out much with a fussy baby..."

Jill shifted the purse strap on her shoulder while sorting through excuses to leave the conversation prematurely. She was eager to see the town for herself, rather than being told about it. "Well, I'd bet-ter—"

"Oh, there's Mr. Tyson." Bob's gaze darted to the elderly man on the corner, struggling to pull a weed from his lawn. "He could use some help." He nodded his cap toward Jill. "Nice meeting you. Maybe I'll see you around again. We can have a longer chat." And then he was off.

Jill soon reached the square and paused to give it the attention it deserved. The holidays were in full swing in Morgan's Grove, with wreaths decorating every lamppost, greenery framing every shop window, and a real-life Santa Claus ringing his bell cheerily at the front door of the library. She remembered the parting gift Lindsey had given her, a spiral notebook small enough to tuck inside her purse. "For note-taking," Lindsey had told her before offering a tight goodbye hug.

Keeping her eyes on the square, Jill felt for the spiral, found it with her fingers, and drew it out. She uncapped a ballpoint pen and jotted down notes, mainly adjectives that popped into her head to describe the scene in front of her. She wanted to paint a picture for the article's readers, and it felt good to have the words flowing easily again.

She capped the pen and clutched the notebook, committing to a leisurely pace as she made her way down one side of the elongated street. It was more of a rectangle, the town square. She noticed details she hadn't last evening when she'd driven through, such as brick sidewalks in a pristine crisscross pattern, storefronts with colorfully striped awnings, old-fashioned lampposts, and tall wastebaskets emblazoned with the same slogan, "Keep Our City Streets Lovely!" Occasionally, she paused and add an adjective or two to her notes.

Jill noticed something else as she walked. Cars would drive through the square, but they never parked. Her eyes roamed the street and saw absolutely no place for parking. A street sign nearby confirmed it: "No Parking at Any Time on the Main Street. Violators Will Be Towed. Ample Parking Behind the Square."

What a strange little town, she thought, *old-fashioned and sweet.* It felt like stepping back in time or maybe walking onto a movie set, and the people seemed... happy. Everyone she passed either nodded or smiled at her. Some even issued a lively "hello, there" or "how's it going?"—usually tinged with a Southern accent.

Eager to reach the founder's mansion, she breezed past the individual shops, deciding to explore them another time. Lucille had given her directions to the mansion, which was only three-quarters of a mile beyond the B&B. Reaching the edge of the main street, Jill slowed her pace and took in the vast countryside as she moved beneath wintry trees. Their branches, some bare and some with brittle leaves still attached, seemed to scrape against the blue sky. She traded her notebook for her phone and snapped photos along the way.

Jill was surprised by the hilly terrain. So much of Texas, as she'd driven through, had been flat and bare. But the road toward the mansion began to dip downward and curve around. And some of the trees were Colorado tall, with thick trunks, standing in groves together.

Jill came across a sign for the founder's mansion and made a right turn onto the property. She passed through an open wrought-iron gate then walked down a wide, tree-lined path. *What would this grand entrance look like during the lushness of spring?* she wondered, taking her time. The empty branches above were clearly meant to create a thick canopy of leaves during the appropriate seasons.

Ahead, she could see an imposing three-story structure at the end of the path. Jill didn't know much about architecture, but as she drew closer, she could easily identify the European influence of Tudor-style features, including dark-brown timbering and steep gables. She snapped a couple of photos then moved ahead, eager to see the interior. The broad stone staircase leading up to the home was lined with white and red poinsettias, and the porch contained a fresh Christmas tree.

Inside, the warmth hit Jill's senses immediately—not only the temperature of the space, but every other detail: the rich wooden floors, the soft-beige color of the walls, the thick Oriental rug beneath her feet, the sunlight streaming in from a stained-glass window above the tall staircase, the rustic Christmas décor of berries and holly...

She noticed the "No Photos Allowed" sign and slipped her phone back into her purse, hoping she could get special permission for photos later on, if she needed them for the article.

"Welcome to the founder's mansion," a voice said beside her. "Would you like to join the tour?"

Jill had been so entranced with the space that she'd almost walked right past the information table. A woman sat with her fingers laced together and peered up at her.

"Oh. Yes. How much?"

"Eight dollars."

Jill handed over the cash, and the woman gave her a glossy brochure in exchange. "Have a nice visit," she told Jill.

Moving forward into the entryway at the edge of the staircase, which had poinsettias on every other step, Jill noticed the cluster of people in the parlor nearby and realized the tour guide had already begun. Part of her wished she'd had the place all to herself, to browse and linger, but she also wanted to hear the detailed history of every room, so she wandered into the immaculate parlor, careful not to disturb the guide. The rooms had been completely preserved—the brochure told Jill the house had remained a family home for over sixty years, until Morgan donated the home to the town, to be preserved as a historical museum.

The tour guide offered basic details about the house: it had fifteen bedrooms, sixteen fireplaces, four bathrooms, a kitchen, a parlor, two drawing rooms, a dining room, and an extensive library. Then the guide shifted her attention to the parlor they were standing in—Jill wondered how many hundreds of times the woman had given the same speech—and rattled off details about the mahogany scroll-arm chairs, the original artwork from European artists, and the marble fireplace imported from Italy.

But as she spoke, Jill did what probably no one else in the room was doing—she pictured the people inside it: her great-great-great-grandfather, his wife, and their daughter, Morgan, the town's namesake. *Did they greet guests here? Have parties here? Relax in the evenings here?* Their images, faint in her mind, were ghosts wandering about the room, nodding, smiling cheerfully, enjoying their elaborate home.

"Let's move to the dining room..." the guide suggested, and the guests followed along.

The tour continued through the bottom level of the mansion then upstairs, where Jill was most interested. Bedrooms were deeply intimate areas of any home, where residents could relax, unwind, remove their social masks, and be themselves. And just as she'd hoped, the rooms were filled with personal items—black-and-white photographs set on nightstands, a decorative brush and hand mirror atop a vanity, old-fashioned dolls placed lovingly on a little girl's bed.

Each room was decorated with a Christmas tree dotted with handmade paper ornaments and stranded with popcorn or ribbons. Jill had stepped back in time and couldn't have removed the smile from her face if she tried. She wondered if, a century before, the residents of the home had any idea that a future relative would be stepping where they had.

"... and feel free to move around at your leisure," the tour guide was saying, wrapping up. "We hope you've enjoyed your visit to the Stout family mansion."

The small crowd dispersed and began to shuffle back downstairs, but Jill stayed behind, clutching her brochure.

The tour guide approached. "I'm happy to answer any questions you might have." The thirtysomething woman wore a navy blazer, and her dark hair was pulled into a neat bun.

"I was curious about the family," Jill said. "You mentioned that Morgan Stout was the last family member to reside here..."

"That's right."

"And she had two children?"

"Three, actually. Melissa, and then two boys, Brandon and—"

"Cody."

The woman's eyes widened. "I'm impressed. Most tourists don't know that information."

"Oh. Well, I read up on the website before I came here," Jill explained. "I'm interested in Cody's children. Do you know anything about them?"

"About Mr. Stout's great-grandchildren? Well, let's see. Cody had three children, I believe."

"One of them was Amelia?"

The woman tilted her head. "That's not on our website."

It was time to come clean about why she was grilling the poor woman. "No, it's not. I guess I need to explain. I believe that I'm a descendant of Amelia's. She married a McCallister. I'm Jill McCallister."

It took the woman a moment to process, and when she did, her eyes danced and her lips parted. "You mean, your ancestors are—"

"Morgan Stout. And Alfred J."

The woman clamped a hand over her mouth. Jill could see her wide smile spilling out from the sides of her fingers. She removed her hand to speak. "I don't believe this. We've known about you, even tried to contact you when we were researching the family history deeper about a decade ago."

"I've moved several times, so I was probably hard to locate. And I'm not on social media," Jill confessed.

"Well, this is amazing. What a treat for me, personally. My name is Jolene Mitchell." She extended a hand, and Jill shook it.

"Nice to meet you."

"May I ask what's brought you to Morgan's Grove? Is it the obvious reason, to learn more about your family history?"

"Yes. As soon as I saw the town online, I knew I had to see it in person." Jill spilled out the details of her recent website search and the decision that led her to the town, to the mansion, but she left out the details of her article. She would save that for later, as she continued her research. Jolene could end up being an incredible source, all on her own.

"I'm honored to meet you." Jolene beamed. "I was born in Morgan's Grove and fell in love with this house when I was a little girl. My mother brought me to visit every Christmas season. It gave me a distinct appreciation for historic homes, so I studied in that field then returned to Morgan's Grove and became its curator a few years ago."

"How amazing."

"I feel like I'm meeting a local celebrity today," Jolene gushed. "We residents love our founder. He created such a lovely town. He was a generous man too. Have you visited the library yet? It's an amazing structure. He built it for his daughter. It mimics an Italian library he visited on a trip overseas." She spouted off a quick list of impressive trivia about the building, including its first-edition collections of classic works, the original wood floors, and its sculptured ceilings and chandeliers.

"It's definitely next on my list," Jill admitted, eager to see the masterpiece of architecture—and to do some extended research on the founder and his family.

"Jolene? Phone call." A voice had drifted in from the hallway.

"I should get that. But please, take as much time as you want here. Wander around, do some exploring on your own."

"I will. Thank you for our chat. It's been very enlightening."

"It was my pleasure, trust me!" Jolene dipped her fingertips into her blazer's pocket. "Here's my business card. Please contact me for any information you might need about the house or the town. Maybe we can even have lunch sometime."

"I'd like that." Jill accepted the card then watched Jolene turn to leave.

Jill realized she hadn't added a single impression of this mansion to her spiral, so while they were fresh in her mind, she scribbled down details, walking through the house again in her mind, room by room. On her way downstairs, passing the gold-framed photos of the Stout family lining the wall, Jill almost felt the urge to wave goodbye, to thank them for their warm hospitality.

"I'll be back soon," she whispered.

Chapter Four

Emerging from the founder's mansion and seeing the shadows spilling around her, Jill was surprised at how much of her afternoon had passed while she was inside. She'd quite literally gotten lost in time.

Making her way back to the town square, Jill heard her stomach growl audibly and knew nothing would satisfy her except food. Lured by the smoky scent of barbecue wafting from a restaurant called The Pit, located prominently in the town square, she made a right turn and let her nose lead the way. She approached the restaurant and pulled on the horseshoe-shaped door handle. Twangy country music floated overhead, and multicolored lights traced the cowboy boots and hats that decorated the walls.

Inside, the restaurant was dark, with floor-to-ceiling wood paneling. Everything about the place was comforting and homey. She could see why it was crowded. Jill entered a long hallway leading toward a register with an enormous chalkboard menu board behind it. The line stood at least ten customers long, even well past lunchtime—always a good sign that the food was delicious.

Jill had to position herself between two tall men in front of her to see the menu board, and when she finally reached the register, she had made most of her menu decisions. She would buy enough food for herself, Lucille, and Rick—an early dinner they could all share.

A robust middle-aged woman with bright rosy cheeks and kind eyes greeted her. "How can I help you?"

Jill peered at the menu again to verify. "I'll take two pounds of brisket, one pound of ribs, and... some sides. Two pints of beans, four corns on the cob, and a dozen rolls. Oh, and coleslaw. Please."

Jill produced her credit card as the woman tapped on the register.

"I don't recognize the accent. Northerner?"

Jill chuckled. "From all over, really. But I'll claim Colorado as my home state."

"Well, how do ya like that?" The woman let out an unexpected cackle. "My family used to visit Colorado every summer. Colorado Springs and the Pike's Peak area, mostly. We'd camp out by the fire, stay in a motor home, do some fishin' for weeks on end—"

"What's that about Pike's Peak?" Another plus-sized woman stepped up to the register, and Jill thought she was seeing double. She glanced back and forth between the women, who had the same button noses, deep-set green eyes, and auburn hair. They even shared similar dimples when they grinned.

"We were talking about the Colorado camping summers, with the family."

"You two *have* to be sisters," Jill noted.

The women nodded in unison.

"Twins?" Jill asked.

The women laughed at the same time, same octave. "We get that all the time," one sister admitted, "but we're a year apart."

"Exactly one year," the other sister chimed in, "to the very day."

"Same birthday?" Jill clarified.

"Yep. But mine comes first. I'm the elder sister. I'm Darlene, and this is Tessa." She pointed with her thumb.

The man behind Jill cleared his throat loudly enough to catch Tessa's attention and bring it back to the register. Jill suddenly realized why the line was so lengthy. The sisters probably bantered with each customer, making the ordering process a particularly long one.

"Oh. Sorry. We get carried away sometimes."

"We?" Darlene smirked. "Speak for yourself." Then she disappeared into the kitchen again.

Tessa scrawled Jill's order on an old-fashioned notepad then swung around to insert the ticket through the cutout window behind her. As she finished tallying up the amount on the register, she asked Jill, "What brings you all the way from Colorado?"

"I needed some holiday cheer, and I read about this place online. Arrived yesterday." Jill had her standard answer practically memorized.

"Found a room at the B&B, then?"

"Actually, I'm staying at an apartment. Lucille's house." Jill had no idea why she was spilling all this personal information to a stranger, but Morgan's Grove seemed to bring it out of her.

Tessa paused. "Lucille Wright? Fantastic lady. You tell her I said 'hey.' Haven't seen her here in months. Well, even longer than that. Since before Frank passed away. He used to come in twice a week for ribs during his route. Like clockwork."

"His route?"

"He was our sheriff, as long as I can remember. Folk 'round here loved him. Tough as nails on the outside, but heart of gold inside. He's sorely missed."

Suddenly, Jill wondered if she'd made the right decision to stop at The Pit for dinner. *Will the food trigger sad memories for Lucille and Rick? Memories of Frank?* But it was too late to back out.

Tessa continued, "Frank's favorite dessert was always the Mississippi Mud. In fact—let me check somethin'." She gave a side glance toward the end of the counter, where plastic shelves held large blocks of something chocolatey. "Yep, two slices left. You're lucky—we run out of Mississippi Mud every day. People love a homemade dessert. These two will be on the house. You tell Lucille they're from The Pit sisters."

Jill only hoped the dessert was more appetizing than its strange name.

IF NOT FOR THE STURDY cardboard box that held the piping-hot bags of barbecue, Jill would certainly have burned her fingers by the time she arrived at the house. As she walked the distance, Jill could smell the mixture of tangy sauce and sweet corn. When she approached Lucille's kitchen door, she shifted the box to free up one hand for a knock. No answer. She knocked again, but still no answer.

She recalled Lucille's insistence to "Come on in!" but Jill had never in her life walked into someone's dwelling only a day after meeting them. She couldn't bring herself to do it. The weight of the box had created an ache between the backs of her shoulders, and she wondered if she should set it down and try the front door instead.

A series of loud barks forced her attention back to the kitchen. Through the door's window panes, she could see the corgis bounding toward her from the other side. Someone followed them, and Jill raised her eyes to see Rick talking on his cell phone while trying to appease the dogs.

He saw Jill through the window, gave a nod, then opened the door, still talking.

"Shh," she told George and Gracie, wading through the corgis and hoping she hadn't completely ruined Rick's probable business call. "It's only me."

"Fine. I'll call you in the morning when I get the schedule," Rick said into the phone after closing the door. He hung up with a sigh.

Jill carried the box to the island as the barking softened into whimpers. She set down the barbecue then knelt to extend a hand to the dogs. "You remember me," she told them. "I'm Jill."

George and Gracie sniffed her palms, then a wave of recognition came over them. Suddenly, they nuzzled into her waist, nearly knocking her over.

Rick extended a hand to Jill. "Sometimes I wish they'd be a little *less* friendly." He smirked.

She accepted his help with a soft laugh—she'd never been so lovingly attacked by small dogs before—and he lifted her to her feet with one strong and fluid motion.

"They're killing me with kindness," she said.

"They mean well." Rick motioned toward the corner. "Go," he told the corgis. They obeyed, scampering to their spot with wagging tongues.

"Sorry about interrupting your call. I should've tried the front door instead."

"It's fine. I'm used to the noise level around here. What's all this?" He took a peek inside one of the paper bags.

"I know it's too late for lunch and too early for dinner, but I bought some barbecue for us, from The Pit."

"I'm starved, actually. Haven't eaten since the gingerbread breakfast. And I haven't had The Pit in ages," Rick admitted. "What's the occasion?"

"A thank you. I expected to come to Morgan's Grove and feel like a stranger the whole time, honestly. But on my second day here, I'm feeling really welcome."

"Yeah, this place can have that effect." Rick raised an eyebrow and gave a half-grin. "Too much, sometimes."

"What do you mean?"

"Small towns can be like a big family, which means they also gossip about each other. It's inevitable."

When it was clear Rick wouldn't elaborate, Jill changed the subject. "Wanna help me unpack the food? Maybe we can lay it out before Lucille comes in. Surprise her."

"She's upstairs paying bills, I think. We should have enough time."

Rick unpacked the items while Jill washed her hands. Then together, they opened up the Styrofoam containers of steaming vegetables, scrunched-up foil with brisket inside, and a white box filled with yeasty rolls. As she arranged the food into a neat-looking buffet, she could hardly wait to dive in.

The only item she'd kept wrapped was the dessert—she would have to gauge how the meal went before revealing Frank's favorite. She wanted the food to be a pleasurable surprise, not an unwelcome reminder.

"I'll get the paper plates," Rick offered, knowing where to find them inside the pantry. Next, he retrieved the iced-tea pitcher from inside the refrigerator while Jill hunted for plastic tumblers and placed them on the counter.

By the time Lucille came downstairs and entered the kitchen, the buffet was complete. Jill did a "tah-dah" with her hands while Rick stood at the other end of the island.

"What have you two done?" Lucille drew closer, examining the food and inhaling deeply. "It looks positively scrumptious."

"Jill's idea," Rick told her.

"I hope it's not too late to eat. Or too early," Jill told Lucille.

If Lucille had been unnerved by the meal coming from The Pit, she was too gracious to show it. She flashed a glance at the kitchen's wall clock and pursed her lips. "I do have a birthday party in a couple of hours, but there's still time for this."

"Are you sure? I can easily pack it all up and refrigerate it, no trouble," Jill told her.

"No, it's fine. The party isn't a dinner party—only light snacks and such. So this will work out well, eating beforehand. Let's dig in, shall we?"

Fifteen minutes later, they had all settled in at the round breakfast table, their plates piled high. The dogs sat in the corner, quiet but staring intently at the humans in case a crumb or two should fortuitously fall from the table.

"How was your afternoon?" Lucille asked Jill, reaching for a paper napkin.

"Perfect, actually. I spent most of my time at the mansion. It was really special." She took a bite of the succulent rib meat—*delicious*!

"Oh, isn't the mansion magical?" Lucille agreed. "Especially at Christmastime. People come from everywhere to see it. I haven't been in ages... I'd love to go again."

"I'll take you with me sometime. I want to go back. There's so much to see."

"Did you meet Jolene, our curator?" Lucille took a significant, juicy bite of corn on the cob.

"Yes. She was extremely helpful." Jill paused, knowing she had a window of opportunity. She decided to take it. "Actually, she helped verify something for me."

"What's that?" Lucille lowered the corn and raised her brows. Rick had paused, too, and stared at her from across the table, fork poised.

"Well... one of the main reasons I'm here in Morgan's Grove is that..."

Lucille dabbed at her mouth with a napkin then intensified her gaze. "What is it, dear?"

"I have every reason to believe that I'm a descendant of Alfred Stout, the founder. So that's why I wanted to see his mansion today."

Lucille's mouth dropped open slightly as she processed the news. "Are you sure? I mean, how would you know that? He was born way back in the 1800's..."

"The internet has all these genealogy websites, and last week, I searched my family history. Alfred J. Stout came up, along with a link to Morgan's Grove. It seems that Morgan was my great-great-grandmother." It felt freeing to give out the information a second time in the course of one day, as though saying it would help her to own it, believe it.

"Oh my stars, this is wonderful!" Lucille gasped. "A relative of our great founder, right here in my own kitchen. Amazing!"

"Jolene helped confirm it today. The genealogy came from my dad's side."

"Does he know about it yet?" Lucille asked. "His ties to Morgan's Grove?"

"He actually passed away years ago, when I was young."

"I'm sorry," Rick said softly from across the table.

"How bittersweet this must be for you, then," Lucille noted.

"It is. He would've loved to know about his roots. It makes me feel even more connected to him now, finding this out."

"That makes sense." Rick nodded.

"We've been interested in doing that too"—Lucille wagged her hand toward Rick— "exploring our roots."

"I'll show you the genealogy site sometime," Jill offered.

"I would love that." Lucille lifted her glass of sweet tea and shook her head. "Famous novelist *and* relative of our founder. You're a double celebrity, my dear. Better get used to it." She winked across the table.

"You can give me your autograph later," Rick teased.

Jill felt that slight flush of embarrassment rise again, as it had earlier with Jolene. She hadn't come to Morgan's Grove to grab a spotlight. But she knew Lucille and Rick could be trusted not to make a spectacle of her. Eager to move the subject off herself, she nudged the conversation toward other topics, starting with the sites she hoped to see tomorrow.

When it was clear they had all stuffed themselves to the brim, Jill stood to clear the plates. "There's dessert," she said, testing the waters.

"Mississippi Mud?" Lucille guessed.

"Tessa gave it to us on the house. Do you want some now? Or I can save it, put it in the fridge. Whatever you want."

"No, now is fine. I'll have a bite or two."

Rick's cell phone buzzed, and he glanced at the screen with a frown then pushed off from the table. "I need to get this. Sorry."

"I'll save you a piece," Lucille assured him, watching Rick leave to answer the call. She leaned in and whispered to Jill, "I worry about my grandson. He works too hard. That phone and laptop always seem to be attached to him."

"He's successful, though, you said?" Jill continued to clear the empty paper plates. "I guess that's what it takes. Dedication."

"True. But he's holding back this time. I can see the worry in his face when he thinks I'm not looking."

It only confirmed what Jill's intuition had told her that morning about Rick and the "something" behind his gaze. She tossed the plates into the trash can then opened up one of the Styrofoam containers at the kitchen island. She was greeted with dark chocolate, layered with a white filling beneath—*marshmallow, maybe?*—then another layer of chocolate. *What is it, exactly? A cake? Brownie? Mixture of the two?* Whatever it was, it did look delicious. Jill cut one of the pieces in half and watched the fudgy topping, still warm, ooze down the sides.

"Dessert is served," she announced, bringing two plates to the table.

After the first bite, Lucille said, "This was Frank's favorite dessert in the world. He died last year. Did I tell you that yet? I can't remember." Her voice was shaky, but her expression was stoic.

Jill chose to feign respectful surprise. "No, you didn't. I'm so sorry."

Lucille's mouth relaxed into a small smile as she stared at her plate. "He used to do this thing. He would hover over his plate to protect the Mississippi Mud then carve his initial into the fudge. Every single time. It became a joke between us." She demonstrated with the tine of her fork and made a sloppy F in the fudgy icing. "Maybe to claim his piece or make sure nobody else would try to steal it away. Silly man."

"He was very well-respected," Jill said. "Around town, I mean. Tessa said he went to The Pit twice a week. She seemed very fond of him."

Lucille talked to the dessert, told it her story. "People *did* love him. He was the kindest man. Tough exterior—everyone else saw that side. But not me. With me, he was a teddy bear. Gentle, loving. And funny." She took another bite, and after a thoughtful pause, added, "He had the biggest, huskiest belly laugh of anyone I've ever known. I can still hear it, even now..."

Jill almost regretted offering the dessert and making Lucille revisit a sad memory.

But then Lucille blinked and told her, "Thank you."

"Oh, you're welcome. I'm glad you liked the food."

"Not for that." Lucille made eye contact. "Well, yes, for that. But mostly for letting me talk about him. I never get to talk about him anymore. People are too scared to ask, or they feel too awkward to listen to the details. They were all very kind after the funeral last year, kept bringing me armfuls of food, sent flowers, invited me over. But soon, well, they stopped. And people went on with their busy lives. As they should, of course. But I was... stuck. Everything in my life came to a standstill. I didn't know what my life looked like without Frank in it. Still don't, sometimes. So thank you. Talking about him helps."

"I'm glad."

"Here's to Frank." Lucille lifted her forkful of dessert a few inches high.

Jill raised hers, too, clinking the edge of it with Lucille's. "To Frank."

Chapter Five

A new day, a new plan.

On her third day in Morgan's Grove, Jill decided she would browse every nook and cranny in the main square. Soon, she would need to conduct some detailed research for the article and visit the library, pore over various sources, formulate specific questions for Jolene, and revisit the mansion for detailed clues into the past. And after that, she would need to compile all her notes and get serious about crafting a first draft. But first, Jill wanted to see the town at her own pace, through a tourist's eyes.

Before heading out on her sightseeing adventures, she tapped on Lucille's kitchen door for a brief hello. Lucille was standing at the sink nearby and answered almost immediately, opening the door with a cheery "Good morning!"

Jill stepped inside the warm kitchen to see the corgis clicking their way toward her without hesitation and without barking. She was no longer a stranger.

"Look at that," Lucille noted. "You're getting the 'wiggle-bottoms.'" She pointed toward the dogs.

"The what?"

"Well, because they have no tails to wag, they make up for it in wiggles. See?"

Jill moved her eyes to the corgis' backsides and realized Lucille was right. They were shaking and dancing in place. Jill had seen the movement before but suddenly understood—they were wagging invisible tails at her.

"Coffee?" Lucille offered.

"No thanks. I was going into the square and wanted to know if you needed anything."

"I can't think of anything. But I did have a question for you. Do you have a minute to sit?"

"Sure. I'm in no hurry."

There had been no sign of Rick around the house yet, and Jill assumed he was upstairs, tapping away on his laptop or conducting a conference call. Lucille moved toward the breakfast table, where Jill joined her, then she folded her hands together, eyes focused on her coffee mug.

"Remember that birthday party I told you about last night? For Doris? Well, I needed to bring along a treat or a snack. And I thought, why not my gingerbread cookies? They're festive and Christmassy..."

"And delicious," Jill added.

"Well, thank you. Apparently, you're not the only one who thinks so." Lucille raised her eyes to meet Jill's and whispered, "They loved the cookies. *All* the ladies did. Gobbled them up until none were left! I had all these compliments, with two of the ladies requesting the cookies for other parties or family gatherings they'll be having in December. Can you imagine such a thing?"

"I told you—they're good enough to sell!"

"That's why I wanted to talk with you. I couldn't sleep last night, thinking about the cookies, the possibilities. And after some careful consideration this morning... I think I want to try selling them. I was remembering my grandmother. She owned a bakery for most of her life—I practically grew up there, watching her bake—and I think in the back of my mind, my whole life, I've always wanted to do the same thing. Share my baking with other people."

"May I ask why you didn't try before now? Was it fear?"

"Oh, probably. And I had a family to raise, plus I worked as a schoolteacher for almost twenty years. And I guess I wondered whether Frank would be supportive. You know, a new business is quite a risk, and he was *not* the risk-taking sort."

"Well, it's never too late to chase a dream. I'll be happy to help, however I can."

"You told me you've got a degree in marketing? Isn't that sort of like sales?"

"In a roundabout way, yes."

Lucille tapped her fingers on the table definitively. "Now, this is only a brainstorming idea, mind you. I don't want to commit to anything yet, and nothing as grand as opening my own bakery, but I want to test the waters. Take a few baby steps. Maybe I could pick your brain for some suggestions?"

"We can certainly do that, but I have an idea right now, to help give you some confidence. Do you still have cookies left over from the other day?"

"Oh, yes. I always make a double batch and freeze the rest. In fact, I was about to freeze them today."

"Well, I have a better idea. Let me conduct an experiment. I was heading into town this morning, anyway. I could take some cookies with me and see if I can sell them."

"Around town? To actual people?" Lucille winced.

Jill snickered. "Yes, to actual people! We could bag them up individually right now, and I could offer the cookies for, say, three dollars."

"Apiece?"

"Apiece! They're huge cookies. And they took hours to make—lots of time and effort. They're worth more than three dollars, actually. In big cities, these types of gourmet cookies sell for as much as six or seven dollars."

"For a *cookie*?!" Lucille looked horrified, turning Jill's snicker into a giggle. "But it's something edible—in their hand one minute, gone the next. I mean, I've thrown together some sugar, spices, molasses, butter. And people would pay seven dollars for that?"

"We won't price them that high," assured Jill. "But like I said, this is only an experiment. It's safe. If it fails, we've lost nothing. You'll still have cookies for your freezer, just like before." She shrugged, hoping to lessen the pressure.

Lucille squinted and rotated her coffee mug a few degrees to the left. "You know what? Many of the shops have special tables—'vendor tables,' they call them—where local goods and crafts are sold. They sell candies and sweets, too. Maybe they would consider selling my cookies?"

"It won't hurt to try. I could offer a free sample to entice them. They might place an order for more. Would you be willing to make another batch if they do?"

"Willing, but I'm not as confident as you are. Still, I guess there's really nothing to lose."

"Do you want to come along? Help me sell them?"

Lucille shook her head. "Heavens, no! I don't think I could bear the rejection face-to-face. Do you mind going alone? I don't want to impose on you. I mean, this is your holiday, your vacation. I don't want you spending it on me—"

"It's no trouble, I promise. It was my idea to offer."

"All right, then. Jill McCallister, you're a Christmas angel sent here at the right time," Lucille said, rising from the table. "Let's go bag up these cookies of mine!"

GRASPING THE CARDBOARD box, Jill rehearsed her sales pitch in her head, but with every step toward the square came growing doubts. She hadn't realized that the pressure to succeed would be so strong. If it didn't go well, she would have to bear the sting of disappointment on Lucille's face when Jill handed back a box full of un-sold cookies.

As she came near the town square's curb, she heard a faint "hello, there" behind her. Bicycle Bob was patrolling the block. He came to a stop and leaned the weight of his bike on one leg.

He can be my first guinea pig! "Hello," she said in her friendliest voice, shifting into marketing mode.

"Jill, right?"

"Good memory."

"Mrs. Haversham tells me we've got a celebrity in our midst. She says you write books!"

"I do. Mystery novels."

Bob scratched underneath his baseball cap. "You know, I've always wanted to write a book. Seems like pretty easy work, jotting down a story, putting pen to paper. I've got plenty of stories. Right up here." He tapped his temple.

"I'll bet you do."

"Maybe someday I could ask for some advice?"

"Well, I'm pretty busy these days. In fact, I've got something to show you." Jill was never more grateful to have a physical distraction in her hands.

"Whatcha got there?"

"Cookies." Jill shifted the box onto her hip with one hand then reached into it with the other. She held out a transparent bag for him to see. "They're delicious. And they're for sale."

Bob squinted to get a closer look. "Are those Girl Scout cookies? Ginger snaps?"

"They're even better! Freshly made gingerbread cookies from Lucille Wright's own kitchen oven. The perfect Christmas treat."

"Lucille—you're her new boarder, aren't ya?"

"Sort of." Jill didn't feel like getting into the details with Bob, who would likely spread them all over town before the end of the afternoon. "I'm selling these cookies for Lucille." Sensing a hesitant interest, she set down the box at her feet then held the baggie between them and coaxed it open in her hand.

"Smells good. How much?"

"Three dollars," Jill said, mentally crossing her fingers.

Bob gave one nod and found his wallet. "Sold! I'll take two, though. One for me, one for the missus."

Elated, Jill dipped into the box for another baggie then exchanged it for his dollar bills.

After tucking away his wallet, Bob tore off the gingerbread man's head to munch on it. "Mmm, these *are* good." Then he sealed up the baggie and dangled both of them from his handlebars. "Tell Lucille thanks. Have a nice day!"

Jill's confidence rose by several degrees as she crossed the street. She found her next customers on the courthouse lawn—two young mothers with strollers, chatting and having coffee on a bench.

"Hi, ladies. I'm sorry to bother you." Jill offered a bright, confident smile. "I'm selling these homemade gingerbread cookies, and I wondered if you'd like to buy one."

The ladies looked at each other skeptically at first then back at Jill, who held out one of the baggies.

"Lucille made them," Jill clarified. "Lucille Wright?"

"Sure, I know Lucille," said one of the women. "I'll have one. How much?"

"Three dollars."

The woman produced the money from her purse without hesitation, and Jill handed over the bag.

By then, two other people walking past the bench had paused out of curiosity and ended up buying two more cookies.

Jill crossed the street toward the shops and entered the candle store, thick with an odd mixture of scents like evergreen, pumpkin spice, summer breeze, and seascape. There was no vendor table, so she made a quick, polite walk-around then pushed the door to leave, grateful for the fresh, clean Texas air to clear her candle-infused senses.

Next, she entered the Stationery Place, an old-fashioned store with endless shelves containing notepads, monogrammed letters, envelopes, quill pens, and ink stamps, with a vendor table in the corner. Before approaching the manager about Lucille's cookies, Jill saw what she was hoping for, a party section on the wall with invitations, gift bags, streamers, cake-toppers, and party favors. Jill snatched up what she needed then walked to the register.

The woman behind the counter, close to Jill in age, tapped out the prices on her register and made small talk. "Lovely cold weather we're having. But there's rain in the forecast, I believe..."

"May I ask you a question?"

"Sure." The woman paused and made eye contact for the first time.

Jill swiveled to point back toward the table. "You sell items by local vendors?"

"Yes! That was my idea, actually. I approached the owner last year, and she agreed. It's been a big hit, I'm proud to say."

"It's a good idea," Jill concurred. "And I have a vendor who might be interested in displaying her product. Her name is Lucille Wright."

"Oh, I know Lucille. My mother was in a book club with her. My name is Angela, by the way."

"I'm Jill, a new friend of Lucille's. I was wondering if you've ever tasted her gingerbread cookies? They're to die for."

"I didn't know she made gingerbread."

"I'd love to offer you a free sample. I have one right here." Jill produced one of the baggies.

Angela accepted the cookie and took a generous bite. Her eyes widened as she chewed. "You weren't kidding. This is the best gingerbread I've ever eaten. Like, *ever*. It's so soft and chewy. And not too spicy..."

"Amazing, right? And award-winning!"

Angela nodded through a second bite, then swallowed and said, "We'll take as many as you have."

Giddy, Jill tried to compose herself and fished out her credit card to pay for her other items. "Great! I only have a sample today. But I can bring some fresh cookies by tomorrow afternoon, if that's okay."

They negotiated the price then exchanged cell numbers.

Jill walked out of the shop with new confidence. She counted the remaining samples—she had enough for the other shops on the block and hopefully for a few more on the block behind the courthouse. The managers of the specialty grocery and coffee shop each placed orders after tasting a sample.

She entered the bookstore next and was instantly recognized by the store's manager. "I can't believe you're in my shop! I have read *all* your books. Twice!" Then she bit her lip and added, "Would you ever consider having a book signing here? We would be over the *moon!*"

Jill wondered if the cookie sales would be contingent upon a "yes," so she gave a strong "maybe," unwilling to commit, and got a cookie order in exchange. Win-win.

Walking through the entire square, store by store, had given Jill more than just the perfect opportunity to sell the cookies. It also handed her a wonderful way to get to know Morgan's Grove deeper, from the inside. She observed the sense of community all around her, overhearing wisps of conversations as she browsed—a woman asked another woman about her son's fever, a grandfather placed a gentle hand on a small boy's shoulder as he scolded him lovingly, two twentysomething women pushed their strollers through the aisles and chatted about brands of diapers. Except for the tourists mixed in, everyone seemed to know everyone else—exactly what Jill had always pictured a small town to be.

AN HOUR AND A HALF later, empty-handed after donating the box to the burger place at her last stop, Jill headed back to Lucille's with a bounce in her step, the bag of Stationery Place goodies swinging from her arm. Not a single one of the shops she'd approached had turned down her sample, and all of them, after tasting, had placed an order. The Pit had even asked for two dozen mini-cookies. Jill had made careful calculations in her head and knew that with two double batches, split apart by a few days' time, Lucille could cover all the orders perfectly. Past that, there were no commitments for more. The rest would be up to Lucille. Jill wanted the venture to be a blessing for her, not a new burden.

"Jill?" she heard someone call from behind.

She twisted around to see Rick walking briskly toward her and paused on the curb to wait for him. In the few seconds before he arrived at her side, Jill wondered how much she should tell him about her outing. Lucille's decision that morning to pursue the cookie selling seemed spontaneous and on-the-spot. Jill doubted she'd even mentioned the idea to Rick yet. Perhaps it was easier to tell a near-stranger about taking a risk than one's own relative, with less chance of judgment or negative input. It wasn't Jill's place to tell Rick about the cookies. She would let Lucille be in charge of the when and how of that conversation.

"Hey," Rick said, a little winded as he caught up to her. They began walking toward Lucille's block together.

She eyed the plastic bag that bumped against his leg. "I didn't peg you as the shopping type."

He returned her grin. "I don't think Christmas lights count as 'shopping.'"

"Lights for the house?"

"Yeah, Gran's were on their last legs, so I bought new ones. There's enough daylight to put them up." Rick glanced skyward then peered down toward Jill's bag. "You were shopping too?"

"I mostly browsed, but I made it through the entire square. I still need to see the library, though."

"There's a lot more to Morgan's Grove than just the square," Rick said. "We've got some nice countryside, ranches with horses, tall trees, rolling hills..."

"I noticed that on my way to the mansion yesterday. I was surprised by the landscape."

"Yeah, the landscape, the weather, the people. Texas isn't as predictable as most outsiders assume it is."

So true. Jill peered down at the sidewalk, stepping on her own shadow, loving *all* the surprises Morgan's Grove had already brought to her in only three brief days.

"Then there's the school, the abandoned church, the bridge. I can take you sometime. If you want."

Jill suppressed a smile. "I'd like that."

As they came to Lucille's street, Jill's thoughts were disrupted by the luscious tones of a jazz trumpet floating through an open window.

"Mr. Anderson," Rick said, seeming to read her thoughts. They paused together across the street on Lucille's lawn and looked toward the second-floor window. "He's sort of... eccentric," Rick continued in a quiet voice while the trumpet played on. "Wears plaid golf pants and a fedora—and smokes a cigar—while clipping the yard. Lost his wife about fifteen years ago. He plays jazz records some nights, loud enough for the whole neighborhood to hear. Gets complaints sometimes. Doesn't care."

"I saw him last night," Jill mused. "I heard Nat King Cole and peeked through my curtain. He was dancing to the music, his hands raised up like he had a partner. But he was alone."

"Yep, eccentric. But a sweet old man." Rick nodded. "Well, I'd better get back to work."

"It seems every time we meet, you're hanging lights," Jill noted.

"Maybe I missed my true calling. Expert lights hanger."

"I'll go say hi to Lucille," Jill said, knowing she was eager to say much more to her than "hi." It had been a challenge to keep her mind focused on a conversation with Rick when all the while, she was bursting to tell Lucille how incredibly well her cookie experiment had gone.

A minute later, through the kitchen window, she could see Lucille standing near the island but knocked anyway, out of courtesy. She opened the door when Lucille waved her in.

"You really don't have to knock," Lucille insisted. "I meant it the other day—come and go as you please."

Jill closed the door and saw Lucille's hands clasped, her eyes expectant.

"The suspense is killing me. How'd it go?"

Jill revealed both hands to show Lucille her empty palms. "This is how it went. No box, no cookies left." She explained first about the paying customers on the street then reached inside her purse for the cash to give Lucille.

"You mean, they actually paid you three dollars apiece for my cookies? No haggling?"

"No haggling and no hesitation," Jill confirmed.

Next, she told Lucille the details of each shop owner she'd approached, then pulled something else out of her purse. "And here are your first official orders."

"I just never imagined... I mean, people want my cookies?"

She watched Lucille open the folded paper and do the math in her head. Before her brow could crinkle as the reality set in, Jill added: "I was careful not to overcommit you." She pointed to some numbers. "I've split this into two deliveries, based on the number that a double batch of gingerbread yields. If you made up the dough tonight, you could actually bake them off tomorrow, giving yourself plenty of time to decorate and bag them up, and I can deliver them before the shops close. And then after tomorrow, you'd get a nice, long break for the weekend and could make another batch by the start of next week to fulfill the rest of these orders. I can deliver those too. Two batches are more than we discussed, but honestly, I didn't know we'd get this many orders. I tried to keep things manageable."

"No, this is fine. I can handle this amount. But, honey"—she placed a hand on Jill's wrist—"I didn't mean to put you to work this way. You shouldn't be lifting a finger while you're here! Delivering cookies, taking orders—"

"You know, it didn't seem like work at all. I got to explore the entire square, see every shop, talk to the residents. I had fun."

"Well, you can back out of this anytime. I can get someone else to make the deliveries, if I need to."

"I don't mind. Besides, there will still be plenty of free time for exploring." Jill remembered something else. "Oh, and look what I found at the Stationery Place." She removed the bag hanging from her arm and spilled out the contents onto the kitchen island. "I bought these festive bags to put the cookies in. They're printed with candy canes. And I got some labels." Seeing Lucille's confusion, Jill clarified. "Stickers to put on the bags. We could write out 'Lucille's Cookies,' your brand name."

Lucille took the labels and studied them. "I have a brand name. I'm really doing this, aren't I?"

"It seems so!"

"I'd better get started, then." She approached the pantry and peered inside, mumbling to herself, then turned to face Jill. "I have the ingredients for another gingerbread batch, at least. I'll whip it up now. No time like the present."

She swiftly collected the flour, sugar, and a jar of molasses in her arms then carried them to the island where Jill stood, double-checking the orders again.

The moment Lucille set down the ingredients, the kitchen door opened wide and Rick appeared, obviously frustrated and staring down at his hands. "Gran, I need some strong scissors. This thing won't budge." He carried a thick knot of coiled outdoor lights in one arm and fiddled with the plastic loop binding them. The thick sweater Jill had seen him in earlier had been discarded, and he wore a white T-shirt that revealed the taut muscles in his forearms.

Closing the door and glancing up, he saw Jill. "Oh. Hey again."

Watching him return his attention to the coil, Jill muttered, "Um, I thought you were supposed to be an expert at this." She couldn't help herself.

The light frustration on Rick's face relaxed into an easy grin. "Yeah, I thought so too."

Lucille had already found the scissors and approached Rick. "Hold still." She clipped the plastic band, freeing the strand of lights.

"More cookies?" Rick eyed the molasses jar on the island.

"Oh, yes! There's a story behind it," Lucille said with a gleam in her eye. She returned the scissors to their drawer then stood near the island.

Rick gripped the lights at his side, patiently waiting as Lucille started from the beginning and took him through the excitement at the birthday party over her cookies, the impromptu brainstorming session with Jill, the experiment of handing out samples to shops, then the overwhelmingly positive response the cookies received.

"We've got twelve orders to fill. So I'm making a double batch for tomorrow's deliveries and another early next week. Isn't it exciting?"

Rick's expression hadn't shifted the entire time Lucille spoke or even afterward, as he processed his grandmother's news.

"Well? Say something," she urged.

Rick ran a hand through his hair. "I'm not sure what to say. I didn't know you wanted to do this, start up a business."

"It's not a *business*. Right now, it's only a hobby I'm curious about. A trial run. That's all."

Rick returned his gaze to the jar of molasses. Jill could tell he was choosing his words carefully. She squirmed from the other side of the island, suddenly a third wheel in an uncomfortable family discussion she hadn't expected to be part of.

"Even so," Rick reasoned, "if you sell food out of your house, even for a short time, you need to consider things like a home-kitchen license and permits. Then there are inspections and sales tax and..." His tone softened. "I'm only looking out for you."

"I know," Lucille admitted, her shoulders slightly deflated. "And I appreciate it. But I'm not ready for all that. Not yet. This is only in the beginning stages right now." Lucille stared down at her hands, flicking her thumbnails together. Then she crossed her arms and raised her gaze to Rick, steadfast. "Let me propose this. I go through with these orders, fulfilling them as promised. And if by next week I still want to do this, and if it's successful, then I'll go about it the right way. I's dotted, T's crossed. Permits, inspections, whatever I need to do. You can guide me through everything. Okay?"

"Fair enough." Rick shifted the coil of lights to lean against his other hip. "I'm just surprised, Gran. All these years, and you've never mentioned wanting to sell your cookies."

"As I told Jill earlier, this was a buried dream. I never had time before, and now, well, there's time." She cleared her throat. "If you want the truth, things get lonely around here without your grandfather roaming around. And this might help. It could fill up my days."

Rick closed the gap between them and kissed his grandmother's cheek. "Fair enough."

Chapter Six

Anybody spying on Jill's work process would've seen a jumble of notes scattered all around the bed, with her at their center, cross-legged and typing away. But Jill saw a method in her own madness, a clear organization of thoughts, ideas, notes, and observations that all made perfect sense in her head.

She hadn't planned to organize her notes yet, not until *after* her visit to the library later in the afternoon, but Miranda's earlier text had sped up the process. That morning, as Jill changed clothes after her shower, Miranda had sent a message checking in on the article, obligating Jill to respond with a brief progress report.

Jill had paused her getting-ready routine to text Miranda back—*I'll send an update shortly*—then retrieved her spiral and laptop. After an hour of combing through her notes, she'd tapped out her overall impressions of the town, the people, and the mansion. She'd even scanned through some photos, chosen a handful of her best shots, and attached them to the email for good measure. She wanted her friend to have confidence in the article, even when Jill herself was still shaky about it.

Jill heard the creak of stairs outside and knew that someone was coming up to the apartment for a visit. Swiftly, she gathered her strewn-out spiral notes and slipped them beneath the laptop. She wasn't ready for anyone but Miranda to see them.

Jill rose from the bed in time to answer the knock that came next. She opened the door to Lucille, who carried a miniature Christmas tree.

"I come bearing gifts!" she said, then paused, staring back at Jill. "Your hair!"

Jill forgot that she hadn't straightened it yet—she had been too preoccupied with the Miranda update. Now, she touched the damp curls and cringed, feeling suddenly on display.

As an adult, Jill only ever wore her hair in its natural state at home, never in public. The years of bullying in grade school had left a permanent mark, so that she viewed her hair as freakish and unnatural, to be ashamed of and hidden away. And so, every morning, with each stroke of the straightener, she would bend her unruly curls to the instrument's will, her way of taming the criticism of those bullies, one by one, even all those years later.

"It's adorable!" Lucille clarified as Jill stepped aside to let her in.

"Thanks. But that's not the word I would use."

"Whyever not?"

Jill shut the door and pivoted. "I actually hate my curls. I've been dealing with them my whole life."

"So, they're natural…"

"Unfortunately, yes."

"I'm envious of you," Lucille admitted, setting the two-foot tree on the table near the window. "I have the straightest, flattest, most boring hair you've ever seen. All my life I've had to *pay* for my waves, sit in a chair for a couple of hours, and have smelly chemicals applied to my scalp, all for a bit of curl." Lucille patted her own gray hair. "I finally gave up a few years ago and cut most of it off. I figure my money is better spent elsewhere."

That notion relaxed Jill—she'd never thought of her hair as something to be *envious* of—and she stopped fiddling with her curls.

Jill eyed the tree, hoping for a change of subject. "So what do we have here?"

"Consider it appreciation for all your hard work."

"It's beautiful. Thank you!" Jill inhaled the fresh scent of pine. "But unnecessary. Yesterday didn't feel like work."

"Even so, I wanted to cheer up your room."

"Well, consider it—and me—cheered. Here, sit." She gestured toward the wicker chair beside the table and sat in the opposite chair. "I'm curious. How do you feel about the cookies, on this morning after? Any regrets?"

"Not a one," Lucille said with conviction as she sat down. "I felt energized when I woke up this morning. There's a strong purpose to my day ahead, which is what I wanted."

"I'm glad." Truthfully, Jill had awakened with doubts. *Did I push too hard yesterday, pressing Lucille into doing something she isn't ready for?* And Rick's solemn reaction to the whole venture hadn't helped. In fact, it had seemed to suck some of the wind from Lucille's sails.

"Your face just changed," Lucille said. "Any regrets on your end?"

"Truthfully?"

"Always."

"Well, I think Rick made some good points yesterday about permits and inspections and taxes. Those things *had* crossed my mind, but I didn't feel like we were at that stage yet. Mostly, I just don't want there to be friction between the two of you... because of me."

Lucille waved at the air and tsked. "You have to take my grandson with a small grain of salt. He means well. But he's always looking at the practical side of things. Plus, it's his nature to be overprotective of me, even more so since Frank passed away. It's a sweet quality to have, but sometimes it can be stifling. Whenever I present what I think is a good idea, I usually brace myself for his negative reaction. The boarder idea, for instance." She nodded at the room's interior. "I thought this would be a marvelous idea, in the scheme of things—spruce up the apartment, bring in some extra income, have someone else around so I wouldn't feel alone—but Rick had his doubts from the start and still does. He doesn't want a 'stranger' living nearby. He's even offered to interview the 'candidates' for me." She chuckled. "I'm perfectly capable of finding a decent, respectable boarder, all on my own. And I told him so. I'm a grown woman. I don't need his permission about the boarder. *Or* the gingerbread."

Jill smiled at Lucille's gumption, as the Texans might call it. "Good for you!"

"His concern comes from a good place, I know. Under the surface, Rick has a heart of gold. He's taken such good care of me. Always has."

Jill believed it. She'd witnessed evidence of their special connection in every exchange between them—the tender tone, the watchful eye, the affectionate humor. They were lucky to have each other.

Lucille began to rise from the chair. "Well, I've got cookies to bake off."

"I'll do some writing here then join you in the afternoon. Maybe I can help bag up the cookies before the deliveries."

"Only if you're sure. As I said yesterday, I don't want to put you under obligation. I can always find someone else to deliver them—"

"No, it's fine. You're actually doing me a favor."

"How so?"

"Well, because of your cookies, I'm getting to know the town up close, which is what I wanted in the first place. The deliveries will give me an excuse to slow down and talk to shop owners and residents, get to know them in a way I never could have if I'd only popped in as a tourist."

"I see what you mean. It reminds me of one summer, when Frank and I visited England years ago. We rented a cottage on the outskirts of this charming village called Chilton Crosse for two weeks. We got to know the locals, took walks around the village every day, browsed the gallery, ate at the pub..."

"Exactly. There's a difference between seeing a town as a tourist and immersing yourself in the culture. That's what I feel like I'm doing here. And your cookies are helping me achieve it."

"Well in that case, I'm glad to help. I'll stop worrying over it."

"Thanks again for the tree."

After Lucille left, Jill remembered her hair and headed for the bathroom to turn on the straightener. As flattering as Lucille's compliments had been, Jill knew it would take much more than a few kind words for her to feel comfortable with her ornery curls in public.

"THESE LOOK SO PROFESSIONAL!" Lucille gaped at the rows and rows of gingerbread, dressed up in their new finery. Jill had spent the past hour helping Lucille prepare the cookies for delivery, tucking the freshly iced cookies neatly inside their decorative bags, the labels already attached.

"I think the store managers will be very impressed." Jill looped her purse over her shoulder then looked up to see Rick, head down and typing out a text as he entered the kitchen. He didn't glance up until he'd finished the message.

"Oh. Hi." His eyes darted between Jill and his grandmother as he lowered his phone.

"That's been happening a lot lately," Lucille said.

"What has?"

"Texting. And more texting." She raised an eyebrow toward his cell. "You need a break from that thing."

Rick shrugged. "Hey, at least it allows me to be here with you. I can work from anywhere, thanks to 'this thing.'"

"Well, I can't argue with that." Lucille's tone lightened.

Jill suppressed a grin, stacked the two boxes filled with cookies, then lifted them up.

"Rick, be a gentleman like I taught you," Lucille chided, nodding toward Jill.

"It's fine," Jill assured them. "These are light as a feather."

Rick set down his phone and met Jill at the door, reaching his long arm toward the knob. His face came unexpectedly close to hers as she turned to whisper, "Thanks." Shaking off his stare, she gripped the boxes and passed through.

She'd expected him to shut the door behind her, but Rick followed her outside into the cold without a jacket.

"I wanted to thank you," he said, his voice husky and low as his brown eyes focused on hers. He folded his arms across his chest for warmth.

"For what?" Not sure how long the conversation would be and anticipating a long walk around the square, Jill took a couple of steps to her left and perched the boxes on top of her car's trunk.

He followed her and paused. "What you're doing for my grandmother. The cookies, the help. The friendship. I haven't seen her this... animated in a long time. I originally came back here early to help her through the holidays. I didn't want her to be alone. But I didn't expect her to be this content. It's almost like she doesn't need me."

"She needs you. I saw her face light up that first morning after you arrived—she's happy you're here. And you don't need to thank me. Your grandmother has helped me too. Dropping her name around the square has made me feel quite important. She's well-loved around here."

"True. But she puts on a good show for everybody. They all think she's doing fine. And she is. But when she's alone in the house, she struggles. And you've helped her this week not to struggle as much."

Jill nodded and returned his gaze. For the first time, she noticed the dark circles underneath his eyes. "What about you? You're the strong one for her, but you've got a lot on your own plate, looks like." She hoped she hadn't crossed a line, making such a personal observation. They barely knew each other. But it was already out there, so she waited for his response.

"You mean the text." He pointed back toward the kitchen.

"The text, the calls, the serious look of concern you think you're hiding. Is everything okay? With your work?" She only knew that he dealt with computers, but beyond that, she wasn't sure what work entailed for him.

"Yeah, I'm on top of it. Only a couple of bumps in the road. Nothing that can't be handled. Eventually."

His mysterious response confirmed Lucille's intuition that something unusual *was* going on at his job.

Rick uncrossed his arms. "Speaking of work, I'd better get back to it and let you deliver those."

Rick took backward steps toward the kitchen door and gave a final wave as Jill took up the boxes again, surprised that he'd followed her out the door in the first place. Rick had abandoned the pull of his phone for a mini-conversation with her.

She headed down the driveway with a tiny smile.

JILL HAD JUST ENOUGH time to deliver the cookies around the square before dusk hit and stores started to close. With each new delivery, she would enter with the cookies, receive the money, and then spend a bit of time chatting with the store owners and sometimes their customers. Each shop had its own selection of Christmas music playing, and by the time Jill had finished her rounds, she was convinced she'd heard every Sinatra or Crosby holiday song ever recorded, multiple times. And as she'd told Lucille, natural conversations *had* popped up here and there between Jill and the residents—Angela from The Stationery Store confided that she hoped to take over the shop one day; Mindy, owner of the boutique, mentioned that her daughter was getting over a bout of strep throat; and Jack, the diner's manager, told Jill a long-winded story about the photo on his wall of him as a little boy fishing with his grandfather. Jill would never have learned those tidbits, save for the gingerbread cookies.

Before heading back to Lucille's with some daylight to spare, Jill approached the grand library, which shared the center lawn with the courthouse. A plaque embedded in the stone exterior told her the library was "lovingly dedicated to Morgan Rose Stout."

Jill touched the familiar name with her fingertips then twisted the doorknob and entered, still holding the empty boxes at her side and hoping no one would mind them. She could've easily been stepping into any ornate library in Europe, with the rich Oriental rugs, the dark wooden walls, the chandeliers above, and the stained-glass windows. All were as beautiful as Jolene had described. She could picture Alfred J. Stout visiting museums and libraries in France or Italy for inspiration then later barking orders over the phone to international merchants while negotiating prices for materials, then even later overseeing the entire building process, eagle-eyed.

Jill found herself standing in the middle of the first floor, over a hundred years after the first stone had been laid, gazing upward, taking it all in, then scanning the rows upon rows of floor-to-ceiling bookshelves.

"Impressive, isn't it?" someone said behind her.

Jill twirled around to see a tall woman around her own age, standing with clasped hands and a welcoming expression.

"I've heard all about it, but to see this building in person... it's amazing," Jill acknowledged.

The woman's lips parted slightly. "You're Jill McCallister, aren't you? I've read all your books! I love how strong and smart your female characters are."

Jill dipped her head. "Thank you. That means a lot."

The woman took a step closer and told Jill quietly, "I'm Chaynie Mayfield, the assistant librarian. I'm also friends with Jolene, and she let me know that you're the descendant of Alfred Stout? Sorry if that's a secret I'm not supposed to know. But the minute you left the mansion, Jolene called me up."

"It's not really a secret. But I guess I'm still getting used to everything. I only found out about my genealogy a week ago. It feels brand-new."

"Well, you're welcome to use our resources here to research the family further. In fact, I hope you don't think this is *too* presumptuous of me..." Chaynie moved past Jill, walked a few feet toward the circulation desk, then leaned behind the counter, where she produced two hardcover books. "After Jolene called me, I pulled a couple of resources, figuring you'd probably visit the library sometime." She held the first book higher. "This one is a detailed historical account of the family and the town. And *this* one"— she shuffled the books—"is Morgan's biography. I browsed through it myself after I pulled it. Some fascinating details inside." She tapped the cover with her fingernail, her excitement infectious.

"Thank you." Jill accepted the books with her free hand. "I can't wait to read them. You have no idea how much this helps." Chaynie didn't know that she'd just handed Jill a huge chunk of her article's research without her having to spend hours digging around for it.

"Do you have time for a tour of the library?" Chaynie asked. "We're open for another half hour. I'm happy to take you around."

"I would love to, but I have a prior commitment." She knew Lucille would be waiting on her report about how the deliveries had gone. Jill's focus would be too divided if she said yes to the tour. "But I'll come back. I promise."

A willowy blond girl approached Chaynie and tapped her shoulder. "I've got Mr. Simmons waiting on line one."

"Okay, thanks. Let him know I'm coming." Chaynie turned to Jill, removing a card from the countertop. "Here's my information. If you have *any* questions while you're here, just ask."

Chaynie slipped the card inside the pages of Morgan's book, then they exchanged goodbyes.

WISHING SHE'D WORN a thicker coat and more comfortable shoes, Jill trudged the final stretch back to Lucille's house, enjoying the twilight hour. The sun had set while she'd been inside the library, and she peered up at the hint of stars above. She couldn't remember the last time she had actually stared at the stars, paid attention to them. Small towns had that effect—they made a person slow down and savor the little things.

As if to prove her point, the colorful glow of Christmas lights dazzled Jill as she rounded the corner and noticed Rick's handiwork. She hadn't seen the finished product yet—Lucille's roof, including the gables, had been trimmed pristinely with bright lights. Rick had even wrapped the porch columns with them, adding to the holiday effect.

Jill set down her boxes and books and found her phone. Snapping a photo, she sent it immediately to Lindsey with a message: *Merry Christmas from Texas!*

When she reached the kitchen door, she could see Rick at the stove, flipping food with a spatula. Lucille stood near him and caught Jill's eye. "There you are!" Jill could hear her say, muffled through the window panes.

Lucille opened the door and ushered Jill inside the cozy space. "You're just in time for supper," she said, helping to empty Jill's arms of the boxes and books. Jill heard sizzling sounds at the stovetop and watched Rick deftly lift a grilled-cheese sandwich from the pan and onto a paper towel. Jill's stomach growled at the sight.

Rick gave her a backward glance. "I made some with ham slices, some without. Which do you want?"

"Either, thanks." Jill removed her coat and noticed three places set at the breakfast table. They were expecting her, including her without a second thought. And something about that warmed Jill up even more, from the inside out. "Can I help?"

"No, no," Lucille said. "Come sit and tell me all about the deliveries while Rick finishes up. He's the designated sandwich-maker. And server." She winked at her grandson.

Jill carried her purse to the table and heard the corgis whining. She moved her gaze to a gate sectioning them off from the kitchen. "Hi, guys." She waved at them, and they whined even louder.

"You two, hush," said Lucille. "You've already eaten tonight." She took a place at the table beside Jill. "How did everything go today?"

"Perfect. The managers were all happy to see me. Most of them had already carved out spaces on a table or countertop and started laying out the cookies right away. I even saw some customers eyeing them as I left. I'm pretty sure we made some immediate sales."

Rick slipped in beside Jill, quietly set an oversized bowl of potato chips in the center of the table, then slipped away again.

"Oh, and I have something for you." Jill opened her purse and produced a manila envelope. She unclasped the brad and drew out a stack of cash and checks. "I meant to separate these, make them all nice and neat, put them into their own envelopes—"

"No need," Lucille insisted, holding out her palms. "I can sort them later."

"I did specify the shop owners, though"—Jill pointed to the mini-sticky notes on each individual payment—"so you could keep track. We can develop a better system later." She looked up in time to see Rick setting down her plate containing a grilled cheese square, perfectly cut into two triangles. "If there *is* a later, I mean. If you decide to pursue this."

Lucille chewed at her lip. "I'm surprised that today went so well. I guess I was worried. Silly of me."

"Not silly. Understandable," Jill assured her. "This means something to you."

Rick set down Lucille's plate then his own. He pointed at Jill's glass as he sat down across from her. "That's *non*-sweet, by the way. Safe to drink."

"How did you know—" Jill brought the glass to her lips for a taste.

"Oh, honey," Lucille said, "I saw the shock on your face the other day when I offered you sweet tea. You couldn't hide it."

Jill shook her head. "Sorry..."

"Don't be! Most Northerners despise our sugary tea. But if you're raised on it all your life, like we've been, I guess you get used to it. It's an acquired taste."

"Well, thanks for accommodating this Northerner."

"So, about the deliveries," Rick began. "Y'all have more next week?"

"Right," Jill confirmed. "Including The Pit. They wanted the mini-cookies. 'Appealing to kids,' they told me. I split the orders evenly to give Lucille a nice break over the weekend."

"Good thinking." Rick lifted his sandwich to his lips.

"This looks delicious," Lucille said. "My grandson, the chef!"

Pausing with his sandwich still in the air, Rick gently countered, "Not sure this makes me a chef, Gran. Anyone can make a grilled cheese." Then he took an enormous, crunchy bite.

"That's not entirely true," Jill said, lifting up one of her cheesy triangles. "My roommate, Lindsey, ruins *every*thing. She tried to make grilled cheese once and nearly burned our apartment down."

"Sounds like an adventure. A dangerous one." Lucille slipped the payments back into the envelope then turned her gaze toward the kitchen island. "You came in with books. Does that mean you had a chance to visit the library?"

Jill had taken a first scrumptious bite of her sandwich, then chewed and swallowed as she nodded. "Briefly. I'll go back another day." She dabbed her mouth with a paper napkin. "I met Chaynie. She'd already heard about me from Jolene... my connections to Morgan's Grove."

"And she knew you from your novels, I imagine?" Lucille wondered.

"That too."

Lucille reached for a handful of chips. "Well, it was bound to get out sooner or later. About your heritage, I mean."

Rick interjected. "And once Bob gets ahold of that information, the entire town will know your history."

"He already got wind of my novels." Jill grinned and selected a chip. "He wanted some writing advice."

"Oh my." Lucille chuckled. "I hope you wriggled out of that one, somehow."

"I did. As politely as possible."

"You don't mind, do you?" Lucille asked. "About people knowing your connection to the town?"

Jill paused to consider it. "I really don't. I think it's sweet, the affection everyone has for the founder."

"Well, you *should* be proud of your roots," Lucille insisted. "You come from a wonderful, beloved family."

Family. Jill hadn't yet thought of her heritage in quite that way. At first, the Stouts and their descendants had just been faraway people in old photos with distant expressions in their eyes, connected to her by DNA. But the more she learned about them, and the more she became immersed in the town that Alfred had founded, the more tangible the connection to those people had started to become. As a single, childless adult, with her father gone and her mother bouncing around the globe, Jill never thought of herself as having a family. But maybe that was starting to change.

As though Lucille and Rick could sense she was having a reflective moment, they ate in silence for the next couple of minutes, enjoying the food. Aside from Thanksgiving and her recent buffet from The Pit, Jill couldn't recall the last time she'd sat down to a meal that hadn't included Lindsey and her boyfriend. Or no one at all. Most meals in Denver, she'd spent alone—hectic lunches at her keyboard or takeout at home because Lindsey and Charlie had gone out on a date.

Rick interjected softly, "Anyone ready for seconds?" He had already polished off his sandwich, and Jill realized most of hers was gone, too.

"I'll take another one," she told him as he rose from his seat.

"Oh, you young people showing off. Appetites with room to spare! I can't handle another bite." Lucille took a generous sip of her sweet tea.

Jill watched her set the glass down then graze her fingers over the envelope with a soft smile that she probably thought no one would catch.

Chapter Seven

Slipping into her flannel PJ's, Jill whispered "bliss" to the air then slipped beneath the sheets, cool and crisp. She shouldn't even *be* so tired, not at barely ten p.m. The day after deliveries had been slothful and peaceful, with nothing special on her agenda. But perhaps the eventful week had finally caught up with her—the long-distance driving and constant flurry of activities had finally taken their toll.

Jill's phone rang beside her, and she tilted the screen to see Lindsey's name. "Hey!" Jill said, propping a second pillow behind her head.

"What time is it there?" Lindsey asked. "I can never remember if I'm ahead and you're behind. Or vice versa."

"Almost ten. We're ahead an hour."

"'We?' Are you officially a Texan now?"

"I'm starting to wonder. I almost said 'y'all' today."

"You did *not*." Lindsey gave a giggle.

Jill asked about her week, and Lindsey gave a quick rundown then added, "Oh, and Tommy got gum stuck in his hair yesterday, and I had to cut it out. That was a first. How are things in Morgan's Grove?"

Jill had already texted Lindsey about the major daily happenings since she'd arrived, so she skipped over those. "Today was a nice pace. I spent some time in the park, ate lunch, then went back to the library, where Chaynie gave me the grand tour. Oh my gosh, Lindsey, you would love the children's alcove upstairs. It's this entire section designed for children. A fantasyland, filled with books, floor to ceiling, and stained-glass windows fashioned with classic children's book characters. And Chaynie has a reading time every day for the kids—they sit in this circle of tiny chairs. I snapped some photos but forgot to send them to you. I'll do it tonight. All I kept picturing when I looked around was Morgan's little-girl face, all lit up and happy that her father had built her that space."

"I'm trying not to be jealous! That sounds amazing. I want to see it someday. How's the article coming? Any breakthroughs since you've been there?"

"I've spent most of my time taking photos, writing down impressions, and getting an overall feel for the community." She glanced toward the book on her bed. "But I think today, I might've found my focus, finally. Chaynie gave me Morgan's biography, and I nearly finished it in one sitting. I've only got a couple more chapters to go. Lindsey, she was this amazing woman." Jill sifted through the facts in her brain, wanting to be accurate. "Morgan went through all these hardships—her daughter died of cancer, age three. And her husband died at the end of World War II. But Morgan somehow turned the challenges into victories. She established the first Children's Cancer Research Hospital in the South. And during World War II, she transformed the mansion into a USO headquarter, where she would host parties for the soldiers and the community."

"Wow. A true philanthropist."

"Exactly. And so for the article, I thought I could focus in on her spirit, her generosity. I asked Chaynie why so many of the details in the book weren't part of the mansion's tour—there was no account of the USO parties or the death of her child. Chaynie said Morgan was humble to a fault. She didn't want recognition for her charitable works. She always did things behind the scenes, never taking credit."

"But why does she have a biography detailing her life?"

"It was written a couple of decades after her death, so she never knew about it. I struggled with it today, about making her the centerpiece of my article, even though she might not have wanted to be showcased that way. But I want her legacy to stay alive. I have a feeling she would approve, knowing where my heart is, knowing my intentions."

"Definitely. I mean, just hearing bits and pieces of her story is inspiring. It makes me want to do something... noble."

"Imagine how it feels to be her great-great-granddaughter. That's a lot to live up to." Jill switched the phone to her other hand then pulled the quilt higher for warmth. "So anyway, that's where I am right now. Making progress. And enjoying the journey of being here." It seemed impossible that she was nearly halfway through her stay in Texas. *Only another full week left...*

"And enjoying someone else's company too?" Lindsey's tone lifted, and Jill could hear the eyebrow-raise implied in her voice.

"Linds, what are you talking about?"

"Well, nearly every time you text me, you mention Rick, the grandson. But you hardly give any details. Spill! He's cute, isn't he?"

Jill rolled her eyes. "You are completely boy crazy."

"Nope, only curious. It's a girlfriend's duty to ask these questions. Part of my job description."

Usually, Jill would have had no problem diving into the silly depths of schoolgirl chatter about "boys" with Lindsey, even at their age. But for some reason, her growing friendship with Rick felt more mature than that, and she wanted to protect it and keep it private for the time being, even from her best friend.

"So? Cute or not cute?" Lindsey asked again.

Jill pictured the dark hair, the thoughtful eyes, the strong stubbled jaw. "He's... rugged. And sort of calm and quiet. And smart," Jill admitted, knowing Lindsey would badger her until she received *some* small nuggets from her. "And he's loyal. I'm glad he's here for Lucille. He's good for her."

"You told me she lost her husband recently." Lindsey's tone became thankfully serious again.

"Yeah, last year. She's tough, though. She's managed to carry on, make a life for herself."

"See? Another strong, inspiring woman. They're all around you."

"They really are." Jill thought of all the female shop owners she'd recently met, and the single mom next door to Lucille. And even Mrs. Haversham, whose son, Jill had recently learned, was on his second tour in Afghanistan.

"Oops. Speaking of strong women, that's my mom, buzzing in on the other line," Lindsey told her. "Sorry, I have to get it."

"Tell her hi for me," Jill said.

"I will."

Jill clicked off the phone, set it down, then scooped up the biography. In the cover photo, Morgan looked about eighteen years old, her eyes full of promise, a wistful smile playing on her lips, her whole life ahead of her.

"I'll do you justice, I promise," Jill told her great-great-grandmother, then opened the book to finish reading.

THE LAST PERSON JILL had expected to see at the bottom of her stairs on Saturday morning was Rick. She'd slept late, showered and dressed, and planned on another outing to the founder's mansion to ask Jolene some follow-up research questions. But as she opened the apartment door, purse in hand, Jill spotted Rick standing below with a hand on the railing.

He saw her and paused. "Hey. I was just coming to see you."

"I'll be right down." Jill locked the door then slipped her key into her purse and tapped down the stairs. Rick waited on the driveway below, wearing a brown leather jacket and jeans. As she moved closer, she noticed he was clean-shaven, revealing a small cleft in his chin.

He looked years younger without his light beard. "Everything okay?" she wondered.

"Yeah. It's just... I've been on conference calls all morning—"

"On Saturday?"

"Mostly international calls, yeah. Anyway, I hung up the last call and stared at the phone and realized that Gran was right. I need a break from 'that thing.' So I put on my coat and walked outside. Left my cell phone on the bed upstairs."

"You rebel!"

"It feels weird. Like part of my arm is missing. Or maybe my brain."

"Where were you headed? Just now, I mean?" She still hadn't put the pieces together of why he was headed up her staircase in the first place.

"I wasn't really sure. Maybe for a ride in the truck—I still keep it in the garage, to use when I'm in town. It's a nice day for a drive."

Jill hadn't even noticed the weather until he mentioned it. She looked high at the peerless, cloudless sky, which was the pale-blue color of a robin's egg.

"I remembered I promised to show you some off-the-grid places around town."

Jill recalled that offer but thought Rick had forgotten.

"But you're headed out too," he noted, gesturing toward her purse.

The mansion can wait was Jill's first thought, and she knew how Lindsey would have interpreted it: *Look at you, postponing plans for a guy!* But it was true. The mansion could wait. Jill had seen it before, and she could see it again. Plus, she'd gotten loads of research done the day before. She could afford an off-the-grid outing with Rick.

"It was nowhere special," she said. "Be my tour guide today. I need to see this town through the eyes of a local."

With a nod and what she thought was a relieved half-smile, Rick headed toward the garage and pushed a button to raise the door, revealing a glossy black truck that dwarfed Lucille's modest white Honda.

"I think I might need a stepladder to climb in." Jill approached his truck hesitantly, only half-kidding. There was no way she could hoist herself up into a cab like that with grace and ease. Thank goodness she was wearing comfy jeans instead of a skirt today.

"It won't be that bad," he assured her, opening the passenger side. "Grab onto that handle." He pointed to it. "Then balance your left leg inside and pull your weight up."

"You can't laugh if I fall." She reached high for the handle, gripping it tightly.

"You won't. I'm here."

She thought she could feel the ghost of his hands near her waist as she propped her left foot firmly on the cab's floor then lifted herself up to the seat.

Rick shut her door then rounded the truck to enter on the driver's side. The engine roared to life, and Jill thought about how appropriate it was to drive around parts of Texas in a truck that positively screamed "Texas."

The heater thrummed at her ankles as Jill clicked her seat belt. Rick eased the truck out of the driveway, backing all the way to the street, pausing to check for traffic.

You can tell a lot about a person by the way they drive, Jill's mother used to say. If that was true, then Rick's driving style showed he was confident but careful as he inched through the town square, watching for pedestrians.

He continued past the B&B then past the mansion's gates, using one hand to flick on the radio. Jill fully expected the twang of country music to float through, but instead, Rick had found a station playing standards—Sinatra, Bublé, Tommy Dorsey. Very *un*-cow-boy-like.

As Rick turned a corner, the truck crested a steep hill, revealing tall oak trees, their naked branches shivering in the wind.

"This is beautiful," she whispered.

"Yeah, there's some nice open country around the outskirts of town."

As he drove along, Jill noticed ranches and farms filled with acres of crops awaiting their future harvests or enormous bales of tightly packed hay. Horses and cattle were a common sight, with the occasional barking dog.

"That's an old abandoned church." Rick pointed through the windshield at a stone structure, overgrown with dried weeds and dead grass.

"Is there a story there?" Jill wondered aloud as Rick slowed the truck to a stop in front of it.

"Not that I know of. It's a mystery why it was never rebuilt or torn down. A relic of the past that just stays around. But kids play here—they think it's haunted."

"I can see why." Though the structure was beautiful, it had a gothic quality about it, hidden partly in shadow beneath a thick patch of trees.

Rick moved the truck along and returned to the two-lane country road. "That's the Peterson ranch," he said as the property came into view.

Two horses, one blond and the other chestnut-colored, noticed the truck and trotted toward the fence.

"Can we stop?" Jill asked on a whim. She didn't ever remember seeing a horse in person, up close. It was her chance.

"Sure." Rick pulled the truck to the side and halted.

She hadn't expected him to dash around the truck bed and appear at her side, but he was there when she opened the door, ready to help her down. She accepted his warm, strong hand and landed on the dried grass next to him.

She led the way to the fence, moving tentatively toward the horses. She had no idea they would be so *tall*. "Are they friendly?"

"Yeah, they're old and sweet-natured. Put your hand out. Let 'em smell you."

Jill could sense Rick following behind and felt safer moving forward. The blond horse whinnied loudly then snorted, dipping its head down and up, down and up.

"It's saying hi," Rick assured Jill as she drew closer.

The darker horse had already approached the fence and extended its head as far forward as it could, curious to see who the strangers were. Rick reached his hand out to the horse for a sniff then stroked its nose.

Taking her cue from Rick, Jill stretched her hand upward toward the blond horse. After it sniffed her knuckles, she slowly flexed her hand to reveal her palm then touched the tip of the animal's nose with her fingertips.

"It's soft," she said in awe. "Like velvet."

The horse nuzzled its nose even closer, pushing Jill's hand away.

"I think he wants more." Rick showed her, patting the side of the chestnut horse, stroking its glossy neck.

She had to step in closer, but Jill was unafraid. They were gentle giants. She copied Rick's motions and petted the horse's neck. The animal blinked drowsily under long blond eyelashes and stood stat-ue-still, clearly enjoying the massage.

"Did you ever ride?" she asked Rick, eyes still glued to her horse.

"Sometimes. Pops, my grandfather, had a friend who owned a ranch, and he'd take me out there when I was a kid. We'd go riding and fishing. Whole afternoons, just the two of us."

"Sounds nice."

In the distance, the revving of an engine spooked both horses, and they followed each other back into the pasture, trotting all the way.

"Guess petting time is over," Jill said, wiping the grimy film from her hands. "That was amazing."

They returned to the truck and settled in, then Rick continued on the country path. They passed a couple of schools and at least four churches. It occurred to Jill that she and Rick hadn't spoken a word since they'd pulled away from the pasture. In that respect, Rick was the opposite of his grandmother. He didn't need to fill silences with chatty banter, didn't seem obliged to. Oddly, the silence was more intimate than talking, as though he trusted her enough to be quiet with her. Still, she wondered what he might be thinking. *Is his mind here, in the truck's cab with me, or back at the house, wondering who might be calling his cell phone?*

Rick broke the silence as he made a slow right turn back toward the square. "I have one more place to show you, but first, let's grab some food. You hungry?" He glanced over at her as he completed the turn.

"Actually, yes. I forgot to eat breakfast this morning."

"Juan's is the best Mexican food in the area. Not that wimpy Tex-Mex stuff, but the real deal, authentic. Can you handle spicy?"

"Sure," she said, not entirely sure she *could* handle spicy, but wanting to try. She was feeling adventurous.

Minutes later, Rick was handing her bags of food which he'd ordered to go. The mixed scents of meats and spices swirled through the cab as Jill perched the warm bags on her lap.

"Have you seen the bridge yet?" he asked, turning the wheel.

"What bridge?"

"It's sort of tucked away. It's not on any map—only the locals know about it. It's got a cool history. Your great-great—"

"One more great—"

"Great-grandfather built it for his wife. There's a table for picnics, but it might be too cold today."

Jill smirked. "You forget where I'm from! This is nothing." She waved at the weather outside.

Rick made another turn, and after a few hundred yards, Jill could see an object ahead, a boxy, hollowed-out building. As it came into view, she noticed the details: it was a covered bridge with a barn-red exterior and slanted shingled roof, complete with a clearwater creek flowing beneath.

"When you said 'bridge,' I never pictured a *covered* one. In Texas?"

"Yeah, there aren't that many of them, maybe a handful in the whole state."

Rick pulled over to the edge and stopped the truck. He exited the cab then came to Jill's side to help empty her hands of the food. The first sound Jill heard when she stepped down was the rushing water of the creek, then a bird cawing in the distance.

"Eat first?" he asked, and Jill confirmed the plan with a nod.

Rick led her to the picnic bench near the creek, where they opened the bags and laid the table with plasticware and napkins. He drew out the food, which included two bottled waters.

"Oh, here," Jill said, reaching for her purse and opening up her wallet.

"Naw, put that away," Rick insisted. "This is on me. It was my idea."

"Well, only if the next one's on me."

She opened her Styrofoam container to view seasoned rice, a side of beans, and the main course, two enchiladas smothered with chili sauce. She had told Rick to order for her. It smelled delicious.

"One's beef and one's chicken," he said, pointing toward them with his plastic fork. "And I told them to use mild sauce. You can graduate to spicy over here, if you want." He pushed the two small containers toward her. "It's better to take this in stages, I've learned."

Jill's first bite of the silky tortilla packed with tender beef was sumptuous. "The sauce is perfect," she confirmed. "Just enough spice for me. This is so good!"

"They make everything from scratch. Family recipes."

"It shows." As she continued to eat, Jill peered around at the dense forest, enjoying the cool wind on her cheeks and watching a squirrel bravely approach a nearby tree, digging for nuts. After a bit, she mused, "I don't think I've had a picnic since I was a little girl."

"Food tastes better outdoors. Something about the fresh air." Rick took an enormous bite of a crispy taco.

Jill uncapped her water and took a long drink. "Thanks for the tour. It sort of filled in the gaps for me about Morgan's Grove. I feel like I know the whole place even better now."

Rick nodded his response, having just taken another large bite.

Jill indented the Styrofoam with the crescent of her thumbnail. "It's bittersweet, though. Being here."

Rick wiped his mouth with a napkin. "How so?"

"It makes me think about my dad. How I wish that he could be here with me, seeing all this for himself."

"Makes sense. What about your mom? She might not be blood related to the Stouts, but she could still be interested, join you here someday. You could take her through the mansion, around town, share it with her..."

"If I can ever *get* her here," Jill quipped. She saw Rick's confusion. "She lives by the seat of her pants, always moving, never in one place very long. It started when my father passed away. Mother kept moving the two of us around, city to city, seven times in eight years."

Rick's eyes grew wide as he paused the water bottle at his lips. "Seven?"

"She claimed she was restless. Always looking for a better job in a bigger town. But my theory is a bit darker than that. I think she was running away from the grief. Every time it started to catch up with her, she moved. Well, *we* moved, sometimes in the middle of my school year."

Rick shook his head. "How did you handle it?"

Jill shrugged and stabbed the enchilada with her plastic fork. "Made the best of things, I guess. Tried to cope. What choice did I have? I was a shy kid and had just lost my father, so the world already seemed less... safe. Walking into a new classroom for the first time was petrifying."

Especially because of my untamable curly hair, she wanted to add, along with the never-ending teasing it brought from kids treating her like an exotic animal at the zoo, with everyone wanting a peek and calling her names.

"I was always the new kid," she continued. "The spectacle, the anomaly in the room. And whenever I would actually manage to make a new friend, it wouldn't last long, anyway, because Mother would move us again. So I learned not to make attachments. Surface-level friendships were easier. Safer."

Rick gave a nod, and something in his eyes told her he understood. *But how could he?* She knew next to nothing about his childhood, but with a grandmother like Lucille and a town like Morgan's Grove, he was bound to have been surrounded by love and familiarity and security most of his life.

"I think I sort of envy people who grew up here," she added. "Having a place to call home."

"Yeah. But small towns can be suffocating sometimes. Everyone knows everything. You can't sneeze without the whole town saying 'God bless you.' And," he added, "it's hard to mess up with the whole town watching. Especially when your grandfather's the sheriff."

"You can't tell me *you* ever got into trouble here."

"More than once," he admitted, opening a foil-covered package in the center of the table. "In fact, a rebellious streak when I was seventeen landed me a night in jail. Pops used it to teach me a lesson."

"What had you done?!"

Rick offered Jill the sugary dessert, a mini-churro, and continued. "Nothing too sinister. Got caught up in some vandalism with a couple of guys. It didn't help that I'd had a beer beforehand. Somebody called the police, and of course, Pops had to show up."

"Oh, no." Jill chuckled at the thought of a teenaged Rick behind bars, being taught a lesson by his stern grandfather.

"Trust me, you didn't wanna get in his way when he was in 'tough cop' mode."

"I'll bet!"

Rick's grin softened suddenly as his forehead crinkled. "Yeah. Things aren't the same around here without him." He stared down at the foil. "Can't believe it's already been a year. Well, almost a year. Monday."

Monday. Lucille's text from the day before was making more sense now. "I wonder why..."

"What?" Rick peered across the table.

"Well, your Gran texted me that she needed Monday morning off from baking. And now I understand the reason. But why doesn't she just take the *whole* day off? She knows we aren't committed to a specific day next week for deliveries. She can start baking on Tuesday, if she wants."

"Gran and I are visiting the gravesite Monday morning. She told me she wants to stay busy the rest of the day. I think baking will be a good distraction. She hasn't been back to see his grave, and neither have I. Not since the service..."

Jill put all the pieces together. Rick probably had piles of work he should've stayed in California to complete, but instead, he'd brought his work with him to Morgan's Grove early for this very occasion—to mark an important, sad anniversary with his grandmother and to stay with her during the holiday.

Rick changed course, ate his mini-churro in one bite, then dusted the cinnamon and sugar from his fingers. "Ready for a tour of the bridge?" He began to gather up the remnants of their meal, shoving them back into the paper bags.

"Sure." Full and satisfied from the meal and from the conversation, Jill ate the churro in a couple of quick bites as she watched Rick toss the bags into a nearby trash bin.

He led her toward the enormous entrance. "C'mon. I'll take you through."

"Christmas lights?" Jill pointed to the roof, where clear bulbs sparkled in the sunlight.

"Yeah, not just for Christmas, though. The lights stay all year round. There's an automatic timer that turns them on at dusk."

When they entered the bridge's interior, Jill spun around to take it all in. The plain wood with unpainted slats that appeared cobbled together was quite different from the pristine, cherry-red exterior. She saw a bird building its nest, high up inside a rafter.

"How old is it?" Her voice echoed inside the beams as she stomped her foot on a plank. "Seems pretty solid."

"1915, I think. There's a plaque somewhere around here..." Rick pointed. "There. Hard to see in the shadows. But residents know the story by heart."

"Tell me." She could read the plaque later. She would rather hear Rick's version, anyway.

Rick rubbed his palms together in preparation as he took slow steps backward and inside the bridge, still facing her in tour-guide mode. "Okay, so Alfred J. Stout—industrial tycoon, as you already know—married a northern girl from Indiana. And after he moved her down here, built her a mansion, and renovated the town, he decided to construct this bridge. He wanted to give her a reminder of her northern roots, so he hired an Indiana architect who'd designed most of the bridges in that state. When it was finished, he surprised her with a reveal ceremony on their anniversary."

"A covered bridge for a present? That's really romantic."

"The plaque doesn't say all that, but the details have been passed down through the generations. Who knows what's true, what isn't?" Rick continued his leisurely pace until they reached the other side.

"I choose to believe the romantic version." Jill emerged into the daylight with him, her eyes adjusting to the brightness.

"Most people do."

"Do you come here a lot? When you're in town?"

"Yeah. Mostly when I need a spot to think. It's a good, quiet place to be isolated, alone. But as a teenager, it was more of a social hangout with friends." He moved to the creek's edge.

"I can see." Jill noticed a collection of initials carved deep into the wooden slats on the outside wall of the bridge. In the center she saw *R.W.* "Is this *you*?" She took a guess, pointing. "R.W. plus... S.W.," she read, squinting.

"Yep, that's me."

"Who's S.W.?"

"Sarah Watkins. We dated in high school for two years. And beyond." Rick looked out toward the bubbling creek and folded his arms across his chest.

Jill walked to stand beside him, hoping he would elaborate.

"We had a game plan after high school—attend UT and settle down here in Morgan's Grove afterward. We talked about marriage, kids, all that."

"Sounds serious."

"Back then, it felt serious. But she changed her mind about UT and accepted an application for an out-of-state school. I guess she got cold feet. We tried to make it work long-distance, but she quit answering my emails and calls after the first month. She was pulling away." Still focused on the creek, he uncrossed his arms and combed through his dark hair with his fingers. "And there was another guy, so we broke up. And that was it. I haven't seen her since."

"She doesn't come back to Morgan's Grove?"

"Her family moved away years ago, and I think she's married, now, with kids. It was only a high-school thing." He paused then gave Jill a sideways glance. "How'd you get all that out of me? I hate talking about myself."

Jill snickered. "A special talent, I guess."

"Well, it's your turn. Tell me about your checkered past. It's only fair."

"It's not that checkered. All the moving I did in high school never left much room for a boyfriend. But I did have one in college who was pretty serious. And another one, semi-serious, about two years ago. He ended up moving to Canada for a job, and that was that." She smiled. "There's that long-distance theme again."

"It's a relationship killer. I'll never do it again," Rick admitted. "It's impossible to stay connected when you're thousands of miles away, even with technology and Skyping. It's not the same as being together in person."

Jill's phone jingled in her pocket. "Sorry. I guess we're not entirely technology free, after all." She saw the name on the screen then answered the call. "Hi, Lucille."

"I promise I'm not trying to bother you, dear, but do you know where my grandson is? That gadget of his has been ringing nonstop for the past two hours! I don't know how to shut it off, so I tossed it underneath a couple of pillows to muffle it then closed his bedroom door."

Jill covered a chuckle with her hand and looked up at Rick. She removed her hand from her mouth. "He's right here, with me. Would you like to speak with him?"

"No, no. He's a grown man. I probably shouldn't have hunted him down this way. But I wondered if the calls were important, that's all. He usually leaves me a note when he's gone." Lucille clucked. "But not this time."

"Well, I'll be sure to tell him about the phone calls."

Lucille clicked off, then Jill pocketed her phone and stared up at Rick with raised eyebrows. "You're in trouble, young man. You can probably expect a grounding from your grandmother when you get home."

"Wouldn't be the first time." Rick gave her a half-grin, then they swiveled together to pass back through the bridge. "Guess playtime is over. Back to real life."

Jill imagined that Rick was already picturing the thousand phone calls and emails he would need to return that evening. "Well, at least we got to escape it for a while."

She stepped through the cool darkness of the bridge with Rick at her side, their soft footsteps the only sounds inside. Jill felt the pull to linger, to stay a few more moments in that peaceful place. With Rick.

Chapter Eight

Exactly a week after Jill had arrived in Morgan's Grove, she sat on her bed, tapping on her tablet to find out more information about a monster storm that was forecasted to hit the western states during the next few days. Things weren't looking good for Colorado—or for Jill, if she stuck to her original plans to travel back home over the weekend. She might have to cut her time short in Morgan's Grove.

But forecasters can be wrong, Jill reasoned as she clicked off the weather website. Storm systems changed paths all the time or even disintegrated before they reached their destination. Besides, Jill wouldn't be leaving for Colorado until Saturday, so even if the storm hit the western states on Thursday, there could still be time for the roads to clear afterward. She wouldn't worry about it. Not yet.

Jill heard chatter below her bedroom window and approached it, drawing back the curtain to peek outside. She watched Rick accompany his grandmother, both dressed in black coats and ducking raindrops as they walked. They disappeared from Jill's view as Rick raised the garage door, and Jill could hear the grinding gears beneath her feet. A minute later, she watched Lucille's white car back out of the driveway slowly, with Rick at the helm, and the gears of the garage door groaned again.

Jill backed away from the window, imagining the two of them picking up flowers then reaching the gravesite and walking through bare winter trees to find Frank's headstone.

Jill knew of people who visited the graves of their loved ones weekly, replacing dying flowers with fresh ones, having a talk with the deceased, and maybe even issuing some prayers for comfort. Jill had only ever seen her father's gravesite once, during the service after he died. Her mother wasn't the type to revisit a grave over and over again—and they'd moved so many times over the years that easy access to the gravesite would've been a challenge. Later, she explained to a teenaged Jill that she didn't need to seek her husband there. He was always in her heart, and that was enough.

But Jill never had the opportunity to ask herself which type of mourner she was, the frequent visitor or the absent kind. That decision had been made for her long ago.

JILL DECIDED TO SPEND most of her morning at the founder's mansion again, browsing the rooms and jotting down more notes. Then she ate a late breakfast of French toast and smoked bacon at a place called Christine's Bistro, right outside the square. In truth, Jill was biding her time and giving Lucille plenty of space before reaching out and offering company or help in the kitchen. She'd planned to text Lucille around two o'clock, but Lucille beat her to it, texting *Starting the cookies!* with a smiley attached. The coast seemed clear for a visit.

As Jill approached Lucille's kitchen door, she resolved not to ask about her morning at the gravesite. If she wanted to talk about it, she would bring it up.

Jill was waved in by Lucille, who stood at the island with Rick. Christmas music played softly in the background while the corgis barked their friendliest barks, and Jill greeted them as she closed the door behind her. They followed her to the island, where Jill recognized the disc of gingerbread dough, ready to be rolled out.

Rick caught Jill's eye then gave a gentle smile. Jill felt her heart lift a little inside her chest, the same way it had each time he'd offered a hand to help her into the truck... or when his gaze had settled on her a bit longer than it should have across the picnic table.

With a subtle eyebrow raise, she issued him a how-did-things-go-this-morning? glance, and Rick seemed to read it clearly, offering a blink and a small nod in return. *We're okay.*

"I'm glad you're here," Lucille told Jill. "And I haven't mentioned this to you yet," she said to Rick, "but an acquaintance found me at church yesterday and asked if I would cater her son's birthday party on Wednesday. With gingerbread cookies! Imagine that."

"Word is spreading," Jill confirmed. "In fact, this morning, three store managers called me, requesting orders. I told them I'd speak with you first."

"I'm open to that," Lucille said. "One more double batch tomorrow? Completely doable."

Jill noticed that the dogs were confused about how they should divide their attention between the humans, so they planted themselves directly in the middle, staring back and forth as if watching a tennis match.

"So you've decided, then?" Rick asked. "That this is a business—that you'll keep baking and selling past today's orders?"

Jill didn't sense disapproval in his tone but more curiosity, as if he simply wanted to confirm Lucille's decision.

Lucille placed a hand on Rick's forearm. "I told you this was a trial run—and it still is. No firm decisions made yet. But I didn't expect more orders to roll in. How can I say no? I'll only commit to these for now. And then midweek, like I promised, we can decide for sure."

"It's your decision, Gran. I just want to be sure it's all done the right way. Looking out for you, that's all."

"I know, son. Thank you."

Son. Jill hadn't heard Lucille use that affectionate word for Rick before.

"Oh! I completely forgot," Lucille exclaimed. "Apparently, Jill's secret is officially out. Or at least, it's *getting* out. I ran into Bob after church, and he grilled me, asking all about Jill's connection to Alfred Stout and whether the rumors were true." She grimaced toward Jill. "I hope it was okay for me to confirm it."

"Totally fine. It was bound to get out."

"That's what I figured. I didn't give him any information that he didn't already know. I confirmed that, yes, you are related to the family, and yes, that's why you're in town. But then..."

"What?" Jill braced herself.

"Bob told me to ask you a question. We're having a town parade during the festival the week before Christmas."

Jill remembered seeing the flyers around the square.

"And Bob wanted to know if you'd be our grand marshall."

Rick snickered into his fist.

"You mean like riding on a float?" Jill asked, slightly horrified. "Waving to people? With some banner around my shoulder?"

Lucille chuckled. "I think that's exactly what Bob meant. And when you put it that way, it does sound a bit ridiculous. But he meant well."

"It was sweet of him. We can tell him the truth: I won't be here that close to Christmas. I'm scheduled to go back to Colorado in a few days."

"An honest answer, but I don't like it, myself," Lucille said. "I don't want to think about you leaving yet, so we'll just enjoy you while we can. One day at a time."

Rick fished his keys from his jeans pocket. "I need to run some errands. Y'all need anything?"

"No thanks," Lucille and Jill responded in unison.

He took a final sip of coffee, placed the mug in the sink, then told the corgis goodbye as he went out the kitchen door.

Jill faced Lucille. "I'm here to help today. With the cookies."

"Are you sure you're free?"

"Positive. I went back to the mansion this morning and did some more exploring. And over the weekend, I devoured the biography about Morgan's life. It's fascinating. Lucille, you should read it. She was this incredible woman, giving and kind and generous. And I'm not just saying that because we're related."

"I've heard bits and pieces about her, but I wasn't sure if it was all rumor. It's interesting, the idea of summing up a person's whole life in one book. When someone's gone, it's hard to pinpoint who that person really was, all the things they meant to others, their impact on this world, the people who loved them..."

It was clear Lucille wasn't speaking about Morgan anymore. She likely had Frank in mind.

Lucille gazed down at the disc of dough as she spoke then suddenly blinked and shifted, turning her attention to Jill. "In any case, yes. I will take you up on your offer to help out. My focus is a bit scattered today, it seems."

"Would you rather postpone some orders? It would only take a couple of calls, and I could—"

"No, no. I *want* to be in the kitchen today. It's good for me." She patted Jill's hand twice then reached for the rolling pin. "Now, this part is more of a one-person job, but you can help me cut out shapes and ice the cookies in a bit."

Jill perched on the stool across the island from Lucille, much as she had her first day in Morgan's Grove. A stack of new cookie bags sat near her, waiting to be labeled and filled.

"Rick tells me he was your tour guide this weekend," Lucille noted, rotating the dough with expert fingers.

"Yes—he showed me some off-the-beaten-path places. Lots of farms and ranches, an abandoned church, and the bridge. We had a picnic there."

"That's what he told me," Lucille confirmed with the curl of a smile.

"We talked about lots of things, about the town, and family. He told me more about his grandfather."

"You've become a member of an exclusive club. It's rare for Rick to open up to anyone." Lucille sprinkled a pinch of flour on top of the gingerbread disc.

"Yeah, I got that sense. I wanted to ask more about his childhood but didn't want to pry. Did he grow up in Morgan's Grove? He said he went to high school here."

Lucille hesitated, even pausing her task in mid-roll. "I'm not sure if I should say much."

"You don't have to talk about it. He's a private person. I respect that. Forget I asked."

Lucille shook her head and softened her tone. "It's not a secret, his upbringing. It's just that... Rick is a complex man. He's got—what do the psychologists call it?—'trust issues.'"

Lucille's hesitation told Jill there was definitely more to know about Rick. She did respect his privacy, but that didn't stop Jill from hoping Lucille would keep going, offer details, and fill in the gaps.

"I suppose trust issues are normal, under the circumstances," Lucille added, setting down the rolling pin. "When Rick was about seven, and I was tucking him in at night, he would reach out and clutch at my wrist without a single word, his tiny fingernails digging into my skin. He didn't want me to leave the room. He worried that I would leave forever, like his parents had."

Lucille suddenly looked wide-eyed at Jill, and it was obvious she'd said more than she'd intended.

"Does that mean that you and Frank"—Jill knew she shouldn't pry further but asked anyway—"did you raise Rick? The two of you?"

It made perfect sense. Lucille seemed more of a mother figure to Rick than a grandmother. And with Frank gone, they only had each other.

Lucille confirmed Jill's suspicions with one statement: "My son and his wife died when Rick was a little boy, so Frank and I took him in, as our own."

Jill was aghast. Lucille had lost her son, and Rick had lost *both* parents as a child. Jill understood grappling with that sort of pain at a young age. But two parents gone at once, she couldn't even begin to imagine. *Every possible security, ripped away. His entire world, changed forever.*

"Lucille, I'm so sorry. About your son."

"Thank you." Unlike her quivering lip when she talked about the fresh grief of Frank's passing, Lucille's expression seemed stoic when talking about her son. Jill imagined that, having been forced to talk about it throughout the years, Lucille had developed an especially thick skin. She had probably felt a tangible distance from the events, watching them from the outside looking in, as Jill sometimes did with her father. But it didn't make the feelings any less painful.

"I shouldn't have asked you about it." Jill looked down at her hands, feeling guilty for pressing too hard, for letting her curiosity get the best of her, and for compromising Rick's trust without him even being there.

"You didn't do anything wrong. I'm the one who let it slip. I don't mind talking about it—it's part of my history. But with Rick here... well, it's part of his history too. Maybe it wasn't my place to say anything."

"I'll keep this between us, I promise," Jill assured her.

"Thank you."

Lucille turned her full attention back to the rolling pin, and Jill suspected it signaled an abrupt end to the conversation about Rick.

She left Lucille to her silence, knowing they would pick up a new piece of conversation soon enough as the baking process wore on.

Jill let her mind process these new details as she sorted mindlessly through the cookie bags in front of her. So much about Rick was making more sense—his standoffishness, his skeptical nature, and his protectiveness over Lucille. If Rick had been raised by his grandfather, then that death had likely made an even stronger impact than a typical grandparent's passing would. Essentially, Rick was mourning his father.

Chapter Nine

At 5:31 a.m., Jill was sharply awakened by the corgis. Their "guard-dog" barks, relentless and urgent, floated upward to Jill's apartment through her slightly cracked window. Jill heaved herself out of bed and shuffled to the window, hoping for some answers. Mr. Anderson's light was on across the street, but the rest of the block was virtually dark.

Lucille's kitchen lights flicked on, and Jill watched the door open. Rick came out with his grandmother—he was carrying her toward the garage.

Without thinking, heart thumping, Jill clicked on a lamp and shoved her bare feet into the nearest pair of sneakers as the garage door's gears began to grind beneath her feet. She rushed out the door without a coat, navigating the steps in the shadows, praying she wouldn't fall.

She halted at the garage's opening and watched through the haze of dim overhead lighting as Rick placed Lucille gingerly into her car's passenger seat. Before he could shut the door, Jill approached them, arms crossed over her chest to stave off the cold.

"What happened?"

"Gran fell." Rick stepped aside so Jill could get a closer look. "I heard her call from downstairs and found her on the floor."

"Lucille!" Jill peeked her head inside the car. "Are you all right?"

"I was a klutz who tripped over my own corgis." Lucille chuckled through a wince. "Imagine that. I came downstairs for a glass of water. I was groggy and I didn't see Gracie—the dogs are always under my feet—and I darted to avoid stepping on her. Next thing I know,

I'm on the ground, calling Rick for help. Thank goodness he heard me."

"She can't put her weight on the ankle," Rick said, his voice deep and raspy from sleep. "So we're going to the ER in Austin to check for a break."

"I really don't think it's necessary." Lucille tsked, but the pain in her eyes told Jill that X-rays were the most logical next step. Lucille was the type to minimize her own pain simply to reassure others and put *them* at ease.

Jill placed a hand gently on Lucille's shoulder. "Is there anything you need me to help with?"

"The corgis—ironically." She placed a hand on top of Jill's. "We might be a while. So the dogs need to be let out and then fed. Their dry food is in the—"

"No worries. I've watched you feed them. I'll take good care of them, I promise."

Jill squeezed Lucille's shoulder gently then shut the door.

"Do *you* need anything?" Jill asked Rick, rubbing her arms, feeling helpless.

"Nope. Thanks. We'll know more after the tests."

She backed away from the car to let him walk around to the driver's side.

Just before he entered, Rick paused and made eye contact with Jill. "I'll call you with an update."

"Okay."

Jill felt the cold air sift all the way through the flannel to her goose-pimpled skin as she backed into the driveway to give them ample room. She watched Lucille wave through the windshield as the car headed toward the street.

Jill walked to the edge of the curb, waiting until the bright-red taillights disappeared around the end of the block. Before walking back to the house, she looked down to realize, in the dim light of a street lamp, what she had on.

"I'm wearing cupcakes." Cartoon cupcakes danced on her pink flannel pajamas, the ones Lindsey had given to her one birthday. *Why couldn't I have remembered to grab my coat, at least?*

"Is she okay?" someone asked from a distance.

Jill noticed Mr. Anderson's shadow directly across the street, standing in a robe at the curb, neck craned for an answer. So that they wouldn't have to yell, Jill crossed the empty street to join him, realizing they'd never been formally introduced. "Mr. Anderson?"

"That's me. And you must be Jill? Descendant of the Stout family, correct?"

Does everyone *know?* "Yes, sir."

"I promise I wasn't spying," he assured her. The nearby lamppost shone down on top of his balding head, and she couldn't see the full picture of his face through the shadows. "I get insomnia most nights, and I like to look out the window, seek out constellations, bide my time. I saw Lucille's light come on and her grandson carrying her."

"Lucille had a stumble," Jill verified, unsure of how much detail Lucille would want her to give in this gossipy town. But he was a concerned, longtime neighbor. Surely Lucille wouldn't mind him knowing. "It's her ankle. They're going to get it X-rayed. Only a precaution."

"Anything I can do?" His gravelly voice was filled with concern.

"Thank you, I don't believe so. Hopefully, we'll know more about her condition tomorrow. Er... later today."

They waved goodbye and parted, and Jill yawned as she walked across the street again. Thankfully, Rick had kept the kitchen door unlocked. The corgis greeted her, circling her feet, wondering where their master had gone. Jill stepped more carefully than usual, not wanting to suffer the same fate as Lucille by tripping over the dogs. Their incessant barks had settled into nervous whimpers.

"She's fine," Jill reassured them as they followed her. "She'll be back, I promise. I'll take care of you in the meantime."

Gracie stared deeply into Jill's eyes, unblinking.

Jill squatted down to the dog's eye level and scratched at her ears. "It's not your fault," she whispered. "It was an accident. She'll be good as new."

Gracie blinked as though she understood, then panted, producing an enormous corgi smile.

Jill moved toward the food bag but remembered the dogs would be off their schedule if they ate *that* early. They usually didn't eat for another three hours, at least.

Jill knew she couldn't possibly curl up in her bed and drift off to sleep until then. She was too antsy and concerned about Lucille. It amazed her that it only took a few days' time to feel genuine concern for a person who had been a complete stranger only the week before.

Jill switched on a nearby lamp and sat at the breakfast table, contemplating how to pass the time. She needed to mull over some things, like what the day might hold. Jill's mind whirred to life as she remembered that it was Tuesday. The original plan had been for her to deliver Monday's baking to all the shops while Lucille made another batch to fulfill the order for the next day's birthday party and the newest shop orders.

No matter if Lucille's ankle was broken or merely sprained, she surely wouldn't be physically able to stand at the island, mix the dough, roll it out, or lift the cookie sheets into the oven. It would be too taxing, and she would need rest. The cookie orders would hang entirely upon Jill's shoulders.

She couldn't help Lucille, couldn't be with her during the X-rays or calm her nerves before hearing the verdict from the doctor. But she *could* take care of the cookies.

HOW DOES LUCILLE MAKE this look so easy? Jill paused the rolling pin over the flattened gingerbread disk. Her arms ached, and she was slightly out of breath.

During the pause, Jill heard Lucille's landline ring for the umpteenth time—concerned neighbors and friends had called all throughout the morning to check on her. Two people had dropped by the house, offering casseroles and comforting words. Jill assumed word had gotten out through Mr. Anderson—and if he'd spoken to Bicycle Bob, that would surely have set the gossip lines on fire.

Jill had let the machine pick up all the calls so that Lucille could hear the messages when she came home. At last count, there were eight. Among them were Bicycle Bob's wife, Margaret, Darlene from The Pit, the pastor from Lucille's church, Mr. Anderson again, and two ladies from some committee. Jill wondered what it must be like to have a town full of concerned friends jumping to checking on her, should some emergency occur.

"Feel better soon," the person told the answering machine in the next room. "Call if you need anything."

Jill contemplated answering the most recent calls to give them the update Rick had phoned with an hour before from the ER—"Her ankle is badly sprained, not broken. She'll need crutches and a lot of bed rest this week." But it wasn't Jill's place to answer Lucille's landline and talk to Lucille's neighbors. Perhaps Rick could phone them back and explain later.

Returning to her rolling pin, Jill resumed her cookie-making mission, which had nearly been derailed before it had even begun. Earlier that morning, Jill realized something: she didn't know where to find the gingerbread recipe. Before she panicked, she searched all the obvious places—kitchen drawers, cabinets, countertops, and even the petite rolltop desk in the corner of the kitchen, where Lucille sat and paid her bills. Jill felt like a snoop, shuffling through someone else's papers and kitchen drawers, but it was all for a good cause. She *had* to find that recipe, or else there would be no cookies for tomorrow's orders. And that was not an option.

When her search produced nothing, Jill leaned against the island, defeated, panic rising as she recalled that she'd never seen Lucille use a recipe card. *This was my great-grandmother's recipe,* she'd told Jill on that first day. She had probably made the cookies hundreds of times and knew the recipe by heart.

Jill didn't want to bother or worry Lucille, even for a couple of minutes, if there was any chance of finding the recipe somewhere in the house. So rather than try to contact her, Jill had continued the search. And finally, on the tip-top shelf of the pantry, she discovered a wooden box with "RECIPES" engraved on the side. She held her breath as she sifted through the cards, dimmed and stained from use. Halfway through the "Cookies" section, she found "Molasses Crinkles," Rick's childhood nickname for the cookies.

After following the recipe precisely, chilling the dough for the required two hours, then rolling it out and praying it was the right thickness, Jill finally began to cut out cookies and place them onto baking sheets. Lifting them into the hot oven, all she had to do was hope that she'd gotten it right.

Waiting on the cookies, Jill could fully appreciate why Lucille enjoyed the baking process so much. It was exhausting, yes, but Jill found herself loving odd little things, such as the squishy texture of a brand-new bag of brown sugar, the satisfaction of a cookie cutter sinking deep into the dough, the glorious scents of allspice and cinnamon and cloves sifting into the batter and hitting her senses, and the wrinkles of the wax paper as she unwrapped the refrigerated dough like a delicate Christmas package. The entire process had a strangely soothing appeal.

Minutes later, she heard a car door slam. Rick and Lucille were home.

Jill had let the corgis into the backyard earlier, which was good timing—Lucille didn't need them jumping on her, causing another fall.

"We're he-ere," Lucille announced as Rick opened the kitchen door for her.

Lucille's left ankle, tightly wrapped in a blue bandage, entered the room first, elevated with the help of crutches. She wobbled on them, and Rick guided her, holding onto her shoulders for security.

"Oh, look at you." Jill gave her plenty of room to maneuver around. Thank goodness for a rather spacious kitchen. "Are you in pain?"

"Not anymore. The doctor gave me medicine to help. We were there for an eternity, though. Some big emergency was going on, and I guess my ankle wasn't important enough to prioritize."

"We should get you to bed," Rick insisted, still hovering behind to make sure his grandmother didn't fall. "I'll carry you upstairs."

"Oh, Rick. Surely you don't need to go to all that trouble."

"For now, I do. You don't want to fall again, do you?"

"Bite your tongue!"

"Plus, you need your own bed. Doctor's orders, to get some sleep. Maybe later, we'll set up a place downstairs, something temporary."

"That's a good idea," Jill agreed, shutting the kitchen door for them.

Lucille paused near the island, nearly tipping over, but Rick caught her in time. Seeing the remnants of cut-out cookie dough, she said, "You've made the gingerbread!"

"Well, I attempted to. I searched your kitchen for the recipe and found it in this box." She pointed to it on the counter. "I hope these will be up to your standards."

"Oh, they'll be fine, no doubt. They smell scrumptious enough. Thank you for taking over." After a beat, Lucille paused and gasped. "Yesterday's cookies we baked... those deliveries were supposed to be today, weren't they? And then tomorrow's party... the birthday! Oh, such horrid timing—"

Jill pushed out reassuring hands. "That's what these cookies are for. It's all covered. And the deliveries have already been made. When the dough was chilling earlier, it gave me time to make the rounds to the shops. No problem."

Lucille let out an audible sigh. "Jill, you're a lifesaver. I'm so sorry for all this."

"None of this is your fault. And it's totally under control."

"What would I do without you?" Lucille suppressed a yawn. "These pain meds are making me loopy. After some rest, I'll try to heal up fast, and then I can help you again."

"We won't worry about that now," Rick prompted, urging her forward toward the hallway. "Your cookies are in good hands with Jill."

"Are you hungry?" Jill asked. "People have been calling all morning—I think Mr. Anderson spread the word. He saw you leave earlier, and I told him you took a fall. Two people brought casseroles, and I put them into the fridge. I could cut you a slice?"

"No, dear, thank you. I'm too tired to eat. But it sounds perfect for after my nap. Heat yourself a slice. You deserve a good, hot meal after all this commotion I've caused."

The timer buzzed, and Jill scurried around the other side of the island to retrieve the oven mitt as Rick and Lucille slowly left the kitchen. Jill coaxed the cookie sheets out of the oven and placed them onto the island.

When the cookies were cool enough, Jill dabbed icing on one of them for a taste test, shoving away the most obvious fear: *What if these aren't good enough?*

She bit off the gingerbread man's head and began to chew. The texture was the same as Lucille's—a bit of a crunch at first, followed by a chewier center. The flavors and spices were a bit subtle but still tasty. Not quite as tasty as Lucille's, though. Something was off. Jill took a second bite and stared again at the card, scanning the ingredients. She had followed the recipe to the letter. *Why aren't these cookies as delicious as Lucille's?*

She didn't have time to create a new batch, chill it, and do the whole process all over again. They were still good, Jill reassured herself, just not Lucille-good.

Rick entered the kitchen as Jill began to roll out another disc of dough. He paused at the island and scratched at his stubbled jaw. His eyes were glazed over, with prominent circles underneath. He looked like a tired little boy.

"These turned out nice." He leaned in closer to examine the cooling cookies.

"Well, I tasted one. And they're... okay. But they're not exactly the same as Lucille's," Jill confessed. She had paused her rolling but kept her fingers perched on the handles.

"I thought you used her recipe."

"I did, but I dunno. Something's missing. Maybe your grandmother has the magic touch, and I don't."

"Doubtful. May I?" His hand was poised over a cookie.

"Sure. I made plenty. But they still need icing. That's my next step."

Rick took half the cookie into his mouth with one enormous bite. After chewing a few times, he shrugged. "I think they're fine."

But I don't want "fine." I want spectacular.

Rick finished the cookie in another big bite then poured a cold glass of milk while Jill continued her rolling. "Want some?" he offered.

"Maybe later."

"Thanks for all this." Rick returned the milk carton to the fridge. "At the ER, I could tell Gran was relieved you were here, looking after things. We'd both forgotten all about the cookies, though."

"I was eager to help. I feel like I'm partly responsible for getting her into the cookie venture. I didn't want to let her down."

"I know that feeling. She has this way about her, where you always want to do your best for her even though she never asks for it."

"Exactly."

After downing the milk, Rick set the glass in the sink then returned to the island. "I would offer to help, but I'm pretty useless in the kitchen."

"I've got it covered. You need some sleep, anyway," she told him.

"You do, too. This is your vacation, and all you're doing is working."

"But I enjoy it. Does that sound weird?"

"Nope, 'cause that's how Gran feels about baking too."

As Rick stifled a yawn, Jill poked gently at his ribs with her elbow. "Go! You're making *me* sleepy now."

"Sorry." He gave a sheepish grin before heading upstairs.

JILL PUSHED A SPATULA deep inside the casserole, a sort of pasta-tomato-cheese concoction that Mrs. Briars had made, and carefully lifted a piece onto a plate. She heard footsteps approaching and saw Rick in the doorframe, hair damp, cotton shirt clinging to his chest, fresh from a shower. He was a much more alert version of the Rick she'd seen a few hours earlier.

"You're still here." He approached her at the island. "That didn't sound right. I meant... You deserve a break from all this by now." His eyes scanned the kitchen and landed on the breakfast table, where the freshly iced cookies sat in perfect rows, waiting for the icing to harden enough to be placed into bags.

"I'll take a break soon, then I'll bag those up, and then the job is done. I wanted to warm up some casserole for Lucille. Do you think she's ready for it?"

Before Rick could answer, a sharp tinkling sound floated down from the second floor.

"I gave Gran a bell to summon me, so she wouldn't have to yell downstairs," he explained. "I'll see if she wants some food. It's probably time for more pain meds."

Jill decided to wait on the casserole—she would heat a slice for herself, and for Rick, too, once she served Lucille.

"Jill?" Rick called from the second floor. "Can you come up? Gran wants to see you."

All the ruckus energized the corgis, who had been keeping watch at the bottom of the staircase. They whined and barked their protests as Jill threaded through them, clicked the safety gate open and shut, then climbed the stairs to Lucille's bedroom at the end of the hallway.

"How are you feeling?" Jill asked, standing alongside Rick at the end of the bed.

"I'm rested. But sore." Lucille sat straight up in her bed, with thick pillows behind her and equally thick pillows elevating her wrapped ankle. Her eyes were brighter than they had been earlier. "Being forced to stay in bed gives a person time to think," she told them. "And I've made a decision."

Looking puzzled, Rick pushed his hands into his jeans pockets, waiting.

Lucille focused first on Jill. "I know everything you've done today—the baking, delivering, answering the doorbell, watching over the corgis. And I'm so grateful. Because of you, we're all caught up with tomorrow's birthday party and those new store deliveries that we've already committed to?"

"That's right."

"Well, when those orders are completed, I want to quit. If anything, this fall has shown me that I'm in over my head. I can't handle all these orders—and you'll soon be gone, back to Denver. Besides, this is your vacation. And I'm stealing it away from you."

"But like I told Rick downstairs—"

Lucille raised a hand in the air to stop her. "I've imposed on you for much too long. Here's my decision, and it's final. No more selling the cookies past tomorrow. Oh, I won't stop altogether—the baking, I mean. I'll always make them for holidays or for friends. But I won't be selling them anymore. It was only a dream. In reality, it's too much hard work. And you'll be free to enjoy the rest of your time in Morgan's Grove as *you* wish to spend it. It's settled." Lucille ended with a firm nod.

"Do I get a say in all this?" Jill asked meekly. She saw Rick's shoulders lift and lower in a silent chuckle.

"Of course. Speak your mind," Lucille replied, softening.

Jill cleared her throat and sorted through her tired brain for her rebuttal: "When I made deliveries today, there were five more shop managers who wanted to order cookies on the spot, before the fresh ones were even displayed. And Chaynie from the library caught me outside to place an order of cookies for a children's Christmas party over the weekend. Lucille, people love these cookies. They offer something comforting and lovingly made during a hectic holiday season. I've seen it with my own eyes. I didn't commit to these orders—I wanted to check with you first—but I *can* handle them, really. I've already planned it out, and I can do this myself, fulfill at least these final orders by the end of the week. Let me do that for you as my Christmas gift."

"That's very kind, Jill, but I saw how exhausted you were, earlier and even now. You try to hide it, but I know the toll it's taken. You did a two-person job today. And I can't ask you to do that again."

"I'm offering. You're not asking. And as far as my vacation goes—I've had a lovely time here. I've already seen the entire town, every square inch of it, twice over," Jill countered. "That was my main goal when I arrived, and it's been more than achieved."

Jill had no specific plans in the week ahead, beyond taking Jolene and Chaynie out for lunch to wrap up her research questions and thank them for their help. Plus, she could still work on the article upstairs at night, piecing together her research, outlining, composing drafts, polishing them. And she still had a couple more weeks to reach the article's firm deadline of Christmas day and to begin crafting her talk for the New Year's Writers Conference in Denver. It would all work out.

"I can help." The statement had come from Rick, and both Jill and Lucille craned their necks to stare at him with wide eyes. "What?!" he asked. "You don't think I can do it?"

"It's not that," Lucille said. "It's just... well, frankly, it's the last thing in the world I ever expected to come out of your mouth. I thought you disapproved of my cookie venture."

"'Disapprove' is a strong word. It surprised me that you wanted to do it in the first place. Plus, I didn't want you to overwork yourself. And Jill is making good points. Why not at least finish these last few orders, if she's willing? It wouldn't be a one-person job with me pitching in. We would share the duties."

"What about your own work?" Lucille countered. "All those conference calls and emails keeping you busy—"

"Jill and I can take turns on some of this stuff—deliveries or bagging up the cookies. I can take short breaks and keep working. Right?" He turned to Jill for confirmation.

"Right," she confirmed, still trying to process his shocking offer of help.

Rick moved his gaze to Lucille. "There you go. Not a single reason to say no. This can be my Christmas present to you too."

Lucille shifted her focus to Jill. "It's up to you. You're the one who only has a precious few days left in Morgan's Grove..."

"No doubts on my end," Jill assured her.

"Well, the pair of you are obviously as stubborn as I am." Lucille beamed up at them. "I'll agree, but I have one sticking point, and I won't budge. Let someone else do the deliveries. That will remove several hours off your plate and make me feel less guilty."

"Fine by me, but who do you suggest?" Jill asked.

"Mrs. Haversham has a niece, Becky, who's been looking for part-time holiday work. I think this would be perfect for her. And it wouldn't take long to train her. She's a bright girl."

"Agreed," Rick said.

"Then it's all set!" Lucille said, her grin widening.

Jill returned the grin, but it started to fade fast. Thinking ahead toward the week, she winced. "Actually, first, I have a small confession about the cookies. I followed your recipe to a T this morning, but... they're not the same. The cookies taste good, but they're not extra-special, the way yours are. What am I missing?"

Lucille pondered then said, "You found my recipe card downstairs. But I haven't used it in years. I've experimented with it the last several Christmases, adding a bit more of some ingredients and holding back on others, only a pinch or two here and there. I didn't add the changes to the card—I've been mixing ingredients from memory. But I can write out the changes for you tonight."

Relief. "That would be wonderful."

As Lucille attempted to readjust her position on the bed, she groaned softly.

"It's time for your next pain pill," Rick insisted.

"And I'll go make you a plate," Jill added. "You need some food too."

"Wait," Lucille said, making Rick and Jill pause in their tracks. "One more thing. A huge thank you. For everything. I don't know where I would've been today without you. Both of you."

Chapter Ten

"**Y**ou look soooo tired." Lindsey leaned her face closer to the tablet's screen. Jill had been in the middle of a deep sleep when Lindsey called for a video chat.

"Gee, thanks."

Two hours before, after making Lucille a plate of food and then one for Rick, who had some business emails to return, Jill had carried her own plate up to the apartment and scarfed down the delicious casserole in a few big bites. Afterward, she'd taken a lightning-quick shower, slipped on a pair of sweatpants and a T-shirt, then slogged over to the bed with still-damp hair and plonked down to disappear into the oblivion of sleep.

"I am," she confirmed to Lindsey. "Very tired. It's not always like this. But Lucille hurt her ankle early this morning, and I pitched in to help with the cookies all day. And now Rick is going to help out the rest of the time..."

"Rick, eh?"

"Yes. He's been a godsend, and that's *all* this is," she fibbed, knowing there *was* more. She was secretly thrilled to be handed an excuse to be rotating inside Rick's handsome-and-slightly-mysterious orbit for the next few days. She steered Lindsey toward a new sub-ject. "What are the local stations saying about the storm?"

"It's bad, Jill. They're calling it the 'storm of the decade.'"

"They always call it that. For dramatic effect."

"This time, they mean it. 'Historic,' they keep saying. I'm worried about you traveling back here. The system is supposed to arrive in Denver on Friday, and it might be headed south after that. You have plenty of time to drive here, safe and sound, if you leave tomorrow, ahead of the weather. But after that, all bets are off. You could get snowed in for a while."

Jill already knew her answer—she couldn't leave the next day, not after her lengthy plea to Lucille a few hours ago about wanting to finish out these orders. And Jill couldn't leave Rick to fend for himself with the cookies.

"I need to stay put. I'll risk getting snowed in. And maybe the storm won't be as bad as they say," Jill reasoned aloud. "Once it passes, the roads could be cleared fast enough for me to come home on schedule. Or close to it."

"Well, whatever you do, stay safe and keep me posted on your plans." Lindsey paused. "I think Charlie's calling me. Sorry to wrap this up, but we're going to a late dinner..."

"No problem. Go! Tell him I said hey."

"Will do. Love you, miss you!" Lindsey blew the screen a kiss.

"You too."

Jill clicked off and watched her friend's face disappear from the screen. While she was in phone-talking mode, she might as well try her mother again, to catch up and see where on earth she was at the moment. Her mother didn't know how to video chat, so they always spoke the old-fashioned way. A minute after dialing her number, it went straight to voicemail. Again.

"Mother, it's me, calling to see how you are and what you're up to. I'm on vacation right now in a Texas town called Morgan's Grove. It's a long story, but Dad's ancestors apparently founded this town! I'll fill you in later. Let's touch base, and I can tell you all about it. Take care!"

Clicking off, Jill didn't even know where exactly to picture her mother. She was only a week into her Bahama cruise, but where she would go after that and what her Christmas plans were was anyone's guess. Jill would have to be satisfied with not knowing.

A few minutes later, praying the iced cookies hadn't dried up too much during her unexpected nap, Jill tapped downstairs and headed to Lucille's kitchen. The original plan was to eat her casserole upstairs, wait about half an hour, then return and bag up the cookies.

When she opened the door to Lucille's kitchen, Jill saw an image she didn't expect. Rick sat at the breakfast table, squinting while he tied a ribbon around a packaged cookie. As Jill approached, she realized he'd bagged up nearly half the cookies already.

"What's all this?" she asked.

"I wanted to get a jump on these." Rick lifted his eyes, but then his face changed. He stared hard at Jill.

Horrified, she realized what he was staring at. Her hair.

After her shower, she'd fallen straight asleep. No makeup, no hair straightening. Heading to the kitchen, she'd assumed she would be entirely alone, that Rick and Lucille would be sound asleep from such a tiring day.

But instead, Rick was observing Jill in her most natural state. She wanted to slink away and make him un-see it, somehow.

Thankfully, she felt the scrunchie still on her wrist and deftly swept her hair up into a bun, tucking away loose strands. *Better, at least.* "You've never seen me like this. My hair."

"You look different."

The kiss of death. *Different.*

"I mean…" He tried to recover.

"I know. It's horrible. Frizzy and unmanageable." Perhaps mocking her own hair might diffuse the awkwardness in the room. "We can apparently blame Morgan herself. She had naturally curly hair, too."

"It's *not* horrible. It's just… not what I'm used to seeing. It's usually straight. I mean, how do you…" He pointed hesitantly toward her head, trying to work it all out.

Jill remembered that men knew next to nothing about women's hair care. At least he was trying to understand. It was endearing, actually, which relaxed her. He wasn't one of the bullies, poised to call her a name. He was Rick, seeing her in a completely different way than he was used to seeing her. Nothing more.

"Well, there's this product called a hair straightener," she explained. "It's like an iron for my hair. Every morning, I plug it in, take my hair in sections, and straighten out the curls." She demonstrated hypothetically by curving her arms up toward her neck and miming the all-too-familiar motion. "Voila! Straight hair. But tonight, I was too tired to mess with it. Sorry for scaring you." She managed a half-grin.

"You didn't scare me. I like it," Rick assured her, every trace of shock in his face having already disappeared.

"You do not." He *had* to be lying to make her feel better. The only other person on the planet who genuinely liked her curls had been her father. She still had a strong impression of herself at maybe five years old on his knee, where he'd wrapped a ringlet around his finger and called her "my little Shirley Temple."

Jill shifted to sit down at the table and peered across at Rick with wide, skeptical eyes.

"I really do. Like it." He was serious. "Curls look good on you."

"I can't believe you're saying this. It goes against everything I've believed. I've had this deep complex about my hair since I was a kid—I was bullied and teased about it relentlessly, called all sorts of names."

"Kids can be cruel. I think you should wear it that way more often. Natural, I mean. To spite the bullies. Don't let them win." Rick set aside the finished cookie and reached for a new one, back to business as usual. "Maybe I'm biased, though. I've always had a thing for curly hair."

Jill felt a blush rising to her cheeks, and she was glad Rick's focus was elsewhere so he wouldn't notice.

One of the corgis sighed deeply in the corner of the room, and after another beat of silence, Jill realized it was the end of the curly-hair conversation. Part of her still felt that old, strong urge to dash upstairs and straighten her hair. But the other part, the one that was starting to trust Rick and feel comfortable with him, won out. She *would* sit there, fighting her insecurities and helping him with the rest of the cookies, wearing her curly bun.

Scanning his accomplishments, Jill realized that Rick had not only carefully tied the ribbon in the same technique she always did, but that he'd attached the label in the right spot as well.

"These are very professional," she whispered.

"Shocked?"

"Let's say pleasantly surprised."

"I've seen you and Gran do this. You don't think I pay attention. But I do."

Jill didn't want to interrupt his process more than she already had, so she began attaching labels to the rest of the empty bags.

"Did you get some sleep?" Rick asked.

"Yes! I didn't know how exhausted I was. I'm a new person."

Rick nodded. "That's always how it is for me. I work myself to the bone some nights, for hours, and then wonder why my brain is in such a fog. But sleep after working hard is the best kind of sleep."

"I totally agree. Especially after I've finished a part of a novel where the creativity is flowing. It's like time disappears. I get exhausted after that, but it's a good exhausted."

"What's it like, writing a book? That's a broad question. I guess I mean—creating characters and worlds, diving into your own story. It must be the best form of escapism."

"It can be." Jill attached a label and smoothed it out with the tips of her fingers. "There are these rare times that writing is this smooth, easy process, when the Muse dictates everything and I'm there to catch it. When that happens, I can spend hours typing chapters, nonstop. I even forget to eat! It's like the world melts away, and it's just me and the page. It's the best kind of feeling." Jill paused and frowned, realizing what she was saying. "Not that I would know, lately. Like I said, it's rare. And I miss it…"

"Yeah, you mentioned you were between books?"

She looked across at him and decided to trust him—again. Jill was tired of holding it in. "Well, that was my subtle way of saying that I have a raging case of writer's block."

"Really?"

She shrugged and tried to look matter-of-fact. "It happens. But it hadn't happened to me until I ended my series. I thought it would come easy, the next book, the next idea. I assumed it would be there, waiting for me. But it never materialized. I mean, I've brainstormed a thousand ideas in the last several months. But all of them stink. I don't like any of them. And it makes me doubt myself."

"How do you know when an idea is good or bad?" Rick slipped another cookie into another bag.

"I feel it in my gut. Whether an idea will work or it won't." She peeled off another label. "It sounds completely unscientific—and it is—but that's the best way I can describe it. I get this… rush, this little high. And when I chase an idea down, when I keep exploring it, and it *keeps* giving me that rush… well, I know it's a good one."

Rick paused his work. "It's sort of that way with me, in business. A deal or a concept can look great on paper, with all the figures and budgets and research. But something in my gut will tell me, ultimately, whether I'm in or out."

"So you do understand." *I only wish my* agent *did*, Jill thought. She sighed quietly at the thought of him, eager, years before, to sign her first novel. But his interest in Jill had waned lately, as well as his inquisitive texts. In fact, he'd recently signed a new and promising author. She wondered if she would soon be replaced, cast aside.

"Well, you'll get there," Rick assured her. "With the new novel, I mean. You've written, what, five of them?"

"Four."

"So, it's not like you're a one-hit wonder. You've proven you're capable of writing four full novels. That's pretty incredible. Most people couldn't do what you do. I know I couldn't. It'll happen. Keep being patient."

Somehow, that unexpected brush of praise from an unexpected source gave Jill's self-esteem a much-needed lift. He was right—she was too hard on herself. She *had* written and published four novels, a worthy accomplishment at her age. And she *could* write a new one. She was capable of it. It was only a matter of time.

"Thanks for listening," Jill told him, feeling suddenly vulnerable, barely able to make eye contact. She realized she hadn't spoken that frankly with anyone else about her writing fears, not even Lindsey, Miranda, or Lucille. But Rick had made it easy.

"Anytime. Creativity is pretty fascinating to me. I don't feel like I have a creative bone in my body. I get that from my granddad, I guess."

"Oh, I beg to differ. Look at what you've done right here!" Jill's fingers grazed the bagged cookies between them. "This process takes loads of creativity."

"Well, I'm not sure about that." Rick grinned.

Jill silently counted the bags and realized there was one extra cookie left over.

"I'm curious…" She picked up the cookie and chomped on its head, letting the flavors settle on her taste buds. When she finished the bite, she admitted, "I was hoping the icing would cover my flaws."

"And?"

"See for yourself." She snapped the rest of the cookie in half and handed Rick the other piece.

He took a bite. "Mm. It's good."

"Still not as good as your Gran's, but they'll do."

"We'll get it right," Rick assured her, "together."

Chapter Eleven

Jill sat on Lucille's front porch with her coffee, marveling at the sudden warming of temperatures, a predicted high of seventy-two. She had slept soundly after yesterday's exhausting events then awakened early enough to make Lucille's dough again, following her updated recipe while Rick made a couple of important business calls. During the refrigeration wait, when Rick was still busy with his work, Jill took her coffee outside, enjoying the squeak of the porch swing as she rocked back and forth.

Her cell buzzed, jostling her back into the present moment as she saw Miranda's name across the screen.

"Hey," she said into the phone.

"You sound refreshed," Miranda noted.

"Do I?"

"I can see why. I finally got a chance to browse your photos. That small town is one cute place! Even makes my jaded New York self want to visit."

"It's even cuter in person."

"From your emails, it sounds like you're making good progress on the article."

Jill set down her coffee on the nearby table and recrossed her legs. "I am. And I'm even thinking of extending my stay here. Mostly because of the pending weather—"

"Storm of the decade?"

"Yep. I've been keeping tabs on it," Jill admitted. "Looks pretty bad."

"It's historic, apparently. Staying put is probably the best idea."

"I think so. Plus, I've sort of committed myself to this gingerbread-cookie venture..."

"Gingerbread?"

"Long story. I'll save it for another phone call. Suffice to say, staying in Morgan's Grove will be good for me—it'll help me to finalize some details and conduct more interviews. I have full confidence that I'll make your deadline."

What she *wasn't* telling Miranda was that she hadn't even started the first draft yet. She'd been rather distracted by the town, the people, and the cookies, and she'd told herself it was all in the name of research. She knew she could pull it off in time—all of the brainstorming and researching, the outlining and interviewing, would come to a head and collect itself in the form of an actual article with paragraphs and sentences. Eventually.

"I have confidence in you too. You've never let me down. I also have confidence that this article will be what we need right now."

"What do you mean?" Jill sensed an ominous tone in her friend's voice.

"Well"—Miranda lowered her voice to a hush through the phone—"our subscriptions have become concerningly low. For the last quarter. And a couple of advertisers have recently pulled out. The competition for online eyeballs is fierce right now. Bluntly, we're headed for trouble if the tide doesn't turn."

"I had no idea. Why didn't you tell me?"

"Embarrassment, I guess. It's not easy to admit possible failure. Even to a friend."

Jill understood well. She hadn't yet told Miranda the true depths of her own novel-writing struggles.

"On the bright side, we've needed stronger articles to draw interest and make us relevant again. And yours, with the genealogy topic, will do that. Hopefully. I'm not sure you're aware, but anytime your name is signed to a piece, our subscriptions for that month jump significantly. And you're apparently getting buzz for the recent veteran's dog piece—I've heard rumors of award nominations. Selfishly speaking, even writing accolades for you can create more buzz for us at the magazine."

Jill brushed off the extra load of unintentional pressure Miranda had just heaped on top of her already-tired shoulders, which carried the weight of the upcoming storm, the additional cookie orders, and her growing attachment to Morgan's Grove. "I'll do everything I can to help."

"Thanks, my friend. It means more than you know."

After they hung up, Jill tapped her phone to find the most recent weather forecast, which was even more bleak and dire than the day before. If the predictions were right, the storm would be wreaking havoc for several days, adding at least another whole week to Jill's visit. And she had absolutely no problem with that. It was what she'd been secretly hoping for: *more time.*

HEARING SOFT SNORES, Jill tiptoed into the living room to see Lucille fast asleep on the pull-out sofa bed. Earlier that afternoon, only a day after her fall, Lucille had insisted on being moved downstairs to recuperate in the living room, so that she could be "in the thick of things."

"It's too quiet to rest up here," she had told Rick.

"*Too* quiet? That doesn't make much sense, Gran."

"Well, *I* know what I mean. And Jill does too, don't you?" she'd asked as Jill handed her a glass of water.

"I do, actually."

And the argument was settled. Jill found sheets in a guest closet and made up the sofa bed while Rick moved some of Lucille's things downstairs.

As Lucille's snoring continued, Jill clicked the remote to quiet the Christmas movie blaring from the TV, hoping she wouldn't wake the corgis slumbering nearby. The colorful tree lights blinked at her from the end of the room, and the fire Rick had made earlier for his grandmother had simmered into a lovely glow. Until she and Lindsey had become roommates, it was a scene Jill was mostly unfamiliar with, something she only saw in movies—twinkly lights, cozy firesides, cinnamon-scented candles, manger scenes.

When Jill was younger, she and her mother were usually still in boxes from their latest move at Christmas. And if her mother could *find* it inside the boxes, Jill was given a petite ceramic Santa Claus to place on her nightstand. That was all. Her mother didn't bother to decorate the rest of the apartment or even to find a tree. She didn't have time for Christmas, so as an adult, that became Jill's habit too.

She returned to the kitchen, where she and Rick had spent the last three hours together, rolling the dough, cutting out the cookies, lifting trays in and out of the oven, and transferring the warm cookies to cool on paper towels on the island. They worked together remarkably well, and there was an ease to their movements. Not once had they disagreed about what to do next or how to do it.

While they worked, there were periods of companionable silence and periods of light chitchat about the weather or the town or the upcoming festival. Anyone peeking in on the domestic baking scene for the first time might assume that Rick and Jill had been making cookies together for years.

As Jill entered the kitchen after checking on Lucille, Rick sat at the kitchen table, preparing to make the icing. Earlier, Jill had tasted a cookie fresh from the oven and was greatly relieved that it tasted every bit as mouthwatering as Lucille's own cookie creations. She was glad she'd risked her pride and told Lucille about her recipe woes.

Before joining him at the table, Jill tapped on Lucille's iPod, which played a cheery "Jingle Bells," and clicked onto another playlist of classical music.

"Had enough holiday music?" Rick asked.

"Yeah, I'm not a huge fan."

"How come?"

He reached for the new bag of powdered sugar and began kneading it the way Jill had shown him, pushing the sugar down toward the middle before opening it.

"I'm just not a big fan of Christmas in general. I usually hold my breath until the season passes."

Rick stopped kneading and looked across the table. "That bad?"

"My father died the week after Christmas." Jill picked up a wooden mixing spoon and twirled it slowly in her hands. "It was a roofing accident. I was only ten. So I guess I sort of associate his death with the holidays. That final Christmas with him was the last happy one I remember." She stepped back into memory and visualized the scene. "He handed me a gold-wrapped present from under the tree. It was a snow globe with a plastic snowman in the center of it. We lived in Arizona, and he knew how much I wanted a white Christmas. He took the globe from my hand and flipped it over with his wrist, and the globe started to snow. It was magical." She set down the spoon and noticed that Rick had been listening intently. "Anyway, the globe eventually disappeared. It got lost in one of our moves."

Jill wondered, in the seconds of silence that followed, whether Rick might finally exchange a piece of his own story with her, maybe talking about his parents and how they'd died when he was young too. But she couldn't give him the chance. She felt the growing swell of emotion underneath the surface and knew it would be more than she could handle. She hadn't planned on baring her soul over gingerbread and powdered sugar.

She tapped the table with the spoon. "I guess we'd better finish up the icing before the cookies dry out." Her eyes landed on the bag of sugar Rick still held, hoping he would take the hint that she was desperate to change the subject.

Rick took the scissors then snipped off the top of the bag. He started to tip it toward the ceramic bowl faster than Jill would have done, herself.

"Oh, be careful," Jill warned, "because the sugar can come out—"

But it was too late. Rick had dumped the entire contents of the bag into the bowl, and in the process, had speckled his black sweater, the table, and the floor with an enormous burst of powdered sugar. The finest particles still lingered in the air between them as white dust.

"—too fast," Jill finished in a whisper then held her breath.

Rick froze, his hands still clutching the empty bag.

This is it, Jill thought, *the moment Rick loses his patience, regrets that he ever agreed to help with the cookies. The moment where he goes back to being withdrawn and hard to read, where he wishes I had never come into their lives.*

But to her great surprise, Rick suddenly cracked a smile, which grew wider and wider until a deep laugh echoed inside the room. "I am *wearing* this sugar!"

Jill joined him in laughter. "And so is the floor!"

Rick's chuckles subsided, but the hint of a smile remained as he threw down the empty bag. "I don't even know where to start." He did the natural thing and wiped the sugar off his sweater with his palm. But it didn't dust off, as he'd likely expected. The stubborn granules only embedded themselves deeper into the fabric, creating long, thick smudges.

"No, wait! Don't wipe it," Jill chided, still giggling. "You're making it worse. There's a trick for this."

"So I'm not the only idiot this has ever happened to?"

"You're not an idiot. It's happened to me. Well, not exactly to *this* degree," she quipped. Jill walked to the pantry and retrieved the miniature vacuum that Lucille charged continuously on the wall.

"How will that help?" Rick asked as she approached. "Are you going to vacuum me?"

"Actually, yes! Hold still."

He raised his hands to give her room, and Jill turned on the compact machine, which whirred to life, then began at Rick's neckline. She gently moved the vacuum a few inches down his sweater and watched the sugared powder get sucked away, leaving almost no trace behind.

Rick arched his neck downward to see her progress. "It's actually working!"

"Your grandmother taught me this," she said above the noise.

Jill realized that the vacuuming activity had brought their faces quite close together and that her hands were incredibly close to his chest. It had become suddenly awkward.

She clicked off the vacuum. "Anyway, you get the idea. Here, you'd better do the rest."

"Is everything all right in there?" Lucille called from the living room.

Jill handed Rick the vacuum then poked her head through the doorway. "Just a baking mishap. Totally under control."

Lucille shut her eyes again as Jill went in search of the broom. Rick switched on the vacuum to finish up his shirt and pants as both corgis tapped their way into the kitchen to see what all the commotion was about. George began sniffing and licking the sugar on the floor.

"No, no. That's not good for you," Jill warned, gently shooing both dogs away with the broom.

They seemed to understand and kept their distance as she finished the job. When it was obvious they wouldn't be getting any special treats, the corgis waddled back into the living room while Rick clicked off the vacuum and examined his efforts. "I'm not sure the inventor of this vacuum ever imagined it would be used for *this*."

Jill put away the broom, washed her hands, then sat across from Rick again. "I got you a new bowl."

He took it and used the tablespoon to gently portion out the mountain of powder he'd dumped into the other bowl. Jill prepped the paper towels, readying them for the iced cookies.

"Gran says you might stay longer in Morgan's Grove."

Earlier, while bringing Lucille a portion of homemade spaghetti from the pastor's daughter, Jill had told Lucille about staying to wait out the storm. "Oh, how wonderful!" Lucille had squealed, which had also answered Jill's next question: *will Lucille mind if I stay in the apartment a few days longer, or does she need it freed up for a potential boarder?*

"Yeah, the storm heading for Denver looks pretty foreboding. Better safe than sorry."

"That's my motto." Rick stirred the water into the powdery mixture, watched it cake up, then added a bit more. *Eyeball it*, Jill had coached him earlier. "Maybe the storm will keep you here for the Christmas festival."

"Maybe."

She said it, even knowing it wasn't likely. The festival started the weekend *after* next, too close to Christmas. Jill didn't see herself staying in Texas that long—she had a life in Denver to return to. But this year, of all years, Jill was actually open to a little brightness in her holiday, a bit of magic in her life. And if any place could produce that for her, it was Morgan's Grove.

JILL NOTICED THE POP of red color in Lucille's lap as she set down the mug of cocoa on a nearby coaster. Lucille had been working on a poinsettia needlepoint piece for the past hour and had just begun the red threads before Jill went to the kitchen.

"How beautiful." Jill sat on the couch beside her, careful not to spill her own drink. She blew on its surface before tasting it.

Lucille paused and tilted the half-finished mesh canvas toward Jill. "I discovered this among the decorations. I had worked on it last year, before Christmas, but then Frank became ill…" She sighed deeply then looked Jill straight in the eyes. "He's been gone for twelve whole months, but sometimes it's as fresh as yesterday, the pain. Some days, I think I'm all right. But other days, his absence hits me in the gut again, as strong as the day it happened. Why is that?"

Jill shook her head and stared down at her cocoa. "Grief is strange. Even decades later, for me, there's this hollow part deep inside, a hole that can't be filled up by anything but my dad."

"That's a very accurate description." Lucille carried on with her poinsettia. "I used to love needlepointing. It was soothing, the rhythm of the needle, the coming together of colors to fill an empty space. I'm glad I've picked it up again. It's giving me something to do with my hands, with my time. I've become restless with this ankle of mine."

Jill nodded toward it, propped up on the pillow. "How is it feeling today?"

"Much better. Still sore sometimes, but the pain is completely gone."

"And the swelling too."

"Yes. Those ice packs did the trick. I only wish I could function fully again. There's so much to do for the holidays, errands and housework and shopping. And of course, cookie baking. But I know you and Rick have that under control. Did Becky do well with the deliveries today?"

"Yes! She's perfect for the job. She knows all the townspeople, and she's friendly and bright. I admit, her handling the deliveries really helped out."

Jill's phone buzzed, producing a text from Rick: *I forgot. Which brand?* He had attached photos of two brown sugar bags.

Jill snickered, swiveling the screen so Lucille could see. "He's shopping for cookie ingredients tonight. He insisted." Jill tapped out her response to Rick.

"It's impossible to picture *my* grandson shopping for brown sugar."

"He's been surprisingly helpful. With everything."

Lucille paused her needlework again. "I've noticed you two getting along quite well. I don't make it a habit to eavesdrop, but I'm only a room away, so I sometimes hear the cordial banter between you."

"We work well together."

Jill's phone beeped with another photo from Rick, a bag of Skittles perched in the shopping cart along with a message: *You can save the greens and purples for me.*

Jill grinned.

"What's that?" Lucille squinted toward the screen.

"Oh, nothing. I had mentioned yesterday that I liked this certain kind of candy. I guess he found it."

I only like the yellows, reds, and oranges, she had told him then. He must've been paying attention.

JILL OPENED THE APARTMENT door to an unusually blustery Friday morning—clouds raced overhead, and tree trunks swayed, losing thin branches to the ground while crisp dead leaves danced along the driveway. Texas would be getting some of that Western cold front, too, it seemed. But surely it would come in the form of winds and thunderstorms, not snow and ice.

She hadn't planned on a grocery run, but as Jill had assessed the ingredients last night, she realized Rick had forgotten one vital component: ground cloves, essential to the spice mixture in the gingerbread recipe. Jill had intended to pop in and out of the store for that one item before Rick and Lucille returned from her doctor's appointment so that Rick would never realize he'd forgotten the ingredient. But on her way downstairs, she watched Lucille's car pulling into the driveway earlier than expected, with Rick at the wheel.

Jill waited until they came to a stop in the garage to approach the car then opened Lucille's door. "No more crutches?"

"Hallelujah, no! But—I have this cumbersome boot to wear now." Lucille tilted her ankle so Jill could see the thick black boot covering her leg from toe to calf. "The doctor said I need to try walking on it."

"He also said that her ankle was improving better than expected." Rick joined Jill on the passenger side. He wore a dark-green, long-sleeved sweater with jeans and had a hint of a shadow-beard, her favorite look on him.

"Well, that's great news," Jill said.

"Yes, and if I can manage this boot thing on my own today, it means I can make my bridge game tonight."

"Bridge?" Jill hadn't heard Lucille mention it until now. "I didn't know you played."

"Oh, I used to all the time. The girls and I had a Friday night bridge game every week for twenty years. We took turns in each other's homes while our menfolk ate TV dinners or had their own poker game together. But ever since I lost Frank... well, I didn't feel much like playing, and the girls stopped trying to twist my arm to join them. But I've missed it. So when the doctor told me I could carefully resume normal activities, I used Rick's phone to call Madge on the way home to ask if they'd have room for one more tonight."

"'Carefully' is the key word," Rick said. "Remember, the doctor said not to overdo it. In fact, I should drive you there—"

"No, no. You've done enough," Lucille assured him. "Madge has already agreed to pick me up. Well, we'd better head for the house. It could take me all day to get there."

Jill stepped forward toward the driveway so Rick could help Lucille out of the car. There was surprisingly ample room for the three of them in the space between her car and Rick's massive truck. Lucille struggled with the boot, stopped to catch her breath, then tried moving forward again.

"What are you two up to today?" Lucille wondered. "More baking?"

"Our final order. It's for the library's Christmas party tomorrow," Jill confirmed, facing Lucille and inching backward. "I have a quick errand first, then I'll get started on the dough. And then—" Her phone jangled in her pocket. "Sorry."

"It's fine. Go ahead," Lucille said. "I need a break, anyway."

Rick helped his grandmother pause and lean against the car to catch her breath.

"It's from The Pit," Jill told them, looking at the screen. She clicked the speaker option to let them both hear the call. "Hey, Tessa."

"Jill! We're having a gingerbread-cookie crisis!" Her voice was light but frantic.

Jill's eyes widened toward Rick. "Crisis?"

"Lucille's cookies are outselling my Mississippi Mud!"

That time, Lucille's eyes grew wider.

"People keep asking for the cookies, and I'm all out!" Tessa explained. "We didn't place a recent order for more, did we? My sister was supposed to call it in, but I guess she conveniently forgot."

"No, I don't have any orders for The Pit. We're about to start a batch for a different order, but it's our last one. We're not taking any more orders after that."

"Gosh, that is not what I needed to hear." Her accent seemed to thicken as her panic deepened. "Listen. Is there *any way* on this planet that I can convince you to add us to that final order? Please? Pretty please with barbecue sauce on top?"

Jill glanced toward Rick while she told Tessa, "Actually, I don't mind making it a double batch today." Rick nodded, so Jill continued. "I'll deliver the cookies to you in the morning."

"Jill, you're a doll! An angel. A lifesaver. A total saint—"

"Okay, okay." Jill snickered. "We're happy to help. It's no trouble."

Clicking off, Jill shifted her gaze from Rick to Lucille, who asked, "Has that happened a lot?"

"Has what happened?" Jill replied.

"Frantic merchants still trying to order my cookies?"

"Actually, yes." Jill hadn't even told Rick about the newest inquiries—she'd assumed it was a moot point. But she did the math in her head. "Since I've cut off the deliveries, I've had four—no, five—different calls from shop owners begging me to reconsider and take orders again."

"You're kidding." Lucille pondered the new information but then shook her head. "Well, it's all very flattering, but look at me." She waved down toward the boot. "I'm still incapacitated. I don't think 'normal activities' includes standing in a kitchen for hours a day, making gingerbread."

"Was I wrong to take Tessa's order?" Jill wondered.

"No, it was sweet of you. But let's keep that door closed on future orders. I think it's all for the best. I'm not as young and capable as I used to be, and that's the truth of the matter..." Her voice trailed off as she reached for Rick's arm again, squeezed it tightly, then attempted another step in the boot.

They followed Jill slowly outside, where the wind howled.

"This Texas weather," Lucille clucked. "It's been mild the past week. But now it's back to its temperamental old self."

"It's hard to know how to dress," Jill admitted. "One day a thick jacket, the next a silk blouse." She touched the fabric of her shirt. The wind was strong, but it was still too warm for a jacket.

Jill parted ways with Lucille and Rick then moved toward her own car. She was already slightly behind schedule—she'd spent part of the morning tapping out the first few paragraphs of a rough draft for the article but wasn't particularly happy with it. The recent pressure Miranda had placed on her seemed to be blocking Jill's creative juices again. But once the final cookie orders were complete, she would have more time to write—that was the plan, at least.

Chapter Twelve

Jill knew it was coming.

When she and Rick had started packaging the cookies, she had recognized that familiar pinch behind her eyes, the lurking threat of pain. It was probably a culmination of the busy week—Lucille's fall, the cookies, the article, the pending storm. Jill had ignored the pain, wishing it away. There was too much left to do.

But as she stared at the cookie in her hand, she could only see the outer fringes of it. The center of her vision was a big white spot of nothing. "Uh-oh."

"What's the matter?" Rick wondered. "Do I need to re-ice it? I got lazy on the last few, I admit."

"It's not that." Jill blinked hard and opened her eyes with the same result. "I think I'm having a migraine. Stupid me, I didn't eat lunch today. I think that's what this is." She tried to focus on Rick but could only see the outline of his hair, not his face. If it had been the first time she'd experienced the optical symptoms of a migraine, the aura, she would've panicked. But she'd had occasional migraines since her youth and knew what to expect. The next stage was usually a searing headache with accompanying nausea.

Rick pushed his chair back and came to her side. "What can I do?"

"I'll be okay." She shut her eyes, preferring the blackness. She could already feel the stab of pain between her eyes, the throbbing at her temples. "I need to get some rest in a dark room. It's the only thing that works."

"Here. Let me get you some aspirin, at least. Hang tight."

As a distraction, Jill paid attention to her own breathing patterns, berating herself for not stopping earlier to take some medicine and eat some food. The migraine could've been prevented. She wished she could sink into a bed right that second, but she had a hundred steps, including a whole flight of stairs outside, before that could happen.

She felt Rick at her side again, his elbow brushing against her arm. "Take these. Maybe they'll help." She opened her eyes enough to see part of his fist. He tipped the medicine into her open palm, and she swallowed them in one gulp, chasing them down with the water he'd brought.

"Thank you," she whispered, trying not to alarm him. The pain in her head was getting stronger.

"You're in no condition to make it upstairs," Rick said. "Gran is at her bridge game and won't be home for hours. Why don't you crawl into her bed in the living room? She won't mind."

A bed a few steps away sounded like heaven, so Jill closed her eyes again and pushed up from the table. She could feel Rick's strong arms supporting her as she leaned into his body while he walked her step-by-step into the living room. Jill could hear the tapping of concerned corgis' feet padding along behind them.

Rick helped Jill into the bed, and after she sank into the mattress, he draped the quilt over her shoulders, tucking it in at the edges. "What else can I do?" he asked. She heard him click off the nearby lamp.

"Can you find me a bag of some sort, maybe a garbage bag? In case I have to—sorry, it's gross, but migraines make me nauseated. And I might need to—"

"Not gross. Just real life. I'll be back."

Jill must have sunk into a deep sleep before he had a chance to return, because the last thing she recalled was Rick quietly telling the dogs to move along as he shuffled toward the kitchen in search of the bag. Next thing she knew, the lovely, cool darkness of the room had engulfed all her senses.

"JILL?"

Somewhere in the fog of sleep, she could hear a man calling her name.

"Jill? It's Rick. You need to try to get up."

She opened one eye to see him standing over her, one hand on her shoulder. He had clicked on the lamp. She opened the other eye and remembered the migraine, the blinding white spot in the center of her vision, the slight nausea. But every trace of the migraine was gone, even the pain. In the lamplight's glow, she could clearly see all of Rick's handsome, concerned face staring down at her.

"I hate to wake you up, but we need to take shelter. There are bad storms heading our way."

"Shelter?" Jill rolled toward him with a small groan. She heard the gusts of wind, the rattle of windows, and the crack of thunder, and bolted up in the bed—she was in Lucille's bed in the living room, she remembered—and gazed up at Rick in confusion.

"We need to move to safety," he confirmed. "We're under a tornado alert."

"In December?!"

"They're rare this time of year, but sometimes we get powerful cold fronts forcing their way in. And when the front hits the heat, it can cause this kind of weather."

The storm of the decade. So it *had* made its way to Texas, even earlier than expected. She hadn't had a single moment that day to check on the storm's path, except to see a text from Lindsey early this morning: *Power out, but we're okay. At Mom's, hunkered down.*

Jill threw back the covers, grabbed a couple of pillows, and accepted Rick's outstretched hand.

"How's your migraine?" he asked, helping her to stand.

"Totally gone."

The lamp flickered beside Jill, and then, poof, the light was out. *All* the lights in the house were out.

"I was expecting that," Rick muttered.

Jill's eyes attempted to refocus through the pitch dark in front of her. She squeezed Rick's hand tighter when she heard another crack of thunder. But Rick had come prepared. He clicked an object in his other hand, and a beam of light pierced the darkness.

"Where are we going?" she asked as he led her toward the hallway.

"The only place we can be really safe. It's the room we always go to."

Her senses snapped awake as she thought of Lucille. "Your grandmother. Is she still at her bridge game?"

"She's safe. I called her a minute ago. They're all taking cover at Madge's house."

Above the winds, Jill heard a wailing siren, warning residents of the danger. It suddenly became real.

Rick's flashlight beam landed on an oddly shaped door beneath the staircase. He pushed the door wide open and let Jill crouch inside first. She heard the whimpers of George and Gracie—Rick had already placed them into their kennel and draped a towel over it inside the cramped space. *How did I sleep through all this activity?*

When Rick closed the door behind them, he also shut out the howling winds, giving Jill a moment of false peace. She situated herself on the floor beside the kennel and made room for Rick, who lowered himself directly opposite her against the wall, his knees bent beside her. Jill wondered how uncomfortable he was, with those long legs in such a tight space. He set the flashlight down between them so that the ray shone straight up to the ceiling, creating enough illumination for them to see most of the space and each other.

Jill poked her finger inside one of the kennel's air holes and received a whimper and a nervous lick from one of the corgis. "It'll be okay," she told them, hoping it was true.

She propped a pillow against the wall behind her and handed the other to Rick so he could do the same. As Jill adjusted her position, she heard another peal of thunder. The storm was getting closer.

Rick produced his cell phone and brought it to life, the screen lighting up his face with an eerie glow. "We're still under a warning. The tornado has been spotted south of us, a couple of miles away. We're right in its path."

That news filled Jill with dread. Images of an Oklahoma summer when she was eleven years old flitted into her mind. Her mother hadn't come home from work yet, and the babysitter was asleep on the couch. Jill had hidden underneath a table while the worst of the storm passed and the city sirens wailed.

"So you've done this before? Used the closet as shelter?" Maybe if Jill got Rick talking, he could distract her from the storm. Awaiting his answer, she pushed her shirt's long sleeves over her fingertips until they disappeared.

"Yeah, it was Gran's idea. She keeps the closet empty for just this reason. A tornado ripped through Morgan's Grove about forty years ago, destroying several homes and part of the courthouse, so I guess she's hypersensitive to them. We've probably crouched in here a dozen times over my childhood, me and Gran. And Pops."

Jill jumped as the thunder inched closer with each crack.

"Did I tell you that they raised me? Pops and Gran." It came out of nowhere. Rick's gaze was steady on the floor.

Jill couldn't believe he was bringing up his past in a cramped storm closet in the middle of a tornado. But the volatile conditions somehow made it an appropriate topic. "No, you didn't tell me." She would keep her promise to Lucille and let Rick tell his own story.

He readjusted his pillow then peered through the flashlight's glow at Jill. "I was seven years old. My parents died in a car crash on their way to see a movie in Austin. Slick roads, bad weather, and my dad lost control. I was staying with Gran and Pops that night, and I didn't know about the crash until they told me the next morning."

Rick's gaze had moved toward the wall behind Jill, his voice unflinching, even a bit robotic, as though he were reading out a newspaper article. Jill recognized it as a defense mechanism.

He made eye contact again in the shadows. "After the funerals, my grandparents started the adoption process. I have these watery images of them in my mind, my parents. My mother's perfume, my dad's briefcase, their laughing together. But for the most part, I don't remember them. They're like characters in a book—distant, far away, not part of my everyday life. I'm sure you know how that feels with your dad."

"Yeah, I remember some vivid details, but they seem to fade more each year. I'm not sure how to hang onto them. Or whether I can."

She understood what she'd read in Rick's eyes from the first day they met. It was subtle, but she had sensed it early on: *Play it safe, keep your distance, don't get too attached too soon.* That was what happened with the early loss of a parent. One learned to hold on loosely to things... and to people.

A shard of white light flashed underneath the door, catching Jill's attention. She braced herself, expecting thunder to follow. When it came, it shook the house. The corgis whined, and Jill gripped the insides of her sweater sleeves tighter.

She wondered if Rick might be grateful for the interruption after spilling his story unexpectedly. He returned to his phone but frowned. "Reception's gone. The page won't load." He gave up and folded his arms across his chest.

"I hope Lucille is okay," Jill said.

"Madge's husband has a safe space in the house, so Gran is just as safe there as she would be here, I guess. But she was worried about the corgis."

"Of course." Jill grinned.

"And you."

Jill heard a clinking on the roof, pounding faster and faster.

"Is that...?"

"Hail," Rick confirmed.

It was a sure sign that the tornado was even closer. She inhaled a deep, lingering breath then pushed it out, resisting that little-girl urge to be terrified. But the images swirling in her head were of every tornado she'd seen on the news or in movies—raging, churning, menacing funnels that destroyed everything in their wake, chewed up houses and cars and people then spit them out. She gathered her knees close to her chest and pressed her arms around them, not knowing what else to do. She hated being at the tornado's mercy.

She felt a warm hand through her sweater's fabric and realized Rick was clasping her wrist, attempting to comfort her. She wriggled her hand out from the sleeve to thread her fingers through his.

"We'll be okay," Rick whispered. And at least for that split second, she believed him.

The next time the lightning hit, a terrifying crash came, followed by a thud that shook the house again. The corgis barked, and Jill sucked in a sharp breath.

"What was that!?" she said.

"Could be a tree falling."

"What should we do?"

"Sit tight, wait it out. This is probably the worst of it, right here."

Jill squeezed Rick's hand harder. The house creaked and groaned under the pressure of the howling winds as hail bashed the roof even more strongly. The dogs made frantic circles in their crate.

Jill breathed in small pants, not knowing where to channel all her anxiety, so she prayed in her mind—panicked fragments of pleas for safety.

In all, the terror lasted only three minutes, if that. But it felt like three hours. And just when Jill was convinced her life would be claimed there, in that impossibly small room with Rick and the corgis, things seemed to calm down. She noticed that the hail had thinned out then stopped completely. Soon, the lightning became less frequent.

And finally, when the thunder faded, rumbling farther and farther in the distance, Jill began to breathe again. She and Rick were still holding hands, and she couldn't seem to let go. "Do you think it's over?" Her voice was small and quiet.

"Almost." Rick paused to listen then turned to Jill. "How are you? How's your head?"

"I'm okay. My heart's beating so fast. But my head's fine. Once a migraine leaves, it's usually gone for good."

A minute later, when she was convinced the worst of it was past and that they weren't going to die, she found her full voice again. "We should check on Lucille."

Rick agreed, releasing his hand from hers, and drew out his phone to dial.

"Tom. It's Rick. How are things there?" He mm-hmm-ed a couple of times then said, "We're all fine here. Please let Gran know." He clicked off and told Jill, "He said they got a lot of wind and rain, but no damage as far as he could tell."

"That's a relief."

Another rumble of strong thunder in the distance told them the storm wasn't *quite* finished flexing its muscles yet.

"We'd better stay put," Rick said. "The winds are still pretty fierce."

Jill knew that just because a tornado had passed, it didn't mean there wasn't potential for more damage behind it. And sometimes, a tornado spawned other tornadoes. But she did feel safer at the moment. Her anxiety had ratcheted down significantly.

Rick stretched his legs to the side and moved his foot in a circle. Suddenly, the closet light flashed on as the electricity whirred back to life. The corgis got excited and barked.

"That's a good sign." Rick checked his phone again and got a signal. After scrolling through the weather radar, he confirmed: "Looks like the worst has passed. I'll survey the damage." He pushed off the floor then offered Jill his hand, and she took it, rising to her feet.

Their bodies were almost touching in the cramped space. On a whim, Jill leaned up toward Rick's shoulders to draw him close in a tight hug. "You kept us safe," she whispered. "Thank you."

She felt his hands cradle her waist in return.

When she backed away, Rick cleared his throat then reached for the doorknob.

"I'll get the corgis," Jill told him.

The minute she opened the crate door, the dogs burst out, tongues flapping, ecstatic to be free.

"Are you hungry?" she asked them, and their synchronized barks said they were.

In the kitchen, Jill gave them treats then joined Rick on the backyard's covered porch, leaving the dogs inside. The drastic drop in temperature made Jill shiver. The rain still pelted down, and lightning flashed in the distance, the remnants of a powerful storm issuing its faint goodbyes.

The porch light didn't illuminate very much of the backyard—it was no match for the dark sky above. But Jill could see the golf-ball-sized hail dotting the yard as well as the main damage done: the great oak tree was splintered down the middle in the shape of a V, and part of its corpse lay a few feet away.

"It's a goner," Rick said as Jill came to stand beside him, her hair blowing in the wind. "Nothing we can do about it tonight. I'll have my friend examine it in the morning, figure out how to clear the tree. The roof needs inspecting, too, with all that hail."

"Lucille will be heartbroken about the tree. But at least the house seems untouched. We were lucky."

Rick turned to Jill. "Want some breakfast?"

"At this hour?"

"You said you hadn't eaten all day. I make a mean omelet. We could call this a post-tornado, thank-God-we-didn't-get-killed celebration."

"Count me in."

Chapter Thirteen

The morning after the tornado, Jill stepped out of the garage apartment and gasped. Overnight, the temperatures had plummeted into the mid-forties, forcing Jill back inside to retrieve her thick eggplant-colored coat along with her matching scarf and gloves.

Thankfully, the cookie deliveries would only take about a half hour, with The Pit and the library being the only orders to fill. After Jill gathered the boxes of cookies from a quiet kitchen—Lucille was snoozing in the living room, and Rick was likely getting some work done upstairs—she walked down the driveway and made her way to the town square.

The storm had made its presence known everywhere. Utility workers assessed damage to power lines, volunteers picked up litter and debris that collected near shops and curbs, an entire strand of Christmas evergreen drooped from overhead, and tree limbs lay scattered on the library's usually pristine lawn.

Jill approached the library's front door, eager to dart out of the cold, and pulled on the handle while balancing the box of cookies in the crook of her other arm. Inside, Chaynie was at the circulation desk and set down her paperwork when she saw Jill.

"Oh, the cookies! You can set them here." She patted the desk with her palm then pushed an envelope containing payment toward Jill. "The kids have been asking me about these all week. Word is getting out about Lucille's cookies."

Jill didn't have the heart to tell her that this was the final delivery run. "I've added a few extras," Jill noted, "for you and the other employees. You've been so kind, answering my questions about the Stout family and finding me those books."

"How are you liking them?"

"I read the Morgan biography in nearly one day. Totally fascinating!"

"I told you!" Chaynie beamed. "She was a remarkable lady."

"Could I keep the books another week? Looks like I might be sticking around longer than planned."

"Of course! As long as you need them."

Before parting ways, they chatted about the storm's damage and how the library was hit particularly hard by softball-sized hail. Chaynie was having the roof assessed later that afternoon.

Jill gathered the remaining box of cookies and headed for The Pit. Even though the restaurant wouldn't open for another two hours, Jill had texted ahead, and one of the sisters had unlocked the door for the cookie delivery. Jill opened the door to the scents of spicy meats and the sound of raised voices.

"It's *eight* chopped beef and four dozen ribs," Tessa told her sister through the kitchen's cutout window as Jill approached the counter.

"Well, don't blame *me*," Darlene sniped. "I can never read that chicken-scratch writing of yours," she grumbled as she disappeared back inside the kitchen.

With wide eyes, Tessa noticed Jill standing there. "Oh. Sorry about all the fussing. *Sisters*. Can't live with 'em, and all that..."

Jill grinned and set the box on the counter.

"Can you believe these temperatures?" Tessa shuddered. "My nose was frozen on my walk to work this morning. We might even get some actual *flurries* this afternoon!"

Jill was tempted to show her the photo of the five-foot snow-drifts that Lindsey had texted the night before.

"And what a storm last night!" Tessa continued. "Word is that the tornado touched down behind the square, missing the elementary school by barely a quarter mile! Tore up some trees from the roots then moved on. How did y'all make out at Lucille's place?"

Jill told her about the hail, the loss of electricity, and the downed tree. "Rick said he'd get a friend to assess the damage. I'm hoping they can save the tree, but I doubt it."

"Rick? Oh, you mean Patrick."

"Patrick?" Jill tilted her head, trying to register the name.

"Yeah. Our biggest town celebrity. Besides you, of course."

"What do you mean?"

Tessa seemed suddenly sheepish, like maybe she'd said something she shouldn't have. "I assumed you'd been told by now. Rick is Patrick Wright... *The* Patrick Wright of Quantum Software."

Jill's eyes grew wide. She wasn't familiar with the Patrick Wright part, but anyone living on Earth had heard of Quantum, a popular file-sharing software. "What do you mean? He works there?"

Tessa chuckled. "Honey, he created that company from scratch. It's all his brainchild. That man is a bona fide zillionaire. I thought you knew."

"Tess! I need some help with these orders!" Darlene called from deep inside the kitchen.

Tessa clucked and shook her head. "Sorry, hon, gotta run. Duty calls. Thanks again for the cookies! You're a genuine lifesaver."

Jill exited The Pit, trying to process the bizarre new information about Rick. Surely, Tessa was mistaken, or it was all a joke. *Rick—mild-mannered, humble, overprotective Rick—a successful zillionaire? A celebrity?* Nothing about him told her it was true. That was not the Rick she had come to know.

Eager to do some quick research, she lingered inside The Pit's doorway, pulled out her phone, then Googled his name in a matter of seconds. And there it was, easily confirmed. *Patrick Wright, creator of Quantum software.* She scrolled through the results and saw a handful of articles. He had a scarce online presence for someone so famous. The one and only picture she could find of him was a clean-shaven portrait from several years back, nothing recent.

Jill pocketed her phone and walked swiftly back to the house, eager to speak with Lucille, and noticed an unfamiliar pickup truck parked at Lucille's curb. After tapping on the kitchen door and getting no response, not even a corgi bark, Jill cracked open the door and walked inside. "Anybody here?"

She heard a jovial shout coming from the back porch. Stepping outside, she saw Lucille covered in blankets and sitting in a lawn chair with her leg propped up on a thick pillow. She was belly-laughing as she watched the corgis wrestle and play in the center of the yard.

"Hello!" she greeted Jill. She shielded her eyes from the bright sky and added, "Join me."

As Jill took a seat in the second lawn chair, she noticed the other activity going on in the yard—Rick and another man stared up at the damaged tree, oblivious to the dogs' shenanigans.

"It's hard to believe we had such awful weather last night," Jill said. "And now this calm, cold day. The dogs love this crisp air, don't they?"

"It's so good for them," Lucille agreed.

George suddenly came to a halt, tongue wagging, then turned to chase Gracie. Jill chuckled. "Looks like they're taking turns herding each other."

"They are," Lucille confirmed.

"So what's the verdict on the tree?" Jill asked.

Lucille gave a deep sigh in return. "I'm still hoping they can save part of it, but I'm doubtful. I keep telling myself it's only a tree, but it feels like more. Frank told me he used to swing from that tree as a little boy—this was his childhood home," she said wistfully. "So I guess it isn't only a tree, not really."

"I'm sorry," Jill offered. "That's heartbreaking."

"Thank you, dear. It's all about perspective, though. I'm grateful the damage wasn't worse and that no one was hurt."

"Things were pretty scary last night. But Rick stepped in and took care of everything."

Lucille moved her attention from the tree to Jill with a wry grin. "You had to be hunched together in that tiny closet for a nice bit of time, I imagine. It was good for you both, I think."

It was, Jill thought, remembering Rick's unexpected confession about his parents' death. But then, on top of that, Tessa's recent shocking revelation echoed in Jill's head—"our town celebrity, a bona fide zillionaire"—and she wondered if she'd ever known Rick at all.

"Mrs. Wright?"

Lucille turned to see Rick's friend, a burly, balding man, approaching the porch. The corgis came trotting along behind him. As the man came closer, Jill could tell he was probably Rick's age. He had a youngish face, but the hair loss made him seem a decade older.

"Lenny, give it to me straight. I can take it," Lucille said.

Rick—Patrick—followed Lenny and paused at the edge of the porch. When he made eye contact with Jill, he gave a small smile but then frowned. He must've read the lingering confusion on Jill's face.

"Well, ma'am, it's gotta come down. The trunk has been compromised. It's basically a dead tree. I'm sorry. I can call Jorge's crew and have him chop it up and clear the stump. He's busy today, so maybe later in the week. The good news is we can chop most of it up for firewood. At least it won't go to waste."

"That's something." Lucille nodded. "Well, as my grandmother used to say, 'It is what it is.' Thank you for coming out quickly this morning. Oh, I forgot—Jill, this is Lenny. He's a police officer who worked with my husband for many years, but his side job is town handyman."

"Nice to meet you," Jill told him.

"You too." Lenny turned to Rick. "I'll give you a call about Jorge."

The two men ended with a vigorous handshake before Lenny left through the back gate.

Lucille noticed the corgis puffing out cold air at her feet. "You two need some water. And some warmth. Let's go inside," she suggested.

Jill stood to help Lucille to her feet. "How's the boot coming along?"

"I'm getting used to it, I guess. It's not as clunky as it was yesterday. Do you want some cocoa?" Lucille offered. "I'm about to make some."

"Sure. I'll be there in a sec," Jill said, watching Lucille enter the house with the corgis.

"Well, I hate to be right." Rick peeled off his work gloves and peered out at the backyard.

"About what?" Jill's mind was elsewhere.

"About the tree."

"Oh. Yeah. It's a shame." She didn't want to talk about the tree anymore. She wanted to talk about "Patrick," but she wasn't sure how to approach it.

"You look preoccupied," he told her.

"I guess I am. This morning, I found out something I wasn't supposed to find out, and now I'm having trouble wrapping my mind around it."

"Something bad?"

"No, just confusing."

Rick's forehead crinkled.

"When I delivered the cookies to The Pit a few minutes ago, Tessa let it slip that your name is Patrick. She said you're the Patrick Wright who started Quantum software." As she spoke the words, Jill realized she hadn't considered his possible reactions until that very moment. There was surely a reason he hadn't mentioned his true identity, even after all the time he'd spent with Jill. She wondered if he would be irritated at her exposing him before he was ready to explain. Or maybe he would shrink back behind his protective wall and cancel out all the progress they'd made.

But Rick's expression didn't show any of those things. He simply relaxed his forehead. "Oh. That."

"I had no idea you were... well, that you were him."

Rick turned to face her squarely, his breath coming out in cold vapors. "I should've told you. I don't know why I didn't." He shrugged. "I guess because, being here in Morgan's Grove, I'm just Rick. And sometimes I forget about that other persona, Patrick. Or maybe I don't want to be him anymore."

"Why not?"

He moved his gaze downward, to the work gloves in his hands. "Because it almost feels like a put-on, that whole lifestyle. California, the tech industry, the publicity that goes with it. I'm not cut out for it. I mean, I'm a country boy from Texas." He grinned that gorgeous grin and shook his head. "I guess I wanted you to know *me* first. The real me."

That was the best answer he could've given Jill, and she almost felt flattered by it. He cared what she thought about him.

"I get it," she said. "But why stay in California with the company? I mean, if you're that unhappy with things."

"I've thought about it for years, actually. But it's all I know. In spite of the headaches of running a major corporation, I'm proud of what we've done. We've made people's lives easier with the software. That's something." He cleared his throat. "Anyway, it's complicated. It's not easy to walk away, even if I wanted to."

But it sounded like he *did* want to, which might involve a move back home to Morgan's Grove. Jill wondered if he'd ever voiced any of his future plans to Lucille.

"I should've told you sooner."

The back door opened, breaking the long gaze between them, as Lucille announced, "Cocoa's almost ready! Who's in?"

"Me!" Jill said, thinking Rick would join them.

But instead, he told Lucille, "Later, maybe. I want to clear some of these branches." Rick slipped on his work gloves again, already assessing the backyard still littered with stray debris.

Jill entered the kitchen then removed her coat and draped it over the breakfast-table chair. "I forgot to ask you the all-important question last night," she told Lucille. "Did you win at bridge?"

Lucille chuckled as she limped toward the stove to retrieve the kettle. Jill thought of offering to help but knew she would be sweetly rebuffed. Lucille didn't enjoy being overly coddled, even when she needed it.

"Yes, in fact! I was the big winner. Well, until a tornado rudely interrupted us." At the island, she poured the steaming water into the first mug as Jill watched the powdered cocoa rise to the top in foamy bubbles. "I'm glad I went last night. Chatting with friends, laughing, catching up with their lives—I've missed it more than I knew. For the first time in a long time, things have started to feel, dare I say it, normal again. And happy. I wasn't expecting to be happy. Not this soon." Lucille filled the second mug. "So, today was the last of the cookie deliveries?"

"It was. Everything went well. But..."

Lucille paused and set down the kettle on the granite. "Was there a problem?"

"No, nothing like that. I found out some information about Rick today. Tessa told me, thinking I already knew."

Lucille gave the same quizzical look that Rick had given earlier.

Jill explained what Tessa had told her, then said, "And I just talked to Rick outside. He confirmed it. He didn't tell me much, though. Said something about wanting to be himself, just Rick, while he's here in town?"

Lucille leaned against the island's edge to face Jill. "I've been waiting to tell you this story, but didn't think it was my place. But now that Rick already knows you know..."

Jill assumed Lucille's account would be *much* more detailed and enlightening than her own Google search could ever be.

"After Rick graduated from UT, he had this brainstorm, an idea for a software company, file sharing or some such. He explained the details and all the complicated technology, but Frank and I didn't understand a bit of it. Still, Rick assured us his company could revolutionize things, make a mark in the world of technology. It was something 'visionary,' he called it. Well, he had my full support, but Frank was wary. He didn't believe in gambling, and that's what he thought it was, taking a great risk. A financial risk. Plus, he never really considered the technology field to be a legitimate career. So he and Rick butted heads over it, and I endured a couple of heated arguments between them. In the end, though, Rick was stubborn, and Frank was too, and neither would change their minds, so Rick pressed on."

Jill was riveted, impatient to hear the rest of the story. It explained so much about the complex relationship between Rick and his grandfather.

"In spite of Frank's dire warnings, Rick started Quantum the very next year with his UT roommate, Mark. They were both only twenty-five years old and sank every penny of their savings into the company. Over the next five years, Rick proved Frank wrong, and the company grew and grew. It became bigger than anyone, including Rick, ever dreamed. He used his given name, Patrick, so that's what the business and computer worlds know him as." Lucille picked up a spoon and stirred one of the mugs. "He's uncomfortable with his status. He never intended to be a millionaire. Rick doesn't know what to do with all that money—in fact, he gives most of it away to charities and individual families in need. You've seen his old truck and the way he dresses. It's hardly the lifestyle of a wealthy man. He lives in a modest beachside house in San Diego. I think the money almost embarrasses him."

"I actually know the company," Jill admitted. "The software is even downloaded on my laptop right now. I can't believe I never put two and two together on my own or that nobody's let this slip before now. I've had dozens of conversations with townspeople, and it's never come up."

Lucille slid the mug toward Jill then began to stir her own cocoa. "This town is gossipy, but it's also *very* protective of Rick. They've known him since he was a little boy. Everyone's proud of him, but they know he doesn't appreciate the notoriety, so they respect his privacy and stay out of his way when he comes home."

Fascinating. Jill struggled to reconstruct the initial image she'd had of Rick when she first arrived in Morgan's Grove. He was nice enough, that first day on the porch, but distant. She'd sensed in him from the beginning a slight suspicion of her, a hesitancy. When Rick first saw Jill, a complete stranger in his grandmother's house, he was understandably leery.

"This town is a sanctuary for Rick. He's safe here," Lucille explained. "He hates the press, detests the spotlight. He gave one interview for *Forbes'* 'Top Entrepreneur of the Year' or some such, but after that, he kept to himself. When he got hounded by the media and even criticized by some, he retreated back to Morgan's Grove. Decided he didn't want any part of the fame. He almost sold the company, backed out altogether. But Mark convinced him to stay. Still, Rick stopped giving interviews, and even now, he goes out of his way not to be photographed. He lets Mark be the voice and face of Quantum."

Rick hates the press. Jill's face flushed hot as she realized she was keeping a secret of her own and how it might look now, under the newly revealed circumstances. Her entire time in Morgan's Grove, she hadn't told anyone—including Rick and Lucille—about the article she was writing for an online magazine. Though it was harmless to him, Jill wasn't sure whether Rick would see it that way, even if Jill wasn't technically the press.

He's safe here. Jill had been living under his grandmother's roof, getting to know both of them well. But he might view it through a different lens if he knew the truth.

"What's the matter, dear? You've gone absolutely pale," Lucille said.

"Can we postpone the cocoa for a minute?"

Jill was already halfway to the back door.

"Of course. But I don't understand..." Lucille said.

Jill opened the door and found Rick at the back fence with a pile of branches cradled in his arms.

"Can you come in for a second?" she called. "I need to talk to you."

He paused with the branches then walked them over to a nearby pile and cast them down. "Sure."

In the few seconds it took for Rick to approach the kitchen, Jill frantically searched her brain for the right phrases she could use to explain, to make him understand.

Rick joined Lucille on one side of the island, and Jill planted herself at the other side in order to face them together. "I've been talking to your grandmother about Quantum..."

"I was filling her in with the details," Lucille explained.

"Right, about how you don't like the press and you prefer to be out of the spotlight," Jill continued. She clasped her hands together on top of the island and realized her palms were clammy. "Well, I have something I need to tell you. But please hear me out."

The confusion in Rick's eyes sharpened.

"When I arrived in Morgan's Grove, I told you both that I write novels. And I do. I make my living from them—they're my main source of income. But there's another writing project I've been working on recently. Sort of freelance." She swallowed, hoping she could get the words out before they both jumped to all the wrong conclusions. "My friend owns an online magazine called *Lifestyle Today*. And part of the reason I'm here in town is to write an article for it."

"Oh dear," Lucille whispered from across the island.

"But—" Jill made a halting gesture in the air between them. "It's not what you think. I promise."

"You're a journalist?" Rick whispered, his tone even.

"Let her explain." Lucille gripped Rick's sleeve.

"No, I'm not a journalist. I'm a novelist. But I worked for this magazine years ago, right out of college, only for a bit. And as a favor to my friend, Miranda, I still write occasional articles for them. It's a good, decent magazine, Rick. It only focuses on human-interest stories and uplifting pieces. Their goal is to inspire and to educate."

"This article," Rick said, his voice growing stronger. "What's it about?"

"That's what I need to explain." Jill could feel her pulse racing inside her temples. She *had* to make him see that she wasn't the enemy. "My assignment was genealogy, so I did an online search and found out about my ties to Morgan's Grove."

"So that part is real." Rick's stare was unblinking.

"Of course it's real. I've never lied to you. Just like you, there was a huge part of my life that I was holding back."

"Why did you hide the article?" Rick asked.

"I needed room and space to do my research. You saw what happened when people started finding out about my novels. I was peppered with questions. And then, when everyone discovered my connection to the Stouts—well, that's the first question on their lips now. And if they'd known I was writing an article, they'd either be hounding me to be part of the article, or they might be suspicious. Like you. It would change the way they looked at me." She softened her voice, pled with her eyes. "Rick, this article was only meant as a human-interest story about *me*. I came here to see the town for myself, research my family's history, and get some inspiration. I've been making notes and brainstorming ideas, but I haven't even written the piece yet. I've been in research mode."

"All this time," Rick said, "you've been gathering material, watching all of us, living here at my grandmother's house, getting to know us."

Jill flashed backward to the night before, wedged up alongside Rick in that cramped closet during the tornado. "But it's not like that." She looked Rick straight in the eyes, unblinking too. "I can see how this looks, which is why I'm telling you about it now. I never came here to do a story about you. I didn't even *know* you were Patrick Wright until an hour ago. This article is about *me* and my heritage. I haven't been spying on you. I can show you all my notes upstairs and prove it to you."

Rick pushed away from the island, shaking his head. "I need some air."

He walked silently to the back door, and Jill winced in advance, expecting a terse slam to go with it. But he clicked the door shut with a quiet, gentle touch, which was almost worse.

Jill returned her gaze to Lucille, and they stood in silence as they heard the garage gears grinding and Rick's engine being brought to life. Through the window, Jill caught a glimpse of his truck backing away. The fact that she was the source of his pain—misunderstanding or not—made her stomach drop to her knees. "I'm sorry," she whispered.

Lucille reached far across the island and clamped onto Jill's hand with her own. "You have nothing to be sorry for. You explained everything perfectly. This is all one big mix-up. He'll see that too."

Jill felt tears prick the back of her eyes. She should've known Lucille would be completely understanding. She only hoped, in time, that Rick would be, too.

Chapter Fourteen

Not good enough. Frustrated, Jill marked a harsh line through the idea she'd jotted down then ripped the paper from its pad and crumpled it into a tight ball. She tossed the wadded paper into the corner, watching it bounce off the growing stack of other discarded ideas.

In the handful of hours since Rick had left the house, Jill had politely declined Lucille's attempts at a diversion—"Let's go see a movie. Or maybe visit the founder's mansion. Or we could even go into Austin, do some shopping!"—and after that, Jill had taken a walk around the block to clear her head then trudged upstairs to the only place she could have some true privacy, the apartment.

She couldn't deny something that had haunted her ever since Rick had climbed into his truck and driven away. Because of Rick's strong reaction to the article, it was dead in the water. She had failed to convince him that the article wouldn't affect him or Lucille in any way, and that he would remain completely unscathed by it. No one would ever connect its content with him or his company. But even if she completed it and submitted it as planned, Jill's heart wasn't in it anymore. The article felt tainted. She couldn't possibly work on it or even approach it without reverting back to that moment when Rick's eyes held hurt and disappointment that she couldn't remove.

So Jill had decided to plonk down on the apartment's floor, with her back against the bedframe and a legal pad resting on her knees, and brainstorm from scratch. She couldn't approach Miranda emptyhanded at the deadline. Jill had committed herself to the article and would see it through. Maybe she could still salvage the genealogy idea, using someone else's life story. But she knew there wasn't time for that. The clock was ticking.

If only Jill had taken Lindsey's advice and returned to Colorado ahead of the storm. She would've left Morgan's Grove none the wiser about Patrick, she could've written a decent article with the research she'd already accumulated, and Rick probably would never have known the article had been written in the first place. But there she was, stuck in Morgan's Grove, licking her wounds, hoping to avoid Rick and feeling slightly awkward with Lucille. Maybe Jill could see if the B&B had an extra room for the next few nights, until the snow in Denver finally cleared and she could return home.

As she was batting that idea around, a brisk knock at the door startled her, and she nearly lost her grasp on the notepad. She'd been so absorbed in her own thoughts that she hadn't even heard the visitor's steps on the staircase.

Jill realized she wasn't in any shape for company, emotionally or physically. Maybe if she held still, the visitor would take the hint and leave.

But a second series of knocks told her the visitor was persistent. The likeliest possibility was Lucille, attempting again to cheer Jill up or distract her with another idea. Jill tossed the notepad aside then hoisted herself up from the floor.

The very last person she'd expected on the other side of the door was Rick, but there he stood, holding a colorful bouquet of flowers. It took her a moment to process the image, to translate what it meant. She had convinced herself that he was done with her, that he'd shut her out and would never speak to her again, believing she'd betrayed him.

"Oh, hi," she said in a small voice. She looked up at his face.

All the hurt and disappointment seemed to have disappeared, and in its place was the old Rick, relaxed and friendly. He even offered a hint of a smile.

What had changed?

"Can I come in?"

Politeness and curiosity won out, and Jill stepped aside as he walked through the doorway. She noticed his quick glance toward the messy pile of wadded-up paper as she closed the door.

"What's this?" Jill heard herself ask as she pointed flippantly toward the flowers then crossed her arms at her waist. She didn't realize until that moment how much of her frustration was directed toward Rick. It had been too easy for him to believe the worst of her. In the beginning, Jill fully understood his stunned reaction to her confession. But as the afternoon wore on, she'd played the scene over and over in her mind. Rick's *first* reaction to the article had been nothing but skepticism and doubt, and it had made her quietly question the momentum she thought they'd been building for weeks.

"It's an apology," he said, inching the flowers forward.

But she didn't take them. *Your grandmother put you up to this*, she wanted to say but didn't. She watched him take a cautious step closer to her, and because of the apartment's small dimensions, she was forced to stand her ground and let him.

"I've had a lot of time to think." His voice was low and resonant. "And I realize I had a stupid, knee-jerk reaction to your article." He blew out a sigh. "Look, I admit it—I don't trust people easily, which is why this hit hard. I assumed the worst instead of really listening to you."

Despite herself, Jill could feel her resolve soften as he took another step closer, still explaining.

"I drove around for a while then went to the bridge to think. I Googled the magazine on my phone. And then I found your articles. That's what I've been doing the past couple of hours, sitting at the bridge, reading every piece you've written in the past few years. And you were right. You're not one of them, a reporter out for a scoop, trying to destroy people's lives. You're an incredible writer, and your pieces aren't salacious at all. They're inspiring. And they're kind. That one about the veteran and his dog..."

She saw the lump in his throat and knew he was being genuine. *That* was the Rick she recognized, the caring one, pushing through his own insecurities to open up to her. All her frustrations evaporated as she continued to listen.

"I was a jackass for thinking the worst of you. It didn't match everything I've seen about you in these last couple of weeks—your compassion for my grandmother, your selflessness. I made a snap judgment based on some bad past experiences that had nothing to do with you. So go ahead and write your article." He paused. "That came out wrong. You don't need my permission. That's not what I meant. Whatever you decide, I'm behind you on it, a hundred percent."

Without removing his gaze from her, Rick tossed the flowers gently onto the bed and took the final step to close the gap between them. She felt the warmth of his hands as he touched her arms, still holding eye contact. "Forgive me?"

She somehow found her voice and told him, "There's nothing to forgive. I caught you off guard. You were starting to trust me, and then I threw the article at you. You weren't ready for it."

"It's no excuse. I should've known you weren't one of them, even without having to read your articles. Because I know *you*."

Jill's heart thumped hard inside her chest, and she wondered if he could hear it. Rick had slowly drawn her closer with his grasp, and part of her wanted to melt into him. But before she could fully realize what might be happening, Rick blinked, cleared his throat, then removed his hands.

"So," he said, taking a small step backward. "Gran wanted me to ask you for an early supper, if you haven't already eaten."

Jill coaxed her heart rate down, trying not to show her disappointment in Rick's diversion from a potentially intimate moment. *Was he going to kiss me? Did he want to?*

"She said it's nothing special, just sandwiches," Rick clarified.

"Okay, sure."

Rick was already taking steps toward the door.

"Tell her I'll be down in a minute."

She watched him open the door and had enough time before he shut it to tell him, "Thank you for the flowers."

Pivoting, Jill lifted the bouquet off the bed, bringing the flowers toward her nose to inhale deeply. Their fragrance was glorious. She shut her eyes tightly and imagined Rick picking them out for her. She took another whiff as the velvet-soft petals touched the edge of her cheek.

FROM THE MOMENT SHE'D stepped into the cold late-afternoon air with the corgis, Jill wondered what she had gotten into. She had offered to take the dogs for a leisurely walk around the square, since Lucille's ankle still made their daily walks impossible. Thankfully, after the flower delivery from Rick as well as Lucille's cordial supper the night before, Jill's Sunday had been surprisingly normal. Earlier in the afternoon, she had tossed all the wadded-up papers into the trash and returned to her article's original notes. Her conversation with Rick had breathed new life into the piece. She'd scanned over her notes with a brisk energy, her confidence returning as she pulled facts and details and observations together. But after a few hours, her brain had finally reached its capacity for clear thought. The walk with the corgis would offer a much-needed break.

Naively, she had assumed it would be a simple task—the dogs were familiar and relaxed with her. But when it came to a walk outside, *they* were in control. Jill recalled what Lucille had once told her: "They're herding dogs. It's in their nature to take charge, so sometimes you have to rein them in."

Easier said than done. Jill's worst nightmare on the walk was for one of the corgis to get loose and run out into the street. So from the beginning, she'd tied both leashes firmly around her wrist for extra security and control. But the corgis' herding tendencies, coupled with their zealous excitement about taking a walk, made them almost impossible to navigate.

She spent the first two blocks being pulled along by them, constantly distracted by children or neighbors or other people's dogs. They were met with nothing but gasps, smiles, and cooing admiration as Jill kept being yanked in another direction by one or both of them, creating awkward entanglements and knots in both leashes.

Finally, mercifully, when they approached the town square, the corgis were too tired to pull anymore. The leashes went slack, and the dogs became "tuckered out," as Lucille would say, with their tongues hanging low, quick breaths coming out in cold vapors, and their ears less alert than before. With the new, slower pace, maybe Jill could actually enjoy the walk.

Usually, when she entered the charming town square, she was either rushing around to complete her cookie deliveries or shopping for specific items at one of the shops. But on her Sunday break, she wanted to be one of the townspeople and take her time, gaze around, window shop, and soak it all up—the twinkly lights, the happy faces, the glitzy decorations in shop windows, the crisp winter air. Though Christmas wasn't her favorite season, her senses could still be dazzled by all that came with it.

A festival poster in the antique shop's window caught Jill's attention. The big event would take place next Saturday, beginning with the outdoor market, then a big Christmas concert, and finally, a parade.

Without any particular agenda in mind, Jill let the corgis continue leading her down the length of the street as the shops began to close up. Gracie's nose picked up something distinctive in the air, and she held it high.

"What, girl?" Jill asked her. "What do you smell?"

Jill's gaze moved ahead, toward a building next to the B&B, where she saw the familiar frame of a tall, lean man. Rick stood beside another, shorter man, peering with great intensity at the empty building. His arms were crossed.

Why is this run-down site so intriguing to them? It was a stand-alone structure, set slightly apart from the uniformity of all the other brick-front shops. It seemed forgotten, left behind, out of place. The windows were boarded up, and the pale-white siding needed some repairs and fresh coats of paint.

Gracie recognized Rick and began to bark. Then George joined in.

Rick swiveled and noticed Jill at the other end of the leashes. By then, the corgis had dragged her to the site, close to where Rick stood. George and Gracie took turns sniffing Rick's boots.

"The gang's all here." Rick squatted down and took George's face in both his hands for an affectionate rub while Gracie licked his gloves.

Jill hadn't seen Rick all day. He, too, had been absorbed with work, even on a Sunday. And since she knew that his work was Quantum, Jill completely understood how intense his job must be. No wonder he couldn't afford to take even one day off. "Lucille said they needed some exercise, so I volunteered."

"Brave of you." Rick stood again while the corgis decided to lie down on the pavement and continue their panting. "Oh. Hank, this is Jill."

Hank held out his hand, and Jill politely reciprocated. "Nice to meet you."

"An old friend from high school," Rick explained.

"Hey, not *that* old!" Hank said with a sharp laugh that drifted away with the wind, then added: "I'll be on my way. Call me when you make a decision." He gave Rick a friendly shoulder slap before leaving.

"I'm glad you're here. There's something I wanted to tell you," Rick told Jill. "Well, I actually wanted to tell Gran too, but I needed your input first."

"You're not making much sense." Jill grinned up at him as he half-rolled his eyes in agreement. She was relieved their easy banter was firmly back in place.

"I know. Here, I have an idea," he told her. "Let's take the corgis someplace more private than Main Street."

Intrigued, she encouraged George and Gracie to stand again as Rick took Gracie's leash, relieving half of Jill's burden. Rick led them all in the direction of the B&B next door, toward a back gate, which he opened wide.

"Are you sure we should be doing this?" she asked meekly, feeling like a trespasser, ducking under his arm to follow through.

"It's fine. I know Mrs. Haversham well. She lets anybody use the space—you don't have to be a guest to be back here. Plus, nobody's using it in cold weather."

Jill had no idea what existed behind the B&B: a beautiful garden, a half-acre or so, with a rolling backyard, lawn furniture, shrubs and perennials, picnic tables, and a gazebo farther beyond. "Wow," she said under her breath.

"It's used as a venue for weddings and parties," Rick said. "I thought the corgis could run loose while we talked." He stooped over to unclick their leashes.

"Good luck getting those reattached later," Jill mused.

She watched the dogs romp around, play-biting each other as they bounded down the hillside.

"A bench?" Rick gestured nearby.

"I'd rather go there, actually." Jill pointed toward the gazebo, where the dogs were headed.

Rick agreed, and they walked toward the white structure draped in lights. When they reached the gazebo, Rick paused to let Jill enter first, and she walked up the stairs.

She peered around at the clean white paneling inside, her shoes tapping on the wood floor. "This is beautiful."

"One of Gran's favorite spots. She and Pops had an anniversary party here once..."

Jill sat on the bench that rounded the gazebo's interior. She patted the space beside her. "What did you want to tell me?"

Rick set down the dogs' leashes then took a seat beside Jill. "It's about Gran's cookies."

Jill had assumed that was a dead topic.

"Remember a couple of days back, when Tessa called you from The Pit?"

"Her cookie crisis?"

"Yeah. Well, I saw Gran's face. She was saying no to future deliveries, but there was something else in her eyes: disappointment."

"You caught that too." Jill nodded, remembering. "I think she misses it, making the cookies and selling them. It felt like she was just getting started, and then she hurt her ankle."

"Right. Well, Tessa's call is significant for another reason. It got me thinking. If the most popular restaurant in town is begging for Gran's cookies, along with other shop owners, I'd say she's got a real hit on her hands. It's undeniable. So tonight I asked Hank to meet me at that building site. He's an old friend, but he's also a contractor. The building used to be a pizza joint that closed down last year, and it's stood empty since. I was asking Hank about how much renovation it would take... to turn it into a bakery. For Gran."

Jill let her mouth drop open.

Rick used his hands to explain. "Look, I know Gran made this big decision to quit the cookies. But that was days ago, when she was laid up in bed, grumpy and unable to function. Even in these last few days, though, she's healed a lot, made progress. She'll be out of that boot and back to full strength soon. She likes the idea of being active with her days. Do you think she'd be open to the idea?"

"Of a bakery? I don't know. I mean, it's one thing to have a quiet dream, but another to make it a reality."

"You can be honest," Rick prompted, lowering his hands, his fingers grazing her knee.

"Okay. Well, what about all the stress of opening a new business? Budgets and payroll and taxes and permits? I mean, if Lucille didn't want that kind of pressure, just baking out of her kitchen every other day, how would she feel about having to run a full-on business in a busy square?"

"I've thought of that. She could oversee things as she wants. But the bakery would be fully functioning on its own. She would be the owner, with her name on the building, but she could be involved as much or as little as she'd want to be. Managers would run the place. I would only hire the best."

Jill extended her gaze past the gazebo, into the yard, watching the corgis run under the glow of a setting sun. She continued to roll the bakery idea over in her head.

"Tell me," Rick prompted.

"Well, the cookies are only seasonal, right? People usually associate gingerbread with Christmas. What if it's a flop when you try to sell gingerbread year-round? Would people actually buy gingerbread during, say, April or August?" She couldn't believe they had reversed roles this way—Rick jumping in with both feet, with Jill expressing hesitant concern.

"Gran bakes other things too, throughout the year—other cookies and breads and brownies. So it wouldn't have to be gingerbread-centered, necessarily. But that could still be the special draw, setting it apart year-round."

"And there's not another bakery in the square."

"There used to be one, but it closed a few years ago." He met Jill's eye line and searched her face. "You like the idea. Don't you?"

Jill imagined Lucille's bright eyes upon hearing the news, and that was all it took. "I love the idea. What a Christmas present for your grandmother. It's a really thoughtful gift."

"I only want to make her happy. And nothing's set in stone until I talk to Gran. It's all her decision. I've notified the owners about my interest, but the paperwork hasn't been drawn up yet."

One of the corgis struggled to climb the steps into the gazebo, ears drooping.

"Gracie, girl, are you exhausted?" Jill asked, watching the dog amble toward her then plonk down on top of Jill's shoes. "I think that's a yes." She chuckled, stooping down to rub Gracie's ears.

"Guess that's our cue," Rick said, standing.

George had approached the gazebo, too, but was struggling to push his stocky frame up the stairs.

Rick handed a leash to Jill, who was thankful the corgis were ready for the trek homeward, past the site of Lucille's potential new bakery.

LUCILLE HAD BEEN SETTLED on the sofa, making progress on her needlepoint, when Jill, Rick, and the corgis burst through the front door, looking cold and winded.

"That was an exceptionally long walk," Lucille observed, craning her neck to view them. Her boot was propped up on the coffee table. "I was about to put on my coat and come find you."

"These two sure gave me a good workout," Jill admitted, unclicking the leashes. "I ran into Rick in the square, and he showed me the B&B's garden at sunset. That gazebo is amazing!"

Rick offered to get the dogs settled in the kitchen and refill their water bowls while Jill shed her coat and joined Lucille in the living room. The sofa bed had been officially retired, so the living room looked neat and tidy again, with the Christmas tree lights glowing from the corner of the room.

"Oh, isn't that garden just the sweetest place? An oasis of solitude," Lucille agreed. "It's also great for parties and celebrations."

Jill was about to take a seat beside Lucille when something caught her eye. She moved toward the fireplace and stared at the new stocking hanging beside Rick's.

"What's this?" She touched the embroidery of her own name.

"When I heard you were staying in town longer, it occurred to me—you need your own stocking."

Jill's smile widened as she joined Lucille on the sofa. "I love it. Thank you."

Rick entered the room to add another log and stoke the fire then sat on the floor with his back to the edge of the fireplace, his long legs crossed at the ankles. "Gran, I want to ask you a question."

Even though Rick had already let Jill in on the bakery idea, this still felt like a private grandmother-grandson talk, so she made a tiny hitchhiker-like hand gesture to Rick, asking if he wanted her to leave the room.

He added, "And I want Jill to stay for this. Her input is valuable."

Lucille set her needlepoint aside. "You've got me curious."

"It's about your cookies." Rick dove right in. "I've done some serious thinking. It's clear how much they mean to you. And I don't think you should give them up. I've watched the way your energy level rises when you bake them and talk about them. You're in your element when you bake. And people all over town are clearly interested in ordering more of them. It's supply and demand, basic economics. Plus, your ankle is healing—"

"I don't understand. You want me to start baking again?"

"Even more than that."

Rick straightened up and leaned forward so he could gesture to explain. He told Lucille about the empty building at the edge of the square, a prime real estate location, then went over Hank's assessment and the possible renovations they could do, which would take only a few weeks' time—they could open by late February. He painted an appealing picture, and by the time he'd finished, even Jill was able to picture a final product.

"I ran this by Jill already, to get her opinion."

"And I think it's a wonderful idea," Jill said. "If it's what *you* want, Lucille."

At first, Lucille was completely speechless. And when she still hadn't spoken, Rick reassured her. "I haven't done anything yet—no papers signed, no decisions made. There's no obligation, zero pressure. But I'm ready to buy the building and start the renovations if you want me to. This is one hundred percent your decision."

Finally, Lucille shifted, watching the flames dance behind Rick. "It's such a generous offer, son. I hardly know what to say. But I'm just not sure about the commitment. I'm not getting any younger. And though I don't mind the work—"

"You can be involved as much as you want," Rick explained, "or as little. You can be hands-on and oversee everything or step back entirely and hire a manager to run the place, someone who will keep you apprised of everything. The bakery will be all yours, with your name on it. But you don't have to shoulder the burden of it."

"This is such a shock. I never dreamed I'd have a business at my age. I'm leery, but"— Lucille's eyes suddenly brimmed with glossy tears—"it's such a sweet offer, really." Her gaze shifted between Rick and Jill. "You're both too good to me. I don't know how I ever man-aged without you here."

This last statement stung Jill's heart, since she knew that she and Rick would be leaving in the very near future, moving on with their individual lives, far away from Morgan's Grove. She pictured Lucille's evenings, even barely a month before, lonely and quiet, with only the corgis for company, living alone in the hollow shell of the house that Frank once occupied.

"I need some time," said Lucille, "to think it over."

"Absolutely." Rick stood then walked over to lean in and hug his grandmother.

When they drew apart, Lucille chuckled. "You two. It seems you're offering me new challenges every day, keeping an old woman on her toes, but I love you for it."

Rick stared at Jill, smiling widely. "Partners in crime. It's a con-spiracy."

Partners with Rick. Jill liked that description very much.

Chapter Fifteen

"I'm calling this meeting to order." Lucille tapped a pencil on the notepad in her lap.

Rick shifted in the cramped wicker chair then sipped the cocoa that Lucille had made for Rick, Jill, and herself before asking them to join her on the porch. The temperatures were low-fifties and chilly but pleasant enough for an outdoor meeting.

In all her adult years, never once had Jill attended a business meeting sitting in a porch swing with a Christmas tree nearby, in brisk weather on a gray day, holding a comforting mug of cocoa. She blew on its surface before taking a sip.

"You have our full attention," Rick said.

Lucille cleared her throat. "Well, I've had some time to consider Rick's generous proposal from last night, the bakery idea. And I could hardly sleep, truth be told, with so many factors to consider. But this morning, I wanted to let you both know that I've come to a decision." Her face was solemn, and Jill was *sure* Lucille was about to turn the offer down with a firm-but-polite no.

But then Lucille's expression broke into a wide smile. "My answer is unequivocally yes."

Rick's face brightened, but before he could say anything, Lucille lifted her finger for a pause. "But there are a few things I want to discuss before we make it official. We need to agree on these points first."

Rick surely knew that his grandmother had to do it on her own terms. "Yes, of course." He set down his mug and leaned forward, elbows on knees.

For a brief moment, Jill questioned why she'd been invited to the meeting—she wouldn't be involved in any of the future plans. In fact, by the time the bakery opened in a few weeks, she would be firmly planted back in her Denver apartment, with Morgan's Grove a distant memory. Still, it was nice to be included, even if the gesture was only a deferential one.

Lucille removed her reading glasses from the nape of her neck, put them on, then lifted the list from her lap.

"Here, let me free you up a bit," Jill said, taking the mug from her.

"Good idea. I need my full concentration on this," Lucille agreed. "Point one. If my name is on the business, I want it to reflect *me*. Cheerful workers, fair prices, excellent treatment of all employees and customers. That's terribly important to me. Point two. The recipes for the gingerbread cookies will never change. I want customers to know exactly what they're getting. No surprises. Point three. The gingerbread recipe must be carefully guarded from everyone except the bakers. It's my great-grandmother's recipe, originally, and that's precious to me. Plus, having a bit of mystery surrounding the ingredients might make people curious about the cookies."

"Now you're thinking like a marketer!" Jill said.

"Is that a good thing?" Lucille asked, peering over her glasses at Jill.

"Definitely."

"Point four. My involvement needs to be flexible. Some days, I might want to garden or relax or read and not even think about the bakery at all. Plus, I'm not sure about my health, and I want to know that the business can carry on flawlessly without me. And finally—" Lucille removed her glasses, abandoned the list, and faced her grandson. "This isn't a contingency. It's a thank you to my darling boy. What a generous, kind, and unexpected..." Her voice quivered and trailed off, but then she found her bearings. "I would be more than honored to accept your incredible, generous gift."

Rick stood from the wicker chair to give his grandmother a strong embrace. "You're welcome," he whispered into her ear, then kissed her cheek and sat down again.

Lucille balanced the notepad on her lap as she wiped a tear from her cheek. "I was thinking about something else. I don't want to wait until the bakery opens before selling the cookies again. What if people forget about them? And besides, it's the holiday season *right now*, and people are asking for the cookies. Why not capitalize on the holidays?"

"Good idea." Jill nodded. "Selling them will keep the buzz going until the bakery opens. Do you want me to drum up some orders this afternoon around the square?"

"No, no. You're too busy with your article. Besides, I don't want to sell the cookies at the shops anymore. The Christmas market is coming up this weekend to kick off next week's festival. I thought I could try to acquire a booth to sell my cookies!"

"Isn't it too late for that?" Rick asked. "People reserve booths months in advance—"

"I phoned Beatrice this morning and left a voicemail," Lucille assured him. "She's on the market's committee and has the inside scoop. Won't hurt to ask."

"What about your ankle?" Rick wondered. "You're still healing."

"Oh, I know it's an enormous job, baking, bagging up the cookies, transporting them, setting up the booth. But I have a plan for that too." Lucille explained that she had already phoned Becky, who was thrilled with the idea of more part-time work. "Becky's out of school for the holidays, so she can help purchase ingredients like she did before. And If I get too tired with the baking, I can guide her in the kitchen to help me out. She can roll out the dough or help me lift the trays and such."

"We could help," Jill said, having no real idea whether Rick could join her. "With manning the booth, I mean. It's only a couple of days. It still gives me time to work on the article."

"Aren't you leaving for Denver by then?" Rick wondered.

"Well, the storm is still wreaking havoc up north with roadway and airport closings, so I was planning on staying for a few more days. At least through the weekend, if that's okay?" she asked Lucille.

"You know it is. I wish you'd stay all the way through Christmas!"

"Count me in," Rick added, "for the booth, I mean. I can shuffle things around and make it work."

Lucille brightened. "This feels right. All of it. I woke up with a new energy today. Once I thought yes to this bakery idea, well, the rest of it fell smack dab into place."

After a pause, Rick clapped his hands together. "I say we get going. There's a lot of work in front of us. I have permits and licenses to apply for. And you, Gran, have a bakery to sign for. The lawyer can draw up the paperwork this afternoon."

"I'm ready!"

THE MOMENT LUCILLE accepted Rick's bakery offer, everyone kicked into high gear. Jill touched base with Becky while Lucille started planning out her baking schedule for the weekend's market. Rick made calls to his lawyer, a realtor, and Hank. By late afternoon, every possible wheel had been put into motion, and all that was left to do was show Lucille the site of her new bakery.

Rick was already at the property, so Jill agreed to drive Lucille there. When they exited the car and approached the building, they could see Rick's shadow through the open door. He waved and approached them on the sidewalk.

"I remember this old place," Lucille told him. "Your grandfather and I used to come here on Saturday nights—date nights. There was a jukebox in the corner, and sometimes, if we had the place to ourselves, I could talk him into a dance."

Jill shared a smile with Rick over Lucille's shoulder.

"Well, it won't look the same as you remember, Gran. It's been hollowed out, stripped of most everything. There's not much to see," Rick warned. "You have to look past the checkered floors and yellow countertops and imagine the potential beyond it."

"I can do that," she assured him.

"And you can start making decisions today. We'll need updates for the counters, floors, and even the stoves and equipment you want. My guys are on standby to start the renovations once you've finalized your decisions. Hank says that since it was a pizzeria, the layout is already food-service friendly with a kitchen in the back, storage space, and an office, but we still need to update all the equipment. I want the best. Top-of-the-line everything." Rick offered his elbow to his grandmother as he led her toward the front door.

"You don't need to sell me on it. I'm already sold," Lucille told him with a reassuring pat of the arm.

Inside, Rick flipped on the light switch. "I had the electricity and water turned on this afternoon."

They stepped farther inside, leaving room for Jill to join them as they paused and took in the space together. It was just as Rick had described, with faded checkered floors, old-fashioned countertops that covered a buffet table, and ghostly fluorescent lighting overhead.

"The jukebox! It's still there." Lucille gasped.

"Yeah, I think the former owners abandoned it because it's broken down. Hank was about to haul it off—"

"Oh, please, Rick," Lucille pleaded, "let's keep it. We can have it repaired, surely. At least we can try."

Rick tilted his head. "A jukebox in a bakery. I'm not sure how well it fits the theme, but whatever Gran wants, Gran gets." He pulled out his phone and started texting. "I'll see if Hank knows someone for the job."

Jill watched Lucille squint, likely viewing the entire space with fresh eyes. Confirming this, Lucille pointed to the floors. "We could install a different color, couldn't we?" she asked Rick. "And maybe even paint the walls? I want something comforting."

"I'll bring home some samples tonight for floors, countertops, wallpaper, and paint colors. The works."

"That sounds fun."

Rick's phone buzzed in his hand, and he frowned at the screen. "I need to get this."

He clicked to answer then moved outside with the call, but Jill could still hear his voice, especially the sharp tone he took. It was the same one she'd heard the week before on another call he'd made in the next room while she was rolling out the cookie dough. Jill stepped with Lucille farther into the bakery, toward the back kitchen, trying to pretend she didn't hear words like "lying to me," and "cheat" waft from Rick's phone call and hoping Lucille wasn't paying any attention. Her silence either meant she was absorbed in envisioning the bakery's potential or that she was eavesdropping like Jill was.

"I wonder what that's about," Lucille whispered, her eyes darting back toward Rick, confirming Jill's suspicions.

"Work, maybe?" Jill asked, hearing Rick's voice thin out and drift away as he took the call even farther outside.

Lucille paused in the kitchen doorway. "He's had a couple of phone calls like that recently, and every time I ask him who it was, he tells me not to worry and that he's handling it, whatever *that* means. I thought at first it was business related, but now I wonder if—"

"What?"

"Well, it maybe could be a girlfriend in California." She lowered her voice. "Or an *ex*, considering the language he's using. Cheating and lying?"

It hadn't occurred to Jill that Rick's tense phone calls might have involved a significant other back in California. She'd assumed the exchanges were all work-related. During the lengthy chats Jill and Rick had been having the past couple of weeks, especially as they baked together, he'd never even hinted about a girlfriend. But it didn't mean that one didn't exist.

"So Rick hasn't mentioned a girlfriend to you?" Jill asked.

Lucille chuckled. "That boy *never* talks to me about his private life. But some of his phone calls sound a little bit... personal. Emotional. Not the way he conducts himself on a normal conference call."

Rick came through the front door, phone in hand, apologizing. "I should've turned this thing off. Sorry. On with the tour! Have you seen the kitchen yet?" He tried to produce a cheerful expression, but Jill caught the flash of anxiety behind his eyes. She wanted to ask him questions, but it wasn't the time or place. Besides, Rick was already whisking past her, entering the kitchen, talking about ripping out the pizza ovens and adding an industrial-sized mixer and special cooling racks. He painted a vivid picture, helping his grandmother envision employees hard at work, measuring out butter and brown sugar, inserting dough into hot ovens, and icing cookies and other goodies with delicate flair.

JILL POPPED ANOTHER lemon Skittle into her mouth, trying not to jiggle the tablet, which she'd propped up with pillows when Lindsey's video call came in a few minutes before.

"This feels like a pajama party and we're in the seventh grade," Jill observed. "I'm *literally* wearing pajamas right now."

"They're cute! New?"

"Yes, I bought them at Mindy's Boutique, in the square." Jill pushed the sleeve of her PJ's closer to the screen, showing off the bright-white stars against the dark-navy flannel.

"Pretty!"

Jill sorted through the Skittles on her plate, in search of a cherry one. "So you're still snowbound at your mom's?" she asked. "Everyone's safe?"

"Yeah. My sister's here with her family, and Charlie's here too. We finally got the electricity back on, and Dad cleared a path from the front door to the mailbox. But the roads are still iced over. School is canceled through tomorrow, at least. You made the right decision to stay put!"

Jill was relieved at not having to spend a few treacherous days holed up in her Denver apartment with no electricity or even at Lindsey's family home, struggling to make small talk with people she barely knew.

"So Lucille was happy today, about the bakery idea? No regrets?" Lindsey asked, also sitting cross-legged in pajamas. Jill had texted her earlier about the morning's porch meeting.

"No regrets at all. She was thrilled, and so was Rick. It's the happiest I've ever seen him." Jill decided it was best to omit the call he'd answered at the bakery's site, not wanting to complicate things or have Lindsey become her usual snoopy self.

Lindsey paused then peered closer into the screen so that her features became huge and exaggerated. Jill chomped on another Skittle, assuming there was a smudge on Lindsey's screen that she was about to remove.

But instead, Lindsey continued to stare straight through to Jill. "Admit it."

"Admit what?"

"You like him. You like Rick."

"Okay, now we really *are* in the seventh grade." Jill chuckled.

Lindsey backed away from the screen and shook her head. "It's crystal clear, maybe to everyone but you. It's the way you talk about him, all dreamy-eyed."

"I do not get dreamy-eyed." Jill was hoping Lindsey would drop the subject, but alas.

"Yes, you do. When you first got to Morgan's Grove, you barely talked about him. But now, somehow, Rick ends up entering every conversation we have."

"Not true." Jill paused her Skittle search. "I talk about other things, too, don't I? The article and the town. And Lucille. And the corgis."

"Yes, but you get this special look when you talk about Rick. Admit it," she pressed. Lindsey wouldn't drop it until she got the answer she was looking for.

"I admit that I misjudged Rick in the beginning and that he's warmer and kinder than I first thought. He genuinely loves his grandmother and takes care of her. You can't say that about a lot of guys. But I also admit that he's more complex than I realized." She hadn't yet told Lindsey about him being Patrick, Head of Quantum. "He's got these deep layers, and I've only peeled back the first few. But the good news is, he's letting me. His walls are coming down..."

"See? Dreamy-eyed."

Jill tossed a Skittle at Lindsey, and it plonked off the screen. "Just because I see someone in a new light does *not* mean I'm dreamy-eyed."

"Okay, okay. I can take a hint. But when a gorgeous, nice man comes into your life, he deserves a second look. They're not that easy to come by. Trust me."

"Linds, I can't give him more than a second look. I'm leaving, and he's leaving. This will all be a memory soon. Back to real life. So what's the use of us being more than what we are?"

"You never know what's right around the corner. Plans can change, Jill. What about me and Charlie? He was leaving to take a job in New York when we met, and then he extended his stay in Denver. And then he stayed, and he stayed, and here we are. Open your mind with Rick. Don't shut the door on any possibilities. That's all I'm saying. Promise?"

"Well, it won't change the fact that I have to finish up my article, then lead a writing panel at a huge conference in Denver—which I haven't even *planned for* yet, by the way—and then cure my writer's block and write a bestselling novel so that my agent won't drop me. But hey, if it'll shut you up about Rick, then yes. I promise I'll keep an open mind."

Lindsey yawned through a giggle, and the yawn was contagious. Soon, they said their goodbyes and signed off.

Full of sugary Skittles, Jill poured the rest into two separate baggies, dependent on the colors—one bag was for her and one for Rick. She set them aside, near the stack of clean laundry she'd done earlier in the evening.

She thought about Lindsey's obnoxious pushing and prodding. Lindsey was one of those girls, part of a happy couple and wanting everyone else to be happy too. But what Jill couldn't tell Lindsey was that she felt herself falling for Rick, and it scared her. She *had* started thinking of him in every part of her day, wondering what he was doing and when she might see him next, and looking forward to it. Whenever she saw him, a flutter started in the center of her abdomen and moved upward to her heart, and she was helpless to calm it. She'd even taken greater care with her appearance, putting more thought into her outfits, her makeup. They were true signs of interest, whether she had acknowledged them or not.

But facts were facts. As they had both admitted at the bridge, long-distance relationships were impossible. They lived in two separate states, and there were no plans to change that fact. Plus, even if logistics weren't an issue, Jill had no idea how Rick truly felt about her. For all she knew, he *did* have a girlfriend back in California and only saw Jill as a descendant of the town's founder and a new friend of his grandmother's. She had no clue whether he might feel a flutter too.

Chapter Sixteen

"Look at you!" Lucille exclaimed as Jill shut the kitchen door.

Jill touched her curls, suddenly regretting her bold decision to do something she'd never done in her entire life—go natural, on purpose.

"I adore it. This style suits you!" Lucille continued, moving in closer, gazing at her hair.

Jill had awakened that morning feeling oddly adventurous. Maybe it was the recent near-death tornado experience, or maybe it was the new bakery venture. Whatever it was, it had her pausing when she picked up her hair straightener as she'd done thousands of times before. During the pause, she'd stared hard at her image in the mirror and imagined her mornings and her life, for once, without the crutch of that tool.

Gathering her courage, she'd switched off the contraption and instead massaged a dime-sized amount of conditioning gel into her hair, coating her curls. Then she'd gently dried them, careful to avoid the dreaded frizz.

Emboldened, she'd flipped her head down, picked at the curls gently, then tossed her head back again and sprayed to set them in place. For a split second, she became her little-girl self and heard all the bullies' name-calling and jabs in her mind.

Don't let them win.

Emboldened, she shoved away the jabs—all of them—and marched down her apartment steps to meet Lucille.

"Thanks," Jill responded, smiling shyly. "It's an experiment."

The corgis entered the kitchen and barked wildly at Jill.

"I don't think they recognize me."

Lucille chided them gently. "You two are silly. This is *your friend.* This is Jill!"

The barking halted as the corgis moved closer, with Jill crouching down to offer a delicate hand. The moment they sniffed her, George and Gracie's hesitation shifted into friendly hand-kisses and wiggle-bottoms.

"Well, *that's* more like it," Lucille told the corgis, then assured Jill, "They'll get used to the new look. And so will you."

As Jill stood, Rick entered the kitchen, absorbed in his phone and tapping out a text. When he reached the island, he stopped short, and his eyes rested on Jill. He blinked and said, "Wow."

"Isn't it pretty, her new hair?" Lucille prompted.

Rick's gaze remained steady on Jill as he answered his grandmother. "Beautiful."

The word hung in the air between them, erasing almost all of Jill's lingering insecurities. *Beautiful.* She nearly believed it was true.

"I think she looks exactly like that Julia Roberts person," Lucille insisted. "In the movie about that prostitute. What's it called? I can never remember movie titles."

"*Pretty Woman,*" Rick and Jill said together, both suppressing snickers.

"That's the one. Oh!" Lucille gave a sheepish grin. "That sounded awful, didn't it? The reference to the prostitute. I only meant that the actress's *hair* in that movie looked the same as Jill's."

"It's fine," Jill said. "I knew exactly what you meant. Thank you."

Flattered by all the compliments but suddenly uncomfortable with being on display, Jill asked Lucille, "Ready for our meeting?"

"Yes. I have coffee and freshly made cinnamon buns at the ready, waiting at the breakfast table! Join us, Rick?"

"I've got another call to make. Sorry." He winced and raised his phone.

"All right. We'll all get to work, then," Lucille said as Rick swiveled and left the room.

Jill joined Lucille at the table but paused when she recognized the edge of a paperback tucked behind the table's centerpiece. Touching the edge, she realized it was *her* first novel. "I thought you were trying out e-books these days," Jill said.

"I am." Lucille took a seat and saw the paperback. "Oh, that's not mine. Well, it *is* my copy from my shelf. But I guess Rick must've pulled it down. I caught him reading it last night."

Jill raised an eyebrow. She was more anxious at the thought of Rick reading and liking— or not liking—her novel than she was with any critic reading it. His opinion mattered more.

"I made some notes last night," Lucille started, flipping through her notepad. And thus began the meeting.

Jill slid the paperback aside and drew her focus back to Lucille. Once the market booth had been secured—Beatrice had phoned Lucille late last night with the good news—Jill had suggested an early-morning planning meeting with Lucille, to help get the ball rolling and to add her marketing skills to the mix. Lucille had already made the first savvy business decision without either Rick or Jill. While on the phone with Beatrice, she had finagled a prime spot for the booth, right outside her future bakery's site, which would drum up interest and would get people accustomed to buying her cookies in that very spot later on.

The morning's agenda was rather hefty with budgets, lists of supplies and ingredients, and ideas for advertising, including ordering posters and business cards in time for the market opening. Surprisingly, Lucille seemed energized by the process rather than overwhelmed. Rick's instincts about buying the bakery had been spot on.

It only took them ninety minutes to make it through the entire agenda. As Lucille checked her list again, George came to sit at Jill's feet and pawed at her leg.

"Hey, little man." She leaned down to grasp his stubby paw in a shake. Gracie saw the exchange and waddled over to vie for some attention too. Jill rubbed their ears with both hands, trying to give them equal consideration. They closed their eyes in corgi bliss.

"How do you get any work done with these two around?" Jill asked.

"It's not easy," Lucille admitted, finishing her second cup of coffee.

George gave a pitiful whine, and finally, Jill understood. "I think they need to go O-U-T."

"You've figured out the corgi code."

Jill rose from her seat and opened the back door for both dogs, who rushed happily through.

As she closed the door, Jill noticed that a photo had fallen off Lucille's memory wall. She leaned over to retrieve the faded image of a young woman squinting in the sunlight with a lanky young man at her side. They weren't touching or holding hands, just standing awkwardly, side by side. "Is this you? And Frank?" Jill carried the photo over to Lucille.

Lucille grasped it then smiled. "Oh, yes. That was taken on the day we first met. Over fifty years ago."

"Fifty years?" Jill sank into her chair, ready to hear more.

Lucille paused to recount the story. "I was eighteen, a ticket-taker at the movie theater in Austin, and Frank and his friend were going to see some awful horror picture. After he bought his ticket, Frank lingered to talk to me and ended up missing the movie altogether! Imagine that. He offered to buy me a coffee at the diner next door, and something told me to say yes, even though he was a complete stranger. Anyway, his friend was a photography major at UT—he always carried that bulky camera around with him—and he snapped this photo right after I stepped out of the booth to join Frank." She stroked the photo with her fingertip.

"I always love hearing stories about how people first met. Yours sounds like a scene right out of a movie."

Lucille chuckled. "Well, I'm not sure it was all that exciting, but I have often wondered—what if I hadn't been on my shift that day? Or what if Frank had bought his ticket at the other window, where Shirley Banks was working? Life is funny that way."

"When did you know that Frank was *it* for you? That he was the one you wanted to be with the rest of your life?"

"That's a heavy question with an easy answer." Lucille set down the photo and searched the air with her gaze, remembering back. "We were at a party together and had only been dating a few weeks. A friend of his told some dumb joke to a group of us, and Frank suddenly exploded with this deep, unexpected belly laugh. It was funnier than the joke! Absolutely infectious. And standing there, drink in hand, watching him try to catch his breath and giggling along with him, I thought to myself, 'I could hear that laugh for the rest of my life.'"

"That's adorable."

"And as the weeks progressed, I got to see his kindness, his loyalty, his integrity. They only strengthened my feelings. Frank had connected with some part of me, way deep down, like nobody else ever had." She shrugged. "That's the best way I can explain it."

"So how do you stretch those feelings out to last half a century? What was your secret?"

"Well, most people think love is roses and candlelight, but it's hard work. It's learning to compromise and live with each other's flaws and staying firm during the hard times, the ebbs and flows of a marriage. You *choose* to stay. That's how a marriage really lasts. You both make the choice, every single day, to stick it out." Lucille paused and stared down at the photo again.

Before Lucille had a chance to get emotional, Rick blustered into the room. "Gran, I've been on the phone with Hank..." His deep voice startled both Lucille and Jill, who turned in his direction. "He wants to set up a time to walk through the bakery site with you." Rick paused, looking from Lucille to Jill then back again. "I've walked in on something. What's wrong?"

"Not a thing." Lucille held up the photo between them. "Jill was asking about this. I told her how Frank and I met, and so we walked down memory lane a bit."

Rick came closer and gazed toward the photo. "So she told you the ticket-taker story?" he asked Jill. "Did she also tell you that a year later, she rejected his marriage proposal three times?"

"Seriously?" Jill's mouth dropped open.

Lucille blushed. "Well... I wanted to be sure *he* was sure and that he meant it with all his heart."

"He obviously did," Jill said.

"You want me to put this back on the wall, Gran?"

"Yes. Thank you, dear."

Rick pinned it back to its spot with ease.

"What was that about Hank?" Lucille asked.

"Oh, he wants to set up a time to go through the site with you."

Lucille consulted her list. "I happen to be free right now. Let's go!"

LUCILLE SAT ON THE living room floor, her foot propped on a pillow near the crackling fire, the corgis snoring soundly beside her. She had been thumbing through the Morgan Stout biography that Jill had given her to browse.

"I've lived in this town for decades and never knew anything about her," Lucille marveled, pointing to the text. "It says here that Morgan crafted individual baskets of food—into the hundreds—and helped distribute them to struggling war widows in Austin."

"Wasn't she amazing? The more I learned, the more honored I felt to be related to her. She's become the main point of my article, in fact."

"I can see why."

Jill joined Lucille on the floor, enjoying the rare silence as Lucille flipped to the next page. After their morning kitchen meeting, Jorge and some other men had arrived with chainsaws to clear Lucille's beloved tree. The minute the mighty trunk hit the ground, the whole house felt it. Lucille was forced to keep the corgis in the kennel most of the day, and she'd lowered the blinds in the kitchen, not wanting to witness the tree's demise. Jill had attempted to work on her article in the afternoon, but at one point, the grinding noise became so obtrusive that she packed up her laptop and took it to Christine's Bistro, where a quiet corner table and a lunch of tomato soup and Caesar salad awaited her.

Lucille continued to skim the biography while Jill focused on the paint samples sprawled out on the table. As she was about to thumb through them, her phone rang inside her pocket. She tilted the screen and saw her mother's name. *Finally!*

It would've been a struggle for Jill to untangle her legs from beneath the coffee table then push herself off the floor in time to answer the call, so she stayed put and pressed the button to answer. She didn't mind if Lucille overheard.

"Darling, hello!" Her mother's voice sounded far away, and the reception was lousy.

"Where are you?"

"I'm on a yacht. South Florida. Some new friends invited me for the Christmas holiday, so I said yes."

She could picture her mother with her phone in one hand, a glass of white wine in the other, and a younger man at her side.

"Mother, did you get any of my messages about my coming to Texas? And about Dad's ancestors?"

"Yes! Sorry—I haven't had good reception until now. You're in some little town called Marshall's Grave?"

"Morgan's Grove."

"Can you repeat that, honey? You're fading away again."

"*Morgan's Grove!*" Jill enunciated her syllables and raised her voice, realizing how ridiculous the whole conversation was.

"What's it like there?"

Before Jill could even form her answer, static invaded the line. Jill thought they'd been disconnected until she heard a faint "… losing you. Happy Holid…!" and the connection went dead.

Jill placed her phone onto the table with a generous sigh.

"Where is she right now? Your mother?" Lucille asked.

"Oh, somewhere in Florida. With 'new friends.'" She added the air quotes with dripping sarcasm.

"Rather than with you," Lucille finished, "for Christmas."

"Yes." She saw the compassion in Lucille's eyes, and before it could shift into pity, Jill added, "But it's fine. That's just my mother. I'm used to it. We'll reconnect sometime in the new year, and she'll tell me all about her holiday adventures and pretend to care about mine." Jill forced a smile. "But now I'm here in this lovely home, with a new project in front of me." She turned her attention to the coffee table and sifted through samples. "Have you narrowed these down yet?"

Lucille set the library book aside. "Actually, I'm overwhelmed. There are too many to choose from! One color looks like the next." She adjusted her glasses then stared again at the hundreds of samples before them. She chose one and held it up. "And look how tiny they are! No bigger than my thumb. How in the world am I expected to imagine an entire room covered in… Evergreen Mist?"

Jill cupped her hand over her mouth to suppress a chuckle.

"Am I amusing you?"

"Yes, actually. Because you're right. This whole system is impossible."

Jill's chuckles caught on, and Lucille let out a hearty laugh. "Oh, look at the two of us. We're hopeless."

Without any warning, not even a whimper or anticipatory growl, the corgis suddenly exploded in simultaneous watchdog barks then ran toward the kitchen door to greet Rick.

"How do the dogs always know?" Jill said. "I didn't even hear Rick pull up."

"It's those enormous ears. Frank called it 'corgi radar.' It's extremely reliable."

Rick stepped inside the living room, brushing the glistening rain beads from his hair.

"Why so late?" Lucille struggled to get up from the floor. "Are there problems with the bakery?"

Jill quietly rose up beside her, offering Lucille a hand to help her stand.

"No, nothing like that," Rick assured her, moving closer and peeling off his coat. "I was just getting some work done after the guys left. They made a lot of demo progress tonight—they ripped out the pizza oven and dismantled the buffet table. It was quiet after that, so I stuck around to have a conference call—"

"At this hour?" The three of them met together in the middle of the living room.

"Yeah, Aaron is in London. We had the call late—well, early for him." Rick held an enormous, flat book at his side. "Samples for wooden flooring." He set it down, balancing it against the sofa.

Jill sensed that Rick was unusually tired from the day, or maybe from the conference call. Or maybe something else.

Lucille must've noticed too, because she said, "You need to go sit by the fire. I'll warm up your meal."

"Need some help?" Jill offered.

Lucille waved her away. "No, no. It's good for me to feel independent again. You two go relax by the fire."

Rick obeyed his grandmother, settling on the floor with his back to the fire while Lucille slowly made her way to the kitchen, still favoring her injured ankle. Jill planted herself on the couch nearest Rick, tucking her feet underneath her.

"Looks like my grandmother's been busy today," Rick noted, glancing at the table full of paint samples.

"She's getting really pumped about the renovations."

Rick leaned forward to scratch Gracie's back in slow, long circles.

"Are you okay?" Jill studied his face for the answer, wondering how much he would give. "You don't seem like yourself tonight."

Rick settled his gaze on Jill. He told her, in hushed tones, "That phone call I took the other day, at the bakery with you and Gran. Well, there's a situation at Quantum. I thought it was handled, but it's this fire I'm having to put out. And the more I try to control it, the more it gets out of control. I'm not sure it can be stopped."

His grim expression was the same one Jill had seen for weeks, off and on, as he answered calls or talked gruffly with someone on the other end. *It isn't a girlfriend he's having problems with. It's his company.*

Jill assumed financial woes but didn't want to pry. He would tell her as much as he wanted to. "I'm sorry. Is there anything I can do?" It was a silly question, but she couldn't think of anything else to say.

Rick stretched his back. "Nope. Nothing anybody can do. I'm supposed to keep the details under wraps, and I don't want to worry my grandmother with this."

"I won't say a word."

An occasional slam or clanking of flatware could be heard from the kitchen as Lucille put together Rick's meal.

"I must've had it written all over my face when I came in." Rick's mouth curved into a half grin.

"Don't worry. Lucille only thinks you're wet and hungry. Nothing a hot meal can't fix."

"I wish it were that easy. Speaking of food, I've been wanting to ask you something. Now seems as good a time as any. Would you... I mean, I was wondering if you'd like to go out to eat with me. There's this Italian place in Austin that's supposed to be good. I just thought you and I might give it a try sometime before you leave."

It was the very last thing Jill had expected from Rick.

He rubbed his palms together. "I thought we both deserved a night off, a chance to de-stress. Maybe tomorrow night?"

"Here we are," Lucille announced in a singsong voice as she came into the room with a tray.

Jill turned confidently back to Rick and whispered, "Yes."

He shined a smile in her direction before standing to help his grandmother.

Chapter Seventeen

"It's a date." Lindsey munched on a granola bar as she stared back at Jill through the screen.

The background wasn't her parents' house—it was Lindsey's classroom. The roads to the school had been cleared of snow, and Lindsey's school had reopened, but passage in and out of Denver was still treacherous as the freezing temperatures and road closures remained.

"It's *not* a date." Jill took a sip of coffee then set it down on the table. "In fact, Rick's exact words were 'We both deserve a night off, a chance to de-stress.' I hear zero romance in that statement."

"He asked you to go to a restaurant, right?"

"Right."

"He didn't ask his grandmother to go with him, right?"

"Not that I know of."

"And he'll do the driving, right?"

"Well, right, because he knows Austin better than I do."

"It's a *date*."

Jill blew out an overdramatic sigh. "Fine. It does seem a *little* like a date, on the surface. But it doesn't make much sense. I mean, have a date and then say goodbye forever? What was he thinking? He knows I'm leaving soon."

"Maybe he likes to live in the moment and not worry so much about tomorrow. And why does it have to be forever?" Lindsey countered. "Look at us." She gestured toward the screen. "Here we are, maintaining a friendship long-distance—for weeks—using technology. People do it all the time."

"But a romance isn't the same. It fizzles fast with distance, even *with* technology. Anyway, we're getting way ahead of ourselves, here. It's just dinner."

"But dinner can always lead to more..." Lindsey raised her eyebrows twice and took another bite of granola.

Jill knew there was no convincing her friend otherwise, so she gave up. "We've talked this to death. Change the subject for me."

Lindsey bit her bottom lip, suppressing a grin. "I can definitely do that." She moved in closer with a whisper. "I was at Charlie's place last night and accidentally saw something."

"Don't keep me in suspense!"

"I was searching his drawer for a pen and noticed a velvet box stuffed into the corner."

"You mean...?"

Lindsey's smile widened. "A ring box. I *had to* crack it open and peek. Jill, it's beautiful. Pear-cut with two small diamonds on each side."

"Oh, Lindsey! It's really going to happen!"

"Christmas, I'm thinking. He's been sort of hinting around."

"Are you going to tell him that you saw the ring?"

"Of course not! I'll play the part, make him think I'm totally surprised."

Jill heard a bell in the background, and Lindsey darted her eyes from the screen. "Gotta go. The students are about to descend. Only two more days until Christmas vacation—I hope I can make it!"

"Keep me posted on things with Charlie."

They clicked off at the same time, and Jill sank back into her chair near the apartment window, peering outside at the gray day. *Lindsey, engaged. Soon to be married.*

Jill wondered how drastically their friendship would change in the coming years. Lindsey's strongest attentions would naturally shift toward bridesmaid dresses and wedding cakes, toward honeymoon venues and house-hunting, and then, eventually, toward maternity wear and late nights with a fussy infant. *Where will I possibly fit into all that?*

AT THE KITCHEN ISLAND, Lucille hummed "God Rest Ye Merry Gentlemen" and counted out the new bags and labels from the Stationery Place while Jill sat at the kitchen table and checked her list. The day was designated as a relaxed prep day before the chaos of cookie baking for the Christmas market would begin. Jill had offered to double-check the required ingredients, confirm their upcoming agenda, and stay on top of the marketing—she'd already ordered business cards, a huge poster to hang inside the bakery's window, and a professional-looking banner for the booth itself.

"That's too much for you to handle," Lucille had protested.

But the night before, Jill had stayed up until two and had finished her article—well, all except the ending, which she had struggled with. She couldn't seem to bring the details together and wrap it up in a way that would leave the reader—or herself—satisfied. The article contained everything she wanted it to: fascinating snippets about Morgan's life, a brief mention of the current residents—not by name, just generalized observations—and her own insight about finding her true heritage. But some element was still missing. Jill hadn't found the beating heart of the piece yet. She hadn't entered that zone where she got sucked into the piece in a rush of emotion until she reached the end. *It will come*, she had assured herself. *There's still time.* She'd clicked her laptop shut and decided to set it aside for the next couple of days as she helped Lucille with her cookie venture.

The plan was for Lucille to be in charge of all the baking, icing, and bagging of cookies, with Becky as her sidekick and Jill filling in the gaps where necessary. The baking would take two full days before the start of the market on Saturday morning, where Rick and Jill would man the booths so Lucille could rest if she needed to.

A question for Lucille about the grocery list was on the tip of Jill's tongue when Rick entered the kitchen, clutching his cell phone. His face was ashen.

"What's wrong?" Jill asked before Lucille could turn around and realize what state he was in.

"I have to go to California."

"Right now?" Lucille asked.

Jill stood and moved closer to join them at the island. The corgis seemed concerned, too, whining at Rick's feet.

"There's no choice."

"What on earth is wrong? You're so pale." Lucille placed a hand on her grandson's clean-shaven cheek.

"It's about the company. It's serious. They need me to handle things, and I can't do it from here. I'm sorry, Gran, but I can't tell you anything until I know more. I'll fill you in when I get back. I promise."

Jill knew it was related to the night before, when Rick had confided his general concerns about Quantum. The situation, whatever it was, had reached its breaking point.

"When will you come back?" Lucille asked. "And can you get a flight on such short notice?"

"My assistant already booked a reservation that leaves from Austin in two hours. I'll try to be back in a couple of days, if I can. In time for the—" His eyes widened as he looked at his grandmother.

She shook her head slightly.

"In time for the market."

Jill wanted to inquire about this odd exchange between them—*is there something else I don't know about?*—but figured it was some sort of nonverbal shorthand between close relatives. And it was none of her business.

"I'll help you pack," Lucille told him.

Rather than reject her offer and insist he could do it himself, Rick simply gave a nod and blinked. Even in his daze, he focused on Jill, his eyes filled with a new concern. "I don't know how long I'll be gone. Rain check for the dinner?" he whispered.

"Of course. Go. Don't worry about us. I'll help out around here."

Seemingly satisfied, he headed upstairs with Lucille.

Twenty minutes later, suitcase in hand, Rick bent forward to hug his grandmother goodbye. "Don't worry about me. Promise?"

"I'll try," she whispered, then backed away and crossed her arms at her chest.

Jill peered up into Rick's handsome face. *This could be it,* she thought. *What if he doesn't return this weekend, and I have to leave for Denver?* She shoved her insecurities aside and boldly leaned in, standing on her tiptoes for a hug. He reciprocated, squeezing her waist.

"I hope everything turns out okay," she told him.

"Me too," he whispered. As he released her, his free hand drifted down to find Jill's. He squeezed it, leaving her with extra reassurance.

After watching him head toward the garage, Lucille shut the kitchen door with a lengthy sigh. "I worry about him so," she told Jill. "It's something unsettling in his eyes. I don't like it."

Jill was grateful that Rick hadn't given her any real details about Quantum the night before. She didn't want to betray his trust by giving Lucille more information or to hold back the details and feel like she was lying to Lucille, so she told the only truth she owned as they moved toward the island together. "I have no idea what's going on. But now those intense phone calls he's been having make more sense, don't they?"

Lucille's eyes widened. "You're right. I never wanted to pry, so I didn't ask him. But now we know they had everything to do with Quantum. Bless his heart..." She trailed off and shook her head.

Rick backed his truck out of the garage while Lucille and Jill watched through the window.

After the truck disappeared, Lucille asked, "What did Rick mean about a rain check?"

"Oh. Well"—Jill hadn't actually decided whether to tell Lucille about their dinner plans. She had been leaving it up to Rick—"he invited me to an Italian place in Austin tonight." She tucked her fingers inside the ends of her sleeves, hoping the information would be sufficient for Lucille, but she could already tell it wasn't.

Lucille raised an eyebrow. "A date?"

"Oh, I don't know... more of a nice meal between friends, probably. Rick was vague about his intentions."

Lucille shook her head. "He's hard to read sometimes."

"Tell me about it."

Lucille locked eyes with Jill. "You're good for him. I've noticed it. Around you, he's... centered. Calmer, somehow. He relaxes when he's with you."

"Well, I can sense my walls coming down too."

"You have walls?"

"I've started realizing that I do." Jill considered a deeper answer and leaned against the island. "When I look back, I see how I've protected myself from getting hurt. I guess everyone does it, to some degree. But I tend to only let people see certain parts of me until I'm sure I can trust them. And the more I get to know Rick, the faster my walls are coming down. I can feel it happening every time we're together."

"You care for him, don't you?"

Jill shifted her weight to one leg. "Well, yes. Sure I do. I mean, he's become a real friend. And he's a good man. You can be very proud of him."

"He *is* a good man, isn't he?"

"He was raised right." Jill paused then chuckled. "That sounded so Texan, didn't it?"

"Yes, it did!"

"But truly, Rick's upbringing will get him through this crisis with Quantum, whatever it is. The lessons you and Frank taught him growing up were invaluable. He'll lean on them now."

Lucille's chin wobbled. "I hope you're right."

Chapter Eighteen

Speculation is a spectacular waste of time.

Jill's grandfather had said that to her when she was younger, whenever she would fret over worries that ended up being nothing at all. But as valid as that statement still was, Jill couldn't help speculating during the twenty-four hours since Rick had left for California. Thankfully, all the baking had kept her insanely busy, with hardly a moment available for fretting.

But when Becky went home for the evening and everything that needed to be done had been done—rows and rows of beautiful gingerbread cookies lined the dining room table, displaying a hard day's work and two double batches—Jill insisted on making some grilled-cheese sandwiches for herself and Lucille, as comfort food and a distraction. Her sandwiches would never be as good as Rick's, but she remembered a couple of tricks he'd used and tried them.

Halfway through the meal, Lucille picked at her potato chips and finally confessed, "I wonder what's happening."

It was a vague statement that came out of nowhere, but Jill knew exactly what she meant.

"I keep picturing Rick's face when he left," Lucille continued. "That hollow expression. He isn't one to overreact. So I'm afraid, well, that his business is crumbling. Maybe he's going bankrupt?"

That had crossed Jill's mind, too, though she didn't want to voice it. Even in the brief time she'd known Rick, she understood that he wasn't the type to overdramatize things. She remembered the tornado and how calm he was, how collected and sure. But when she'd heard the crack in his voice after the phone call sending him to California, and when she watched the color drain from his face, Jill had known it was something dire.

"Maybe not," Jill assured her. "It could be a technical issue, a glitch in the software that only Rick can fix. I mean, companies like his don't just fold. There are safety measures to prevent that sort of thing, I'm sure."

She had no real idea what she was talking about—Jill's focus in college had been primarily on small businesses and marketing, and she knew next to nothing about how multi-million-dollar corporations functioned. But she wanted to reassure Lucille, somehow.

The ringing landline startled Lucille, making her jump. Realizing that Lucille was poised to rush toward the living room phone on her weak ankle, Jill bolted from the table first. "I'll get it, don't worry."

She reached the phone within two rings, but it wasn't Rick. When Lucille approached, Jill covered the receiver with her hand and whispered, "It's Jolene, for you."

"Oh, okay." Rather than simply accept the receiver from Jill, Lucille paused then said, "I'll take it upstairs."

A lot of trouble to go through, simply to talk to Jolene, Jill thought. But before she could question Lucille or convince her otherwise, Lucille was already edging her way up the stairs, leaning on the banister.

"Lucille's getting the other line," Jill explained to Jolene, who then made small talk about the weather until Lucille finally picked up.

"I've got it, Jill. Thank you."

Jill replaced the receiver with a frown. *What's so private that Lucille can't have me within earshot?*

She returned to her plate and continued eating. Lucille rejoined her within minutes, replacing the napkin in her lap and giving no information at all about the call. "I was hoping that was Rick," she muttered, reaching for another potato chip.

"Me too. But we should hear something soon," Jill added, hoping it was true.

BY FRIDAY MORNING, Rick still hadn't called or texted either of them. Although Lucille kept her attention staunchly on the cookie baking with Becky, her cell phone was never more than two feet away, and she was ready to grab it on the first ring.

Jill spent a portion of the afternoon picking up the business cards and posters then returning to the kitchen to fill in as needed. When she saw the exhaustion on Lucille's face, Jill insisted that she go upstairs and take a nap, letting Jill and Becky finish icing and bagging the cookies. Lucille issued no protest, which confirmed how exhausted and worried she actually was.

"I'm excited about the festival," Becky told Jill, making easy chitchat as she smoothed icing onto a cookie.

Becky had been a welcome presence in the house, with her youthful outlook and upbeat attitude. Sophisticated for a seventeen-year-old but not overly so, Becky looked as though she'd stepped right out of a magazine for clean-cut, fresh-faced teens who were vying for valedictorian. Her shiny blond hair spilled over her shoulders as she smiled through her lip gloss.

Jill set aside a finished cookie then reached for another one. As much as she still loved the gingerbread, she was no longer tempted to snatch a piece for herself during the process. The cookies had become just business. "Me too," she replied. "I've never been to a winter festival before."

"Never? Oh gosh, you'll love it." Her twangy accent told Jill she'd lived in Texas her entire life. "There's so much to do. There's a concert and a parade. I'm in it this year, matter of fact. I'm Miss Morgan's Grove High."

"Congratulations," Jill said, and she meant it, knowing Becky would wear the title well.

It only took another hour of work between them before all the cookies were iced. "I'll bag them up," Jill insisted. "You can go on home. It'll be a long day tomorrow with the booth."

Earlier, Becky had offered to help Jill transport all the cookies and necessary supplies to the booth and then to take Rick's place selling the cookies if he didn't make it back to town by then.

When Becky left, Jill felt suddenly antsy. She slipped on her coat, wrapped her scarf around her neck, then stepped onto the back porch with her phone and Googled Quantum. Nothing special came up, nothing new. Then she searched for Patrick Wright. Surely, even as low-key as Rick tried to remain, if his company was in grave trouble, it would've already made the news.

But neither search turned up anything significant. Quantum's crisis hadn't made the headlines yet, which she hoped was a good sign.

She had planned to leave Rick alone and let him contact her first, giving him privacy to work everything out on his own, but she couldn't help herself. She texted him a nonchalant message: *Everything fine here. Ready for tomorrow's market.* She paused then added, *How are things going? We're worried about you.*

It took less than a minute for Rick to respond: *Rough day, but made it through. Thanx for asking. Sorry I can't make it tomorrow. Impossible.*

She read the text twice, sad that he'd confirmed he was staying in California but smiling because he had responded at all. Knowing he was thousands of miles away but could still have an instant conversation with her right there on Lucille's back porch felt oddly intimate to Jill. She pictured Rick during a flurry of stressful meetings, making serious decisions inside a serious boardroom, with possibly his whole company and his whole future on the line. No warmth, no laughter, no home-cooked meals or festive gingerbread cookies to go home to. No corgis, no Lucille. No Jill. She imagined him hearing the beep on his phone, expecting bad news about Quantum then seeing Jill's friendly, inquisitive text instead. And perhaps he had smiled too. Hopefully, her snippet of a message had provided him with a familiar slice of home and of safety, right there in his pocket.

She took a chance and tapped out, *No worries, Becky's helping. A call to Lucille would be nice. She's getting frantic.*

When he didn't respond, she figured he'd already switched off his phone and didn't see the text. But at least he'd received her first one and knew she was thinking about him, that someone, somewhere, cared about what was happening in California. He wasn't alone.

Jill remained on the porch for a bit, gazing out at the darkening skyline.

After a few minutes, when the cold air became too much to bear, she returned to the kitchen, surprised to see Lucille and the corgis entering from the living room.

"Oh, there you are!" Lucille said. "Rick phoned! It was wonderful, hearing his voice."

"How did he sound?"

"We only spoke for a minute—I could tell he was rushed. He sounded exhausted, poor thing. I asked if he was eating and sleeping enough. He said he was, but I don't believe him."

"Did he give you any news about the company?" Jill was hoping for a tidbit, something to grasp.

"Nothing. I tried to pry without prying, but it didn't work. He told me he's been in meetings all day and that he'd eventually have a better idea of how this thing would all pan out. He called it a 'thing'!" She clucked her tongue. "Men. Don't they realize we need details?"

Jill chuckled at Lucille's frustration and Rick's vagueness. At least he had called. That was something.

Lucille shook her head. "I wish he would let me in and tell me what's going on. How can I help if I don't know what's going on?"

Jill walked toward Lucille and clutched her hands for reassurance. "It's his way of protecting you until he knows more. It's all going to work out. We just need to trust him."

As she said the words, she actually believed them. He would know what to do. And when it was time, he would let Lucille in. He would let them both in.

AS JILL CRAWLED INTO bed hours later, her entire body weary from the past few days, she thought of Rick's text again, and a memory struck her of something Lucille had recently said: "You *care* for him."

Jill clicked off the light and rolled onto her side, pulling the comforter up higher and curling her hands underneath her chin. She stared out the window at the slice of moonlight shining through. She thought about Rick and saw his dark eyes, which could flash from empathy to mystery in a single blink; his thick, rumpled hair with a tiny hint of gray forming at the temples; his capable, masculine hands that could roll out cookie dough, clear away debris after a storm, wrestle playfully with the corgis, or tap out brilliant business ideas in an email. Then she thought of his heart, damaged from the loss of a mother and father he never really knew, vulnerable from a grandfather's tough love, and untrusting because of people who were only interested in his wealth or fame.

Her mind drifted over the past couple of days without Rick. She'd experienced a nagging pull the entire time, a sense that a valuable piece of her day was missing, an empty spot in her life that kept waiting to be filled. Each time she had entered Lucille's kitchen over those two days, her mind immediately pictured Rick somewhere inside the house. But he wasn't there, and it seemed jarring. Something was out of place.

"You care for him."

Jill shifted onto her back and stared at the ceiling. The empty sensation she'd felt a moment before was more comfortable than the bigger question Lucille had posed. *Of course I care for him. But how much? To what degree?*

She wanted to examine it rationally, to remove her emotions from the equation and remain objective. Naturally, she had become accustomed to seeing Rick on a daily basis, even on weekends. It was a habit, a pattern. And when anything, be it technology, an activity, or a person, was removed from one's usual routine, it would be missed. It made perfect logical sense. And for her, that "anything" happened to be Rick. Nothing more, nothing less.

Satisfied, she rolled over to her other side and closed her eyes.

MELANCHOLY OVERCAST skies, gusty winds, and forty-eight-degree temperatures were not the most ideal conditions for kicking off a cheery holiday festival. But nothing would stop Jill and Becky from selling the cookies, not after all their work and effort.

Suffering from a mild headache, Lucille agreed to stay at home and recuperate. Perhaps she would visit the market and booth that afternoon, if she felt better. Meanwhile, it took Becky and Jill three individual trips to load up both of their cars with cookie bins, a tote containing the flyers and other essentials, two folding chairs and a table, the box for petty cash, and a mini-cooler Lucille had packed the night before with lunches. The town square's rules relaxed during the festival, and cars were allowed to park briefly at the curbs while vendors unpacked their wares. Jill admitted to herself, as she lugged her end of the table into Becky's ample SUV, that she wished Rick was there. He'd been such a big part of the whole endeavor—the future bakery, the market ideas, the overall support—and he was missing it. And she was missing him.

At the bakery site, it only took a few minutes to unload everything, but setting up the booth presented its own set of problems. Jill battled with gusts of wind as she struggled to secure her posters and prevent the business cards from flying away. At one point, when Becky had clamped her hand down on one end of the tablecloth and Jill had lost control at her end, Becky started to laugh and couldn't stop.

"Look at us," she said between gasps. "It's like we're part of a wacky sitcom!"

Jill had to stop and laugh, too, which broke the tension. After that, the setup was easier, and they took it in stride, not caring if things went wrong. They were there and the festival was about to begin, and that was all that mattered.

As Jill unfolded her chair, planning to catch her breath for a moment before selling the cookies, she realized hordes of people were already starting to arrive, thirty minutes before the official opening time. Adults and children had begun to stream through the square, eager to take it all in, itching to get the festival started. The wind had begun to subside, and the clouds had parted, letting in an actual ray of sunshine.

The entire town was dressed up in its finery. The square seemed even more Christmassy, if that was possible, with dressed-up elves walking around and jingling their cap bells, and a madrigal standing on the corner of the courthouse, practicing Christmas carols. Then there were the booths—white tents, open on all sides. The tents lined the blocks around the courthouse, spaced perfectly apart, and Jill imagined the committee members' husbands putting them together in the wee hours of the morning, measuring the feet in between. Every business in the square had set up elaborately decorated tables inside their tents, which displayed their wares. Some offered free hot chocolate or free lollipops or face painting for the children.

"All we have are *cookies*," Becky whispered to Jill. "Maybe we should've brought candy canes to hand out to the kids. Bribe them to come to our table. Oh! We should've brought Lucille's corgis!"

Jill chuckled. "Trust me, they would be too big a handful for us. I think the cookies will stand on their own. Once word gets around, we'll be swarmed."

Jill was right. The moment they'd set out the boxes, it was bees to honey, with practically everyone in the town visiting the booth along with some tourists from out of town. Most of the customers noticed Jill's sign attached to the window of the upcoming bakery behind the booth—*FUTURE SITE OF LUCILLE'S COOKIES!*—and asked questions about the new business. Jill recognized many familiar faces amongst the customers, who felt more like old friends than new ones, including Bicycle Bob, Mr. Anderson from across the street, Tessa and Darlene, who bickered over how many cookies to purchase for themselves, and the Cox family with all five of their young children.

Mrs. Haversham from the B&B had been one of their first customers. "I'll take a dozen," she'd said, fishing out the cash from her wallet. "For my son," she added.

Jill remembered that Mrs. Haversham sent care packages to him in Afghanistan every week, containing snacks and books and letters. She even kept an open cardboard box near the B&B's front door for townspeople who wanted to contribute items. Jill could picture him opening up the fragrant package of gingerbread and sharing with his fellow soldiers as they celebrated a bleak Christmas Eve overseas. When she'd labored over the cookies the night before, Jill had no idea they would be making a trip all the way across the world. And for a moment, they weren't just cookies anymore.

"Put your money away," Jill told Mrs. Haversham quietly. "These are on me."

IN THE EARLY AFTERNOON, Lucille stopped by, free of her headache, to check on things. "These are all you have left?" She peeked inside the plastic tub, which contained fewer than twenty cookies.

"That's all," Jill confirmed, handing change to a customer. "At this rate, we'll have to make a decision. Do we pack up early and save tomorrow's cookies for tomorrow, or go back to your house, get them, and use them up today?"

Lucille chewed her lip and considered it. "I say we finish strong today, early, then save the others for tomorrow. We could leave out the posters and make people curious. Even if they pass by the booth and there's nothing here this afternoon, maybe they'll come back tomorrow."

Jill agreed. "Nice strategy. And it's a good problem to have, running out of cookies earlier than expected."

"Indeed, it is."

An hour later, their voices hoarse from talking to customers, cheeks sore from smiling, and bodies weary from stooping over the table and lifting tables and chairs, Jill and Becky headed back to Lucille's.

Inside, Lucille spooned out generous portions of vegetable soup for herself and for Jill. Becky declined the invitation to eat but promised to be back at the house early for the second day of selling cookies. Lucille sent Becky on her way with a tight thank-you hug and a Tupperware bowl of soup.

Rather than feeling the deep exhaustion in her bones that she had expected, Jill realized she felt strong and happy. It had been a satisfying day's work, a team effort with successful results. Earlier at the booth, she had pulled out her phone then texted Rick: *Success! Sold all the cookies.* She hadn't heard anything from him yet and hadn't expected to, but she still wanted to catch him up on the day's events.

"Did you hear anything from Rick?" Jill asked Lucille, who poured sweet tea into her own glass before sitting down.

"Not a peep." She grimaced. "Maybe no news is good news."

"Let's hope so."

Lucille folded her hands together in her lap. "I have a proposition for you. I know it's been a busy day, and we have another one tomorrow. But we deserve a break, don't you think? The last thing I want to do is sit in this house and worry about Rick or laze around and watch movies. I've been cooped up too long with this foot of mine, and it's finally on the mend. The cookies are all set for tomorrow, and there's nothing else to prep. What do you say—are you up for a night out?"

"What did you have in mind?" Truthfully, staying indoors and watching movies under a thick blanket had sounded ideal to Jill after a day like the one she'd had.

"The founder's mansion. I haven't been able to visit this season, and I'm dying to see it at nighttime, all decorated. We can wait until nightfall—get a little rest beforehand—then be all primped and ready to go."

"Primped?"

"Sure, let's make it fancy. I'll wear my gold dress with the sparkles."

Just for the mansion? Jill pictured the usual tourists there, dressed in their jeans and flannel jackets. "Is there a fancy dress code at night?"

"No, just something I felt like doing. It's a rare night when I go to a ritzy mansion and play the part."

Jill did a quick mental assessment of her limited wardrobe upstairs. When she'd packed for Morgan's Grove weeks before, she hadn't added any formal attire. There had been no need. Then she remembered: "I bought a 'fancy' dress at Mindy's Boutique." Jill had kept it tucked safely in its wrapping paper at the back of the closet, prepared for its eventual drive home to Colorado. "I saw it in the store window and had to have it. I had planned on wearing it to the cocktail party at the writing conference in January. In Denver. But I could wear it tonight, I guess..."

"That's the spirit!"

Still puzzled by the elaborate dress code, and by Lucille's extreme sudden interest in seeing the mansion *that night*, Jill wanted to be a good sport and play along. It actually sounded fun, a spur-of-the-moment drive to a beautiful mansion with glittering lights. Besides, she'd been meaning to visit the mansion one more time before she left Morgan's Grove, anyway, and she hadn't seen it yet at night, all sparkly and lit up.

"Okay. Count me in."

Chapter Nineteen

Jill pivoted toward the full-length mirror attached to the apartment's bathroom door and took a lingering look at herself, head to toe. Her hair was tamed to curled perfection, her makeup enhanced for the special evening, and the forest-green dress hung just below her knees, as beautiful as she'd remembered at the boutique. She found her thick black coat then headed downstairs, where Lucille waited inside the kitchen door.

"Well, aren't we a stylish pair tonight?" Jill remarked, seeing Lucille dressed in a long skirt and a thick tan coat that covered a sparkly blouse.

"Dressed to the hilt!" Lucille agreed, gesturing toward Jill.

And off they went.

As Jill's headlights shone down the elongated entrance toward the stately manor, she noticed at least two dozen cars parked all around. "We're not the only ones who had this idea tonight," she noted.

"Oh, yes," Lucille assured her. "Seeing the mansion at night is very popular. It's a Christmas tradition for a lot of folks."

"I can see why." Jill gazed up through her windshield toward the lights adorning the gables and porch.

They exited the car, then Jill helped Lucille up the short staircase to the porch, halting at the sign posted outside the door: *"MANSION CLOSED FOR PRIVATE PARTY."*

Jill's shoulders sank. *All this trouble for nothing.* "Oh well," she told Lucille. "Maybe we can try again another night."

"Nonsense," Lucille answered with a sly grin, her eyebrows slightly raised. "We have an invitation."

"We do?"

Lucille pushed the door open to a puff of warm, soothing air and stepped inside. Past her shoulder, Jill could see at least forty people facing them, clustered together near the staircase, each dressed in semiformal attire and holding a wine glass.

"Merry Christmas!" they shouted collectively as Lucille shut the door behind them.

Jill assumed it was a yearly traditional party thrown for the town—*but why all the secrecy from Lucille?* Jill's eyes roamed above the guests' heads to a banner hanging from the staircase, which gave the answer: *"For Jill, Honorary Resident of Morgan's Grove."*

"I don't understand," Jill whispered to Lucille.

"This is all for you," she explained, smiling. "A party in your honor. A descendant of our founder."

Jolene appeared from within the crowd and handed Jill a glass of champagne. Then Jolene pivoted to address the whole group. "We all adore our founder, Mr. Alfred J. Stout, and his family. And here, in his home, where he first discovered our little town of Morgan's Grove, it's appropriate that we honor Jill McCallister, one of his direct descendants." She turned toward Jill and spoke more softly. "We're so glad you found us and that you've spent time here. You fit right in, and you will *always* have a place here. Consider Morgan's Grove your second home."

"Hear, hear!" shouted Bicycle Bob from the corner, and others joined in, raising their glasses high.

Still dazed from such an unexpected outpouring, Jill managed to skim the crowd and see many familiar faces: The Pit sisters, Chaynie from the library, Mrs. Haversham, Becky, and many of the shop owners she was used to seeing on an almost-daily basis. Jill put the pieces together—Lucille had been acting strangely, pressuring her to visit the mansion and insisting on dressing to the nines. Suddenly, even that odd phone call Lucille had received from Jolene the other day made perfect sense. *How long had they been planning this?*

Jolene cleared her throat for one last announcement. "I have a special gift for Jill, on behalf of the founder's mansion and the town of Morgan's Grove." She handed her glass to a nearby guest then produced a flat, velvety box the size of her palm. "This was the necklace that Alfred gave to his daughter, Morgan, on her sixteenth birthday. It's her birthstone. The necklace has lived in this mansion for many decades, under glass. But the board members discussed it, and we've unanimously decided that this piece of jewelry deserves to have a new home and a new owner."

She handed the box to Jill, who gave her glass to Lucille. With all eyes watching, Jill tipped open the box while sensing the uniqueness of the moment. She wanted to slow down and savor it.

Inside the box, lying daintily on a velvet pillow, she found a pear-cut amethyst hanging from a silver chain. Jill let out a gasp and touched the jewel. She told Jolene quietly, "I can't accept this."

"Oh yes, you can." Jolene carefully removed the necklace from its case. "It's yours by birthright. We all agree."

Jill accepted the gift wordlessly then let Jolene drape the chain around her neck.

As Jolene clasped it securely with nimble fingers, she explained to the group: "There's a legend that goes along with the necklace. Alfred purchased it during one of his European travels. The piece was originally created for a beautiful duchess, who lived a long and happy life on the outskirts of London. The legend says that before passing the piece down to her granddaughter, she proclaimed, 'The wearer of this necklace will experience love in her life for all the days of her life.' This was true for Morgan Stout, and may it also be true for its new owner."

Jill raised her fingers to touch the delicate amethyst. "I don't know what to say." She looked out toward the residents of Morgan's

Grove, who'd gone to so much trouble to surprise her. Then she glanced toward Lucille, whose eyes were glistening.

"Thank you," Jill whispered to her. Then, more loudly, toward the crowd, she said, "Thanks to you *all* for this. For everything. For making me feel welcome here."

Another burst of merry cheers erupted, then Jolene announced to the group: "There's food in the dining room—help yourselves. The mansion will stay open until nine, so feel free to mingle."

"I'm shocked by everything. When did you put all this together?" Jill asked Lucille, still touching the amethyst while the guests dispersed and wandered toward the buffet.

"When I learned you were snowed in and would be staying awhile, I thought this would be a perfect way to let the town show you how special your visit has been. You are a resident of Morgan's Grove, and you always will be."

"Thank you."

"And Rick helped too."

Lucille pointed far into the corner to where Rick stood, wearing a navy suit. He raised his glass toward Jill. He'd been there, hidden at the back of the crowd, all that time.

"He didn't want to miss it," Lucille explained as Jill kept her eyes locked on Rick. "He texted me earlier, let me know he was on his way. I wasn't sure he would make it—he must've come straight from the airport." She patted Jill's arm then made her way toward the dining room, leaving Jill and Rick alone in the wide entryway.

They met each other in the center, near the Christmas tree. Jill felt a wave of shyness as she looked up at him. He was clean-shaven and wore a crisp suit and light-gray tie. She'd never seen him so dressed up and professional. Finally, he looked the part of multimillionaire, but his eyes held a mixture of fatigue and anguish. He'd aged five years since Wednesday.

He managed a smile. "Surprised?"

"Completely. I can't believe you're here."

"It was time to come home."

"Are things okay? With Quantum?" She said it softly.

Rick's body language gave nothing away. "It's a very long story. But I can tell you later. This party is about you. Gran wanted to do something before you left, to show what you've meant to the town. And to her."

Jill hadn't welled up once, not during Jolene's speeches or all the cheers, or even with the gift of the necklace. But with Rick standing there, knowing what it cost him to be there and hearing about the time and trouble Lucille had gone to, Jill felt the hint of tears. "I'm honored. Your grandmother is such a special woman."

"So are you." Rick leaned in to graze her cheek with a lingering kiss. She closed her eyes and accepted it, aware of his lips close to hers. He backed away, holding his soft gaze steady on her.

"Where's our guest of honor?!" she heard Bob shout from the other room.

Jill shook her head and grinned. "Guess I'm being summoned."

"Sounds like it. Would you mind if I slipped out early? I've got a couple of calls to make, and—"

"Of course, go ahead."

"I'll meet you and Gran at the house later."

He stroked her arm before walking past her and out the front door. A hint of his aftershave remained in the air as she walked toward the dining room filled with people who were eager to make her the center of attention once more.

NORMALLY, AFTER AN evening filled with light music, polite conversation, and bubbly champagne, Jill would have peeled off her coat, kicked off her shoes, and sunk into her bed with a satisfied sigh.

But the moment she and Lucille left the mansion, every nerve in her body teemed with anxiety as she thought about Rick and wondered how his trip was—how *he* was. He had bravely given nothing away at the mansion, and even Lucille hadn't had the chance to speak with him. Jill drove slightly over the speed limit, hoping Lucille wouldn't notice, then brought her car to a careful halt in its driveway spot.

As she helped Lucille out, Jill noticed Rick's shadow through the kitchen window and coaxed her heart rate down. They opened the door to the sight of him snacking on a sandwich, his coat removed, his tie disheveled. Jill immediately noticed the absence of dogs swirling at their feet—Rick must have let them outside. He abandoned the sandwich to accept his grandmother's tight hug.

"I'm glad you're here," she muttered into his shoulder.

Backing out of the hug, she kept her hands on his arms and looked him straight in the eyes. "How are you?"

Instead of giving a reassuring nod and saying he was okay, he shrugged. "I need to talk to you about everything. Let's go sit." He pointed toward the living room as Lucille released her grasp and moved in that direction.

When Rick pivoted toward her, Jill whispered, "Maybe this is a conversation for just the two of you. She needs you right now..."

But Rick grasped Jill's hand gently. "I want you here. Stay. Please."

When she nodded, he led her into the den, where Lucille sat straight-backed, waiting. As they approached her, Rick took a seat beside his grandmother while Jill sat on the loveseat nearby.

"I'm not sure where to begin." Rick shifted forward, rested his elbows on his knees, and let his tie dangle. He stared at the floor then cleared his throat. "It all started three weeks ago, when I came to Morgan's Grove to surprise Gran. I got a call from James, my vice president. A discrepancy had been found in the records by Lily, our head accountant. James said that Lily would follow up on it, do some digging. I told them to keep it quiet between the three of us, and I trusted them to work it out, hoping it was just an error that could be corrected. But a week later, James called again, saying the discrepancies were worse than we first thought. Enormous, in fact. They amounted to hundreds of thousands, maybe even a couple million over the years. Stolen."

"Oh, Rick," Lucille whispered.

"It gets worse." He raised his eyes to his grandmother. "At that point, it became a legal issue. James and Lily met with the authorities, and then, because of the amount and because it was clearly an embezzlement case, the feds got involved. I've had multiple video conferences with them over the weeks. They needed my testimony, though I didn't have much to contribute. I hire people to take care of the finances. That's not my thing. Looking back, though..." He ran his hand through his hair and moved his gaze back to the floor, whispering, "Man, maybe it should've been. Maybe all this wouldn't have happened."

Lucille clasped his hand, and Jill saw him squeeze it before continuing. "After my interviews, there was nothing more we could do but wait. The feds had things under control on their end and kept on with their investigation. And we had to keep it quiet. Nobody knew about it. Only myself, Lily, James, and Mark."

"Who's Mark?" Jill asked.

"My partner. We started Quantum together, after UT."

"Oh, your roommate. Right."

"So anyway, the call I got on Wednesday, the night I went to California, was the federal prosecutor updating me on their investigation."

"Did they find the thief?" Lucille asked.

"They found everything. Dates, bank account transfers, dummy accounts. It wasn't a one-time thing. This had been carefully planned and executed over years."

"Oh my stars. I can't believe this." Lucille's face was pained. "Who would do such a horrible thing?"

"That's the part you won't believe." Rick stared hard at his grandmother. His voice cracked as he said, "It was Mark."

Lucille's mouth fell open as she blinked hard. "That's impossible."

"I thought so too. But all the evidence pointed straight at him."

"This doesn't make sense. You mean, Mark sat there for weeks, knowing this whole investigation was going on? He didn't have a conscience and come clean to you? Or panic and try to leave the country?"

"He did try. The feds found him packing when they arrested him."

Lucille's expression shifted from shock to anger within seconds. "Mark. It's unreal. He was your friend. Your very best friend. Your roommate and partner. How could he—"

"I don't understand either, Gran. I never will."

Jill didn't know Mark, but she didn't have to in order to see how painful it was for Rick. She couldn't imagine trusting someone that much, knowing someone for years, then being bitterly betrayed. It was unthinkable.

"This is devastating. I'm so sorry." Jill knew how shallow it sounded under the circumstances. "How does it stand now? What happened during your trip?"

"The feds needed me there to finalize their investigation before pressing charges, and conference calls weren't enough. I spent a couple of days with them privately, being interviewed. I also met secretly with James and Lily, planning out how to do damage control and reassure our investors. And figuring out how to rebound from all this as a company. Mark was arrested early this morning."

Rick was clearly in business mode, using a matter-of-fact tone to explain everything. But Jill wondered if he had even tested the waters inside himself to understand what the betrayal meant to him, personally.

Lucille was sniffing back tears as Rick stretched his long arm around her. "Don't worry, Gran. We'll be fine. Really. The financial loss didn't do any permanent damage. Quantum will recover, stronger than ever. I'm not worried."

"But *Mark*..." Lucille shook her head. "He's been in this house, eaten my food, and attended parties here. I've known him since he was ten years old and considered him a member of this family. It's such a betrayal of all of us."

"I know." He patted her shoulder.

She snatched a tissue from a box nearby to wipe a falling tear. "Did you speak with him after the arrest? What on earth did he have to say for himself?"

"I went to see him at the jail this morning, before my flight. I had to look him in the eye, see for myself. He sobbed most of the time, kept apologizing. He's ashamed, claimed he has a sickness. That he did it for the thrill. Explained it as an addiction, something he couldn't control." Rick shook his head. "I don't understand it."

"You mean, like a mental disorder?" asked Jill. "Kleptomania?"

"On a grand scale." Rick nodded. "The biggest shame of it is, he has a family—a wife, two kids. And it's not their fault, what he did. They had no idea about it. I'm going to see that they're taken care of. They shouldn't have to pay for his mistakes."

"Oh, Rick." Lucille took in a deep breath. "What a nice gesture."

"It's the right thing to do. And like I said, the company will recover just fine, eventually."

"But will you?" Lucille asked.

After a pause, Rick said, "Yes. I will be fine. What else can I be?"

"What happens next?" Jill asked. "A trial?"

"It depends on the lawyers and their process. It could go to trial, but it'll take a while—months at least, maybe years. He'll get at least a five-year sentence. That's minimum."

"I wish you hadn't gone through this alone," Lucille said, half-scolding. "I can't *believe* you didn't say anything!"

Jill couldn't believe it, either. For all the weeks she'd known him, Rick had been quietly enduring the trial of his life.

"I couldn't talk about it," Rick explained. "I was bound. But it'll be all over the internet soon, Mark's arrest. It's why I wanted to come to Morgan's Grove and avoid the press as long as I can."

"I'm glad you did. You're safe here," Lucille reassured him. Her spunky tone was back. It was a put-on, a mask, but she was doing it for Rick as a show of solidarity. "And I'll bet you're famished."

"I was having a sandwich when y'all came in."

"Nonsense. I made soup this afternoon. You need something hearty and comforting in your stomach."

"Food. The perfect cure for everything, eh?" Rick quipped.

"You're darned right!" Lucille insisted. "Sometimes it's the only cure."

Rick squeezed his grandmother's shoulder and whispered "thank you" before she rose to prepare the meal.

When she left the room, Jill turned toward Rick. "I don't even know what to say. I'm sorry that I can't do anything to make this better. I feel sort of helpless."

"It's okay." He gave her a soft smile. "It's enough for me to be here, at home. It's all I need."

Chapter Twenty

Standing in the middle of Lucille's living room, Jill scanned the tote bags, the cookie containers, and the cash box to make sure she'd included all the items they would need for day two of the festival. She didn't want to forget anything.

Rick hadn't emerged from his room yet that morning, and Jill hadn't expected him to. The night before, he'd eaten an enormous bowl of Lucille's soup and some crusty bread, taken a sleeping pill, and gone straight to bed. But as Jill picked up a plastic tub of gingerbread cookies, she heard Rick call out to her.

"Here. Let me get that."

He stood at her side, showered, shaved, and wearing a coat and gloves, ready to go. He relieved her of the tub.

"What are you doing up? It's early."

"Not that early for me. Couldn't sleep much."

"Any new developments with Quantum?"

Rick propped the tub against the sofa's arm. "Nothing new. I'm still fielding frantic calls and texts from nervous investors and employees. It'll be like that all day as the word gets out. But I can't stay up in that room anymore. Put me to work."

"Well, you could help me load all this." She gestured toward the rest of the items that she had planned to lug to the car by herself. Becky had kept the table and chairs in her SUV the day before and was going to meet Jill at the booth for setup.

"Sure. And I can sell cookies too, just as we'd planned."

Jill couldn't believe his casual offer to man the booth when everything had changed. The night before, she had let her curiosity pique as she scrolled online to see what the media might already be saying about Quantum. It only took a few seconds for Jill to see that Rick was right, unfortunately. The media had pounced on the story and were devouring it like hungry buzzards on a kill. Jill had scrolled through story after story, and the dominating image was a photo of Mark being yanked away in handcuffs from his family, who stood in the background at the doorway of their home, his wife sheltering their two children.

Jill wondered how the press could be so heartless to seek the man out at his home, snap such a photo, and spread it all around the world. She finally understood why Rick despised those so-called journalists and had worked hard to avoid them. She was surprised they weren't already on Lucille's doorstep, clamoring for an interview.

And yet, instead of hiding indoors, Rick wanted to participate in a public festival. *Shouldn't he still be upset about Mark? Shouldn't he be making more calls, checking on his corporation, worrying about the fallout, and wringing his hands over everything?* But there he was, back in action and offering to help as though nothing else mattered more than selling gingerbread at a booth in a small Texas town.

But perhaps that was the point. The festival and the cookies could become a shaft of light in a dark tunnel, a way out of the misery of the embezzlement scandal. The town could provide an escape hatch, even if only a temporary one.

Rick gave a half grin. "Why do you keep looking at me like that? Did you expect me to stay upstairs forever?"

"No. But... honestly? This festival isn't your thing—sitting for hours, chatting with people, selling cookies while festive music plays in the background. I just didn't think you'd be in the mood for it, especially today. Becky and I have it covered. It's really okay."

"Hey, I can be sociable," Rick countered, "when I want to be. I made it to the party last night, didn't I?"

"You certainly did." Jill could still feel his kiss on her cheek.

"*What* are you doing?!" Lucille came into the room and stood with hands on hips in front of her grandson.

"I told you I'd participate in the festival, so here I am. Participating."

She softened. "But that was before all the stuff with Mark happened. Rick, you need more time off. Take the whole day—lounge, breathe, sleep. It's why you came back home, to rest."

"Gran, that's the last thing I need. I'm fine, trust me. There's nothing I can do to change the Quantum situation. Why sit around and get maudlin over it? I need to stay busy."

Lucille shook her head. "You are so much like your grandfather."

As if to prove her point, Rick lifted the tub. "It's a done deal, Gran. Jill and I will handle the booth for you. Won't we?"

"We've got this, Lucille. I promise. And Becky will help out too, when we need her."

"Well, all right. Only if you're sure."

"We are," Rick and Jill said in synch.

AFTER THREE HOURS OF selling cookies, Jill and Rick were down to one plastic tub. Rick had been jovial to all the customers, chatting when needed, answering questions about the soon-to-open bakery, wishing them a merry Christmas, and acting like he meant it.

During an unusual lull, as Jill counted the rest of the cookies, she felt Rick's stare. She gave him a side-eye. "What?"

He set down his bottled water. "Nothing. I was thinking that you're really good at this."

Jill abandoned the tub and turned to face him squarely. "Good at what? Counting cookies?"

"That and everything else. You have a knack for things—marketing savvy, communicating with people, baking. You make everything look easy."

"Well, I learned the baking part from Lucille. I had zero interest in it before I came to Morgan's Grove."

As she spoke, Rick had reached toward her neck to close a gap in her scarf. "I like your hat. It matches your eyes."

Her hat wasn't anything special, just a chocolate-brown knit cap with a silly puffball on top. When she'd slipped it onto her head and looked in the mirror, she watched her curls spill out over her shoulders. And for the first time in her whole life, she actually loved her hair. "Thanks," she told him, feeling that familiar flutter again.

A man cleared his throat nearby, a new customer.

"I'll get this one," Rick offered.

Before she returned to her cookie counting, Jill noticed the sun peeking out, spreading thin shards of light through gray clouds over the square.

"Beautiful," she whispered then remembered that she'd forgotten to snap pictures of everything: the sky, the cookies, the busy square, even Rick. She had promised Lindsey a pictorial essay about the festival.

As she snapped the final photo, she realized that Rick had struck up quite a lengthy conversation with a rare male customer—the majority of festival-goers were women and children.

They were discussing basketball, and Rick was smirking. "Yeah, their defense is a joke this season. They sure didn't get their money's worth with the new coach."

The customer was in his mid-thirties and dressed in khaki pants and a dark jacket. "Exactly. And what about Tyler? Talk about a joke. Certainly not worth the money and hype."

Jill never understood the appeal of sports, but it always fascinated her to watch two men discussing it as if it was the most important thing in the world, as though people's lives depended on the statistics and scores and plays. And it created a unique sort of temporary male bonding, sometimes between total strangers. At least Rick was being given a small break from all the mothers and kids who'd been visiting. He finally had another guy to talk to.

"So how many would you like?" Rick asked the man, rubbing his hands together.

"How many?" The man seemed to forget why he was at the booth. "Oh. Umm. Yeah. Cookies." He fished around inside his pocket. He produced a small wad of cash and a cell phone. "Guess I'll take one."

Rick handed over the bag. "That'll be three dollars."

The man counted out the bills then said casually, "Hey, so, you're Patrick Wright, aren't you? Owner of Quantum Software."

Jill saw Rick stiffen. "Why do you want to know?"

The man held his phone higher between them and said, "How does it feel, knowing your partner was stealing money from you all those years? Looking back, were the signs evident?"

That cell phone wasn't just a phone—it was a recording device. The overly friendly basketball-loving guy wasn't a customer at all. He was a sleazy reporter in disguise, charming his victim before moving in for the kill. It made Jill's skin crawl.

"No comment," Rick said, his tone sharp and terse.

"You need to leave," Jill told the man, her eyes narrowing. The customer line was growing again, and she didn't want a scene. "We're here selling cookies. That's all. Leave us be."

But the man planted himself, locking eyes with Rick. He wasn't going anywhere. The phone came even closer, a few inches from Rick's mouth. "But the people want to know. Do you feel betrayed? Angry? And how can the shareholders ever trust Quantum again? Will this shake the customers' faith in the company?"

"Look, pal—"

"You were once roommates with Mark Sullivan. Did he show any criminal tendencies back then?"

At that, Rick took an angry step forward, his thigh bumping the table between them.

When Jill saw Rick's hand rise to snatch the guy's phone, or maybe even to slug him, Jill grasped Rick's elbow. "Rick..." she whispered gently.

Breathing fast, Rick froze, his icy stare still focused on the reporter. Then he lowered his hand. "You need to leave," he told the man through clenched teeth. "Now."

The line grew even longer as approaching customers gawked, riveted by the exchange. It was quickly becoming a spectacle and had to be defused.

"Listen to the man," said a voice from behind.

Lenny, dressed in his crisp police uniform, came to stand beside Rick, his giant arms crossed tightly across his massive chest. He stared down the reporter. "It's time to move along."

The reporter hesitated then glanced around at the waiting customers, whose expressions were as stern and protective as the policeman's. "Fine. But the people have a right to know!" He lowered the phone and took a step backward. He slinked into the crowd and disappeared, likely to go and write a piece that contained nothing but pure speculation and lies.

Jill's hand was still clutching Rick's elbow. She let go of his sleeve and watched him turn to Lenny.

"Thanks, man."

"No problem," Lenny said. "Let me know if you see any more of those vultures. I'll be here in a flash." He shook Rick's hand then turned to go.

Rick was as flustered as Jill had ever seen him. His eyes darted around the crowd, probably looking for more reporters. He backed away from the table and began walking toward his truck parked on the other side of the B&B nearby. Jill held up a gentle hand to the customers. "Be right with you," she assured them.

Rick was her first concern, not the cookies.

Jill managed to match his pace and walk in front of him. He halted when he noticed her. "Let's get out of here," he pleaded.

It wasn't that easy—people were still waiting, expecting cookies. Jill couldn't abandon them altogether. But she and Rick couldn't possibly slap smiles on their faces, pretend everything was fine, and get back to business.

"Okay. I'll meet you at the truck in a sec," she told him.

He continued walking while she tapped out a quick text then returned to the table.

"Sorry about that," she told the waiting customers. "Can I help you?" she asked the next person in line.

Two minutes later, as she'd hoped, Jill felt a gentle tap on her shoulder. It was Becky, who'd received her text for help. All that needed to be exchanged between them was a fast "I'm here" and "Thanks. I'll text you soon," before Becky stepped forward and took her place behind the table.

"How many do you need?" she asked the next customer. Jill knew the booth was in good hands.

When she approached the truck, Jill had expected Rick to be in the driver's seat. But he was slumped inside the passenger side, one hand massaging his temple. Perhaps he didn't trust himself behind the wheel just then. Jill opened the driver's side, hopped up with some significant effort, and noticed he'd already started the engine.

Jill always hated driving someone else's car, especially with that person sitting beside her, but Rick's massive Texas truck would be a unique challenge in itself. Still, she clicked her seat belt, adjusted the seat much closer to the wheel, then asked, "Where should we go?"

"Anywhere."

Pulling away from the curb and away from the square, she heard the peaceful whoosh of the powerful heater. She guided the truck into the rural part of Morgan's Grove and down tree-lined back roads she had become familiar with over the weeks. From her peripheral vision, she could see Rick staring out his window.

Jill felt guilty because every question that awful reporter had shoved toward Rick was a question she'd been dying to ask him herself. Even more questions, deeper ones, piled on top of each other as she drove. *Is he planning to return to California for good? Doesn't he need to be there now, cleaning up the mess instead of selling gingerbread cookies at a festival? How is he dealing with the betrayal of his best friend and partner? Does it make him want to reexamine all relationships in his life, even trusted ones?*

She wanted answers, but not in order to sell newspapers or to quench a salacious curiosity. It was because she cared about him. She didn't want Rick in turmoil and didn't like seeing him cover up the pain.

Up ahead, she saw a familiar turnoff and slowed to follow it. She'd already checked behind them to make sure they hadn't been followed by that reporter or another one looking for a story. She made the turn and parked next to the creek, close to the table where she and Rick had shared a picnic two weeks before. She thought maybe the covered bridge, peaceful and remote, could help him somehow.

Jill switched off the engine and waited for Rick's cue. He stayed motionless for a couple of minutes, unblinking. Then he reached for the door handle and pushed himself out of the truck. Jill followed his lead, hopped out, and watched him walk toward the bridge's edge and peer out over the gentle stream. The bubbling water sounded blissful in Jill's ears. There surely couldn't have been a more peaceful place, even on that dark day.

After a moment, Rick inched forward and sat down at the creek's edge with his feet close to the water. Jill had no idea if he wanted her to join him there or not, but she did anyway. Dried leaves crackled under her jeans as she lowered her body onto the cold, hard ground beside him. She left some room between them in case he still wanted his space. She pulled her knees up, rested her cold hands on top of them, and watched the water gurgle and foam around slick black rocks.

Finally, Rick looked over at Jill as though he wasn't aware she'd been with him the whole time. His eyes were vacant, emotionless. She wanted to touch his face and offer some comfort, but he probably wouldn't accept it.

He blinked then stared out at the water. "Did I tell you that Mark is on suicide watch? I can't remember if I told you." His tone was flat, detached.

"No, you didn't."

"We talked through Plexiglas, using handheld phones. Mark wouldn't make eye contact with me. Then he spilled everything in one long, rambling sentence about how he took the money, all the years he did it, all the lies he told. I've never wanted to punch somebody and hug somebody at the same time. And then he started sobbing. I know he was contrite, but that level of betrayal is just"—he pushed out a deep breath—"it rips me in two. I don't know who he is anymore. Did I ever?"

Rick was talking toward the stream, staring at the bubbles as he spoke. "I mean, you trust someone. You live with them, spend time with them. You listen to their stories, and they listen to yours. For years. Then you chase this dream together, build a company from scratch. And even when success comes and money and fame, he's still the *only* one you can really count on. The only one who was with you from the beginning. And then you find out that for all these years, it was just a lie and that you were gullible enough to believe it."

Jill felt that instinct to reach out again. And so, she did. Nothing too overt or disrupting, only a hesitant hand on his back that she doubted he could even feel through the fabric of his jacket.

"My grandfather was right." He said it so softly she almost didn't catch it.

"What do you mean?"

He squinted sideways at her. "He was the one who warned me about Mark all those years ago. It's the reason Pops was never in favor of the company. Well, one of the reasons. 'Never go into business with a friend.' I can still hear him say it. He said Mark was too flaky. Shady. That there was something in his eyes you couldn't trust. But I defended Mark. I got angry, fought with Pops about him, lots of times. And seeing how things ended up... He was right all along." He returned his gaze to the ground, where his boot stomped a dried leaf, crushing it.

Jill removed her hand from his jacket and slipped it back onto her knees. "I don't think it's wrong to trust somebody. It says a lot about your character that you would. And Mark's sins aren't *your* failure." She leaned in closer and waited until he made eye contact again. "You didn't fail. *Mark* did. It's all on him, and he knows it."

Rick pushed up from the ground, clearly frustrated. Jill stood, too, watching him take a few steps toward the bridge with his back to her. She wished she'd just listened, not talked. Advice and platitudes weren't what he needed. He only needed someone to vent to. She wasn't being the friend he craved.

She watched him pause and wondered if he was ready to leave. But when he swiveled around, he didn't move toward the truck—instead, he walked straight toward Jill and stopped, inches away and out of breath, his dark eyes filled with pain.

"Don't you understand?" he whispered, his fingers touching the tips of her curls. "My failure was in trusting Mark in the first place. If I hadn't done that—if I had *listened* to my grandfather—I wouldn't be where I am right now. He always knew, deep down, that the company was a bad idea, that I would ignore his advice and screw things up. I *did* fail. I failed my grandfather. I'm just glad he's not here right now to say 'I told you so.'" Rick caught himself and shook his head. "I didn't mean to say I'm glad he's not here."

"I know." Her heart beat faster, and she wanted to turn away. It had all become more intense than she'd bargained for.

But as she peered into Rick's eyes, one thing became crystal clear—he needed her. He was responding to her. So she stood her ground and offered him a new perspective. "Your grandfather was trying to protect you. That's all." Jill realized that she'd been grasping at his coat sleeves and that once she'd committed to staying, to helping him, she was desperate not to lose their connection. "Rick, he loved you, aside from any disagreements or issues you had. Isn't that the only thing that matters?"

Rick took in a breath to ponder her words. His expression changed, the edges starting to soften.

"Frank only wanted the best for you, like any parent would. He spent all those years raising you as his own child. And that's all you need to know. He wouldn't judge you if he were here right now. You know that. He would only love you."

Rick looked hard at her then moved his eyes past her, far away. He seemed to be taking it in, kicking the new idea around in his head. Maybe his grandfather *was* on his side. Maybe the fatherly love rose above everything else. Jill could see him working it out, struggling to let go of years' worth of fallacies, habits of thoughts. He had trouble holding an intimate gaze with her, perhaps because there were tears starting to form in his eyes.

Before she knew what was happening, Rick had leaned down to gather Jill into his arms, catching her in a tight embrace, pressing his face into her shoulder. She felt his breath on her neck and his grip tightening around her waist. She sensed his despair, the turmoil. She wondered whether he had allowed himself to cry since his grandfather's passing or if he'd kept a year's worth of grief inside until that moment.

They stayed locked together until his breathing finally slowed and turned shallow and she could sense his frustration physically melt away. He was letting go. By clinging so tightly to her, he was finally letting go.

Too soon, Rick backed away and released her. She saw him rub his jacket sleeve against his cheek in one quick motion, wiping away tears. Jill hoped he wasn't embarrassed and that he wouldn't take the easy route and bolt, pretending it never happened. To her surprise, he stayed right where he was, inches away, in no hurry at all.

He slowly touched her cheek. The tenderness was such a contrast to the intensity of that embrace. It was the calm after the storm. "Thank you," he said, his voice weary.

They remained locked in a stare, lost in each other.

Just as Rick moved his hands down to her waist and clasped her hips, Jill heard gravel crunching under tires. Rick steered Jill as far out of the road as possible as they watched three cars pass, going too fast, then park on the other side of the bridge. A group of rowdy teenagers climbed out, yelling, laughing, and apparently claiming the bridge as their own for the afternoon.

No more privacy.

"I guess we'd better get back to real life," Rick told her.

She tossed him the keys to his truck as they walked toward it. As he opened the door for her, Jill was curious about what could have happened, had the teenagers waited even a few seconds longer to blast their way through the intense moment she and Rick had been in the middle of sharing. She would never know.

Chapter Twenty-one

The next morning, Jill pushed the mascara wand into its container then stared at her face in the bathroom mirror. The image faded as she stepped back into the memory of that embrace at the bridge, with Rick's arms, strong and full of raw urgency, and his face coming closer to hers. She felt that mixture of elation and anxiety all over again.

Setting down the mascara tube, Jill put on a light sweater then left the apartment, eager to see Rick and curious to know his current state of mind. She hadn't seen him since they'd driven away from the bridge and he'd dropped her off to finish selling the cookies with Becky. So, Jill was grateful when, moments ago, Rick had texted to invite her for breakfast downstairs.

When Jill arrived in the kitchen, the glorious scents of bacon and coffee mingled together as she waded between the corgis.

Rick pushed back his chair when he saw Jill. "I made us breakfast. There's plenty."

He met her at the island and handed Jill an empty plate.

"Thanks. Did you get some sleep last night?" Her voice was hushed and intimate, as though they were sharing a secret.

"Enough." His expression didn't tell her much, but it did tell her he wasn't closed off. His eyes were bright, and his mouth was relaxed. They hadn't lost that connection they'd discovered at the bridge.

"Rick was just telling me about the reporter incident from yesterday," Lucille said from the table.

Rick cleared his throat. "Yeah, I told Gran about Lenny, how he helped us out. I called him last night and asked him to put an officer on patrol in the neighborhood. I don't want those reporters creeping around. Or bothering Gran. Or you."

"Good idea." Jill began filling her plate with eggs and bacon. She followed Rick to the table, where he pulled out her chair.

Rick picked up his fork but hovered it above his plate. "You know, I don't mind reporters doing their job. I get it. Quantum is a big story. But shoving a recorder in my face or pretending to be a customer... it's going too far. And they don't even bother to get the story right. They speculate and twist the truth and lie. All for profit."

"Do you have a PR person to issue statements and help set the story straight?" Lucille wondered.

"Sure, but I've told her to stick to the script and not give too much information. But maybe that's the wrong strategy."

"How so?" Jill prompted, pausing her eating.

Rick put down the fork and addressed them both. "The irony is, I've been upset with the press, dodging and avoiding them for years. But maybe I need them on my side right now. Investors are restless, customers are worried, and they're reading all this misinformation. I wish I could tell my side of the story somehow."

"Why don't you?" Lucille asked, then gestured toward Jill. "You've got a top-notch writer sitting here, in this very kitchen."

Jill raised her eyebrows, wondering how she'd suddenly become front and center in the conversation.

"And she's someone I trust." Rick moved his gaze toward Jill. "Through her, I could control the narrative. Get out in front of this thing, correct the rumors..."

Through her. Jill could see where his thoughts were headed. "Oh, no. I'm flattered, but I don't work for that kind of magazine, remember? My friend only publishes educational or inspiring pieces."

"I think this could be *both* inspiring and educational," Lucille urged.

"It could be sort of a profile piece," Rick explained, "with Patrick Wright coming out of the shadows, telling his side of the story. They could see the real me."

For a moment, Jill let herself push past the fear to see his point—she was known for finding the heart of a piece. She *could* be the one person to get Rick's story out there, with his permission. She was in a unique position to help, and she knew Miranda would probably grab a chance for an exclusive with both hands.

"Are you sure," Jill asked, "about being so open? And about me being the one to do it? I've never written anything like this before. I'm not sure I'd be the best fit."

Lucille clamped a hand down on top of Jill's. "Honey, I spent some time reading your magazine pieces last night—Rick showed me how to access them—and you are the *perfect* fit for this. Your articles are kind and humane. You would do the story justice. I have no doubt."

Jill let her eyes roam to Rick, who was patiently awaiting her response. He seemed as sure as Lucille. Jill reached for her coffee cup and took a long, thoughtful sip. The more she let the idea sink in, the more she knew it was the right one—the only one.

"I'll do it," she told Rick. "If you're sure about this. I mean, it's all happening so fast—"

"I trust you. And something like this—my story, my words, well told by you—would give me some sort of power back. I wouldn't feel like this thing is spiraling out of control." He gave a nod. "If you're willing, then I'm sure."

"That's all I need." Jill removed her napkin from her nap. She could eat later.

"What's the next step with the magazine?" Rick wondered.

"I'll explain it to my friend and see what she thinks. There's a chance she might want the story all to herself, or to give it to a writer who's more experienced in profile pieces and interviews. But I'll fight for it."

"Tell her I won't give an interview to anyone but you."

"Okay. I'll go make the call."

"*The* Patrick Wright? The mysterious millionaire? You're telling me you've basically been living under his roof this entire time in that Podunk town? Why didn't you *tell* me?" The questions came fast and loud, as Jill grinned and held the phone a few inches from her ear. She'd decided to return to her apartment for privacy to make the call.

"Miranda, I didn't know he was that Patrick until a few days ago, honest. And even then, I was respecting his privacy. I never considered writing a piece on him. But this morning, he asked me to write one, and I called you right away."

"Do you know what this means? An exclusive interview with Patrick Wright? It's a game changer for this magazine."

"I know." Jill hadn't let herself consider all the ripple effects until she dialed Miranda's number. With the profile piece, *Lifestyle Today* would be thrust into the spotlight, their readership would skyrocket, and advertisers would be begging for space in their magazine. Rick had seen the interview as Jill doing *him* a favor of sorts, but honestly, he was doing her friend and the magazine a favor, too.

"Well, it's a no-brainer. If you want it, this one's yours. But it has to be quick so we can get the exclusive. Sooner the better. This week?"

Jill smiled at the thought of being handed yet another valid excuse to stay in Morgan's Grove longer than planned. In fact, a few more days would lead her right up to the door of Christmas. Jill imagined herself in town through the weekend, spending Christmas day with Lucille and the corgis. And with Rick.

"I can do it. But... I've never written anything like this profile piece or done an interview this important."

"You can pull it off. I know it. Use that razor-sharp insight you have, the one you use with all your other pieces. Let Patrick tell his side. You'll become his mouthpiece, giving him a chance to quell the rumors. And if this thing goes the way I think it will... Jill, you may have just saved this magazine."

THIS ISN'T WHAT AN *interview with a millionaire should look like*, was all Jill could think. She sat in comfy sweatpants on Lucille's couch, her feet curled under her, a notepad in hand, and her pen poised and ready. Rick had sat down on the same couch and draped an arm between them, his body angled toward her so that his knee touched hers. He wore relaxed attire, too, that same flannel shirt and jeans she'd seen him in when they'd first met on Lucille's porch.

"You'll do fine," she whispered, waiting for Rick to make eye contact. His shallow breaths and serious gaze told her he was nervous. "Any regrets?" she asked when he finally looked at her.

"None. Let's do this."

They had each spent the better part of the afternoon in separate spaces, preparing for the interview. Jill had stayed in her apartment after hanging up with Miranda, nervously crafting interview questions and trying to anticipate the direction of Rick's answers for possible follow-up questions. She'd even done a crash course on the history of his company, researching online to make sure she had the full picture in her head. She avoided the salacious pieces entirely, reading only the legitimate news sites.

Rick had spent the afternoon in his bedroom, likely pondering his role in the piece and figuring out what he did and didn't want to say while fielding more calls and questions from shareholders and employees.

Lucille had already coaxed the corgis into their kennel and insisted on going upstairs to give them complete privacy for the interview.

"I'm going to record this," Jill told Rick, reaching for her phone. "This is *only* for me, for when I'm compiling the piece after we're done. I want to be sure I get the details absolutely right. I'll delete the recording afterward. Okay?"

"Okay."

She clicked the button to record then returned to her notepad, where she would write down the key points for herself. Jill began with the biggest question of all: "What do you want people to know about you, the company, the situation?"

Rick cleared his throat before answering. "That there's misinformation out there. Rumors are being spread about me and my company. And I'm here to clear them up."

As he continued, his voice grew in volume and in confidence. He seemed to become unaware of the recording and swiftly turned the interview into a conversation with Jill, just the two of them falling into an easy back-and-forth. His body language relaxed as he gestured, and his voice pattern fell into the natural rhythm Jill recognized and knew so well. She nodded occasionally as she jotted down key phrases. Rick talked about the origins of the company, the intent behind it, and the initial enthusiasm. Then, with Jill's follow-up questions prodding him, Rick shifted to the progress and successes over the years.

Finally, he addressed the main crisis with Mark. "Mark is a good man, but a troubled man. He will always be my friend." It was the only point in the interview when his voice began to quiver, and Jill wondered if he could continue or whether he might call the whole thing off. During a long pause, Jill moved her finger toward the phone, prepared to cut off the recording, but Rick shook his head. "No, I'm fine. Let's keep going."

He was careful to protect Mark's privacy, not giving details about his mental state or his family. But he issued a warning to reporters: "I plead with you to leave his family alone. He has a wife and children, and they have done nothing wrong. They deserve to live their lives without the press hounding them. I'm appealing to your humanity."

Rick ended the interview by talking about Quantum's bright future, his hopes for its success, and his confidence in its current leadership. "We will move past this crisis and will be stronger for it."

When it was clear Rick was finished, Jill clicked off the recording. "How do you feel?"

Rick stretched his arms above his head and blew out a sigh. "Good. That was weirdly cathartic."

"I think you did great. You gave me a lot to work with." She scanned her pages of notes.

"Now what?"

"Well, I thought I could take some headshots of you to add to this casual vibe we've got going."

"I'm wearing flannel."

"Precisely. People need to see you out of your suit." She stopped herself short and grinned. "Um, that came out weird. I didn't mean..." She saw Rick's grin matching her own and felt a blush rise higher in her cheeks. "Anyway, what I meant to say was that *this* is who you are. Flannel and boots, the Texas boy turned successful entrepreneur. You said you wanted the public to see you. Well, this is you."

"Good point."

"Plus, if these don't turn out well or Miranda doesn't approve, we can always use your usual professional headshot." Jill set the notes aside then pushed off the couch. "How about some natural light? Maybe near the window? Or even outside?"

He rose, too, then followed her out the screen door to the porch.

Jill maneuvered him by grabbing his sleeve with one hand and peering at her phone screen with the other, comparing the different shades of light. Rick took a few steps backward as she guided him nearer the porch swing.

"There. That's the spot," she said. The sun was setting, and the glow of it created beautiful lighting.

"What do you want? Serious? Smiling?"

She shrugged. "Try both, maybe? Whatever's natural, relaxed."

"Forcing myself to look natural and relaxed," he said with a half grin. She snapped his photo at that moment, without him knowing. "That should be easy."

He posed, clearly uncomfortable, smiling in one shot, removing his smile in another, looking at the camera, looking away, trying anything and everything. *Surely one of these shots will be the one...*

"Okay, all finished. I'll put you out of your misery." She lowered her camera to scan through the photos.

"So about that rain check."

Jill paused and looked into Rick's face.

"For dinner?" he clarified. "Did you already forget?"

I thought you *had,* she wanted to say. "No, I just—so much has happened..."

"Since the profile piece is keeping you in town a little longer, maybe after you've submitted it, we could celebrate."

"I'd like that."

The screen door opened behind Jill, and she swiveled to see Lucille's head peeking through. "Is it safe to come out?"

"Of course." Jill gestured for her to come outside. "We're all finished. It was pretty painless, I think."

"It was," Rick concurred. "There's nobody else who could've brought all that out of me. No way."

Lucille joined them. "Now what?"

"Well, I need to disappear to the apartment again," Jill said, "so I can bring together my notes with Rick's quotes and create the big picture. The interview was the easy part for me. Now, the real work begins."

Chapter Twenty-two

Jill stretched her back and let out an audible groan, tempted to take a break and run around the block in the crisp midnight air to keep herself awake—the coffee wasn't doing its job anymore. She had pulled numerous all-nighters over the years, trying to meet her publisher's stringent editing deadlines, so the sluggish fatigue was completely familiar to her. However, the specific level of intensity and pressure she felt was not. The time crunch toward her deadline felt more personal. She had to get the piece right—too much depended on it. It wasn't about fictional characters she'd created or scenarios she'd made up in her head. It was real life. And it was Rick.

After that afternoon's interview, Rick had offered to do a quick drive-by at Juan's, his treat, so Jill accepted then took her tacos up to the apartment to get to work while Rick disappeared to return some calls. Lucille had told Jill she could stay in the kitchen and work at the table, but Jill knew that the possible distractions—loud dogs, unexpected phone calls, Lucille watching a movie—would multiply if she stayed inside the house.

Scanning the current draft of her piece, Jill realized she'd made more progress than expected. After listening to her recording multiple times, pausing at certain points to jot down exact quotes, Jill had created a basic blueprint of how the piece would progress, including which quotes she would use and where. As it all came together, she discovered it was actually much easier than penning her other articles. Rick was the obvious focus, so she wasn't forced to find a certain angle or explore a particular aspect of her subject. Using Rick's words and his perspective was powerful enough on its own. She wanted him to do the talking. She wasn't so much the writer as the conduit for what he wanted to say.

Jill hovered her fingers over the keyboard and reread her last paragraph. As she began to type, her phone buzzed with a text from Rick: *Need a break? Gran made apple cider. And I have a decision to share.*

Curious, Jill saved her work then slipped on her shoes and wrapped her coat around the flannel pajamas she wore. She'd already removed her makeup, but she knew Rick and Lucille wouldn't care about her bare face. She felt comfortable enough with both of them, by that point, to walk into the kitchen with confidence no matter what state she was in.

As promised, Lucille had apple cider waiting in the kitchen, both in a steaming pot on the stove and in individual mugs, and asked how the piece was coming along.

"Very well," Jill told her, uncertain if Rick's decision was about to change that. She wondered whether he regretted certain comments he made during the interview. *Will he want to soften parts I've already typed? Or has he changed his mind about it altogether?* There was no use speculating until she heard him out.

Lucille secured her robe tightly around her waist then walked with Jill into the living room, where Rick waited on the sofa, also in comfortable attire, sweatpants and a white T-shirt, but his face was all business.

"Did I wake you with my text?" he wondered.

"No, I'm pulling an all-nighter. Seems we all are," Jill observed, feeling oddly comforted by that notion. She wasn't the only one awake so late. "You've got my curiosity piqued."

Lucille had already sat in the chair nearest the corgis, so Jill joined Rick on the sofa, careful not to slosh her cider as she sat. She shifted her legs underneath her then reached up to touch the amethyst—a new habit she'd formed was checking to make sure it was safe and sound around her neck. The night of the surprise party, Jill had toyed with keeping the precious antique jewel tucked away inside the apartment, but it was meant to be worn, and in the past three days, it had become a natural part of Jill's wardrobe. Jolene was right—the piece, a slice of Morgan's Grove's history, belonged with her.

"I'm in the dark too," Lucille said. "Rick wouldn't give me a clue until we were all here together. I don't know if my heart can take any more dramatic announcements. I hope it's something good?"

"It is," Rick assured her. "I decided it tonight, and I wanted y'all to be the first to know. I'm handing over the reins of Quantum to James, the VP. I just got off the phone with him."

His announcement was met at first with silence, except for the crackling fire.

Finally, Lucille spoke up. "Do you mean quit the company? Oh, honey. Isn't that a bit drastic?"

Jill watched Rick's face, looking for any sign of hesitation or second guesses. But she only saw confidence.

Rick shook his head. "Not as drastic as it sounds. I won't sell off my shares and won't step down officially yet. I'll become a sort of silent partner, behind the scenes for a while. James has agreed to handle the day-to-day elements, but he'll keep me in the loop until I step away for good someday. I need to do this gradually so I won't scare the shareholders. They need to see a united front right now. But by the end of next year, I plan to walk away entirely. I'll announce it then."

"What brought you to this point?" Jill asked. "I mean, was it all because of Mark?"

"His arrest was the catalyst. And then talking to you this afternoon, hearing myself say it out loud, talking about the company. I think I've wanted to walk away for a long time but didn't have reason enough. Or courage enough, maybe. I haven't been happy at Quantum for a long time. I'm a computer guy, not a CEO. I never liked the business side of things, but gradually, that's all it became for me. I'm still proud of what I built. But I've lost that creative spark somewhere, and I want it back."

"What will you do now?" Lucille asked. "With your time, with your days? You love to work, to stay occupied."

Rick shrugged. "I could eventually start another business in Austin or even create a nonprofit. The pressure of running a company this size… I didn't realize how it was eating away at me. I never really got time off from it. Even if I wasn't doing actual work, I was worrying about the company's welfare, day and night. Never a real break. And I don't want to live that way anymore. Being in Morgan's Grove has influenced me more than anything. A simpler life, a slower pace. It's reminded me of who I used to be. Who I want to be."

"Does this mean," Lucille asked with a timid voice, "that you're moving back home?"

"I can't commit to that yet, but probably. Maybe. There's still a lot to sort out in California with the beach house, the company, and all the technicalities and paperwork. My whole life is out there. Or was. I'm not sure anymore. It's time to reevaluate things."

"One step at a time is the smartest way to tackle a new path." Lucille nodded firmly. "I'm proud of you for thinking it through, making the hard decisions. And I can't say I'm disappointed that Morgan's Grove is a possibility. I've missed you." She stretched her hand out between the sofas, and Rick grasped it. After a beat, Lucille let go. "I need to warm up my cider. Anyone else?"

Rick and Jill both gave a polite "no."

Lucille left the room, and Rick looked toward Jill, half his face glowing in the light of the fire. "How's your piece coming?"

"*Our* piece," she corrected. "It's good. Truth be told, I thought you were about to throw me a curveball tonight, like maybe you changed your mind about my writing it."

"Nope. Won't happen. It's still the right thing to do. I haven't wavered."

Lucille reentered the room with her mug and some strips of paper, which she waved as she sat down on the sofa. "Guess what these are!"

When Lucille held them steady, Jill made a guess. "Tickets to something?"

"Precisely. I bought them this afternoon. Three tickets for Thursday's concert." She turned to Jill. "You'll still be here? In Morgan's Grove?"

"I'll be here," she confirmed.

"Do you know what barbershop music is?" Lucille prodded.

Jill pictured the only cliché she knew, a group of four men, each wearing greased, sculpted moustaches and red-and-white striped suits, singing an old-fashioned tune. "Sort of."

"Well, our local quartet, Then and Now, is performing. People come from all over to hear them. They've won awards at our local and state contests."

"Impressive," Jill said then finished off her cider.

Rick chimed in. "They've been together"—he shifted toward his grandmother for confirmation—"thirtysomething years?"

"Thirty-five." Lucille handed the individual tickets to Jill and Rick as she spoke in wistful tones. "Frank loved to hear them sing. In fact, he's the one who took credit for forming them in the first place."

"I never knew that," Rick said.

"It's true. He heard Stan humming one day and thought of two other men interested in creating a musical group. Frank suggested Stan to them, they added another fella, and voila! Instant quartet."

"Like *The Music Man*," Jill added. "You know, the part where he asks the guys to sing, then they harmonize, then they do nothing but walk around and sing together the rest of the movie."

"Right!" said Lucille. "Well, when they first got together, Frank came up with the name and even helped manage them for a few years, finding them bookings and such. I think he was living vicariously through them. He always wanted to be musical, but bless him, he couldn't carry a tune in a bucket." She chuckled. "So what do you say about the concert?"

"I'm in," Jill said.

"Me too," Rick agreed.

Lucille clutched her ticket and said softly, "I was telling Jill the other day how I hadn't expected this holiday to feel very Christmassy. I knew it would be sad and lonely. In fact, I almost wanted to bow out of the whole experience." She raised her eyes to Jill and Rick. "But spending it with the two of you this way... It's been an unexpected blessing, hasn't it?"

Tears stung the back of Jill's eyes, surprising her. She remembered her own Thanksgiving a few weeks before, spent with Lindsey's boisterous family. She'd felt out of place and isolated even in a room full of people. And Jill had been dreading Christmas even more, anticipating spending it alone.

But as she sat in the presence of such kind, newly familiar people, Jill felt the very same way as Lucille, unexpectedly blessed.

AFTER THREE DAYS AND nights spent writing multiple drafts of Rick's profile piece, making minor changes, rearranging a couple of sections, then editing and polishing it, Jill had finished. She'd sent the final copy to Lucille and Rick that morning and would await their input and prepare for their critiques.

Perfect! Lucille's text read. And Rick's was *Great. All of it. Wouldn't change a word.*

With that, Jill had reread the piece one final time, attached the candid photo of Rick she'd taken on the porch, then sent it off to Miranda. Instead of a text, Jill received a call minutes later.

"It's fantastic. It flows well, has just enough direct quotes. And you've managed to put some heart into it too. Take this the right way: this piece seems personal."

"It is," Jill admitted.

"Well, it shows. And that's what will draw the readers in, knowing the writer cares about her subject. Listen, I'll get this edited pronto," Miranda said. "We might be able to post it online tonight. And Patrick has read and approved, right? No surprises there?"

"None. He's on board."

"Excellent. Hey, about the genealogy article... Why don't we put that on the back burner for now, no deadline? If you want to finish it someday, send it to me. But you've worked hard enough on this profile piece. It's all I need from you."

"Are you sure?" Truth be told, with all the Rick drama over the past several days, Jill had practically forgotten about the other article.

"Positive. I'll still publish it anytime you're ready, but there's no rush now. Not with this new Patrick piece. So, take a breather. Enjoy your holiday."

"That sounds like a nice idea," Jill admitted.

She thought Miranda was about to hang up, but instead, her friend added, "It's really fallen into place for you."

"What has?"

"Everything. I mean, who knew that your trip to Texas would produce all this? Finding out about your heritage, then meeting Patrick Wright, and now the profile piece. It all feels meant to be."

Jill had the same sensation earlier. "I know. It's weird. When I look back, it all feels like puzzle pieces clicking into place."

"Exactly. See? You're a wonderful writer. Even when you're not writing."

Jill giggled. "That makes no sense. I think you need some coffee."

"Now, *that's* an understatement. It's been a whirlwind few days. Take care, my friend. A million thanks. And a Merry Christmas."

"You too."

AFTER THE PAST WEEK, Jill was ready for a break and glad to have the luxury of time while getting ready for the barbershop concert. After she'd hung up with Miranda that morning, Jill had spent a leisurely afternoon shopping with Lucille around the square, where Jill had bought a lovely handmade shawl for her mother, some kitchen towels and baking gadgets for Lucille, candy-cane-shaped toys for the corgis, a "Teachers Are Special" pen set for Lindsey, and a new laptop case for Rick.

As dusk fell, Jill returned to her apartment and tried on a couple of outfits, experimenting with her curly hair then cracking open a new eye shadow. She was primped and ready twenty minutes before she'd agreed to meet Rick and Lucille to leave the house.

Jill had chosen a dark suede skirt and a burgundy sweater to wear. She'd pulled back some of her curls and fastened them into a barrette at the top of her head, not to hide the curls, but to emphasize them in a new way. She'd darkened her makeup with a bit more color than usual on her lids, her lips, and her cheeks. Finally, she'd sprayed on a hint of fragrance, selected her coat, and grabbed her purse.

When Jill clicked open the kitchen door, she saw Rick standing at the island, tapping on his phone. He wore jeans and a chocolate-colored blazer with a dark-green shirt underneath. He swiveled to see her then looked her up and down.

"You look nice."

Jill shut the door and walked toward him.

"You too." She touched the edge of his blazer as he set down his phone to give her his full attention.

"Oh, good. You're both here." Lucille, out of breath, rounded the corner from the living room, clutching a manila envelope.

"Are we late?" Jill asked. "I thought we still had a few minutes."

"We do." Lucille had gone all-out Christmas, wearing a red sweater decorated with a wintery snowman scene. She stopped short and glanced at Jill and Rick standing at the island. "Aren't you both gorgeous?! It's like you've stepped right out of a fashion magazine together."

"I think I'm overdressed." Jill tugged at her sweater.

"You're perfect," assured Lucille.

"What's that?" Rick pointed toward the envelope.

"Oh!" Lucille's eyes brightened as she turned the envelope over in her hand then set it on the island delicately, as though it were some ancient artifact she'd been searching for and had finally found. "I was rummaging around at the back of my closet for this sweater and noticed it had slid right off the hanger and onto the floor."

Jill wondered what the sweater's connection was with the envelope but remained patient.

"When I stooped down to get the sweater, there it was, this envelope, tucked away into the farthest back corner of the closet. I had to get on my hands and knees to reach it. I knew it wasn't mine—nothing I recognized, at least. And when I looked closer, I realized it belonged to Frank."

She swallowed then pushed the envelope closer to Rick. "You need to see what's inside. I had no idea your grandfather had been collecting these."

Rick, clearly puzzled, did as his grandmother instructed and slipped his hand inside the envelope. He removed a thick stack of papers, some glossy, some newsprint, and sorted through them one at a time. Jill stood at Rick's side and peered at them, too. They were all clippings of interviews, photos, and articles about Quantum, dating back years, from the very beginning of the company's creation.

"Don't you see?" Lucille prompted. "Your grandfather was following your successes. I had no idea he was keeping these tidbits about your company for all those years."

Rick paused, holding up the most recent article, from the year before. He looked sideways at his grandmother. "I wonder why he didn't tell me. Or even why he didn't tell you."

Lucille clucked. "Oh, Rick. People are complicated. Your grandfather was an incredible man, but he wasn't perfect. It took a lot of effort for him to offer compliments, to show support. You know that. He was a proud man. It didn't come naturally to him, expressing his feelings. But look!" She touched the corner of the article Rick held. "He *did* care about your company. Otherwise, he would never have gone to the trouble to find all these, clip them out, and save them. It's undeniable proof, right here."

"Fair point," Rick acknowledged. "He was hard on me all those years, but I guess I've been hard on him too." His voice had lowered to a near whisper as he shifted toward Lucille. "I'm just like him, aren't I? I hide my feelings, guard myself too much, take people for granted..."

Lucille clutched his elbow. "You resemble him in some ways, yes, but that was learned behavior. You learned it by watching him all those years. Rick, you have a heart the size of, well, Texas, and a sensitivity that Frank chose not to show. He showed it to me but nobody else. Maybe it came from years of being a police officer and not being allowed to show emotion on the job. You guard yourself, too, but not so much that you cut people out of your life. And you show me every day that you love me, in a million different ways."

Rick dipped his head and nodded, acknowledging he'd heard her. He slid the clippings back inside their paper shell and secured it with the brad. "Can I keep these?"

"They're yours." She patted his arm. "Now, let's go to a Christmas concert, shall we?"

AS LUCILLE HAD PREDICTED, the entire town seemed to turn up for the quartet's show. Even though they arrived early, Rick had trouble finding a parking spot at the high-school theater located a half mile behind the square.

Inside, Lucille was able to find three empty seats together and led Jill and Rick into the aisle. When Rick sat beside her, Jill noticed that he had trouble getting his long legs to fit comfortably in the snug space, his knees tapping up against the seat in front of him. Jill shrugged out of her coat as Rick helped pull on the sleeves.

As they settled in, Jill observed the buzz of activity: people gathering for the show, finding seats, and tapping on phones. The stage was flanked by two gigantic Christmas trees.

As Lucille's church and bridge friends noticed her, they waved and started gushing about her gingerbread.

"I can't get enough!"

"My grandkids ate up every single one!"

"When does the new bakery open?"

"This is good for her," Rick whispered into Jill's ear from her other side, his breath sweet and minty. "I haven't seen Gran this happy in a long while."

The house lights flickered in the auditorium, urging people to find a seat. The show was about to begin. The curtain lifted, displaying even more decorations onstage, nutcrackers and dressed-up snowmen. Jill noticed the thunderous applause when the quartet emerged, and it was apparent before they even opened their mouths to sing that the group of men was beloved by the town. One of the gentlemen stepped forward, introduced himself in a low, resonant timbre as the bass, then introduced the rest of the men. Then they sang song after song of classic Christmas tunes, both secular and religious.

Perhaps because there were no other instruments involved, or perhaps because the vocal arrangements and harmonies were so unique, Jill enjoyed the festive music more than she could have imagined. The atmosphere suddenly felt old-fashioned, and she was transported to another time, a gentler time, where men were gentlemen and ladies were admired and cherished. As the quartet sang, she painted a picture in her mind of ballrooms in the forties, packed with couples dancing at a glitzy party, gliding to the sounds of big bands. The men wore slicked hair and tailored suits while the women donned red lipstick, heels, and polished updo hairstyles.

As they sang, the quartet blended perfectly with every note, using soft dynamics then getting louder to build emotion, ending each song with power chords. *This is anything* but *Podunk*, Jill thought.

Rick's sleeve brushed against Jill's wrist, which was perched on the armrest, and her attention shifted completely. She became distracted from the stage, distracted from the cheery music and from the dreamy forties ballroom. She was transported back to her seat, strongly aware of Rick beside her.

The quartet launched into a beautiful, moving rendition of "Have Yourself a Merry Little Christmas," first explaining to the audience that the lyrics were purposely somber because the tune had been written in 1944, at the height of World War II. Jill experienced the song in a whole new way, listening closely to the lyrics, picturing families torn apart, spending Christmas without each other, praying to be reunited the next year.

As she hummed along, Jill felt something graze her hand. She thought it was a mistake, maybe Rick shifting in his chair again, accidentally touching her fingers. But his hand was near hers on purpose. It stayed there, hovering for a reason, like an open question.

And when Jill slowly flipped her hand to meet his, Rick had his answer. His fingers inched steadily closer until they interlocked with hers.

And there in the darkness of the theater, as the lyrics of a bittersweet song floated through the auditorium, Jill wasn't aware of anything but Rick's hand, tender and comforting. She smiled in the darkness, feeling thirteen again, a giddiness rising inside. She couldn't even recall the last time someone had held her hand in a theater. It had been much too long.

When the song ended, the audience gave a hearty standing ovation. Rick released his grasp, and they joined in the applause. And with that, the concert was over.

Turning to gather her coat, Jill noticed Lucille's expression—she was smiling through tears. She probably missed Frank, especially hearing that final song's melancholy lyrics about not being able to spend Christmas with the ones we love. Jill offered her a knowing glance, wishing she could do more.

Back at the house, the corgis greeted them with jovial barks. After letting them outside, Lucille asked Rick about his plans for the rest of the evening.

He was already preoccupied with his phone. "I've got some important emailing to do."

"Anything worrisome?" Lucille wondered. "Any new word about Mark?"

Lucille and Jill had tried to steer clear of that topic and let Rick have some space, but Jill was still glad she'd asked. She was curious too.

"Naw, these emails are regular business, mostly with James, trying to figure out the details of my new role." He leaned forward to kiss his grandmother on the cheek. "Thanks for the concert."

After a pause, Rick took a couple of steps toward Jill and bent down to kiss her cheek too. "See you tomorrow?" he whispered.

"Tomorrow."

Lucille watched her grandson leave the room, her eyebrows raised high. "What's tomorrow?"

"It's that rain check he's been promising for the dinner in Austin."

"Oh, the *date*!" Lucille's whisper contained the same hopeful lilt in her tone that Lindsey's had.

Jill suppressed her grin, gave a slight eyeroll, then whispered, "I don't want to define it. I like being with him. Can't we just call it two people having dinner who like each other's company?"

"Well, it's a mouthful compared to 'date,' but I'll call it whatever you want." Lucille gave a wink then reached for the coffee pot.

Chapter Twenty-three

J ill had assumed she would sink into bed after the barbershop concert, close her eyes, and fall fast asleep. But near midnight, she found herself sitting in the apartment's chair near the window, restless, scrolling through photos on her phone. She started with her very first day in Morgan's Grove, and the images left her smiling: the town square and that beautiful library, the stately founder's mansion, the old-fashioned covered bridge. And the people, too: Bob waving to a neighbor from his bike, The Pit sisters handing over an order to a customer, Becky making a cookie delivery, Mr. Anderson raking leaves while wearing his fedora. And the final photo was a candid shot taken of Lucille feeding the corgis a treat in the kitchen while Rick stood in the background, making a meal.

Jill swatted away the unthinkable reality that she would soon leave Morgan's Grove. It felt like being forced to awaken from a lovely, extended dream.

She set the phone on the table and peered through the open curtains toward the night sky, where diamond-like stars sparkled. *This town, these people...* They had come to mean so much to her in a short space of time. She didn't want to leave them behind yet.

A seed of an idea occurred. *What if I don't have to?* Maybe she could still keep some part of Morgan's Grove alive. She'd been searching for months and months for a new story. It could be right in front of her, just like Lindsey suggested weeks ago.

Jill's heart thumped faster as she followed the idea further down its path. A town, rich with quirky but lovable people, each with their own story to tell. Maybe she could fictionalize the town, create characters loosely based on Morgan's Grove residents, and craft individual storylines for them. Pushing out of her chair, Jill found her legal pad then plopped down on the bed and began writing snippets of brainstorms, fragments of thought, idea after idea—they came tumbling out faster than she could catch them.

She had entered the zone.

She broadened her vision, opened up the possibilities. It could even become a series of novels, with each additional book focusing on a new main character.

Jill's pen only stopped minutes later when her hand began to cramp. She took a break to stretch out her fingers and skim her notes. Her heart was *still* pounding as she read them over, which was a very good sign that she was onto something.

But she knew how it worked. Sometimes, a seemingly great idea that hit late at night would look ridiculous the following day, much like a dream that made perfect sense in the subconscious but became a questionable mess in the light of morning. She also knew that getting swept up in the whirlwind of a few minutes' brainstorming didn't necessarily mean that a feasible, workable idea would actually result from it.

Jill decided to sleep on it, revisit her notes the next day, and see whether they were her writer's salvation or merely the midnight ramblings of an exhausted mind struggling with insomnia.

"YOU'RE A FAMOUS JOURNALIST!" Lindsey squealed.

Jill snickered, adjusting her phone between her shoulder and ear, using her hands to fluff the tissue paper on Lucille's gift bag. She'd spent the morning wrapping the presents she'd purchased the day before in the square. "I'm not technically a journalist, and I'm not exactly famous, either."

"Well, I disagree. I'm sitting here, looking at a piece that my friend wrote online. It's officially gone viral. If that's not fame or real journalism, I don't know what is."

Jill had texted Lindsey the link to Rick's profile piece when it went live that morning, and Lindsey had texted back a series of shocked emojis then added: *You didn't tell me how gorgeous he was! Wow!*

Jill had also texted her mother the link but hadn't gotten a response yet.

"I still can't believe you kept this to yourself," Lindsey mused. "Rick's true identity, his trouble with Quantum. I should be mad at you for not telling me, your best friend. I had to read about the details along with everyone else."

"I'm sorry." Jill set Lucille's gift bag aside. "But I had to keep it quiet out of respect for Rick. He was trusting me, and that's not easy for him."

"Yeah, I get it. Charlie says you may have helped save Quantum's reputation with this article."

Jill wanted to humbly deny it as overstatement, but she knew that the piece probably *was* having a positive impact on the company. And on her own career. All morning, Miranda kept filling Jill's inbox with the rave reviews the article was already getting from colleagues, readers, and the media. She'd also received two separate requests to speak at national writing conferences in the month of January. Even Jill's literary agent had *finally* texted her with congratulations and a message that read, "Let's talk about your next book after the holidays." Instead of a shaming tone, his message held a hopeful one.

Jill's eyes wandered toward her legal pad, which she'd tossed onto the side table the night before. She paused her gift wrapping and picked up the pad. All morning, she'd been too afraid to face her late-night brainstorming. *What if it's not good enough? What if it's not what I need it to be?* But with Lindsey as her support, she could be brave enough. At the least, she needed to hear her own ideas aloud and bounce them off of someone else.

"Can I tell you something?" she asked Lindsey, skimming her scribblings.

"Of course."

"I did something last night. I couldn't sleep, so I started scrolling through my photos of the town, and I had an idea."

"For a new book? I *knew* it!"

"Well, I *think* it's a new book, but it's too early to tell. I just scribbled down some notes, some seeds of ideas." She told Lindsey the core notion of a town similar to Morgan's Grove as a possible series.

"So this wouldn't be a true story?" Lindsey asked.

"Right. It would be a fictionalized version. More 'inspired by' than 'based on' Morgan's Grove."

"I love it. What would the first book be about? Where would you start?"

Jill hadn't thought that far ahead but decided to brainstorm aloud. And the most obvious answer came to her first: "It could begin with a story like mine. A wandering young woman searches for her roots, her family. And she finds all that and more in a small town. The first book could start here, with me. Or, rather, with a character *like* me."

"I think you really have something. It sounds like a book I would read."

And with that, Jill knew she had something feasible in her notes. Lindsey's enthusiasm only confirmed Jill's own gut feeling that it was a story worth pursuing with confidence.

Jill set the pad back down and blew out a breath. "Thank you for letting me talk it out."

"I'm glad you did. Will you tell Rick and Lucille?"

"Not yet. I need to sort out the details, make this more concrete. Lots of work ahead. But I will tell them, when the time is right."

They shifted the conversation back to their holiday plans—Lindsey was packing up to leave for Utah, where Charlie's family would be celebrating.

"And you're in Morgan's Grove for Christmas?" Lindsey confirmed.

"That's the plan. Leaving on Christmas day, in the afternoon."

"Christmas day? Can't you wait a couple more days to leave?"

"No choice. I have to get ahead of the holiday traffic. And plus, I checked the weather, and *another* big storm is headed toward Denver midweek. I can't stay stuck in Morgan's Grove during the writer's conference. People are paying a lot of money to attend. I have to be there. It's a long-standing commitment."

"Well, at least you still have your date with Rick tonight."

"It's not a—"

"I know, I know. It's not a date. Dinner, then."

"Yep, it's tonight."

"So how does this work, exactly?" Lindsey wondered. "Have dinner with a handsome man that you've grown to care about, share an intimate holiday with him and his grandmother, then leave forever?"

Lindsey probably meant it lightly, but put so bluntly, Jill realized how crazy the whole idea sounded. "That's about the size of it," she quipped, but it was a question Jill had asked herself multiple times in the past couple of days. In fact, when she awoke that morning, she had almost cancelled the dinner. Part of her brain kept nagging: *What's the point? I'll be gone in forty-eight hours anyway. I'll probably never see him again.*

Ultimately, the other part of her brain—the part that told her to follow through on a promise, the part that knew the evening was still valuable in the scheme of things and that it *could* be the last time she was with Rick—had won out. All the more reason to see it through.

Somehow, Jill would manage to compartmentalize the dinner, to let it exist all on its own, in a separate dimension of time and space apart from everything else, with no expectations or presumptions. It could be an isolated evening where she rested in the moment, rather than jumping two steps ahead in her mind.

"Well, what*ever* tonight is," Lindsey said, "I hope it's a night to remember."

"Me too."

"DON'T YOU LOOK BEAUTIFUL?!" Lucille said as Jill entered the kitchen and shut the door.

Lucille must have let the corgis outside, and Jill was grateful. She didn't need doggy drool on her new heels or well-meaning scratches on her bare legs.

"Thanks." Jill was unusually confident in her appearance. She'd decided on an upsweep for her hair, a loose bun of sorts that still let her curls breathe.

"Your dress—it matches the necklace, doesn't it?" Lucille noted.

Jill flicked open her coat to show more of her new jewel-toned dress to Lucille. "Isn't it the perfect color? Mindy picked it out when she saw the amethyst. I bought the dress at her boutique."

While Rick and Lucille had been busy at the bakery that afternoon with an important walk-through, Jill had spent the better part of her day around town, saying goodbyes. She'd visited The Pit ladies and some of the shop owners, returned her library books to Chaynie, chatted with Jolene at the mansion, bought the dress from Mindy, and then attended the parade.

Truth be told, Jill's expectations were a bit dashed. The parade had been talked up so much by Lucille and other townspeople as the slam-bang ending of the Morgan's Grove Festival that Jill was half-expecting a long string of ornate floats and balloons with fireworks at the end. Instead, the entire parade lasted about ten minutes and consisted of four trucks decorated as floats, followed by a few horses, some goats, and a tiny high-school marching band bringing up the rear. Still, the energetic crowd cheered as though it had been the Macy's Thanksgiving Day Parade. Bicycle Bob gave a shout-out to start the event: "This day is in honor of our founder's descendant, Miss Jill McCallister!" It had been unexpectedly heartwarming as the crowd cheered her on.

"Oh, I haven't told you about the walk-through at the bakery." Lucille's eyes danced. "It's all coming together. There are so many details to consider, but I can't believe the progress, already. Rick says we're ahead of schedule."

"Rick says what?" he asked as he entered the room. He paused when he saw Jill.

"Tell her she looks pretty," Lucille whispered, as though Jill wasn't standing right beside her.

"She does. Very pretty."

Jill felt like a girl leaving with her date to the prom. She imagined Lucille whipping out a camera and pushing them together for a picture.

Rick came to stand between them. "My phone's been blowing up all day."

Lucille frowned. "Did it stop working?"

"No, Gran, it's slang that means people keep contacting me. I've been getting texts and calls about the profile piece Jill published."

"Oh, yes! Mrs. Martin stopped me on the street today to talk about it. People are buzzing about it around town." Lucille turned toward Rick. "And it's done what you wanted? To help the company?"

"It's done exactly what I wanted. Some of the weight of this thing has been removed."

"Well, you've helped my friend too," Jill told him. "Miranda says the piece is going viral and that advertisers are clamoring for ad space. I think you've single-handedly saved the magazine."

"You were a mighty big part of that too." Rick clicked off his phone. "I'm going off the grid tonight."

As he slipped the phone inside his pocket, Jill took in the sight of him, clean-shaven and wearing a black jacket over a dark-eggplant-colored shirt, with his hair combed back, the perfect length. She'd noticed it had grown a little shaggy in the weeks since he'd been there, but he must've had it trimmed that afternoon.

"I will too." Jill reached inside her clutch for her phone. She turned it off and placed it facedown on the island, not even wanting the device in her presence. She wanted all her focus to be on Rick.

"Have fun tonight. And drive safe!" Lucille waved before leaving the room.

"Ready?" Rick asked, holding the kitchen door open for Jill.

They walked toward his truck, parked conveniently in the driveway, and she noticed it had been spruced up for the occasion, as well, with a shiny, waxed exterior, and a pristine, vacuumed interior. When he offered his hand to help her inside the cab and placed a secure hand on her waist, Jill could no longer deny it: *Yes. This definitely feels like a date.*

IT TOOK HALF AN HOUR to reach the restaurant. Rick had been wise to time the dinner for after Austin's rush-hour traffic and only hit a couple of minor lags on the highway. But it also meant that Jill wouldn't be properly introduced to Austin by daylight. She would have to settle for bright headlights and flashes of huge strip malls, huge churches, huge everything. Entering Austin was entering an alien land, especially compared to the coziness and warmth of

Morgan's Grove. She'd nearly forgotten what a big city felt like, with the energy, the crowds, and the rush of things.

But as Rick exited the highway, the trees thickened and the traffic lessened, and the city became utterly charming. After a few blocks, he turned onto a secluded lane that led to Portofino's Italian Restaurant. Several bare winter trees, as well as the building itself, were laced with tiny white lights, a theme that continued inside, with strands placed delicately on tall topiaries. She wasn't sure whether the lights were Christmas inspired or whether they were year-round touches, meant to add to the romance.

Jill and Rick were seated at a corner table and given oversized hardcover menus. The selection was immense, and Jill was clueless. Though she enjoyed Italian, she only ever ordered Parmesan chicken or linguini. That night, though, she was feeling adventurous.

"Order for me," she told Rick, closing her menu.

"The pressure..." he quipped, scanning the menu. "Toasted ravioli for an appetizer?" He peered over the menu for her approval. "Or calamari?"

"Fried octopus?" Jill crinkled her nose.

"Squid, actually. I'll take that as a no?"

"A very polite no," she confirmed. "But order it for yourself, if you want."

"That's okay. We'll go with ravioli. And maybe chicken marsala for the entrée?"

She found it adorable that he wouldn't firmly decide without peering over the menu, eyebrows raised, to gauge her reaction first. He obviously didn't want to misstep.

"Perfect," she affirmed.

She sipped the sparkling water the server had just poured, amazed at how relaxed she was, probably due to the drive over, which had felt like an easy, everyday occurrence. They had chatted about light topics such as the progress of the new bakery, the parade—Rick agreed about its hokey charm and hadn't even attended—and the concert.

Jill always hated first dates. They were usually glorified job interviews, stilted and fake. But on the way to the restaurant, during their relaxed chitchat, she'd realized that it wasn't a *first* date. She knew Rick, his history, his background, his favorite desserts, even the triggers that might start a bad mood or a bad memory. All those hundreds of hours she'd spent with him and all the talks and interactions over the past weeks had been, in a sense, a long series of other dates leading up to this one. And as he drove, she'd remembered that it was just Rick. She was safe with him—safe to be who she was and not have to fake her way through the meal. She gazed at Rick across a white tablecloth between tall candlesticks and realized that they could've easily been in jeans and T-shirts, eating appetizers and playing a round of pool.

The server took their order. "Excellent selection, sir," he said then disappeared again.

A quick flash of light nearby caught Jill's attention. She glanced to see a couple, heads together on the same side of a booth, smiling as they snapped a photo.

She chuckled softly. "Can't escape selfies, even at nice restaurants." She adjusted her position in the stiff-backed chair. "Actually, that reminds me—I had this idea, and I kept forgetting to run it by you. It's about the bakery."

"Let's hear it." Rick leaned back and settled in.

"You know that wall in your grandmother's kitchen, with all the photos? The memory wall. And now that she wants to model the bakery after her own kitchen"—Lucille had recently made her way through Rick's samples and chosen colors and textures that echoed her kitchen at home—"I was thinking. Why can't you create a memory wall at the bakery too? You can leave the wall's location up to Lucille, or maybe do it yourself and surprise her when the renovations are finished?"

"Interesting." He crinkled his brow. "But what kind of photos? Our family photos?"

"The wall could be anything she wants it to be. Maybe customers could bring in personal photos or even ones taken there, at the bakery. You know how some restaurants do that, with framed photos lining the walls?"

"I see where you're going. A sort of scrapbook of the bakery, memorializing people's experiences and commemorating them... What's the word I need?"

"Maybe celebrating?"

"Yeah. A celebration wall. People could take pictures of moments in their life—at home, or at the bakery, anywhere—when they're celebrating."

"Sure! Happy times like birthdays, parties, graduations—"

"Holidays."

The server approached the table politely then set down the appetizer between them. Jill cut a ravioli in half with the side of her fork then tipped it into her ramekin of marinara. Her first bite was chewy and warm, with silky cheese melting inside. "This is delicious."

Rick took a bite, agreed, then set down his fork with a clank. "I have an idea about this celebration wall of yours." He fished around in his pocket and produced his cell phone, bringing it back to life. "If it's good enough for them"—he nodded toward the selfie couple—"how about it?"

"I thought you were off the grid tonight."

"This'll only take a sec. We'll call it research."

Rick had abandoned his chair and headed over to Jill's side of the table. She didn't need to be prompted to smile for the camera—she was smiling already at the thought of a Rick-and-Jill selfie, especially since she'd just gently mocked another couple for doing the same.

Rick bent down with a hand around Jill's shoulder and leaned in until they were cheek-to-cheek.

"Say 'fettuccini,'" Rick whispered.

They said it together as Rick snapped the photo.

"I'll send you a copy now." He returned to his chair then tapped his phone. "And later, I'll have it printed." He shut off his cell before slipping it back into his pocket. "It can be the first photo on Gran's new wall."

"I love it."

But even as she said the words, it struck Jill again that she wouldn't be in Morgan's Grove to see the wall or the bakery for herself. She would be far away, in Colorado, immersed in her old life, busy with new projects and opportunities—thanks, in great part, to Rick's profile piece.

She picked up her fork and ate the rest of her appetizer, unable to shake the notion that it was more of a goodbye meal than a first anything.

When the appetizer was cleared away, the waiter brought out the main course. Jill cut into her chicken and tasted it. "This is so succulent. It melts in my mouth. You were right about this place."

"The reviews online were outstanding. I'm glad they were accurate." Rick paused his fork in the air. "I'm sorry about something."

Jill cocked her head. "What could you possibly be sorry for? I'm having the best time."

"Not about tonight. Something else. When we first met, I wasted time." He made stronger eye contact. "In the beginning, I sort of pushed you away. I don't know if you even realized it, but I was suspicious of you and wondered how you got close to my grandmother that quickly. But I didn't know you'd turn out to be so..."

She waited patiently, staring at him through the candlelight.

"So *you*. Easy to talk to, smart, and kind. When I watch you with my grandmother, the way you treat her, how you've supported her and been this rock for her, I just... well, I think you're pretty amazing. That's all."

She couldn't sustain his gaze after all that flattery. She didn't know what to do with it. "Well, I have a confession of my own," Jill admitted. "I made some early presumptions about you, too, and I'm happy to say they were incorrect."

"So I've proven my worth?"

"Over and over again."

When the desserts came—chocolate cheesecake for her and tiramisu for him—Jill realized their time was nearly over, and she suddenly wanted to linger over her dessert and try to slow down the ticking clock. She scrambled to find ways of filling the conversation but came up empty. The only topic on her mind was leaving. There was no more denying it: their evening was rapidly coming to a close.

After Rick paid the check and helped Jill with her coat, they went out into the crisp December air. Rick handed his ticket to the valet, and while they waited for his truck, Rick rested his hands on Jill's shoulders. "Cold?" he whispered down to her.

"Yes!"

He rubbed her shoulders, and she leaned back against him. He reached around her in a backward embrace as they rocked gently. She could've stayed that way for hours, hearing him breathe, safely cocooned in his arms. But too soon, the truck appeared, and Rick released Jill to open her door and help her inside. She scooted to the center of the truck's seat and clicked the belt around her waist.

During the ride back to town, Jill raised her bare hands to the heater. When she lowered them to her lap, Rick found her hand in the dark and caressed her fingers as they listened to soft classical in the background. They hardly spoke a word the entire drive. She usually enjoyed contented silence with him, but that night, the silence broadened inside the cab, filling every crevice and adding to her insecurities. Instead of being satisfied with the silence, she was left to wonder what he was thinking.

And then she let her own doubts come. *What had I expected from tonight? That he would kiss me, beg me to stay? Ask me to abandon Denver and make a life with him in Morgan's Grove?* It was crazy to hope for it. Rick wasn't even completely sure of his own future plans, and he hadn't hidden that fact. Still, she couldn't stop wishing that he would offer some hint, some glimmer that he was interested in keeping the relationship alive beyond the current moment.

But as she went over the evening in her mind, Jill realized that aside from some hand-holding and an embrace that she had initiated, Rick had made no verbal overtures in that direction. She had no concrete evidence that Rick saw their relationship as anything more than an affectionate and temporary friendship or that there was any future for them.

A small, brave part of herself still wanted to tell him how she felt, take the chance, and run the risk of heartbreak, but something stopped her—a vivid memory of what Rick had told her only weeks ago at the bridge: "Long-distance is a relationship-killer. I'll never do it again."

Nothing she might confess to him would change his mind. It was futile. It *was* a goodbye dinner, a friendly rain check that had turned into a thank-you meal for the profile piece, merely an obligation fulfilled.

When they came to Lucille's house, Jill remembered: "My phone is still on the island..."

They walked into the kitchen, where Jill noticed the absence of corgi barks—they must've turned in early, along with Lucille.

Jill found her cell right where she'd left it, facedown on the countertop. She placed it into her bag and looked up at Rick in the shadows of the lamplit room.

"I enjoyed tonight," he told her.

"I did too."

He stood near her but didn't reach out or come closer. He didn't lean in or smile. He only paused. There was a sudden formality about him, a rigidity she didn't recognize or understand.

The longer the pause drew out, the more Jill recognized it as Rick's polite signal to her. The evening had clearly come to an end.

"Thanks for everything," she replied. "The food was amazing."

Rick stared at his feet, rocking slightly side to side before making eye contact. "I wish we had more time."

"What do you mean?" Jill tried to temper her expectations.

"Everything just feels"—he shook his head and blinked—"I don't know, rushed. Like we ran out of time."

Jill stared up at him, willing him to say what he was thinking. It was their chance. The whole evening had been their chance, if something was to come of a future together. But when the long pause returned and began to grow between them, it was clear that nothing else *would* come. He'd given his answer.

Jill waited another beat then whispered, "I know."

A bark came from upstairs, then another and another as both dogs joined in.

"Shush!" Jill heard Lucille tell them. She pictured Lucille trying to wrangle the corgis and keep them quiet. She'd likely retired early with them on purpose, to give Jill and Rick privacy when they returned.

But they didn't need any more privacy, it seemed. The silence had said everything.

"I'd better go," Jill told Rick with a small shrug.

"I'll walk you outside," he offered.

"You don't have to. I'm only a few steps away."

He opened the kitchen door for her, and she walked out into the cold night air.

Even before she reached the apartment's staircase, tears had formed, and it took everything in her to suppress a sob as she walked upstairs and heard the kitchen door click behind her.

After closing the apartment door, Jill leaned against it and choked back tears. Needing a distraction, she found her phone and glanced at the screen, viewing Lindsey's text through blurred vision: *How did your date go???*

Jill knew she couldn't make it through a phone call with Lindsey—and besides, she was already in Utah with Charlie's family, and Jill didn't want to bother her.

A text would have to do. Jill stepped farther into the apartment, blinking and sniffing away tears, tapping out her feelings as they came in a rush: *Restaurant, beautiful and romantic. Food, perfect and delicious. Conversation, relaxed and easy. Rick—*

Jill paused and studied the floor. *What about Rick?* A million things entered her mind about the evening, about the awkwardness in the kitchen, about leaving him behind. And even further back, she remembered him pulling away from an almost-kiss in her apartment, right where she stood. Rick *had* given her signs, if she looked hard enough for them. He was letting her go.

She typed out the truth: *Just friends. He made it clear. Nothing more. I have to accept it. He doesn't want me.*

Jill read over her text, mouthing the words, feeling tears form again. Then she sniffed them back and deleted each word, letter by letter, replacing the message with: *Rick, the perfect gentleman.*

She clicked Send then tossed her phone on the bed and peeled off her jacket. And the only thing that came to her as she stepped out of her heels and unbuttoned her dress was: *Why stay?*

The profile piece was done, the genealogy article could be finished at any future date, the roads back to Denver were clear, and she had a conference to prepare for and a new book to write. Nothing was keeping her here. Another day and a half spent in Morgan's

Grove couldn't possibly matter, in the scheme of things. Remaining would only make things harder, as she played house with Lucille and the corgis and Rick, pretending they were one big happy family. But they weren't. Morgan's Grove was never meant to be permanent. *How did I trick myself into believing that it was?*

Feeling foolish, Jill turned all her energy and frustrations toward two crucial tasks, cleaning and packing. She would break the news to Lucille in the morning, somehow, some way, and make her understand. Through the haze of the evening's confusion, Jill had established one harsh truth: she couldn't stay in Morgan's Grove another day. Rick was right. They had run out of time.

Chapter Twenty-four

Before the non-date with Rick, Lucille had texted Jill about having a big Christmas Eve breakfast the next morning. But Jill knew she couldn't possibly tell Lucille her news—*I'm leaving today*—then endure a long, sit-down breakfast with the two of them. She would rather slip out of town, get on the road, and move along before she lost all her nerve. Her car was completely packed, and the apartment was back to its pristine condition, the same as the day she'd first entered, ready for Lucille's future permanent border.

Jill used the house key Lucille had given her and unlocked the kitchen door. She said a quiet hello to the corgis then placed the key onto the kitchen island, listening for movement in the house but hearing none.

"Wanna help me out?" she asked the dogs. She tiptoed down the hallway to tuck presents underneath Lucille's tree.

As George and Gracie watched, Jill wedged Rick's gift into an empty spot beneath a branch then tucked in a special gift for the dogs, filled with all their favorite treats and toys. Finally, she set down Lucille's bag of kitchen goodies, along with a check for the remaining amount for Jill's stay at the apartment. She knew Lucille might wave it away if she offered it in person.

When she rose and swiveled around, Jill noticed an item sprawled over the back of the sofa—Rick's dark jacket, the one he'd worn the night before. She touched its collar then pressed the fabric between her thumb and finger.

"What's all this?" Lucille asked, walking down the last step to approach Jill.

"I'm spreading a little Christmas cheer." Jill could also hear Rick moving around upstairs.

Lucille noticed the purse slung over Jill's arm. "Are you going somewhere? The shops are probably closed for Christmas Eve."

This is the hard part. Jill took a couple of steps toward Lucille, held eye contact, then paused. "I actually need to get going back home, to Colorado. I'm sorry."

"Right *now?*" Lucille's frown deepened in the creases of her forehead. "I don't understand. You were going to stay through tomorrow, at least, and spend Christmas day with us."

"I wanted to. But I—"

The corgis woofed at a commotion in the hallway then sprinted in Rick's direction as he came down the stairs, wearing a T-shirt and sweatpants, his hair rumpled from sleep.

He scratched at his unshaven chin and came to stand near his grandmother.

"Jill's leaving," Lucille whispered, peering up toward Rick.

"Today?" Rick's confusion matched his grandmother's, and Jill nearly lost her nerve. She wanted to drop her purse down, remove her coat, and stay put.

"Well, there's another big storm headed to Colorado," Jill explained, realizing her words were tumbling out faster than she'd intended, "and I can't get snowed in again. I'm speaking at a big writing conference after the holidays."

"I remember you mentioning that." Lucille nodded.

"And also, my agent wants to have a chat with me about a new book, so things are looking up. Seems like I'll be staying pretty busy in the new year." Jill had rehearsed the explanation a couple of times that morning, but as she spoke, her thin reasons for leaving sounded incredibly hollow.

Jill could see Lucille turning over the new developments in her mind. Finally, she spoke. "Well, isn't that wonderful news? I'm happy for you."

After a beat, Jill managed a glance in Rick's direction, but he gave nothing away, gazing at the air between them and blinking, expressionless.

"Well," Lucille finally said, breaking the silence. "If I can't convince you to stay, maybe I can at least send you off with a big breakfast. French toast and bacon? Or a quick plate of scrambled eggs? I know the way you like them best—not runny and topped with a hint of cheese and a dash of salt. You can't leave on an empty stomach."

Jill almost said yes, merely to appease Lucille and accept her hospitality, but as she stood there with Rick, who *still* had no noticeable reaction to Jill's news, she knew she couldn't possibly endure much more. It was time to go.

"I'm sorry," Jill told her. "I snacked on a granola bar earlier. I'm just... I need to get on the road." Jill rubbed the amethyst between her fingers and realized she'd been clutching it since Rick had come down the stairs.

"Well, then, I guess this is it." Lucille stepped closer, and Jill was reminded of the first time they'd met on the porch, weeks before, when Lucille had offered that same warm and welcoming tone. She'd had no idea, that day, what Lucille and Morgan's Grove would come to mean.

"Do you have enough cash, some bottled water? And a full tank of gas?" Lucille wondered.

"Yes, thanks. Plenty of everything. I'm all ready."

Lucille grasped Jill's arm. "I'm afraid *I'm* not ready. I can't believe how time has flown and that you're leaving us on Christmas Eve, of all days!"

"I know the timing is unexpected, but it feels like we've celebrated Christmas—all week, really—and it's been lovely." Jill felt a lump forming at the back of her throat. It was what she'd hoped to avoid at the breakfast table, but it was happening anyway. "I'll miss this place. All of you. Everything."

"Well, I was selfishly hoping you would change your mind," Lucille spouted with a half grin. "And that you'd decide to stay here in Morgan's Grove permanently and become the manager of my little bakery."

"It's very tempting. But I—"

"Need to leave for Denver," Lucille finished for her. "You have to do what's best for you, and I respect that. But it doesn't mean we can't stay in touch through technology. That video-chat thing. Rick can show me how it works, can't you, dear?"

Rick gave a small nod of acknowledgment, his dark eyes brooding.

"We can talk long-distance," Lucille told Jill, patting her hand. "It'll seem like you're still right here in my own living room."

Jill only wished that were true, but she knew how long-distance friendships generally worked. Rick was right: the best of intentions kept people active in each other's lives for a few weeks. But after that, real life would intervene, and the texts and calls would trail off until they dropped away to nothing. It was inevitable.

"Oh, I have something for you." Lucille pivoted to search the outer edges of the Christmas tree then produced a thick tote bag, covered in cartoon corgis and filled to the brim with presents. "Merry Christmas from all of us, even George and Gracie."

"You didn't have to do this," Jill protested, but she still accepted the bulging bag.

"Oh! And your stocking. Can't forget that..."

While Lucille turned her back and threaded through the sofas toward the fireplace, Rick grasped Jill's hand and moved his eyes toward her. He whispered, "Are you sure? About leaving now?"

Before she could respond, he had released her hand, and Lucille had placed a thick stocking into Jill's arms. "For you to open tomorrow morning."

"Thank you," Jill managed to whisper.

"Rick, let's help Jill with her luggage. I'm sure it's heavy down those apartment stairs."

"I've already loaded the car." Jill clutched the stocking and the tote.

"Well, then"—Lucille clasped her hands together—"I guess there's nothing more to do. This really is goodbye. Let us at least walk you to the door."

It took everything inside Jill to brush past Rick, then to patter through the corgis toward the kitchen. At the back door, Lucille turned squarely to Jill and brushed a curl gently away from her shoulder.

"You drive safe, okay? Let us know when you arrive in Denver. You need someone looking out for you." Then she reached up to hold both sides of Jill's face gently. "You are always welcome here."

Jill bent forward for a tight hug. "Thank you," she whispered into Lucille's shoulder, "for everything."

When they parted, Lucille stepped out of the way, shooing the corgis into the kitchen and giving Rick his space.

He turned to Jill, searching her face. "Do you need anything? I mean, do you have what you need for the trip? I can check your tires, your oil…"

Jill shook her head. "I had a maintenance check yesterday at the garage outside the square." She locked eyes with him. "Thank you for always taking care of people. That's your quiet gift, I think."

Rick shrugged, and before he could swat her compliment away, she had leaned up into his arms for a tight embrace.

"Stay safe," he whispered as she pulled out of the hug.

Rick twisted the doorknob to let her outside, and a blast of frigid air hit Jill's face.

"Merry Christmas," she told them weakly as she exited the kitchen and walked toward her car, packed and waiting.

Jill climbed inside the driver's seat, clicked her seat belt, and started the engine, aware she was being watched through the window. She couldn't manage another smile or wave, so she pulled out into the drizzly, melancholy morning with only the quickest glance at the house in her rearview mirror before she rounded the corner for good.

THE MAIN ADVANTAGE of driving on Christmas Eve was that Jill only had to share the highway with a handful of other cars. At first, the ride was a soothing one. The glow of the dashboard lights punctuated an overcast day, and the talk radio quietly droned in the background. She had the oddly adventurous sensation that she was going somewhere, while most people were stagnant and hunkered down in their homes.

But after four hours of driving, Jill found solace in none of those things. The dashboard glow seemed eerie, the radio voices became irritating, and the empty road only felt isolating.

Up ahead, she saw a Texas-sized gas station with an enormous storefront, called Luckee's, providing the perfect excuse to stretch her legs and abandon her car for a few minutes. After filling her gas tank at one of the dozens of pumps, Jill wandered inside the fluorescent mega store, where twangy banjo music played overhead and shelves were decorated with cheap lights and colored tinsel, filled with every possible "I Love Texas" souvenir—hats, stuffed toys, mugs, stickers, candy bags. Jill shook her head and remembered the stereotypes that had filled her mind on her first journey into Texas, weeks before. But as she touched a stuffed toy armadillo wearing a cowboy hat, she knew it was a caricature, a false representation of a genuine and down-to-earth collection of good-hearted people. At least, that's what Morgan's Grove had taught her about Texas.

After a restroom break, Jill grabbed a chilled bottled water and a bag of chips then headed to the register, feeling a tug of empathy for the youthful worker behind the counter, who would probably rather be with her family on Christmas Eve. Instead, she was ringing up Jill's items, one by one.

"On your way home for Christmas?" the girl inquired cheerily.

Home. When she asked, the girl probably had images dancing in her head of cordial greetings from family members, a shared meal of turkey and dressing, and wrapped presents beside a Christmas tree. But that was certainly not the description of where Jill was headed. Actually, it was what she was leaving behind.

"Headed back to Colorado," Jill responded, hoping that would be enough to satisfy the girl's question.

"That's a long way from here. Well, have a safe drive." She handed over a plastic bag stamped with Luckee's colorful emblem.

The temperatures had plummeted since Jill had left Morgan's Grove. Perhaps Texas would actually see a white Christmas. Back inside the car, she started the engine and uncapped the bottled water, bracing herself for the second leg of her journey. The plan was to drive for another four hours, find a hotel to stay the night, and drive into Denver on Christmas day.

As she replaced the bottle's cap, Jill's gaze settled on the seat beside her, which contained the corgi tote bag she'd plonked there hours ago, before pulling out of Lucille's driveway. A wrapped box peeked out at her, and she noticed the gift tag: "From Rick."

She shifted to reach for the palm-sized box and pulled it from the tote. The paper was a shiny silver, the sides fastened with tape that still showed through, with an uncentered bow stuck on top. *He must've wrapped this himself.*

She removed the wrapping and tossed it onto the floor then wedged her thumb into the cardboard slit to open the box. As she lifted the lid, she saw something dome-shaped, made of glass. She reached deep inside the box with her fingers then let out a small gasp as she lifted out the gift—a snow globe almost exactly like the one she had described to Rick weeks before, the one her father had given to her as a little girl. Jill clutched the base and dipped the globe downward then up again, watching the snow swirl around inside. Mesmerized, her eyes followed the flakes as they drifted down, down, down, until they settled inside the base once more.

"Rick," she whispered as the snow globe turned wavy through her tears.

She clutched the gift to her chest and let the tears fall. She was tired of holding everything in, tired of pretending and being strong. Besides, she was in the middle of Texas at some ghastly tourist trap on Christmas Eve. It didn't matter if she cried. No one was watching, anyway...

The release felt cathartic, a rush of bottled-up confusion and frustration flowing outward instead of churning inward. As her breathing finally started to calm and the sobs softened, Jill wiped her tears and found her phone, tapping out a number robotically. She didn't even know if Lindsey would answer, since she was likely busy with her soon-to-be in-laws in Utah. But Jill had to talk to someone, even if she wasn't sure what to say.

"Jill? Hey! Merry Christmas!" Lindsey's familiar voice lilted through the speaker, soothing Jill's ears. "I got your text this morning."

"Am I interrupting? I didn't know what you were doing right now."

Jill could hear a clatter through the phone then a sound like a door sliding shut in the background.

"No, it's fine," Lindsey replied. "I'm at Charlie's parents' ranch. They're making dinner, but I have a few minutes for my best friend! I'm stepping onto the porch. I'm glad you called!"

"I had to talk to someone." Jill sniffed and wiped her cheek again.

"Hey. You've been crying?"

"A little bit," she admitted. "Okay, a lot."

"You're not usually a crier. Tell me what's wrong."

"I don't even know where to start... I guess I'm feeling lost." Jill gazed through the misty windshield at the flashing neon convenience-store sign. "Not literally, but just... I feel like I don't belong anywhere."

"Where are you right now?"

"A gas station in the middle of Texas."

"You've left Morgan's Grove? I thought you were staying through tomorrow."

"I wanted to, but it would've been too hard, knowing I'd have to leave anyway. So I packed the car this morning, said goodbye to everyone, and started driving. I'm sitting in my car, and I noticed this present that Rick had snuck into my bag... Lindsey, it's a snow globe like the one that Daddy gave me." She brought it forward again and dipped it down, watched the snow fall, reflected in the dashboard lights. "It's magical."

"What a wonderful gift."

"It is. He's wonderful. They're all wonderful. I just... don't know what I'm doing anymore. I don't know where I'm going or why." She felt tears forming again.

"Jill, listen to me." Lindsey's voice suddenly took on that serious-teacher tone she used whenever she wanted to hold someone's attention. "I have a theory about why you're crying. Do you want to hear this? 'Cause it might sound a bit harsh."

"I need the truth." Jill's pulse throbbed at her temples. She knew how important her friend's advice might be, and she was ready to listen. "Tell me."

"I think you're running away, just like your mom did for your whole life."

Jill frowned, feeling her defenses rise. "Lindsey, that makes no sense. I'm doing the exact opposite." She carefully lowered the globe into her lap. "I'm in my car, on my way to Denver to fulfill my commitments... A writing conference, a new book. How on earth is that running away? I mean, if this were three years ago, I would probably agree with you. I *was* like my mom."

Jill flipped through the pages of memory and recalled specific reasons for certain moves her mother had put them through: a breakup with a boyfriend, difficulties at a new job, dissatisfaction with the city itself—they were all the same reasons Jill had used as an adult to move from city to city when she felt that itch of dissatisfaction. "But I've matured, learned my lesson. I've changed. Denver is security for me—it's the longest place I've ever lived. You *know* that. I'm proud of that. And things actually seem to be turning around for me with my writing."

"Jill, you're missing my point. You're running away from *Morgan's Grove*. From Rick and Lucille and all the people there. How many times over the past few weeks have you told me how welcome you felt? How comfortable and happy you were?"

"Well, sure. But Texas was only for research and my own curiosity about my heritage. I can't just stay there. That's crazy. I mean—"

"*Why* is it crazy? Jill, you adore that place. They've accepted you, almost like family. Don't you see? Morgan's Grove has become your home, and you're running away from it, back to Colorado. That's why you're crying. That's why you're so lost and sad. Your heart is someplace else."

Jill squeezed the phone tighter and tried to process what Lindsey was telling her. The new theory toppled Jill's entire viewpoint of things, and she wanted to reject it. But as she pondered it, as she balanced her choices on a mental scale, Jill knew that Lindsey was exactly right. Over the past few weeks, Morgan's Grove had become a sanctuary, a familiar, comforting, welcoming place. It *had* become home.

"I can't believe I didn't see it," she whispered, not even knowing if Lindsey was still on the other end. She had no idea how long she'd stayed silent. "But what about Rick?" she heard herself ask. "He barely said anything when I told him goodbye."

"You caught him off guard. Maybe he didn't know what to say. Isn't it worth the risk to find out?"

In one heartbeat, Jill knew the answer, and her entire purpose changed. Her confused frown had curled into a small, hopeful smile through tear-stained cheeks. "Thank you," she told Lindsey. "You have no idea what you've done for me. I needed to hear it spoken out loud, all the things I already knew but was too afraid to face. I know what I need to do now."

"Tell me how it all turns out. Merry Christmas, my friend. I love you!"

"Love you too!"

After they signed off, Jill gingerly tucked the snow globe back inside its box then into the tote bag for safekeeping. Her smile grew wider and brighter as she clicked her seat belt and pulled away from the gas station.

She was headed home.

Chapter Twenty-five

Jill pulled up to Lucille's house at dusk, but the only evidence of anyone at home was a golden shaft of light coming from the squares of window panes on the kitchen door, cutting through the cold gray evening. For the past few hours of travel, the weather had been misting off and on, creating glistening beads on Jill's windshield. She parked the car in its usual spot and turned off the engine. She'd been playing the moment over in her head since hanging up with Lindsey, but now that it had arrived, now that she was back in that familiar space again, Jill felt frozen, having no idea what to expect or how it would go in reality.

When she approached Lucille's kitchen door, she saw the corgis through the window, bounding toward her, barking all the way. Lucille followed them and stared at the door with confusion. She wasn't expecting company on Christmas Eve, and she certainly wasn't expecting *Jill*.

But when they locked eyes through the window, Lucille gave a noticeable gasp. That was Jill's cue to twist the doorknob and walk inside.

"What are you *doing* back here?" Lucille squealed, leaning in for a fast hug then grasping Jill's arms as she studied her face. "Did something go wrong? I thought you'd be halfway to Colorado by now. Did you have car trouble?"

"Nothing's wrong. No car trouble. I was on the way to Denver, but a few hours in, I couldn't go any farther. I did some serious thinking, Lucille. It sounds crazy, but I needed to be here again, in Morgan's Grove. I'm sorry to be vague—I'll explain everything in more detail later, I promise. But right now, I have to find Rick. Is he here?"

She had half expected him to round the corner as she and Lucille were speaking.

But Lucille crinkled her eyebrows as she loosened her grasp on Jill. "I haven't seen him all day, not since you left. The minute you pulled away, he changed clothes and took off in his truck. I've been trying his cell all afternoon to tell him dinner would be ready soon and to ask if he would attend the candlelight service tonight at church. Finally, about an hour ago, he answered his cell and said not to worry, that he would come home later, after the service. He switched off his phone again after that."

"Can you remember anything he said? Any clue that might tell us where he is?" Jill felt an urgency deep in her bones, as though facing one of those now-or-never moments that only happened a handful of times in a person's life.

"He said—what was that phrase?" Lucille looked skyward, trying to jog her memory. "Something about how he needed a spot to think." She returned her gaze to Jill. "He needed to be alone. 'Isolated' was the word he used."

"I know where I can find him. Thank you!"

She kissed Lucille's cheek then paused with her hand on the doorknob. "Do you still have a job at the bakery open for me?"

Lucille sucked in a breath. "Does that mean what I think it means? You're staying?"

"I am." That was another decision that had been immediately clear to Jill on her drive back to Morgan's Grove. She would stay, and it would be permanent. The minor things would take care of themselves. She could return to Denver soon, to pack up the apartment and attend her conference as scheduled—or even Skype in for her session, if she got snowed in. And early in the new year, she could find a house of her own in Morgan's Grove and become involved in the bakery, even part-time, using her marketing and business skills. And she could still make time to write. She could do it all.

"Hallelujah!" Lucille clapped her hands together.

As Jill hurried out the door and back into the frigid air, she heard Lucille call out, "And good luck with Rick!"

JILL PARKED AT THE edge of the covered bridge but didn't see Rick's truck as she'd expected. She squinted through the windshield—the evening had quickly darkened, with only a soft glow of the sun's remnants still on the horizon. But everything before her was still, with no movement, no evidence of human activity anywhere. *He's not here.*

Still, she stepped out of the car to make sure. The exhaustion of her long road trip caught up with her all at once, and her legs turned to jelly. She clicked her car door shut and immediately noticed the quiet. The only sound she heard was the quivering of a branch above as a robin thrust itself into the atmosphere for flight. There was no breeze, no sound of animals rummaging or birds singing. The air was hushed, as though nature was holding its collective breath.

She considered hopping back into the warm car and scouring the town, driving around until she found his truck. She could go back to Lucille's until he eventually returned. But something told her to slow down and look around the area before giving up completely. There was still another side to the bridge that wasn't visible from where she stood.

She hugged herself and took slow steps toward the bridge, trying to imagine the words she would choose when she eventually saw Rick. In all those hours spent driving back to town, she'd played various scenarios in her mind, all involving some big, romantic speech she might give him, but the doubts seeped in as sharply as the cold air on her face. *What if Rick doesn't see his future with me? What if he doesn't feel the way I feel?*

As Jill walked toward the bridge, a burst of light hit her senses, and she halted midstep. All at once, a thousand white bulbs lit up the night sky, outlining the covered bridge and illuminating her way. It was the most beautiful sight Jill had ever seen.

Dazzled by its brilliance, Jill remembered her original purpose then scanned the edge of the creek, hoping Rick might be crouching there, doing some thinking.

No sign of him anywhere.

In a last-ditch effort, she cupped her hand to her mouth and called out his name as loudly as she could: "Rick! Are you out here, Rick?" Her voice cut through the stillness, echoing through the bridge's interior. If he was on the other side, he surely would've heard.

But the only echo she received in return was silence. Giving a final sweeping glance around the bridge, she decided it was futile.

As she made the first hesitant steps back toward the car, she heard her name being called. She pivoted and sucked in a breath.

"Jill!" Rick called again.

She saw the shadow of his tall frame as he walked toward her inside the bridge, from the other side.

He halted a few inches from her as they met at the bridge's entrance. "You're here." Confusion showed in his eyes as he touched her hair. "What happened? I thought you'd be out of Texas by now."

"I had a change of heart." She touched his gloved hand. "How long have you been out here?"

"A while. I tried distracting myself with work, but I got restless and didn't know where else to go. I've been beating myself up all day."

"Why?"

"For letting you go." He shifted his weight and shook his head. "All this time, I thought we were building something. I even kidded myself into thinking you might change your mind and not go back to Denver, or that I would have the courage to ask you to stay. It was on the tip of my tongue last night and this morning, but I couldn't get the words out. And then you were gone." He pushed out a heavy sigh. "When your car turned that corner this morning, and I thought I'd never see you again, it hit me hard. I'm in love with you. But it was too late—you made your decision, and I had to respect it. I mean, you have your life back in Denver. And you hate long-distance relationships like I do. So I thought we didn't have a chance..."

Jill peered up into his dark eyes. "Wait a minute. Go back to that other part. You're in love with me?"

"I've known it for a while but fought it, thinking you were leaving."

"I'm in love with you too. That's why I came to find you. I didn't know how you felt about me, though. You're pretty hard to read sometimes, and—"

Rick closed the space between them, cradled Jill's neck, then leaned down and kissed her. His lips were tender but firm, intense but soft, as his kiss went deeper. Jill closed her eyes and let herself drown in it. The kiss was everything she'd waited for.

When he backed away, Jill opened her eyes and watched him lean in to tilt his forehead against hers. For the first time since she'd found him at the bridge, his mouth had formed a smile. She touched his face, his stubbled jaw, the dot of a dimple in his chin.

"Well, *that* wasn't hard to read." She grinned.

Rick backed away a few inches to ask, "This change of heart—does it mean you're staying in Morgan's Grove?"

Jill nodded her answer. "It's home now." She skimmed back over her experiences, which were all rolled into one sweet, warm collection of memories. "My roots are here. I belong here, in this place, with these people. With you."

Then she took the initiative, tugging on Rick's jacket, drawing his face closer to hers. She kissed him slowly, taking her time. He responded, tightening his arms and pulling her into him.

Something cold brushed Jill's cheek, and she broke the kiss to find the source.

"Snow?" She turned her face to the sky and saw the evidence. White flurries headed downward, covering her hair, her jacket, and her hands.

Jill pressed her body against Rick's as they faced the bridge together, watching the flakes fall faster from a dark sky, set against the bridge's twinkling lights.

"My very own snow globe," she whispered.

"OH, YOU SHOULDN'T HAVE," Lucille squealed. "But I'm so glad you did." She clutched the oven mitts that Jill had given her.

Jill sat with Rick on the long sofa, surrounded by discarded tissue paper and empty boxes, as they opened their gifts after a Christmas morning breakfast. The corgis were busy munching on the rawhide bones Jill had given them, and Rick was touching the smooth leather of his new laptop case he'd just opened from Jill.

"I have another little surprise for Lucille." Jill rose from the couch. "Actually, it's for both of you. I'll be right back."

Lucille gave a quizzical look as Jill darted behind a chair to retrieve the papers she'd printed off earlier that morning. Pushing down her nerves, Jill stacked the papers neatly then handed them to Lucille, who reached toward the nape of her neck and accepted the gift.

"Looks like I'll need my glasses for this one."

Jill returned to sit beside Rick, finding his hand and interlocking their fingers. Her eyes remained on Lucille as she examined the front page.

"Untitled, by Jill McCallister. Chapter One." Lucille peered across her glasses at Jill. "Is this what I think it is?"

"My new book," Jill confirmed.

"Really?" Rick asked beside her.

"Well, the start of it. A couple of nights ago, I got totally inspired," she explained. "I was glancing at my photos of Morgan's Grove, of the town, of you both and the corgis. And it hit me. *This could be a story.*" Before they could jump to conclusions, Jill clarified that her book would be fictional, merely inspired by the town.

Lucille hugged the pages to her chest with a beaming smile. "I love this idea."

"Thanks. I wasn't planning on starting the book, but last night, the words were coming fast, so I had to obey the Muse and type them out before bed. This morning, I sneaked in here early to print them off. Hope you don't mind."

"Mind? I'm honored! And I'm excited for you," Lucille assured her.

"I am, too, actually. For the first time in forever, I feel energized about my writing. I think Rick's article jumpstarted things. Well, and being in Morgan's Grove. The story was here all along, right under my nose."

"I can't *wait* to read this." Lucille pushed her glasses higher and perused the first page again.

Rick squeezed Jill's hand and shifted toward her. "I knew you'd break your writer's block. It was just a matter of time."

"You were right."

As she leaned in to kiss him, she heard, "Shush, you two." Lucille waved at them dismissively with one hand and grasped the chapter with the other. "I'm trying to concentrate over here."

"You're reading it now?" Rick asked.

"Of course!"

Rick chuckled then stood, still holding Jill's hand, and led her over to the far corner of the living room, near the tree. Through the curtain, Jill could still see a glorious winter wonderland from the snow the night before.

"Merry Christmas," Rick whispered.

He leaned down for a kiss, and his soft lips tasted like the candy cane he'd eaten earlier. When he backed away, Jill took in his face, half of it lit up by the tree's lights, then released his hands and swiveled inside his grasp. She leaned back against his chest as he wrapped his arms snugly around her. She took in the entire scene: Bing Crosby singing in the background, fire burning in the fireplace, empty stockings hanging—including Jill's, back where it belonged—and Lucille flipping to the next page in the chapter with both corgis lying contentedly at her feet.

It was the best holiday she'd ever had, next to that final one spent with her father. And even though he wasn't with her anymore, Jill felt his presence as she realized she'd found her new home because of him. The search for his relatives had brought her to Morgan's Grove in the first place, to these people, to this moment. Perhaps it was her father's gift to her, this Christmas.

Lucille's Gingerbread Recipe (aka Molasses Crinkles)

Printed with the permission of Sharon Stephens
Note: Be sure to adhere to exact measurements of spices to avoid overly spicy cookies.

¾ c dark molasses

½ c brown sugar

1/3 c cold water

¼ c butter (lightly melted)

1 tsp baking soda

½ tsp salt

½ tsp ground allspice

1 tsp ground ginger

½ tsp ground cloves

½ tsp ground cinnamon

Mix all the above first, then mix in 3½ c flour

Cover with wax paper and refrigerate for 2 hrs

Roll dough ¼ inch thick on floured board and cut out cookies with cutters of your choice

BAKE 10 min. at 350 degrees (ovens vary). Or, for even softer cookies, bake at 340 for 9 minutes.

ICING/GLAZE: Pour half a bag of powdered sugar into a medium-sized bowl, then pour a couple of "glugs" of room-temperature water and stir to taste. If the mixture is too thin, add more powdered sugar. If it's too thick, add more water.

This recipe yields about fourteen large-sized gingerbread men/women. I usually double the recipe and use both large and small cutters, for variety.

Acknowledgements

To my family, whose support and encouragement mean everything.

To beloved family members who are no longer with me and have recently made their exit to heaven: Daddy, Maw, Pa-Paw, Grammy, and Pappy. They would have been so supportive of this new book and new series. I miss them every day.

To my dearest friends, and to those who continue to be supportive of my writer's journey: Augusta Malvagno, Linda Bratcher, Becky Bray, Karen Peterson, Doris Lininger, Sue Willis, Sheree Webb, Deanna Markham, Stephen and Laurie Stine, Carla Krae, Rebecca Sanders, Rae Champagne, Leigh Ann Olejnik, and Silvana Vierkant-Waller, as well as my TJC friends and colleagues and my beloved Commandos.

Special thanks to my publisher, Lynn McNamee, whose professionalism, knowledge, and ambition have helped to create an amazing publishing company that produces high-quality books. I'm honored to be on board with Red Adept.

Also special thanks to my line editor, Kate Birdsall. Her careful input and guidance has heightened the quality of this book. She made the editing experience informative and enjoyable.

To the entire Red Adept team, but especially Erica Lucke Dean, Streetlight Graphics (particularly Glendon Haddix), and all the proofreaders and formatters. This novel is what it is because of your diligence and dedication and talents. I'm so grateful to you. And I *love* my cover.

To Sharon Stephens for lending me her scrumptious gingerbread recipe (it really *is* prize-winning! I use it every Christmas!) and for inspiring her students. She taught me that baking and entertaining has the wonderful ability to bring people together.

To Clint Jones at Motophoto for my author photo.

Finally, all thanks to God, who makes everything in this life worthwhile. He is the Source.

Other Books by Traci Borum:
The Chilton Crosse Series (in order)
Painting the Moon
Finding the Rainbow
Seeking the Star
Savoring the Seasons
Book 5 Coming Soon
The Morgan's Grove Series
Love Starts Here
Book 2 Coming Soon

Don't miss out!

Visit the website below and you can sign up to receive emails whenever Traci Borum publishes a new book. There's no charge and no obligation.

https://books2read.com/r/B-A-LDS-YXOEB

BOOKS 2 READ

Connecting independent readers to independent writers.

Did you love *Love Starts Here*? Then you should read *In a Jam*[1] by Cindy Dorminy!

Andie Carson has to do three things to inherit her grandmother's lottery winnings—sober up, spend a month running her grandmother's Georgia coffee shop, and enter homemade jam in the county fair. If she can't meet those terms, the money goes to the church, and Andie gets nothing. She figures her tasks will be easy enough, and once she completes them, Andie plans to sell the shop, take the money, and run back to Boston.

After a rough breakup from his crazy ex-fiancée, Officer Gunnar Wills decides to take a hiatus from women. All he wants is to help make his small town thrive the way it did when he was a kid. But

---

1. https://books2read.com/u/4jwnQv

2. https://books2read.com/u/4jwnQv

when wild and beautiful Andie shows up, Gunnar's hesitant heart begins to flutter.

Gunnar knows that Andie plans to leave, but he's hoping to change her mind, fearful that if her coffee shop closes, Main Street will fold to the big-box corporations and forever change the landscape of his quaint community. But convincing her to stay means getting close enough to risk his heart in the process. Even though Gunnar makes small-town life seem a little sweeter, Andie has to decide if she's ready to turn her world upside down and give up big-city life. One thing's for sure—it's a very sticky situation.

Read more at www.cindydwrites.com.

Also by Traci Borum

Morgan's Grove
Love Starts Here

About the Author

Testing One Two

About the Publisher

Dear Reader,

We hope you enjoyed this book. Please consider leaving a review on your favorite book site.

Visit https://RedAdeptPublishing.com to see our entire catalogue.

Don't forget to subscribe to our monthly newsletter to be notified of future releases and special sales.

www.ingramcontent.com/pod-product-compliance
Lightning Source LLC
Chambersburg PA
CBHW030534190726
48283CB00006B/1913